TO - SUE

Happy Reading

Best Regards

Don Mang

ONE NATION
UNDER GOD

Mine Eyes Have Seen The Glory
Of The Coming...

A Novel

DONALD J. MANG

iUniverse, Inc.
New York   Bloomington

ONE NATION UNDER GOD
Mine Eyes Have Seen The Glory Of The Coming...
A Novel

Certain characters in this work are historical figures, and certain events portrayed did take place. However, this is a work of fiction. All of the other characters, names, and events as well as all places, incidents, organizations, and dialogue in this novel are either the products of the author's imagination or are used fictitiously.
iUniverse books may be ordered through booksellers or by contacting:

iUniverse
1663 Liberty Drive
Bloomington, IN 47403
www.iuniverse.com
1-800-Authors (1-800-288-4677)

Because of the dynamic nature of the Internet, any Web addresses or links contained in this book may have changed since publication and may no longer be valid. The views expressed in this work are solely those of the author and do not necessarily reflect the views of the publisher, and the publisher hereby disclaims any responsibility for them.

ISBN: 978-0-595-45059-6 (pbk)
ISBN: 978-0-595-69376-4(cloth)
ISBN: 978-0-595-89371-3 (ebk)

Printed in the United States of America

iUniverse rev. date 11/21/08

For Jesus and Mary

I'D LIKE TO THANK

John Heiser, Historian, Division of Visitors' Services, Gettysburg Military Park, Gettysburg, Pennsylvania for his invaluable information and expertise in Civil War military matters

Sister Betty Ann McNeil, D.C., Archivist for the Daughters of Charity, Province of Emmitsburg, Maryland, with gratitude for consultation and advice

Father Alfred R. Pehrsson, C.M., whose spirituality and influence was a significant inspiration

Mary Rosenblum, award winning author, whose comments and encouragement from the beginning were of great value

Christopher, my son, and his wife, Barbara, for their technical assistance

Sandy, my daughter, for encouraging me to "follow my dream"

Millie, my dear wife, without whose assistance and encouragement I could not have completed this novel

and

Warmest thanks to my grandchildren who prayed every night for publication of this book:
Michael, Patrick, Michael, Shawn, Caitlyn and Christian Anthony

DEDICATION

▼

To show my heartfelt appreciation to those who have protected and defended this great nation, the United States of America, I dedicate this book. I am eternally grateful to every patriot who ever donned a uniform and served in the U.S. military, from the frozen plains of Valley Forge in the First Continental Army to the scorching deserts of Iraq. I, myself, presently have a grandson serving in the U.S. Army.

As a young boy, I remember watching very old Civil War veterans marching down the main street of our little town in the annual Memorial Day parade, dressed in their Union blue uniforms of the Grand Army of the Republic. I have seen the weapons they carried—one-shot, muzzle-loading guns. And now, we live in the period of the horror of nuclear weapons.

Let us never forget the cost of our freedom. Many of our brave sons who gave their lives that we may live free, still lie in far-off graves on foreign shores. We have fought for our own freedom in 1776 and again from 1861 to 1865 in our Civil War, furthering that cause. We have defended the rest of the world in two World Wars and have sacrificed valiantly in Korea and Vietnam. We have liberated Kuwait and continue to fight for the freedoms of the Afghanistan and Iraqi peoples.

(And) As in every war, there are many unsung heroes such as those who care for the dying and the wounded. The exemplary work represented by the Daughters of Charity after the battle of Gettysburg is portrayed in this fictional account. Many young soldiers did, in fact, receive the tender, loving care and died in the arms of these holy women. And furthering their noble work, they also cared for the many orphans left in the wake of that war and continue to give of themselves today. And to these dedicated sisters, may God bless them abundantly for their corporal works of mercy.

Contents

PREFACE

▼

The red, white, and blue flag rose slowly above the parapet and snapped briskly in the wind, but it no longer represented the *United* States. The colors were the same, but the configuration was different. It was the new Confederate flag—seven stars representing the seven states that had seceded from the Union. Old Glory had been replaced after four thousand shells smashed into Fort Sumter, forcing its surrender. Nothing would ever be the same again. At that moment, the country could not imagine what lie ahead. That young country, just eighty-five years old, was about to undergo its greatest test. Could it withstand the tumultuous tearing apart, the vast spilling of blood, the endless drain of resources? Could it survive? It had survived the Revolution and proved its mettle, standing up to the great country of Britain to obtain its liberty and independence. But that was when it was united. This time our fledgling democracy would be tested as never before in a bitter trial.

But these questions were far from the mind of the average citizen, especially the younger ones. Young men from both North and South looked upon it as a great adventure. "It'll be over in a few months." "One battle an' we'll show 'em!" They came from farms, shops, schools, plantations, factories, shipyards, big cities, and little towns. They were mountaineers, seamen, politicians, and firemen. Some wanted to escape the drudgery of the farm, the boredom of the shop, or the hard labor on the docks. But they all had one thing in common. They all believed they were going to fight for a just cause—and they were going to win!

A few short years before, most of these young boys who would fight and die for their cause were barely old enough to shave. But the fire was lit, and nothing could stop that boiling cauldron from spilling over, igniting the greatest battle ever to be fought on the American continent.

This is how it was in the Spring of 1861. Everything was put on hold—college careers... jobs... marriages. The future was frozen in time—until that great conflict could be settled one way or the other. Some would resume their lives when it ended. Six hundred thousand would never return. Over two million men in blue and gray took up arms to vanquish one another. And the lives of three million, five hundred thousand slaves were also at stake.

And within this vast multitude of armed men and Negro slaves there were four young people caught up in this life-and-death struggle—Patrick, Joshua, Lou Ann, and Nathan. This is their story.

CHAPTER 1

▼

FROZEN DEATH

Darkness fell on that little plain covered with his country's colors—the white snow splattered with red blood and carpeted with blue uniforms. Patrick O'Hanrahan lay on the frozen earth, numb and seeming unable to move. He was surrounded with his dead and wounded comrades who had earlier charged the enemy that horrifying, cold December day, in Fredericksburg, Virginia, in 1862.

The last thing he remembered was a burning sensation, like a hot poker, plunging through his thigh. Then all went black. Sometime during the night, cold flakes of snow settling gently on his face temporarily revived him. He drifted in and out of consciousness throughout the night, as the rolling fog created an eerie blanket over the dead. Images of his sweetheart, Beth, ice-skating with him in Central Park last winter, flashed before him. Screams and moans from this ghastly field of suffering, maimed, and broken humanity, jolted him to full awareness of his surroundings. Would he ever see her again? The blood oozed from his leg, but the pain was numbed by the penetrating cold night air. He remembered her soft, warm hand clasping his as they skated around that winter wonderland way back home in New York City. Would he ever enjoy the happiness of those New York winters again, or would he be just another frozen corpse by morning? He prayed as he never did before. What would it be like if he died? Fear began to overwhelm him. He moved his arms. I'm still alive. He remembered his grandfather's words. "Trust in God, son. He is always with you." That old Irish tenacity he inherited from his grandfather came back to him. I will survive... I must survive. Thank God the killing has stopped. Will it start up again tomorrow? He remembered his friends using dead comrades' bodies as shields to protect them from the relentless fire coming from the Rebel's position behind the stone wall. The Union soldiers had moved onto that plain, bent over at the waist, as if they were walking into a driving rain. But it wasn't rain—it was hot lead spewing death from a thousand muskets, dropping men by the hundreds. That damn General—sending us men into that inferno all day. His Irish temper briefly took over his mood.

The glory and the flag-waving were gone now. The eager, young men who once paraded down Broadway to the tune of marching bands, feeling so courageous and proud, were decimated, humiliated, and defeated. Was this the end of the Union? Has our cause been defeated? Or will we rise to fight another day?

He clutched his medal dangling from his neck. It was very different than most religious medals. It had the Star of David with the cross affixed to it. But that was long ago when he and Joshua had made a boyhood pact to always remain blood brothers. The jeweler had thought it peculiar that they had asked him to combine these two symbols into one on Joshua's medal, and to make another just like it so they would have identical medals. But they had saved enough money to pay him—that's all he needed to know.

Joshua was only eleven years old when his family moved to Virginia. Where could he be now, Patrick wondered. Memories and visions of his young life raced through his mind. Will morning ever come?

Suddenly, a figure appeared through the fog, rummaging over the bodies all around him. This ghostly figure was removing the clothes from the dead and anything else he could find. Patrick fumbled for his bayonet and removed it from his musket. He lay there waiting, hoping he had enough strength to ward off certain death if discovered. He waited, heart pounding, cold sweat running from his brow. The figure came out of the fog and began to bend over him. He could barely make out the butternut-gray uniform worn by the scavenger. He mustered up enough strength and plunged the bayonet into the man's body. A slight grunt and rush of air came from the Confederate's mouth, and he collapsed on top of him. Patrick quickly realized he must get out of there before more of the enemy arrived. He couldn't move with this dead weight on top of him, so he struggled to slide out from under him. The fog was his ally. He crawled cautiously and slowly across the plain, over the dead and wounded, fearing a bullet in his back at any minute. He occasionally crawled over a man in pain who would let out a scream as he slid over him. That rattled his senses. He grew weaker and weaker as he made his way over that sea of writhing souls, some screaming for water and calling for God's mercy. When he thought he couldn't go any further, he wedged himself between two bodies for protection from the cold night wind. As he lay there envisioning his mother calling him in for dinner while he was having a snowball war with Joshua, he realized how loosely he had used that term—war. A horrifying thought came to him—these men on either side of me—their mothers don't know yet. He again struggled to crawl back to the Union lines. He could see a dim light coming through the fog from a small campfire. That must be our lines—if only I could make it there, I ... Once again he blacked out.

CHAPTER 2

▼

LILACS IN DECEMBER

A blurry figure again appeared before him. He panicked and reached for his bayonet. It wasn't there. This is it, he thought, as he began to pray. He braced himself, when suddenly he heard a soft female voice, as his eyes began to focus more clearly. A young woman's face slowly swam into view.

"You're going to be all right," she said. "You're safe now." A faint odor of lilac drifted from her long brown hair, which was loosely covered with a dainty blue scarf. It matched her sky-blue eyes that seemed to smile as she spoke. "Here," she said. "Take this. It will warm you up," as she handed him a cup of hot tea. He couldn't speak for a moment, suddenly realizing he was in a tent.

"You were carried here by some men from your regiment. You're in a field hospital, Sergeant."

The hot tea helped. He was beginning to feel sensation in his feet again. He pressed his large strong hands tightly around the cup to warm them. I feel almost human again, he thought to himself. A shooting pain through his leg caused a deep moan to escape his lips. He looked down at his bandaged leg, hoping it was still in one piece. He had seen many other soldiers having their limbs amputated right out in the open in front of the field hospital, as his regiment was forming into line for battle. Oh, the sick feeling in his stomach, as he and his comrades were all writing their names on pieces of paper and pinning them to their uniforms, hoping to be identified if killed in the impending action.

"The surgeon says you're going to be all right," the young woman explained. "He says the bullet went clear through your leg, just missing the bone." She settled back into a chair, brushing a strand of hair from her face. He tried to push himself up on the pillow with one hand while balancing his cup in the other. "Here, let me help you," she said as she rose from the chair and fluffed up the pillow behind his head. The cold air blew through the makeshift tent, people constantly opening and closing the flaps as they passed in and out. He was covered with two blankets but couldn't get warm.

"Are you a nurse?"

"Not exactly," she replied. "I'm a volunteer with the Sanitary Commission." She was standing over him now, holding a book in front of her. It looked like a Bible. Her long, flowing dress fluttered every time a gust of wind blew in. She looked quite warm and comfortable standing there in her long blue dress and black cape. "If there's anything you need, I will gladly get it for you." He was thinking of Beth, and how much she reminded him of her—same height—same stature—same color of hair.

"Oh, I could use something to eat." He couldn't remember when he ate last.

"I'll go and get you something." She got up and quickly disappeared through the flaps of the tent. As he looked around, he saw dying and wounded everywhere. Most had no cots. He was one of the lucky ones. The rest only had straw or pine needles between them and the frozen earth. Some were moaning. Some were just staring into space. New litters were coming in frequently, and some were going out with the dead. He shuddered. Thank God—he had made it this time. Where were his men? Did any survive? He tried to get up, but the movement of his leg caused intense pain. He settled back down, but was unable to rest. Gruesome images of the carnage from the day before flooded his brain. He had to find out about his men. Maybe a nurse would know.

"Hey, nurse!" he hollered every time one passed by, but they were all too busy to stop. He *had* to find out about his men. The sweet lilac fragrance was gone, and the pungent odor of blood, sweat, and other acrid smells permeated the whole tent.

The young lady appeared at his bedside as quickly as she had gone, carrying some warm muffins and a few strips of bacon in a small basket. He didn't ask where she got them. Devouring the food ravenously, he was about to ask her if she knew anything about his regiment.

"I have to run along now. Take care of yourself. Hope you feel better soon." She walked away briskly, head erect, with the Bible in her hand. He slid back under the covers and fell into a deep sleep.

The next few days dragged on. The awful smells, the intermittent screams of pain, the cold draft blowing in through the tent flaps, and the lack of decent food were getting on his nerves. He was determined to get back on his feet. The sixteen year old boy in the next bed had had his leg amputated and cried most of the time. He felt sorry for him and tried to console him; but the boy, a private in a Pennsylvania regiment, just kept whimpering. Pat was a compassionate man to a point, but feelings of anger and frustration crept over him as the boy kept sobbing. At one point he blurted out, "Get a hold of yourself, man! Thank God you're still alive." He felt guilty after saying this and didn't talk to him much after that. He forced himself to sit up on the edge of the cot. The pain was tolerable now. A nurse came in and changed the dressing on his wound.

"Coming along fine," she exclaimed. Then off she rushed on her daily rounds. No use talking to the private either, he thought, rather disappointedly. There were a few short dime novels someone gave him, but he read them quickly and became bored again.

As he was praying his rosary one morning, he smelled the fresh lilac scent once again. "Good morning, Sergeant. How are you feeling?" She approached him with a big smile, a bright blue bonnet on her head and a plate full of cookies in her hands. "I thought you might enjoy these," she said as she sat down in the chair next to his bedside.

"I'm feeling much better now, thanks." He reached out and took the plate from her. He no longer needed to ask her about his regiment, since a few of his friends had paid him a visit the day before. They had told him that half of his regiment had been killed and many more wounded. He had taken the news very hard. His friends had never seen him cry before, as he usually hid his feelings. This time, however, he had just sat there, his tall frame hunched over, his head in his hands, a few locks of black hair falling over his eyes, and wept openly.

"You don't look too well, Sergeant. Can I help?"

Glancing at her, then down at his leg, he responded, "I'm O.K. Just a little homesick."

"I didn't get your name," she said quizzically.

"Patrick."

Before he had a chance to ask, she exclaimed, "Mine's Lou Ann. My father's name is Louis and my mother's name—Ann," she proudly stated.

She was the first female he had spoken to since he had joined the Army in '61, and a seemingly caring one at that! He wanted to know more about her and blurted out, "Where are you from?"

"Pennsylvania. A small town called Gettysburg. Ever hear of it?" She straightened out her long, full skirt and shifted slightly to one side.

"No, I can't say that I have." He lifted a cookie from the plate and bit a large piece out of it. "I notice you carry a Bible with you," he went on, as he gazed at her delicate hands resting on the book in her lap.

"Oh, yes, I read it every day. Would you like me to read a passage for you?"

He was a faithful believer, but he wanted to find out more about *her* just then. "Sure," he replied, however, not wanting to disappoint her.

She began Psalm 91. *"You who dwell in the shelter of the Most High..."* He paid extra attention when she read the part, *"No evil shall befall you, nor shall affliction come near your tent."* Strange, he thought—I've heard that psalm before but it never had such meaning—lying here in a tent like this. The last few lines of the psalm drifted by his ears, as he was distracted by the aroma of her lilac cologne. "Where in New York are you from?" she asked, closing the cover of her Bible.

"How did you know I was from New York?"

"Oh, I was here when they carried you in... one of the men told me you were from a New York regiment." She continued, "Where about in New York?" repeating her question.

He focused on her striking looks and felt overwhelmed by her beauty. He stammered for a moment... "New York City."

"How interesting. I've never been to New York City. There must be a lot of things to do there," she went on.

He felt a little uncomfortable, suddenly realizing he had been staring at her. He'd always been a pushover for a pretty face. "Oh, yes, there are," he replied, turning his gaze away from her.

"I come from a small farm community—nothing much to do there. The war came along, and I wanted to do something to help. So here I am. I'm not a nurse, but the other ladies and I do what we can for you boys. We have magazines and newspapers and also supply bandages and crutches. Can I get you something to read?"

He answered without hesitation. "Do you have any New York newspapers?" He propped himself up on his elbows, eagerly awaiting her answer.

"I'll check and see. If I can find some for you, I'll bring them by tomorrow."

"You know, I haven't even had any mail from home in months."

"Oh, I imagine the mail has been delayed on all the trains with the war and all. Don't worry—you'll probably receive a letter soon."

He slumped back in his bed, folding his hands on his chest and staring at the tent above him, rippling in the wind.

"I do hope the war is over soon," she went on. "I've never seen so much misery in my life," as she glanced around at the other men and then at the earthen floor beneath her feet.

He stroked his long black mustache with his forefinger, as if attempting to smooth it out. "Well, it *is* over for many of *them*," he remarked as he pointed to the outside and the battlefield beyond. He stopped abruptly, cautiously catching himself so as not to share his feelings of disappointment and anger over the hard-fought battle and all of the good men that were lost. For the first time, he doubted the cause he came to fight for. Sometimes it had become blurry in the past, but he had been able to easily dismiss these doubts when they came. Now, however, after this horrifying battle, his resolve had been weakened. In his most private thoughts, he could now even understand why some men deserted. But one thing always brought him back to the reason he was there—simply that his country was attacked and he was defending it—and that was all there was to it!

She tried to cheer him up. "I'm glad you're going to be all right. Have you written home yet? I can get you some stationery and envelopes."

"Thanks. I'll probably write to my folks tomorrow," purposely leaving Beth out of the conversation.

"Well, Patrick... may I call you Patrick?" she asked with a twinkle in her eye.

"Please do."

"Well, I have to go now," as she fastened the tie at the top of her cape more tightly. Standing at his bedside, she took his hands in hers. "I'll bring you a newspaper tomorrow," she exclaimed. She slowly stepped back from his bed, pausing for a moment, as if she didn't want to leave. Her hands had radiated a warmth which flowed up his arms and into his brain and sparked feelings he hadn't had since Beth's hands held his that day at the train station.

Lou Ann departed. He closed his eyes and only wanted to sleep—that morpheus of the dreamer. Beth... Beth... Her hands had gripped his tightly, desperately, holding on as his train had begun to pull away to war. He had watched her face on the other side of that misty window, tears trickling down her cheeks. Trying to hold her long dress up from the ground, she began to run alongside the train. He waved helplessly through the glass, wanting to reach out and grab her up in his arms. As the train gained speed, she ran faster and faster until she couldn't run any further; and her figure slowly dissolved into the steam and darkness like a pebble sinking beneath the surface of the water.

His mind wandered. How many more battles? How many more of us will it take? He remembered the current popular saying, "It's a rich man's war but a poor man's fight," as he prayed for sleep to dull the gruesome images of the battlefield.

The next morning he was aroused from sleep by the loud, sharp voice of a nurse. "Wake up, Sergeant!" as she nudged him on his shoulder. "Moving out day for you!" He sat up, rubbing his eyes and thinking he would be going back to his regiment. "You're going to Washington for awhile. Maybe they want you to talk to the President about ending the war," she said with a bit of laughter in her voice. He loved humor but hadn't heard much lately. Had he been fully awake, he would have had a good retort. "They're shipping you up there to a hospital 'til you're fully recovered," she continued.

Washington, he thought. Maybe Beth can come down. Pondering this possibility filled his heart with hope and happiness.

"Here, try these on for size," the nurse said as she thrust a pair of crutches into his hands. "I think you can try to walk with these," she said, as she helped him to his feet. He struggled to stay on his feet, wincing with pain as he did so. He was a little shaky at first, but soon was able to negotiate with them. As he hobbled up and down the aisle, he wondered if Lou Ann would return with his newspaper. He wondered if he was more interested in the newspaper or in her. Probably won't see her again. Just as well— becoming a bit too fond of her. Besides, maybe he'd see Beth again soon.

A brisk cold wind was blowing as he left the hospital tent for the first time since he had been wounded. He made his way to a spot overlooking the battlefield across the river and found a large pine tree to lean against for extra support. He gazed across the water. Small shafts of sunlight beamed down through the clouds onto the battlefield. A sign from God they were at peace now? The bodies of his comrades had been removed, and Marye's Heights looked very peaceful except for the bloodstained earth. Will anyone remember? So many... so many. He trembled, feeling weak and nauseous, as he lowered himself down to sit on a tree stump. It was like a dream— more like a horrible nightmare, he thought as he peered through the early morning haze.

On his return to the hospital tent, he noticed several corpses lined up on the side of the tent covered with blankets. He felt a chill go up his spine.

"Oh, there you are, Sergeant," the nurse said, as he clumsily entered the tent. "A teamster was just here looking for ambulatory patients," she continued while folding a pile of blankets on a small table. "You're supposed to be boarding a train for Washington soon. I'll see if I can find him, or you might miss it."

He nodded his head in acknowledgement and moved himself slowly to the bedside of the boy with the amputated leg. "Here—take this," he said with a warm smile, handing the boy his rosary. "Sorry for losing my patience with you. This is all I have to give you. Just think about it—you'll be back home in no time." The boy, forcing a meager smile, reached out to accept the gift.

"Thanks," he said. "You've helped me more than you know."

"Good luck, lad." He shook the boy's hand in his large hands and returned to his own bed to pick up his haversack.

A few minutes later, he heard the teamster's loud voice—"Whoa!"—and the clatter of his ambulance wagon pulling up in front of the tent. "How many you got for me this time, Nellie?" he shouted. She ignored the driver and helped Patrick over to the wagon and onto the back of it.

"Good luck, Sergeant. I think you'll like it up there. Heard the food's much better," she whispered, cupping her hand to the side of her mouth as she spoke.

CHAPTER 3

▼

NORTH TO WASHINGTON

The short ride to the train station was pure agony. The deeply rutted roads brought moans from the wounded. Some amputees let out chilling screams. Patrick felt fortunate as he looked around at the soldiers who had lost an arm or a leg.

The train station wasn't much better. Scores of men lay on litters, exposed to the cold wind and freezing rain. He, however, was able to move about on his crutches to some shelter beneath a tree and its umbrella-like branches. "Thank God," he murmured to himself as he heard the shrill whistle of the train. At least these poor souls will have some shelter now. He was mistaken. Most of the train consisted of flatcars with no shelter whatsoever.

The cold wind grew colder as the train picked up speed. He sat among his broken comrades, freezing rain pelting their faces. He spoke to a few men that he knew from his regiment. They didn't want to talk much about the battle.

"Hey, Pat, is that you?" he heard from somewhere in the midst of the carpet of bandaged bodies. Someone was waving his arm, motioning him to come closer. He maneuvered his way by crawling around the others, dragging his crutches behind him. Too much pain, he thought. Shouldn't be doing this.

"Danny boy," Pat shouted. "You made it!"

"Well, not all of me," he answered, pointing to the stump where his leg had been. He began to cough, as he reached out to shake Pat's hand. Pat noticed the dark circles around his eyes and the bandages around his head.

Poor lad, he thought, as he took off his coat and held it over Danny's head, blocking the wind and rain from his face.

"Got hit twice," he said, coughing some more.

"I saw you go down with the flag," Pat remarked. "Didn't know if you made it or not." He was referring to the emerald green flag with its golden harp, the Irish Brigade emblem.

"Can't keep a tough Mick down, you know. The ball just grazed me." He pointed to his bandaged head. "But this one hit its mark!" as he placed his hand on the stump.

"You'll be as good as new and out of this God-forsaken war now!" Pat exclaimed, wondering if his friend would make it home. He noticed Danny's cough became more frequent as they spoke.

The train jostled them as it wound its way around the hills and river-banks.

Danny grew quiet as he looked down at the space where his leg used to be.

Attempting to cheer him up, Pat remarked, "Just think, Danny, when you get home and hug your colleen with one arm and be holdin' a wee nip of whiskey in the other, you'll be in all your glory!"

"You're right, Paddy," he went on. "If we had a taste of the crature, I'd drink to that now! What more could a man ask for?" His eyes lit up with a sparkle.

Patrick's coat became heavier as the rain soaked through it. His arms were tiring, but he wanted to shield his friend lying there so helpless. The pain in Pat's leg grew worse. They became silent as they listened to the clack-ety-clack of the train wheels, pondering all that had happened to them.

"We're almost there. I can smell the river from here," Pat exclaimed.

The train rounded the bend and slowly came to a halt, jerking the wound-ed one last time before it stopped. It let out a final hissing sound from the engine's boilers. A small band of soldiers and civilians came over and started to carry off the most helpless men. Pat picked up his crutches and cautiously lowered himself to the ground.

"Don't leave me, Paddy," Danny hollered as two soldiers carried his litter off the train.

"I'll be at your side the whole way." He hobbled over to him, trying to keep up with the litter bearers. The boat landing quickly filled up with the wounded. He sat down next to Danny under an eave of a small building. "Well, Danny, at least we got some cover here." He watched the rain dripping down off the roof as he tried to shake his coat dry. "Bet ya can't wait to get back to the old neighborhood."

"Yeah—it's goin' to look mighty good." He paused for a moment, a slight smile on his face. "Seems like a century since we left. Funny we never crossed paths in the old neighborhood and never met till after we joined up—on the train, wasn't it?" he asked quizzically.

Pat barely heard Danny's last remarks. His thoughts were back on the battlefield. He half-heartedly answered him—"Uh-huh." He muttered something Danny couldn't make out.

"What was that you said, Paddy?"

"That damned wall—that damned stone wall!" he kept repeating, his voice becoming louder as he spoke. "We were so close—I could almost touch it. Never shoulda tried it. That damned General don't know crap. Murderous slaughter it was. An idiot could see there wasn't a chance. Them Rebs thick as thieves behind that wall. Them Minie balls whizzin' all around like bees on honey. Murder! Just plain mass murder—that's what it was. Like shootin' fish in a barrel. Wave after wave—mowed down. All those good men—never had a chance. I hope they hang that bastard!"

"That... that's not like you," Danny stammered. "But I'm with you," he said quickly. "I wish they would hang him from the highest tree! Where was he hiding when we got ours?" Pat, attempting to calm himself down, reached into his haversack and pulled out the few cookies he had saved from Lou Ann and offered Danny some. They both sat there chewing on their delicacy, waiting for the boat to arrive. The hours passed slowly, the rain diminished to a fine drizzle, and quiet descended on this small band of demoralized and broken humanity.

The rhythmic splashing of the paddle wheel grew louder, as the mercy boat approached the dock. The few men who had dozed off from sheer exhaustion were abruptly awakened by the repeated blasts of the boat whistle announcing its arrival. Relief from the cold rain never came for many. A fortunate few officers found cover inside the cabins; but the numbers were so many, the majority was relegated to the open decks and exposed to the elements, including Pat and Danny. Danny fell asleep, and Patrick covered him with his long blue coat. It was good he was asleep—no pain. Leaning on his crutches, he hobbled over to the railing. As he stared out at the cold, swift waters of the Potomac, he felt hope for the first time in quite a while. Going North—maybe see Beth. A warm feeling engulfed him. The boat provided security—out of harm's way—like a mother's arms to a newborn. Maybe that's why boats usually have female names, he thought. The full moon cast its bright glow on the water and painted it with silver streaks that glimmered across this highway to safety. He didn't want to take his eyes off this majestic scene and return to the reality on the deck behind him.

By now, Beth occupied his thoughts more than ever. The year since he had become a soldier had been nothing but drill... march... fight... drill some more... march some more... fight some more... survive... constant moving... freezing... running... sweating... blood... praying... dirt... mud... swearing... dodging bullets... falling over from exhaustion. For a time this was all behind him. Now he had time to think. He hoped to see Beth and his family soon. Beth could surely make it to Washington to see him. He had some money for train fare if she needed it. He was a different person now. The year before, when he left New York City, he was just a boy looking for adventure. One single year had turned him into a man. He could explain his physical and mental hardships to Beth but could never find words to describe the slaughter and carnage of the battlefield, nor would he want to. Death and destruction—that about summed up the past year in his mind. As the mercy boat slowly made its way up the river to his nation's capitol, his anticipation of seeing Beth heightened as each rotation of the paddle wheel propelled him closer to her. He glanced upward at the gradually clearing skies, as the gray clouds drifted away, like the curtain going up on a play in the theatre. The departing clouds opened up a dazzling, starlit sky. As he searched for the North Star, he thought of the last time he went on a boat ride.

He and Beth had taken a steamer cruise up the Hudson River on a similar starlit night. It was summer. He remembered the words she spoke to him after he had proposed marriage.

"Oh, Patrick, we can't get married yet. We're too young and besides, there is all this talk of war. I really want to marry you, but let's wait a little while." He had looked into her deep blue eyes and gently brushed her wind-blown hair from her cheek, caressing her ever so gently.

He replied, "My mind knows you're right but my heart doesn't want to listen. I know the war is coming and I'll be leaving you behind—and you're right! What if I don't come back?"

"Oh, stop that nonsense! I know you'll come back to me. Besides, maybe by some miracle, the war won't come."

He wanted to give her something, like a ring, but he was so poor he couldn't afford one. He tried to think of something—then he remembered the medal—the Star of David with the cross on it. He thought for a moment about his boyhood friend, Joshua, who had moved to Virginia years before. Probably never see him again. He took the medal from around his neck.

"Here. Would you take this and wear it for me as a token of my love?" He then placed it around her neck.

She pressed her hands around it and looked down at it. "It's beautiful and I love it." She hesitated, then continued, "But I can't take it from you. I know how much this means to you. I believe it will keep you safe from harm and bring you back to me. I just know you'll come back and you can give it to me for a wedding present." She removed it from her neck and returned it to his with tears in her eyes.

The pungent odor of blood, forming small pools on the deck around the wounded men, was carried on the wind and swept its way into his nostrils. He was jolted from his warm memories of Beth. The fine mist spraying over the bow, however, invigorated him. After a full year of dusty roads and knee-deep mud, it gave him a cleansed feeling.

Funny, he thought. I'm cold and wet but I feel good. The rain on the many marches and battles he had lived through were heavy and depressing. This wasn't like that. It was a hopeful rain, a rain coming from the North, New York City, home, and Beth. He was headed that way.

As he watched the dark landscape of the Virginia countryside passing by, outlined in a haunting silhouette in the moonlight, he thought of his many young comrades that lay in their shallow, dark and lonely graves. He also remembered the impressions he had of the South when he was a young boy, pictures he had seen and things he had read about that picturesque land—the well-dressed men with their fine suits, vests, and walking canes; the beautiful Southern belles with their fancy hoop skirts, frilly bonnets, and parasols; colored folk singing in the cotton fields. Where were these fine ladies and gents now? He hadn't seen any of these ladies yet. The only Southern belles he had seen had been scowling at him as his regiment marched through their towns. And the only Southern gentlemen didn't have walking canes—instead they had been on the other end of a long musket or twelve pound cannon, hurling fiery balls of death at him and his comrades. "So much for Southern hospitality!" he mused to himself. The few colored folk he had met, like Nathan and his family, were wretched, hopeless, and downtrodden souls who lived like animals under the oppressive yolk of their masters.

Patrick's first encounter with Nathan had happened after a skirmish with the Rebels on the plantation where Nathan's family lived. It happened a short while after he had joined the Army. The fight swayed back and forth all afternoon and the Rebels finally retreated at dusk. The slaves were all huddled in a cellar, their women crying over the loss of a loved one. Nathan's father had been shot and killed in the crossfire. Nathan, himself, had been wounded; and Patrick had taken him to the regimental surgeon for aid. Pat couldn't forget how childlike the slaves had been, calling him "Massa," and how many times they had thanked him for his kindness. He was beginning to understand their plight, as he saw a race firsthand in a way that wasn't in the history books. He had heard that Abraham Lincoln had recently made a preliminary proclamation called Emancipation. All slaves were to be freed. Until now, this had meant nothing to him. After his encounter with Nathan and his grieving family, however, he saw things differently. It was a far cry from that portrait of slaves singing in the fields. The only colored people he had seen were working menial jobs back home. They were house servants, bootblacks, or caretakers of animals. They were just there, like part of the landscape. He never really had occasion to talk with them. He hadn't thought much about them before. But now, seeing them frightened and helpless in the cellar, shook him inside. He saw them now as people with feelings and emotions like himself. To see them subjugated and owned by others was a revelation to him. No longer did he have the single thought that he was only fighting because his country was attacked. Flesh and blood was now attached to his cause. A new dimension had entered his psyche. Now he had a tangible, more concrete reason to endure this war, to suffer it and see it through to the bitter end. He just couldn't get the image of that family out of his mind. He would carry it into every battle after that.

His leg began to throb and the pain grew worse. Standing too long. Better find a place to sit down. He had been deep in thought and forgotten his wound. Slowly he made his way to the spot where Danny was lying and lowered himself down onto the wet, wooden deck. He felt so very tired and just wanted to sleep.

Hours passed before he was awakened by excited voices and the stirring of others walking or hobbling to the railing.

"Washington! Washington!" Their shouts became louder. He made his way over to them. He couldn't see much as he stared out into the darkness. Above the trees and beyond, he suddenly saw the glow of light from the gaslights in the city, illuminating the cloudy night sky. He hadn't seen that much light in over a year. Nighttime in the bowels of the Confederacy had only been lit up by small campfires creating shadows around the men, while nights on long marches were pitch black. In an instant the railing was filled with more men straining to see the lights.

This band of wounded, bloody, and ragged soldiers were again placed on a dock and remained there without shelter, food, or drink. They were mostly quiet and didn't complain. After a long wait, some ambulance wagons drawn by horses backed up to the dock and the men were loaded aboard. Patrick stayed by Danny's side on their way to the Armory Square Hospital.

CHAPTER 4

▼

THE YOUNG AMERICAN

Shelter… warmth… dryness… Building #10… Ward B… Bed #7. Pat realized the comforts he had gone without for so long. He had been baptized in blood—not only his own, but that of his comrades who were mostly either crippled or dead. He hadn't been inside of a building since the last campaign began… it seemed strange to him. He sat on the edge of his cot and felt the soft mattress as he gazed around at the stark-white wooden ceilings and walls. Three wood-burning stoves were in the middle of the floor at about twenty-five foot intervals. There were long rows of beds against the walls on each side of the room. Something caught his eye at the far end of the room, hanging over the Exit door—it was a large Christmas wreath. Christmas! he thought. How could I have forgotten Christmas? He had forgotten many things while out in the field, but Christmas was his favorite time of year. He was given dry nightclothes after scrubbing the grime and dirt of war from his body. An orderly brought him a full meal, which he ate ravenously. He flopped down on his bed from sheer exhaustion in his new warm and secure surroundings. But he couldn't sleep.

His early years unfolded before him as he glanced back again at the wreath. He was ten years old. It was Christmas. He was walking down the street where he lived in New York City. He had just bought a present for his mother, Bridget, and was bursting with joy—he couldn't wait to give it to her. It was a heart-warming night, even though the snow was falling in large, wet flakes and becoming deeper as he walked. He loved his mother dearly, yet still had much sadness and pity for her in his heart, although six years had passed since his father's disappearance. He had tried to be the "little man" for her. Their life together, with Michael, his older brother, had been very hard. They struggled to survive every day since he could remember. He had come from a long line of survivors, though, his parents and grandparents having come from Ireland during the potato famine. He was three years old when they arrived in the United States. They had all been on the verge of starvation and considered themselves fortunate, since thousands were dying in Ireland. One big disappointment in the New World, however, was the discrimination they encountered. Many stores and shops had signs in the windows that read, *"Irish need not apply."*

After some time, however, his father did obtain work loading ships at the docks. He was a good man who faithfully brought his paycheck home each week. He left for work one day and never returned home. His mother was frantic! She talked to some of his fellow workers, made visits to the morgue, and wrote letters to relatives in Ireland to see if he had returned there. She was desperate! No one knew anything. Patrick overheard a conversation between his mother and grandfather one evening about the possibility of foul play. One theory was that his father's boss at the shipyard, who owned a nearby tavern, was insistent on the workers spending a fair amount of their paychecks at his establishment. Having the power to hire and fire, it put great pressure on the men. Patrick's father, they thought, would have tried to organize the men in a rebellion against this and was murdered. They never found out what became of him. Consequently, the family had to find ways to survive.

Patrick's mother took in laundry and scrubbed office-building floors to make ends meet. He learned very early in his young life how to survive. He had been beaten up one day as he was delivering clean laundry for his mother. Mrs. VanHuesen lived uptown in a large Victorian home, so unlike his own surroundings. His delivery route to her house took him through Hell's Kitchen, an area, he soon found out, that was filled with gangs, thieves, cutthroats, and murderers. He managed to escape that day, returning home bruised and battered, his heart sore at the loss of the laundry that would have provided the monies for bread for their evening meal. After that, he found other routes to safely complete his deliveries. Some days he would search the train yards and pick up coal for their stove to heat their humble apartment. Bridget spent many hours in bread lines to keep the family from starving. His brother, Mike, seven years older than Pat, couldn't find steady work. He became bitter and began to drink. He fell in with one of the gangs and became a thorn in his mother's side. Pat then took a job selling newspapers on the street corners.

That Christmas was very special to Patrick, as it was the first time he had enough money to buy his mother a present. He never forgot the look on her face as she opened it and found the beautiful pink and white shawl. She smiled in delight, something she didn't do very often.

"Oh, Patrick," she said as she draped it over her shoulders, "this will keep me warm on cold winter nights. Thank you, son. You even knew my favorite color—pink." She went over to him and hugged him as she kissed his forehead.

"I wish I could give you more, Ma. When I get older, I'm gonna buy you your own house." Just then, Patrick's maternal grandfather, Shawn O'Malley, entered the room from the back of the house. He and his wife, Teresa, had moved in with them recently, as they couldn't pay their rent in their old apartment. They sold everything of value that they had. After moving in, however, he did find work digging ditches, a hard job for him since he was in his late fifties, but he had no other choice. It was a day-to-day struggle for all of them. Going to bed with a full stomach was a great accomplishment!

"Paddy, me boy!" Shawn exclaimed. "Did ya come inta some money, lad?" he asked with a chuckle in his voice. "That's a fine present ya got there for your Mom. It's a grand lookin' shawl, it is!"

"Thanks, Grocky," Pat replied. "I've been savin' my newspaper money for it."

"Yer a good lad, ya are."

Pat remembered the mixed emotions he had at the dinner table that night, since he didn't have enough money left to buy presents for the others.

Times were changing and Patrick was growing up with the city and with the nation—a nation going through growing pains with war about to fracture it in two! He, like many others at the time, was either too young or too busy to realize the underlying currents moving and churning which were about to break upon their newfound America, creating a tidal wave of blood and sacrifice.

There was another side to his life, which brought him hope and happiness. He had been too young to remember much about his father, but his Mother, grandparents, and school friend, Joshua, were very dear to him. But above all, he valued his faith. Patrick never missed Mass on Sundays and grew strong in his faith, striving to understand and share it with everyone he could. He loved being an altar boy, lighting the candles, and serving the priest with the little cruets of water and wine. Most of all, he enjoyed holding the paten under each parishioner's chin as the priest gave them Holy Communion.

Some things began to improve when Patrick was eleven years old. Grocky had become like a father to him, teaching and guiding with much love. The boy prayed nightly that his grandfather would find an easier job, seeing how very dirty and tired he was when he returned from working all day. His prayers were answered sooner than he had ever expected.

It was a rainy day, and Pat had returned home about dinnertime after selling his newspapers. Grocky arrived home at the same time, soaking wet, his clothes covered with mud. He was anxious to tell the family about his experience that day.

"Ye'll not be comin' inta this house draggin' that mud behind ya. Ya take them dirty clothes off ya in that hall before ya come in here, Mister O'Malley!" Teresa yelled from the kitchen.

"Faith and begorrah, Mrs. O'Malley! I wouldn't think of traipsin' through yer palace without changin' me duds, me darlin'."

After finishing their Grace Before Meals, Grocky started right in to tell of his exploits that day.

"Ya'd never believe what happened ta old Grocky today," Shawn blurted out. "Ya see, me pal, Timmy, an' me were diggin' a trench in front a City Hall fer the new water lines an', lo and behold, I hears some lady screamin' in the street. Well, I jumps up outta the ditch an' sees a team a horses pullin' a runaway wagon an' they were runnin' like blazes an' headin' straight fer this little girl who had wandered out inta the street. I whips off me coat an' starts flappin' it as fast as me arms could go right in front a them runaways."

By this time, he was waving his arms up and down, knocking a glass over as he did so and never realizing it. "Well, ya wouldn't believe it!" He paused to catch his breath, then continued, "Them critters suddenly turns an' runs up to the steps a City Hall an' stops cold. Me heart almost jumps outta me chest!" He paused briefly, then speaking in a calmer tone, he went on. "When I gits me wits together, I sees the little girl, still standin' in the street, holdin' her hands to her face an' frozen in her steps. Just then, her mom runs inta the street an' grabs her up inta her arms an' comes over ta me. 'Oh, thank you sir!' she says. 'Oh, thank you! God bless you,' as she takes me grimy hand an' shakes it. 'You saved my daughter's life. How can I repay you?' "Well, I didn't know what ta say. There I was, still shakin', fulla mud an' dirt, smellin' like a sewer rat, an' standin' there with this finely dressed lady wearin' a fancy big hat an' a fur cape over her shoulders. After I catches me breath, I finally says, 'You don't owe me anything, Ma'am. I'm just glad

I was there ta help. How's the little girl?' She says ta me that she'll be fine once she calms down. That little girl has her little head buried in her mom's chest all this time, still sobbin'. Well, I tells her I best get back ta work before me boss gits after me; and when I turns ta go back ta the ditch, some people starts clappin' and congratulatin' me. Saints preserve us! Well, I was embarrassed ta beat the band. All these people standin' there, lookin' at me. 'Oh, sir,' the little girl's mother says, would you give me your name and address? I would like to send you a little something to show my gratitude.' I says, 'Well, ya don't have ta do that, Ma'am.' Then she says that she was gonna insist on it, 'cause her daughter would a been killed if it wasn't fer me. 'Well, Ma'am, if you insist,' I says. She gives me a piece a paper an' I writes me name and address. I tells her I don't want no reward—that savin' that little one was enough reward fer me. Praise be, I'm still shakin' a little." He lifted his beer mug to his lips and took a big swig as he settled back into his chair.

"It was a grand thing ya did, but ya coulda been killed," Teresa said, as she placed her hand over his large, calloused hand, squeezing it as she did. "Your guardian angel must have been with you. Thanks be to God you're still in one piece. I don't know what we'd do without ya."

Patrick smiled, sitting silently at the other end of the table and feeling proud of his grandpa and thankful that he had him. I hope to grow up to be brave like him, he thought.

A few days later, there was a knock on the door. Patrick opened it to see a well dressed man standing there holding an envelope in his hand. "Is this the O'Malley residence?" he asked in a very business-like manner.

"That's my grandpa," Pat said. "He's asleep right now."

"Would you give him this when he wakes up?" the man asked with a slight smile on his face.

"Yes, sir," Pat said, as the man turned to leave. He looked down at the envelope in his hand. It read, "Mr. Shawn O'Malley". He went over to Grocky, still sound asleep in his chair, and gently placed it on his lap.

Pat was crawling into bed when he heard Grocky exclaim in a loud voice, "Praise be Jesus!" He ran into the living room and saw his grandpa handing the letter to his grandmother, then grabbing her by the arm and dancing her around the room in an Irish-jig fashion.

"What is it?" Pat inquired in anticipation, squinting his eyes from the light.

"The Mayor!" Grocky blurted out. "It was his daughter I saved from the horses! Praise be! He wants us fer dinner next week!"

The next few days were filled with nervous excitement over the Mayor's invitation. Grama and Grocky were rummaging through their skimpy wardrobes to find something decent to wear, while Bridget, his mom, didn't seem to care very much. By now, she had become a frequent visitor at the pub down the street. She had never liked people in any position of authority. "What's the big fuss about?" she asked. "He's only a high-falutin' politician." Her drinking caused many arguments between the grandparents and her. They didn't have the money to spend on alcohol, and she was becoming less of a mother to Patrick. His brother, Mike, was rarely home, and cavorting in the streets with the roving gangs most of the time. Grocky wanted to kick him out but Teresa wouldn't hear of it. Mike had taken to drinking up the little money that he begged, borrowed, or stole. He hadn't helped the family in over a year.

The mayor's carriage pulled up to their door on the designated night, and Pat and his grandparents climbed in. "Would ya look at yerself, Mother. Ya look like the Queen of Sheba, dressed in those fancy duds!" Grocky exclaimed.

"And you, sir, look like the King himself." She beamed.

Pat was sitting across from them and taking it all in. "Then *I* must be a prince!" he chuckled as they proudly rode down Broadway, feeling like royalty and anticipating the dinner and conversation with "His Highness", the Mayor.

They were ushered into the Mayor's mansion by a butler, led into the library, and offered a drink. Glancing around the room in awe, Patrick surveyed the high walls lined with bookcases. The volumes of books contained therein were interspersed with beautiful green plants and figurines of a nautical flavor. His eyes became riveted on the large three-masted sailboat and the lighthouse collection to the right of the entryway. It was incomprehensible to him that one person could own so many books, for he had never owned even one. He couldn't resist tapping the worn sole of his shoe on the shiny, deep brown, hardwood floor. They sat there, Grama and Patrick drinking tea, and Grocky savoring the finest whiskey he had ever had. "Never had anything as good as this in the old sod," he quipped. A few moments later, they heard footsteps growing louder on the hardwood floors, and Grocky gulped down the last drop and licked his lips, carefully consuming the last vestiges of this precious liquid.

A stout lady appeared in the doorway dressed in a long blue gown adorned with sequins. It looked as though it were two sizes too small for her. Her hair was pulled up into a bun and fastened to the back of her head with a golden arched comb. "Mr. O'Malley, how good to see you again. I'm so pleased you could come. I presume this is your wife and son," she said, nodding her head in the direction of Mrs. O'Malley and Patrick.

They all stood up, and Grocky gestured toward his wife. "This is the Mrs." And looking at Patrick, he proudly stated, "And this is Patrick, our *grand*son", smiling at Teresa as he spoke, amused by the error.

"Your husband is a very brave man, Mrs. O'Malley. We are so fortunate that our little Sarah wasn't hurt that awful day."

"Thank you, Ma'am. I believe it was an act of Divine Providence it turned out the way it did," Teresa replied.

"Your son—I mean *grand*son—is a lovely looking boy. How old are you?" she asked, bending over slightly to shake his hand.

"I'll be twelve next year." He stretched out his hand to take hers, feeling a bit shy in her overwhelming presence and the lavish surroundings like he had never before encountered.

"Well now, I believe dinner is ready. Shall we go into the dining room? My husband is just finishing some business and will join us presently." She led them into the dining room, and Patrick's eyes opened wide as he looked around the room. He first noticed the large, brilliant, crystal chandelier hanging over the table and the soft, plushy carpet under his feet. He gazed around the room at the fine tapestries hanging on the walls and the shiny silver service on the buffet. They were then seated in chairs designated by the mayor's wife. He glanced down at the china in front of him and marveled at the gold trim on the white plates and the fine silverware and linen napkins placed strategically around each setting.

"Good evening, folks," the mayor said as he entered the room, meticulously dressed in a three-piece herringbone suit. Reaching into his vest pocket, he removed his gold watch, which was attached to his watch fob. "We're right on time, I see. It is an honor to have you in my home, sir. And this must be your lovely wife and son, I presume?"

"*Grand*son, sir. He's me daughter's boy."

"Oh, I see," the mayor replied.

The mayor thanked Grocky two or three times during dinner for saving his daughter's life. Little Sarah, who was five years old, was quietly eating, as Grocky relived the incident. Patrick was totally immersed in all the pleasures of this culinary feast. He had a few servings, as did Grocky and Grama, heaping the fork-tender roast beef high on his plate and smothering it with the gravy. After dinner, the ladies retired to the library while the men stayed at the table and talked. The mayor offered Shawn a cigar, and they both sat there contented from their meal. Pat stayed seated with them, figuring he should be with the men. He was at that curious age and listened intently. Besides, no one had asked him to leave. He was glad he was able to stay. After several minutes of small talk, he and Grocky were astonished when the mayor offered Shawn a policeman's job. Of course, Grocky had told the mayor a sob story, some of which was true, but he had embellished it with a few extra muscle aches and hardship stories.

Grama, Grocky, and Patrick felt like the "cats that swallowed the canary" as they sang and laughed and cried on the ride home that night in the mayor's fancy carriage.

Life changed for the better for Pat and his family after that. The police job provided them with a good living, and the table was no longer of meager fare. They had been the lowest of the low in Ireland, barely scratching out enough to eat from the small plot of land they were allowed to cultivate. When two years of drought came, the potatoes rotted in the ground, and their only source of food had dried up. Patrick's grandparents had seen many friends and neighbors starving to death. They had no choice— to stay was to die—to leave held some hope. America, they thought, would be their salvation—and it was! The family not only survived but now had what they considered to be a prominent place in society. Grocky had steady work and the prestige of a police officer in the community. Pat was so proud the day his grandfather came home wearing his new uniform. He had come bursting in the door hollering, "Ya better all behave or I'll put the long arm a the law on ya!" chuckling as he spoke. Standing there in his blue cap and coat with shiny brass buttons and gray trousers, he looked as proud as a peacock.

The next few years were happy ones for Patrick. Grocky had received free passes and took him to America's first World's Fair on 6th Avenue and 42nd Streets. He never forgot the huge Crystal Palace made of iron and glass in the shape of a Greek cross with its high dome glittering in the sunlight. He marveled at the Cyrus McCormick reaper on display, along with marble statues, glassware from Austria, silks from France, Italy, Turkey and India, and the many European cultural exhibits. After they had finished their tour of the Palace, Grocky took Patrick across the street to the Latting Tower that stood 350 feet high. It was the first time they rode on an elevator, a new steam elevator that took them up to heights they had never been before. They stood on the upper platform and took in the spectacular view of the city. They could see the new construction of buildings and the large, granite block foundations, the new Russ pavement and gaslights installed on the new streets along with the telegraph poles. They also saw the tall ships and paddle wheelers sailing up the East River. Grocky pointed to the wharf on South Street where he had taken Patrick to see the launching of the racing yacht, *America*, two years earlier. Afterwards, P.T. Barnum's Museum on Broadway offered many strange exhibits for them as they gawked at the cherry-colored cat, the Fiji mermaid, and Tom Thumb, the world's smallest man. How thrilled Patrick was to be a part of this new and growing nation. He was caught up in the excitement and promise this new land held for him.

As he entered his teen years, he worked hard at two jobs and helped support the family. In addition to his newspaper job, he began to work at Mr. Schuler's Meat Market in the German section of town. Grocky walked the beat there and had become friendly with the shop owners, which helped get Patrick the job. He learned the butcher trade quickly and became an asset to Mr. Schuler. Grocky told him, "Work—work hard. Save yer money. Become yer own man. Don't be beholden ta anyone. We never had a chance in the old country. We were like slaves—no chance ta better ourselves—always at the mercy of the rich landowners and lords. You've got a land here just fer the takin', Paddy— as good a chance as anyone, lad. Keep yer shoulder to the grindstone and be on the lookout for opportunity. You kin see it all around ya—just waitin' fer ya ta take it. Ya got a damn site better chance than *I* ever had. Ya know, lad, in the old country, land was everything. If ya owned land, ya were rich; an' the more of it ya owned, the richer ya were. Well, I see somethin' different here in these United States of America. Don't git me wrong, Paddy." He emptied the cold ashes from his pipe into the metal ashtray, creating a clanging sound as he tapped it. "Ownin' land is still a way ta become somebody and make a lot a money, but there's somethin' else here ya gotta grasp hold of."

"What's that, Grocky?" Pat inquired, as he lay on the living room rug, head propped up on one hand with his elbow resting on the floor.

"There's more than one way ta skin a cat, boy. There's business an' sellin' an' buyin' an' money flowin' all around ya! Look at some a those rich gentlemen uptown, livin' in those mansions. Do ya think they own land? No sir. They made their fortunes sellin' stuff ta people. Knowledge, Paddy—that's what ya need ta make a success of yerself. Learn somethin'—somethin' that just a few people know. Do that and you'll be a better, richer man fer it! Yes, sir, that's the secret! That there is yer land, not the kinda land that ya can pick up and sift through yer fingers or the kinda land ya can let people live on and charge 'em high rent they can't pay an' then kick 'em off, whole families at a time, an' let 'em starve ta death. It ain't that kinda land an' it can't dry up on ya and git parched so nothin' kin grow on it. Paddy, I'm tellin' ya..."

He looked straight into Pat's eyes. "You'll see the future is yers. Ya kin become anything ya want ta. Learn all ya kin an' keep yer eyes open. This is yer land, an' don't ever let anyone stop ya from gittin yer fair share."

Young Patrick grew to love his family dearly. His grandparents became like parents to him, having no father and a mother who was seldom home. She spent most of her time at McGinty's Tavern, and left the burden of raising him to Grocky and Teresa. He loved his mother in spite of all her faults but couldn't get much love back from her.

He was getting older now and began to take an interest in current politics. A tall man who wore a black, stovepipe hat came to Patrick's city that year. His curiosity about Abe Lincoln was aroused from reading about him in the newspapers and from hearing his grandfather talk about him. He came to speak at the Great Hall of Cooper Union on a cold February night, and Pat went to hear him. He mentioned his grandfather's name to the police guards on duty and managed to squeeze through the crowd, closer to the podium. His first impression of Mr. Lincoln was not very flattering. As he observed this politician from Illinois, he couldn't help but notice his large ears and very long arms. His voice had a higher pitch than a man of his height would seem to have. As Pat listened to him speak, he became more interested in what he had to say. Patrick heard many eloquent words in Lincoln's speech that night, many of them about slavery. With his limited vocabulary, he couldn't comprehend all of it, except that slavery was a bad thing. What he did understand very well, however, was the fact that Lincoln sought to hold the country together at all costs. Pat left the crowd and walked home through a snowstorm with Lincoln's words ringing in his ears. *"Let us have faith that right makes might; and in that faith, let us to the end dare to do our duty as we understand it."* Pat was very impressed with the man in the tall hat.

Pat's thoughts became divided, as the country was also becoming divided. Much of the time he thought about Beth, a young lady he had recently met and was growing fond of. These were warm and hopeful thoughts. But the climate of war was growing fast. How could he think about the future when this ugly monster called war was looming over the nation—*his* nation—the *United* States—*one* nation—*indivisible*. How could this be? He understood the Revolutionary War from history books—fighting England—another country. But how could he fight his own countrymen?

He, like many others, became fearful and unsettled. However, an air of patriotism was also growing, as the call to arms was rapidly enveloping the hearts and minds of all his fellow countrymen.

CHAPTER 5

▼

BETWEEN HOME AND HELL

Patrick's musings were abruptly interrupted by the doctor standing at the foot of his bed. "How do you feel, son? Heard you took a ball in the leg." Before he could answer, the doctor was throwing back the covers.

"Still getting pain," Pat responded.

Taking only seconds, the doctor removed the bloody bandages. "You're damn lucky, son—another inch and your bone would have been shattered. Probably would have had to take your leg off. You'll be as good as new in a few weeks. I'll leave you in good hands," he said as he instructed the nurse to clean and dress the wound. Then he left as quickly as he had arrived.

Patrick asked the nurse if she could get him some writing paper and a pencil so he could let Beth and his folks know he was alive. As she finished applying fresh bandages to his wound, she said, "It just so happens we received a new supply of paper and pencils this morning. I'll get some for you."

A few minutes later she returned with a few sheets of paper and two pencils— "Just in case you break one."

"Thanks." He picked up the pencil to write but didn't know where to begin. Many, many thoughts and images of war shot through his mind quicker than the bullets that had recently flown around him. Finally he began:

My dearest Beth,
It is with mixed feelings of sorrow and joy that I write to you. I am in a hospital in Washington, D.C. recovering from a bullet wound

in my leg, but I will be all right. I miss you terribly and hope you might be able to come down and visit me. I have enough money saved up that I can send you train fare.

I cannot describe to you what war is really like, nor would I desire your innocent blue eyes to fall upon the words of horror which would surely be invoked if I were to attempt it. It is enough to say that I have lost many good friends in the battle of Fredericksburg, Virginia.

There is not a day that passes that I do not think of you. You are in my heart, mind and soul every moment of the day and night. I thank the Almighty Creator of the Universe for sparing my life. I know that one day we shall be together again. This awful war will end soon, I hope.

It is my sincere wish that you will be able to visit me. I would come home to see you when my leg gets better, but they have suspended all furloughs. I could write volumes to you, but they are turning the lamps down right now and I can barely see what I am writing. We will be able to talk all day when you arrive here. Please let me know your response soon. I am not sure how long I will be here before I return to my regiment.

All my love and affection,
Patrick

He mailed the letter the following morning, then waited for Beth's reply. The days passed slowly. Every morning he hobbled down to the mailroom on his crutches. Each day he returned to his bed without a letter. He wrote to his folks and they had not responded either.

Danny was in another ward, and Patrick visited him on a daily basis. His stump was healing well and he was soon to be released to return home. Pat envied him a little— until he glanced at that stump. They talked for hours about the old neighborhood and shared funny stories about their childhood. Danny appreciated the company, and it helped Patrick fill in the time while waiting with so much anticipation to hear from Beth.

They exchanged goodbyes the night before Danny was to be released. Pat had asked him if he would go to visit his folks and Beth to assure them that he was doing well.

Pat found himself becoming restless and bored after Danny left. He had a great deal of time to think. Murder and guilt had settled into the back of his mind. That man— the one he had killed with his bayonet—did he *really* have to kill him? All of the enemy he had shot had been at a distance. He never really knew whom he had hit or if his bullets had hit *any*one. That was war without a face. He couldn't shake the image of that Confederate soldier from his mind, though. The young Rebel had breathed his last breath into Patrick's face. This was as close as war could get! He wanted to go to Confession. He needed absolution, he thought. One day he saw a priest enter his ward and approached him. Before he could speak, the priest introduced himself.

"Father O'Reilly's my name, son. And what would your name be?"

"Patrick O'Hanrahan, Father."

"And what can I be doing for you, lad?"

"Well, Father, I... could you hear my confession?"

"Well, sure'n I'd be delighted to. Why don't we step into the nurses' station—it's more private there."

Patrick had always gone to confession at church, kneeling behind a screen. There weren't any kneelers or even chairs to sit on now. He felt uncomfortable when Father O'Reilly told him he could hear his confession standing up face-to-face. But his desire to confess was so strong, he felt he could undergo this minor act of humiliation. Patrick stood next to the priest, head bowed, with hands folded in prayer and began.

"Bless me, Father, for I have sinned. My last confession was about three months ago." He went on, confessing a time when he became so angry that he took the Lord's name in vain and some immoral thoughts he had silently entertained in his loneliness, but he saved the big one for last.

"Father, I killed a man."

There was a brief moment of silence before the priest responded. "Well, son, you are a soldier in war, and a justifiable war at that!"

"Father, I know about that, but I don't know if this man I killed with my bayonet— well—I just don't know... "

Patrick described how he plunged the bayonet into the Confederate soldier scavenging on the battlefield that cold night and expressed his feelings that maybe it was murder.

Father O'Reilly gently placed his hand on Pat's shoulder and looked at him with compassion. "Did ya ever hear of self defense, Patrick?"

"Yes, Father, I have."

"From what you tell me, you were seconds away from being killed by this enemy soldier. I've talked to many lads like yourself, and you should know about some of their stories—are ya listening ta me now, Patrick?"

"Yes, Father."

"Since this was your first really big battle, I believe you told me, there is something you should know. There have been many eyewitness accounts of enemy soldiers who killed the wounded after a battle. They took their clothing, valuables— anything they could find. You could have been one of them— layin' there in the cold—all naked and dead, without a stitch on ya."

"But Father, I saw his face—and he didn't seem to be armed at the time."

"Now listen to me, lad. Horrible things happen in war. Would ya like to be a statistic? Would ya like your parents to have lost a son? Or your sweetheart her beau?"

"No, Father."

"Well, now, that Rebel soldier had no business takin' things from the wounded and poor dead lads on that battlefield. Is nothing sacred anymore? Now be at peace, son. You didn't ask for this war. It was thrust upon you; and besides, your actions were not premeditated. You were merely defending yourself while in a most vulnerable position—a spontaneous response of self-defense, I would say. Some things that happen in times of war would never enter our minds during peacetime. God knows your heart, and He is a most merciful and forgiving God. Your mere presence here and your openness is in itself a sign of repentance. Are you sorry for all your sins?"

"Yes, Father."

"For your penance, say three Our Fathers and three Hail Marys. Now make a good Act of Contrition."

"Oh, my God, I am heartily sorry for having offended Thee, and I detest all my sins because I dread the loss of Heaven and the pains of hell. But most of all, because they have offended Thee, my God, who art all good and deserving of all my love. I firmly resolve, with the help of Thy grace to confess my sins, to do penance, and to amend my life. Amen."

Father O'Reilly raised his right hand and made the sign of the Cross over Patrick. "I absolve you of all your sins, in the name of the Father, and of the Son, and of the Holy Ghost. Pray for peace to come to this battle-weary nation, Patrick. Now go in peace to love and serve the Lord." Father shook Pat's hand and smiled. "I'll be prayin' for your safety, lad." As he began to walk away, he stopped momentarily and looked back at Patrick. "Oh, and lad, it wouldn't be hurtin' to say an occasional prayer to St. Michael—he's the patron saint of men in uniform, you know." He then left to continue his rounds to the other men.

A heavy load was lifted from Pat as he hobbled over to his bed and prayed the rosary on his fingers, as he had given his beads to the boy in the field hospital.

Christmas came and went with little fanfare. Still no letter from home. A nurse had put up a scrawny Christmas tree in the corner of his ward. A big fat soldier, dressed in a Santa Claus suit, handed out some Christmas cookies baked by the local women. He had a large red nose and wore a red hat with a round white tassel that he repeatedly pushed away from his face. He weaved down the aisle and smelled like a brewery.

Patrick's positive attitude was slowly disintegrating. He became sullen and very lonesome. Here Christmas had come and gone, and he still had not heard anything from Beth. Maybe it would come by New Year's. Danny had gone home, and he didn't have a good friend to confide in. The few men with whom he had struck up friendships had also been released to go home or sent back to their regiments.

As the New Year approached, Pat made his way to the mailroom once again. It was the last day of the year, and he was still anxiously awaiting her letter.

"Patrick O'Hanrahan, you said?" the mail clerk asked.

"Yes, sir. Is there anything for me?"

The clerk sorted through the mail for a few moments and returned with a letter in his hand. "Got one here for you, Sarge," as he handed it to Pat. "Hope it's good news."

"Thanks." He hurriedly limped back to his bed to read it in private. It was from Beth. His heart pounded with excitement and anticipation. He began to read the letter quickly, hoping that she could come and visit him. A feeling of warmth and joy came over him as he read of her love for him and how much she longed to see him again. As he continued on to the second page, however, his mood changed in an instant. His hands, still holding the letter, dropped into his lap; and he gazed up at the stark-white ceiling. She couldn't come, explaining that her mother was sick and she was needed there. He became more depressed.

New Year's Eve, he thought, and here I am in this stinking hospital. Nothing to look forward to. The whole world's celebrating and having a good time. He remembered someone telling him about a pub a few blocks from the hospital. By now he was able to walk with a cane. The money he had saved for Beth's train fare could now be used to buy a little happiness. Why not? He would somehow have to obtain a pass in order to get out of the hospital.

He looked into the mirror and saw an older-looking, weather-beaten face. He hadn't shaved in a long time, and his beard had grown thicker and longer. He had been ready to shave it off before Beth came down. He had also received a new uniform from the quartermaster, wanting to look his best for her. Now, he thought, why bother? Walking around the hospital grounds outside, he breathed in the cold winter air and tried to gather his thoughts. He looked at the many white barrack-like buildings in the area and was surprised at the large number of them in the compound. So many wounded and dying men. He thanked God that he was spared but couldn't shake the deep loneliness he felt. The wind grew colder, and a light snow-fall dusted the grounds and buildings around him. Everything's white, he thought. Looks like a no-man's land—barren—without color—just like my life. He fought the loneliness but felt he was losing the battle. He pulled up the collar of his new blue overcoat and limped along with his new cane. A chill enveloped him as the brisk cold wind brought back memories of the battlefield. He wanted something to warm his insides. The cocoa, tea, and hot cider were well appreciated for a while; but for the first time in his life, he needed something stronger. He made up his mind to go to the pub—pass or no pass—after dinner—after dark—after crumpling up Beth's letter. He would definitely get out of this *prison*.

As he entered the building and made his way over to his bed, he noticed something on his pillow. It was purple—a stark contrast to the white pillow, sheets, ceiling and walls. It was a sprig of lilac. He picked it up, closed his eyes, and inhaled deeply. The aroma was intoxicating. Lou Ann… it was that heavenly scent he experienced when regaining consciousness in the field hospital when he opened his eyes and gazed upon what he first thought was an angel. He felt a slight exhilaration and a ray of hope—someone to talk to—someone very beautiful and sweet smelling—someone he might toast the New Year with. He felt life returning to his weakened body—color in his life—his blood coursing through his veins once again. Beth was far away. Lou Ann was not!

He had just turned to place the lilac on a small table next to his bed when he heard light footsteps quickly approaching. He turned to see Lou Ann coming down the aisle with a small vase in her hand. "Happy New Year, Sergeant. Do you like lilacs?" Her smile warmed his heart.

"Oh… yes… I do. How are you?"

"I'm just fine, but how are you? How is your leg?"

"It's coming along fine, thanks. I'm off my crutches, and the doctor says I should be as good as new in a few more weeks."

"Well, aren't you going to wish me a Happy New Year?"

"Oh… oh, yes… Happy New Year."

"I'm so sorry I missed you back at the field hospital. I looked for you to give you some New York newspapers I collected, but you were gone when I got there. I didn't think you'd be transferred so fast."

"How did you know where I was?" He propped his cane up against the table and sat down at the foot of his bed.

"Well, it wasn't hard to find you, Sarge—I mean, Patrick. We ladies from the Sanitary Commission get to most of the hospitals; and, besides, the nurse from the field hospital told me you had been sent here."

"Would you care to sit down, Miss?" He reached over to pull a chair closer to where she was standing.

"Please call me Lou Ann,"as she placed the lilac in the vase. "Lilacs need water, you know." She grinned. "There you are—a little something to cheer you up. I love flowers, don't you? Lilacs are my favorite." She sat down, glancing over at Patrick, her sparkling blue eyes meeting his for a brief moment. It was a soft look, a hard-to-describe *I want to get to know you better* look, a look of invitation. Pat caught himself gazing into her eyes but glanced away as he felt he should. After all, didn't he recently profess his unwavering love in his own handwriting to Beth? This was a new, awkward and unsettling feeling. Neither one spoke for a moment. She broke the silence. "I'm so glad your leg is better. Do you know how long you'll be here?"

"I'm not sure. Maybe a few more weeks."

"Heard anything from home?"

"Yes, I have." He had received a letter from his grandparents stating everything was well at home. His brother Mike was fighting with Grant in the Mississippi area. "Everything's fine there." In a way, he wanted her to leave. It would simplify matters. But she was pretty and it *was* New Year's Eve. Besides, he was awfully lonely. His thoughts swayed. How many more battles? Would he come back in one piece? Or not at all?

He was determined not to look into her eyes again. He would look elsewhere as he talked to her—maybe her hair or over her shoulder. Instead, he found himself staring at her lips. This was a mistake. They looked more sensual, redder, and inviting than any he had ever seen before. He felt trapped—trapped in a web of desire enveloping him—an exciting web! He thought it might be hard extricating himself from it. He had always prided himself as a young man of good character, a man loyal to his country, family, faith, friends, and *Beth*. A tinge of guilt and fear came over him—fear of losing his character and loyalty, prompted by a long gaze into a pair of deep blue eyes. What did he have to fear? He had escaped the clutches of murderers and thieves in Hell's Kitchen as a young boy. He had survived a thousand bullets flying in his direction at Fredericksburg. Thinking too much. Have to lighten up. Haven't said or done anything wrong. Maybe one evening won't hurt.

"You seem miles away, Patrick. Thinking of home?"

"Uh, no. Nothing in particular," resting one leg on the bed and gingerly placing his hands under the wounded leg, pulling it up onto the bed. "How are things with you, Lou Ann? I'd like to hear about things outside of this hospital and this war."

"Oh, everything is well. Most of my time is spent in hospitals, too. So many wounded and homesick boys."

He began to wonder why she had chosen *him* to show so much attention to. Or was she like this with other men? Maybe she's just a really caring person... or... maybe she's just a big tease! He really didn't know.

"You know, Patrick, we never had much time to talk back at Fredericksburg. I would love to visit longer with you; and, being New Year's Eve, wouldn't it be nice to go somewhere more pleasant?"

"Well, to tell you the truth, I was thinking about getting out of here tonight myself." Now I did it, he thought. Should have said no. Oh, what the heck!

"Did you have any place in mind?"

"Oh, just a little place I heard about down the street."

"Have you been out in this neighborhood yet?"

"No, not really. Just heard about this place from one of the men."

"Well, it's not a very nice neighborhood. You know, they built these hospitals in a pretty bad section of town. I think the guards are here to keep the undesirables out more than to keep the soldiers in."

"Oh—the guards! I just remembered, I don't have a pass. Besides, I'm..."

She broke in. "You won't need a pass. It's New Year's Eve, and the guards know me. You know, my work brings me here often. Don't worry about it." She smiled confidently at him. "I don't make it a practice to socialize with the patients here; but this is a special night and... well... I think we could both use some relief from this awful war. Is there any reason you don't want to go?"

"No. Not really."

"Then it's settled. I think it will do us both some good. I have a few patients to see in another ward. Why don't you get dressed, and I'll be back in an hour. I have a carriage and driver waiting outside."

Pat thought to himself, a carriage and driver—hmmm—sounds well off—out of *my* class.

He responded, "That's fine with me. It's been a long time since I've seen anything of civilian life."

"See you in an hour then," she said as she rose from her chair and straightened her dress. Strolling out of the ward, she glanced back briefly and smiled at him.

He pushed the guilt into the back of his mind and prepared himself for an evening of enjoyment and relaxation with a beautiful woman he hardly knew. He washed up, trimmed his beard and mustache, and donned his brand new uniform. He thought of his grandfather on that night he had come home so proud, wearing his new policeman's uniform. He felt good as he gazed into the mirror and saw a well-groomed, well-dressed, young soldier about to embark on an evening of frivolity. This is how people should live, he thought. More like home—not that hellish business of war and killing. He opened the drawer of the little table next to his bed, searching for his comb, and saw Beth's letter lying there where he had left it. He gently pushed it back to retrieve his comb. His heart pulled one way, as his mind moved in the opposite direction. It didn't seem long before Lou Ann returned.

"Are you ready, Patrick?" she asked as she approached him. "My, you look so handsome in your uniform."

He turned to greet her and smiled.

As they approached the gate where the guard was stationed, the soldier on duty greeted them. "Good evening, Miss Sommers." He looked at Patrick. "Can I see your pass, Sergeant?"

Lou Ann broke in—"Happy New Year, Harry. Here's a little something to keep you warm." She handed him a small bottle of liquor she had concealed in her purse. "It's O.K. He's with me," she said.

Harry's eyes lit up at the gift. "Happy New Year, Miss Sommers." He looked at Patrick. "Have a good time, Sergeant."

Chapter 6

▼

Uncharted Waters

Patrick helped Lou Ann into the waiting carriage. With much difficulty, he was able to manipulate himself up behind her with the help of his cane. She instructed the driver to take them to the Willard Hotel. The carriage was enclosed and had windows in both doors that frosted up as their warm breath came in contact with the cold night air. She pulled a blanket from the corner.

"I don't want you to get sick and have to spend more time in the hospital now," she said as she tucked the blanket around their legs.

He wiped the frost from the window to see what he could of the nation's Capitol, and memories began to seep into his brain. He thought of the carriage ride to the mayor's house with his grandparents when he was a boy. Then, repeatedly wiping the window, visions of Beth waving goodbye at the train station began to flood his mind. He could envision her face on the other side of the steamy train window that night he went off to war.

"You won't be able to see much at night, Patrick. Maybe we could go out sometime during the day," Lou Ann offered. "I can show you the White House, the Capitol building, and all the interesting sights."

"That would be great! I'd like that. By the way, what is this Willard Hotel we're going to? I mean, what kind of a place is it?"

"Oh, you'll love it there, I'm sure. It has one of the finest restaurants in town. The food is delicious."

He did have money with him; but he became a little nervous, thinking this may cost him more than he had bargained for. He hated cheapskates and didn't want to sound like one; however, he was committed now and hoped for the best. He glanced over at Lou Ann while blowing his warm breath into his cold, cupped hands. "How long have you been working for the Sanitary Commission?"

"Oh, shortly after Bull Run when I heard of the many wounded after the terrible defeat of our boys there. I wanted to do what I could to help. I'm not a nurse, so I joined the Sanitary Commission to help the cause in another way. Besides, I wasn't doing much good at home."

"Did you live with your parents in..." He hesitated for a moment. "Where did you say? Pennsylvania, wasn't it?"

"Yes. Gettysburg. It's a small farm town." Pulling the blanket up over her lap and securing it around her hips, she continued. "I was thinking of leaving home even before the war started. My mother can pretty much take care of herself, and we have relatives there if she needs anything. There wasn't much for me to do there."

"Is your father living?"

"Oh, yes. He's a doctor. He has a practice here in Washington. We couldn't live on his small practice in Gettysburg, so he works here during the week and goes home on weekends." She shifted the subject to him. "So tell me about yourself, Patrick. New York—I'd like to visit there some day. Sounds so exciting!"

"Well, it is all of that." He thought for a moment. "But it has a dark side too."

"How do you mean?"

"There are plenty of poor people living in shanties." He felt uncomfortable and avoided mentioning his destitute beginnings. "Did you know there are thousands of street arabs there?"

"What are street arabs?"

"They're children living on the street, mostly abandoned. They do anything to stay alive—even steal or mug people."

"Oh, that's horrible," she said as she placed her gloved hand over her mouth in a gesture of surprise.

"Well, that's the bad side. We also have very rich people living in mansions. There are all kinds of stores. And we have many ships loading and unloading cargo at our docks. It's a real crowded city with a lot of people. Your town sounds nice and peaceful to me."

"Tell me about your family. Do you have a large family?"

"I live with my mother and grandparents. My only brother, Mike, is in the Army too—out West somewhere last I heard."

"And your father is he... ?"

"He disappeared when I was four. Don't know what ever became of him."

"Oh, I'm so sorry to hear that. Must be hard not to have a father."

"Well, my grandfather has been like a father to me."

"Did you join the Army when the war started?"

"No, I didn't turn eighteen until later. I joined up in December of '61."

"Then you weren't in the battle of Bull Run?"

"No. I heard it was a rout." He wiped his frosted window once again, trying to look out. "Well, Fredericksburg was a catastrophe compared to that! A slaughterhouse!"

"Yes, I know. I saw enough wounded and suffering men like you to last me a lifetime." He didn't respond as he gazed out the window, trying to get his mind off the war. She sensed that he was feeling sad about the battle. "Why don't we agree not to talk about the war tonight. Let's just have a good time—all right?"

"You don't have to twist my arm about that." He smiled as he looked over at her. "That's a deal!"

The Willard Hotel was the fanciest place he had seen since his grandparents and he had visited the mayor's mansion in New York City. They entered the ladies' entrance on the side of the building and were escorted by the headwaiter to a booth situated on the back wall. Patrick was impressed at the lavish red velvet tieback drapes, partially concealing each booth, and matching the plush cushions on each side. A white linen cloth covered the table; and a thick, red candle held by a brass holder had been placed in the center of it. From his vantage point, he could see a short stairway descending to the main barroom below. It was filled with men, mostly officers—too many officers, he thought. He reached over to help Lou Ann slide her coat off her shoulders. "You come here often?"

"I've been here a few times," she answered as she removed her hat with its large brim and placed it on the seat next to her. "How do you like it?"

He thought for a moment. "Well, it sure is beautiful... except..."

"Except what?" She looked over at him with a quizzical look.

"Oh, I don't know if... I mean... I might be out of place here. Looks like mostly officers here." He pointed to the barroom.

"Oh, don't let that bother you. It's a free country..." She quickly caught herself. "Well—almost free." They looked at each other and realized that common phrase had taken on a new significance.

A young waiter with a limp approached their booth. He looked frazzled. His white shirt was hanging over his trousers on one side. His red vest was slightly soiled, but he smiled and seemed to be doing the best he could to handle the large holiday crowd.

"Good evening. Can I get you a drink, folks?" He pulled a pencil from behind his ear and removed a small order pad from his vest pocket. Patrick was ready to order a beer when Lou Ann unhesitatingly spoke up.

"Champagne—a bottle of your best!"

"And a beer for me."

"Beer? On New Year's?"

"I'll join you in the champagne later. But you know, I've been in camp and in the field for a long time, and I've been dreaming of a long, tall, cold beer."

The waiter smiled. "One bottle of champagne and one bottle of beer, thank you. Coming right up." He limped away.

When he returned, he poured the champagne for Lou Ann and placed the bottle of beer and a glass in front of Patrick who immediately began to pour it slowly into the frosted glass. He carefully watched the foam rising up until it was filled to the brim. He raised his glass and proposed a toast.

"Here's to you, Lou Ann—the angel of the battlefield—the first person I laid eyes on when I realized I was still alive."

"Thank you, Patrick, but I don't deserve that title. Let's drink to a better New Year and peace for our beleaguered nation."

They clicked their glasses together, and Patrick took a long swig and savored the taste he had been anticipating for months. They ate quietly, enjoying their steak dinner. Pat couldn't remember when he had last eaten so well. White beans and hardtack. Hardtack and white beans. That had been his usual diet in the field, although they did get an occasional bit of salt pork or bacon. This is like heaven, he thought.

Lou Ann began asking him about his regiment. When was it formed? Did he know what other states had regiments represented at Fredericksburg? Some other questions followed. He thought it unusual for a young lady like her to inquire about such matters. He answered some of her questions, but he didn't know the answers to others. He wanted to dismiss this subject. "I thought we agreed not to talk of the war." He looked over at her while wiping the foam from his beer off of his black mustache.

"I'm sorry, Patrick. I didn't mean to…"

"That's okay. I just wanted to enjoy our evening together."

The night wore on, as they continued their conversation, sharing their past histories with one another. At one point, a high-ranking officer approached their booth. "How do you do, Miss Sommers?"

"Oh, I'm just fine. And how are you, Colonel?"

"I'm fine, thank you."

"This is Sergeant O'Hanrahan," gesturing over at Patrick. "And this is Colonel Peterson," looking back at the officer.

"How do you do, Sergeant?"

"Fine, sir," Patrick responded, as he began to raise his right hand to salute him.

"Oh, forget that, Sergeant—we're not on duty now." He smiled as he raised a glass of liquor to his lips. "Are you both having a good time?"

"Yes, sir. It's the first time I've been out of the hospital since..."

"Fredericksburg, Sergeant?"

"Yes, sir—caught one in the leg."

"You're lucky, lad. That was the worst battle yet. But don't worry—we'll lick 'em next time. Rumors are we're getting a new commanding general. Hooker—Fighting Joe Hooker they call him."

"Now, Colonel, the Sergeant and I agreed not to talk about the war."

"I'm sorry, Miss Sommers. That's a good idea. Well, I must get back to my friends. I don't want them to think I deserted them. Good seeing you, Miss Sommers." He glanced over at Patrick "Good luck, Sergeant. We may meet again—hopefully after we win one!"

"Good to meet you, sir." He watched the Colonel attempting to drink from his glass while walking away in a slightly tipsy manner. "Where do you know him from?" Patrick asked.

"Oh, I've seen him in various hospitals on a few occasions. He's some hospital administrator or something."

That figures, Pat thought to himself. We'll lick 'em, huh? He probably never even set foot on a battlefield.

Reaching into his pocket, Pat removed his watch. The crystal had been cracked sometime during the confusion of battle. Maybe that Confederate soldier had done it when he fell on top of him. It still kept perfect time, though, and Patrick placed it on the table in front of them to wait for the New Year to arrive.

"Patrick, what happened to your watch?"

"I'm not sure. It was fine before Fredericksburg."

"What a shame. It's such a beautiful watch."

"It's okay. At least it still keeps time."

It was eleven-thirty. Half an hour and that God-forsaken year would be history. The worst year of his life was coming to an end. By now he had had a few drinks and was slipping into a mellow mood. He became more relaxed and placed his one arm on the top of the booth behind Lou Ann. She set her glass down on the table after taking a sip of champagne, leaned over to him, and whispered in his ear. "I'm glad we came here, Patrick. I mean—I'm having such a good time." Her warm breath on his ear aroused him. He hadn't felt like that in a long time. The steak... the drinks... and now a beautiful girl so close to him. He weakened. Those pleasures became overwhelming and tempting. His world of character and loyalty faded. *Now* was the only time he could touch and feel. This bubble of time captured and enraptured him. That red velvet secluded booth with all a man could desire. It might just as well have been ejected into outer space, light years into the galaxy, suspended and, for all he cared, frozen in time. This time he looked directly into her comely blue eyes.

"You're just what the doctor ordered. You're not just an angel, but a healing angel at that, Lou Ann. I'm having a great time, too."

"Is it getting close to midnight?"

"A few more minutes."

Those two strangers suspended between war and peace, life and death, and for him, what he considered between home and hell, accepted that brief time together and were grateful for it. At the stroke of midnight, the loud clamor coming from the barroom became an explosion of noise but was as a distant din to Patrick's ears. The only sounds that he heard were the soft words emanating from Lou Ann's inviting lips. "Happy New Year, Patrick."

"Happy New Year, Lou Ann." He hesitantly placed his rough, strong hand on top of her soft delicate hands, still folded on the table. She turned her palms upward to grasp his hand and gently squeezed it. She tilted her head slightly and slowly leaned toward him, her soft blue eyes projecting a loving radiance meant just for him. He slid his arm down from the top of the booth behind her until it rested on her shoulder and pulled her gently to himself. There wasn't any thinking or reasoning in his mind—everything seemed automatic. Their eyes met, and the magnetism, once begun, couldn't be stopped. Finally their lips met and Patrick forgot everything. She placed her hand around the back of his neck, embracing him in her total consent of his kiss.

They toasted the New Year and talked the night away. Some time in the wee hours of the morning, a young, smartly dressed civilian man with a mustache and goatee came over to their booth, interrupting their intimacy. He was slender and stood with perfect posture. "How very nice to see you, Miss Sommers. Happy New Year."

"Happy New Year to you, Mr. Booth. I would like you to meet a friend of mine—Sergeant O'Hanrahan."

"Sergeant." He nodded briefly to Patrick. Pat reached out to shake his hand but saw that the gentleman wasn't going to reciprocate. His attention was totally centered on Lou Ann. Pat quickly withdrew his hand, as the man proceeded to speak.

"Haven't seen you at the theatre of late. Are you still interested in acting?"

"Well, sort of. I hope to get back to the stage some day. I'm working for the Sanitary Commission now—that's more important."

"Well, you certainly have promise, Miss Sommers. I think there is definitely a future for you in the theatre."

"I didn't know you were in the theatre," Patrick exclaimed, as he looked at her in surprise.

"Oh, I've had a few small parts—nothing serious—a hobby of sorts."

"Oh, my dear, you underestimate your potential. I think you could go far in the business." Booth continued to ignore Patrick as he spoke and never once took his eyes from Lou Ann.

Patrick could see that she felt uneasy in Mr. Booth's presence, as she repeatedly glanced over at him and away from the intruder. Pat could sense a sinister presence about the man—a phoniness, perhaps. Usually he could read people. This man wasn't genuine. He was afraid this might spoil their perfect evening together and was about to suggest leaving to Lou Ann, when two young ladies approached. Their appearance was disheveled and they were giggling loudly. One of them tripped as they came nearer but managed to stay on her feet. It was quite apparent they had had too much to drink. They each locked an arm through Mr. Booth's arms.

"Ha-a-a-p-py New Year!" they both shouted in unison.

Mr. Booth was obviously embarrassed at his "friends'" appearance. He said goodnight to Lou Ann, as he lifted her hand and kissed it. "Hope to see you at the theatre soon, my dear." As the trio made a hasty exit from the table, Booth's voice took on a tone of anger as he was heard chastising his friends for rudely interrupting his visit with Lou Ann.

"He's some character. Have you known him very long?"

"About two years now, I guess. I always liked the stage, and my father suggested I go to the Ford Theatre to see if I could learn dramatics." She went on, "He's a character, all right. Quite a famous one at that. You never heard of John Wilkes Booth before?"

"No, I'm not much for plays or the theatre. Never had time for such things."

"Oh, yes, he is very famous in this town." She looked down at her champagne glass, as she ran her finger around the rim. "He did coach me in a few small parts. He seems so eccentric. Oh... I don't know... I just don't trust him. There's something about him..."

"Well, I wasn't very impressed with him. He looks sneaky to me."

After deciding to leave, Lou Ann asked the waiter to summon their driver from the barroom; and they rode back to the hospital in her carriage.

"This is a fine carriage you have, Lou Ann."

"Oh, it's not mine. It belongs to my father. He lets me take it sometimes."

"Do you live with him?"

"Only when I'm in town. As you know, I travel most of the time tending to you boys in the field."

Pat held her hand and began to pull her closer to himself, anticipating another kiss. The champagne and beer were now controlling his impulses. She gently withdrew and placed her fingers over his lips, as she said in a soft tone, "You're a nice man, Patrick. I like you a lot." Just then, the carriage wheel hit a large hole in the road and she was thrust over to him, her head falling on his shoulder. He took advantage of the moment, lifting her head up by the chin and stole a kiss before she could regain her composure. "Patrick!" she exclaimed. "You're a naughty one!" She sat up straight, pushing her hat back evenly on her head and moving away from him.

"Well, it *is* New Year's Eve, you know, and I thought another kiss for a lonely soldier boy who's defending your freedom wouldn't hurt anything."

"Oh, Patrick, you've got that Irish blarney about you," smiling in his direction.

The carriage came to a stop sooner than Pat wanted it to. He climbed down, holding the door with one hand and balancing himself on his cane with the other. He paused for a moment, leaning on the door and looking up at her. "Will I see you again?"

"Yes, soon," she replied. "I had a lovely time, Patrick. Good night... or should I say 'good morning?'"

"So did I. Good night, Lou Ann." He closed the door of the carriage and watched it trail off into the early morning haze until it was out of sight.

He limped back to his ward, passing the sergeant who had dozed off in the guardhouse, his legs propped up on the desk and the empty liquor bottle setting on it.

Patrick smiled and wondered how the guard would feel in the morning. He threw a stone at the guardhouse just before entering his own building, hoping to arouse the sleeping sentinel so he wouldn't be caught by the sergeant-of-the-guard.

Patrick awoke the next morning with a hangover. Holding his head in his hands, he muttered to himself, "Never mix champagne and beer again!" He felt like a heel in breaking his trust with Beth. He loved Beth deeply but wanted Lou Ann. He wanted to see her again and couldn't shake that desire. He felt the web closing in on him, and never in his life had he felt so out of control.

An officer in charge at the hospital had assigned him some light duty running errands and doing what he could for the other patients. His leg was almost healed, and he expected to be given orders to rejoin his regiment at Fredericksburg at any time. He knew his place was with his regiment. There was a war to be fought, and he would see it through to the end. Talking to the other men and helping them was good therapy for him. It took his mind off his problems. In his spare time in the evenings, he would write letters to Beth and his family and read newspapers. A headline in an old newspaper caught his interest one evening. The article told of a woman named Belle Boyd who had been arrested as a Confederate spy. He was surprised that a woman would be a spy; but then again, he thought, nothing should surprise him in this crazy war.

He secretly looked for Lou Ann each day and realized that she had never told him where in Washington she was living. A week had passed and she hadn't come to visit him. The following Sunday morning, after attending Mass in the chapel, he took a walk around the grounds outside the hospital. It was a mild, sunny morning for January, and the exercise felt good. He knew that he wasn't in good shape and wanted to prepare himself for the inevitable long marches to come. He resolved to walk around the hospital complex five times, trying to use his cane minimally. On his third round, as he was walking parallel to the street, he heard the sound of a horse-drawn carriage approaching. It stopped at the front gate just up ahead. Lou Ann stepped down from the carriage, assisted by the driver holding her arm. She wore a light blue dress with a matching bonnet and carried a lace-edged parasol at her side. She waved at Patrick as she quickly entered the gate and began to walk toward him. "It's good to see you up and around on this fine day," smiling with a bubbly presence about her. This was a trait of hers that Patrick was especially attracted to.

"I didn't catch the name, Miss," he said, holding back a smile.

"Oh, Patrick, you're a big tease! I'm seeing another side of you I haven't seen before," she laughed in amusement.

"Come, Lou Ann, walk with me, would you? I have more rounds to make. Trying to get in shape, you know."

She slid her arm through his and replied, "I would like that," as she opened her parasol and laid it on her shoulder. They strolled around the grounds, seemingly unaware of the dying and wounded men inside those stark white buildings. For now, they were each other's whole wide world, at least from Patrick's point of view. As they finished walking, they entered the canteen where he sat Lou Ann down at a table and proceeded to get two cups of coffee for them.

"Did you have any plans for today?" she asked, picking up her cup to sip the steaming brew.

"Well, I thought I might pay a visit to the President," he joked.

"Maybe you can see the First Lady, too," she chuckled, going along with his mirthful mood.

As they finished their drinks, Lou Ann leaned over toward him, resting her chin on her hands and looking directly into his eyes. "Well, Patrick, I doubt if you can *really* see the President, but I can show you where he lives. I have my father's carriage outside."

"What are we waiting for?" he said eagerly.

This time she had a different carriage; it was open and had no roof. "I thought you might like a tour of our Capitol, Patrick. It's a nice day for a ride, don't you think?"

"You sure know how to please a fella. This is great!"

The driver knew the city well; and, with a few instructions from Lou Ann, they were off. They passed by the Capitol building that had recently had its dome completed. She identified many of the other government buildings. Then they slowly rode along the Potomac River. As the afternoon wore on, she took him down Pennsylvania Avenue and stopped in front of the White House. They sat in the carriage, neither one of them speaking, and just took it all in. The driver turned and pointed to the President's home. "This is where the boss-man lives."

"It's very impressive. Can you imagine the weight on his shoulders? I mean—the war and all," Pat remarked.

"Yes, I think of that every time I pass here. The decisions he must have to make must be so, so difficult."

"Well, I sure hope he makes the right ones. We *have* to win this war."

"Yes. We should pray for him," Lou Ann offered.

"Oh, I do. Every night I say the rosary. I pray for him and for the war to end."

The day turned cloudy and a cool breeze began to blow. They had seen most of the sights and decided to go back to the hospital. They had only traveled a few blocks from the White House when they noticed a shiny black carriage approaching from the opposite direction. There was an entourage of soldiers on horseback in front of and behind the carriage.

Lou Ann seemed delighted. "It's the President, Patrick!" As the carriages slowly passed each other, the President smiled and tipped his tall hat in their direction. Behind Lincoln's smile, Pat detected a heavy-looking sadness in his deep dark eyes. The First Lady sat across from the President, looking straight ahead, her round face showing no expression whatsoever. Patrick, overwhelmed by that chance encounter, saluted his Commander-in-Chief and forced a smile, hoping it was the right thing to do.

After they had passed each other, Pat blurted out, "Can you beat that? I don't believe it! Wait till I write home and tell the folks and Be..."

"And who? You said your folks and who?"

"Oh, ah..." His thoughts raced. "Ah... I was going to say, 'Bet they won't believe me.'" That was a close one. He had never lied like this before. Why didn't he just tell her about Beth? After all, he didn't have any commitment to Lou Ann. Maybe he was afraid she wouldn't see him again. Well, in any event, he had a date with the war soon, and his holiday was coming to an end. Patrick laid his head back, breathing in the fresh, cool air, and watching the government buildings slowly passing by. They were all draped in the National Flag—Old Glory! He had seen many of his comrades fall at Fredericksburg, carrying that banner into battle. As one would fall, another would pick it up and take his place. Many died that tragic day, trying to protect it. He believed the sadness in Lincoln's face had been caused by eleven of those stars falling from Old Glory— falling from their rightful place and taking up residence on a new flag, an imposter, created by his prodigal brothers from the South. They called it the Stars and Bars or the Southern Cross. In reality, eleven states had seceded from the Union, but the sad-looking man in the tall, stovepipe hat must have known something that others did not.

He had never had the stars removed from the flags that flew in the Northern states. Somewhere deep down in his heart, he probably knew that they would return to their proper place and once again be united with their brothers. His thoughts quickly shifted back to Beth, and he wondered how badly she would be hurt or if she would leave him if she knew about Lou Ann. As Beth tugged at his heart, he could feel Lou Ann tugging on his sleeve and shaking him out of his deep thought.

"Thinking about the President? That was quite a surprise, wasn't it?"

"Oh, yes. We couldn't have timed that better. He's a kind looking man... I mean... honest looking, don't you think?"

"Yes. I saw that in his eyes, too."

Pat never forgot that incident. He had seen Lincoln in New York City before the election, but this time he was almost face-to-face with the President of the United States. January turned to February. Patrick was found fit to return to duty. His wound had completely healed, and he no longer needed his cane. Lou Ann had visited him a few more times and told him that she would be leaving Washington soon also. Her services were needed once again in the field.

The lilac in the little white vase had long since withered and had been discarded. As he lay in the darkness one night, looking over at the empty little vase illuminated by the bright moonlight streaming through the window, he thought of Lou Ann. He felt that he owed her something—the truth, maybe. Truth, he thought. That's a two-way street. Some doubts about Lou Ann had built up in his mind ever since she brought him the lilacs in December. Where did she get them in the wintertime? Could she have gotten them down South? Why had she asked him about the other regiments that fought at Fredericksburg? He had thought a lot about the woman spy in that newspaper article and, after all, Lou Ann *was* an actress. Could *she* be a spy? He tried to dismiss this immediately from his mind. He couldn't bring himself to believe anything like this. But he had a wild imagination that seemed to come alive when he laid in bed at night in the quiet and had time to think. But she's such a nice person. No, it couldn't be. His eyes grew heavy and his doubts evaporated into the moonlight as he continued to gaze at the little white vase.

Patrick saw her one last time before leaving the hospital and returning to his regiment. They said their goodbyes in the canteen at a small table in the corner of the room. It was the only place that provided a little privacy. The room was plain and drab. It had a few tables with chairs, and hot water and coffee were set up on a counter against the wall. It was unfinished like all the rooms in these hastily built buildings—same white walls and ceilings and a wooden floor with a wood-burning stove in the middle. This room, like the rest, was always drafty in the winter. Except for two young nurses sitting on the other side of the room, they were alone.

"You know, Patrick, I've been wanting to tell you something for awhile now. I'm not sure how to say it." She laid her Bible down on the table while she removed her bonnet. Folding his hands in front of him, he looked at her in anticipation of her next words.

"What is it, Lou Ann?"

"Well, since this is our last time together—I mean, for a while—I just wanted to tell you..." She paused.

"Tell me what?"

She reached across the table and clutched his hands. A slight blush came to her cheeks. "Oh, Patrick, I've grown quite fond of you. I just wanted you to know that before you went away."

Patrick only wanted to grab her up and caress her as he became swallowed up in those beautiful blue eyes. Instead, he leaned across the table and kissed her gently on her mouth. The two nurses glanced over at them and giggled softly. He loved hearing those words from Lou Ann but had dreaded this moment, as he fell deeper into his own dilemma and felt guilty as sin for allowing this to happen. "You are truly an angel, Lou Ann. You were there for me at Fredericksburg, and you have been so very good to me here in Washington." He didn't know what to say next. All doubts about that spy business vanished from his mind. He could only think of her as a beautiful, caring young lady whom he constantly restrained himself from loving. He wanted to say he loved her but couldn't. Finally he spoke again. "Lou Ann," he said as they continued to hold hands, "you have become very dear to me also, and maybe..." He stopped in mid-sentence. He was going to say they could write to each other but that wouldn't do. He couldn't perpetuate this budding romance any longer. This seemed like it might be a good time to end it.

"Maybe? You were saying?"

"Oh, maybe we will meet again."

"Well, I just *know* we will." She gave him a piece of paper with her address on it. Always happy, fun-loving, and gregarious, she suddenly became quiet and looked sad. He noticed tears welling up in her eyes. His heart felt heavy and full of guilt. He thought to himself—how many kinds of love are there? Is there a marrying kind of love? Is there a kind of love that a lonely soldier boy has for a pretty young girl who cares for him? Are there degrees of love? He was confused and saddened by her tears. Just a little more than a year ago, he had been so very sad when he left Beth at the train station in New York City. It seemed so long ago... so distant. It was like living two dreams, separated by a nightmare of warfare in between. "Patrick, please write to me." She blotted the tears trickling down her cheeks with a small handkerchief she had pulled from her sleeve. She rose from her chair, placed the bonnet on her head and tied it beneath her chin. She kissed him on his cheek, picked up her parasol, and said, "I promise you we *will* meet again," and quickly walked away. He watched as she scurried out the door, relieved that this goodbye was short-lived. He hated long goodbyes, especially when they concerned matters of the heart and could tell that she probably felt the same by her hasty departure. He looked down at the piece of paper and read it:

Miss Lou Ann Sommers
C/O Sanitary Commission
110 Madison Avenue
Washington, D.C.

He wondered if he would ever see her again. If so, would he be able to tell her of Beth? As he stood up, he noticed she had left her Bible on the table. He grabbed it and hurried to the door. He was too late; she was gone. If he ever met her again, would their relationship blossom? Or would it whither and die like the lilac in the little white vase? He opened the Bible; and tucked into the flap of the back cover, he found a list. It was a record of Union Divisions, Brigades, and Regiments, listed by states in alphabetical order.

CHAPTER 7

▼

WINTER CAMP

The boat slid out from the dock into the deeper waters of the Potomac, heading back to uncertainty. It was a bright, sunny morning, and Patrick watched as the buildings on shore slowly faded from view. The soldiers on deck were mostly silent except for some new recruits who were huddled together at the stern of the ship. They laughed and joked about something; but Patrick, having already been in battle and "seen the elephant," was more somber. He was wondering if he would survive this war.

Then his thoughts turned to Lou Ann. A spy? Maybe he was kidding himself. The list of Army units in the back of her Bible aroused greater suspicions than he had previously had. He felt used and stupid for getting involved with her. All he wanted was the truth. He didn't need all of these doubts and guilt right now. Why hadn't he confronted her about these suspicions before he left? A man should have peace of mind before he goes to his Maker. It *was* possible—half of his regiment was killed at Fredericksburg. Can't think like that.

He had received two letters from Beth while in the hospital. Her mother still needed her, but she missed him terribly and couldn't wait to see him again. He had changed and he knew it. He was a different person since his battle on the plantation when he had obtained medical aid for Nathan, the slave. A further change came over him after Fredericksburg. And most certainly he had changed once again after his stay in Washington. When he had entered the Army less than two years earlier, he was a boy—a boy who saw the world as black and white. But now there were many gray areas. In that short time, his experiences had aged him. He had seen the worst of mankind in the most horrible acts of killing and brutality. And now he saw another side to himself—living a lie with two different women.

The journey from Fredericksburg to the hospital in Washington had been wet and cold, and his leg had ached terribly when he had tried to protect his friend, Danny, from the pelting rain. On this, his return trip, however, he was inside the cabin—alone, warm, and dry. But now his heart ached. It ached mostly for Beth, but… what was this new little spot in his heart that was occupied by Lou Ann? He wondered how it would have been had there been no war—if he had never left home—he would never had met her. For now, he would try to think that way and how pleasant and uncomplicated things would have been. He tried to keep his mind on Beth; she was still firmly rooted in his heart. But the fresh memory of that friendly, charming, warm "angel of the battlefield" kept creeping back into his thoughts. He really didn't know if he could ever forget her.

As he drifted into a dream-like state, he was jolted by a loud voice. "Okay I sit here?"

Pat looked up to see a giant of a soldier standing in front of him. The man was pointing to the chair beside Patrick's. "Help yourself."

The big man plopped down on the chair and crossed his long legs, making himself comfortable. Pat anticipated the chair buckling under his weight.

"My name—Sven Jorgenson. I'm private in Army now. What's your name?"

"I'm Patrick O'Hanrahan—Sergeant in Army."

"Oh… you big boss! Maybe *my* boss!"

"I don't think so. What outfit are you assigned to?"

"Number 69—I think."

"Where did you come from?"

"I from Sweden; way across ocean."

"No, I meant what state are you from?"

"I now U.S. citizen. From New York State."

"Whereabouts in New York?"

"New York City. Big place!"

"That's where I'm from, too."

"You from there, too? By golly! Me too!" The big Swede turned in his chair and gave Pat a forceful slap on his back. Pat winced briefly, as he felt like an anvil had fallen on him. "You Irish boy? You look like Irish."

"Yes, I am, Private."

"You first one call me Private. I like that. But you call me Sven or call me Swede. Everybody at home in New York call me Swede."

Patrick looked over at him and could see that he was a new recruit, wearing a brand-new uniform. It was about two sizes too small for him, and his sleeves ended halfway between his elbows and wrists. "When did you join the Army?" he asked, amused at the man's appearance.

"I join last week. Been waiting to go down and whip them Rebs, by golly! We show them what for!"

Patrick was thinking about how many big men had been brought down by a small bullet smashing into their bodies.

"I like Irish. I live in Irish neighborhood. I have lots Irish friends."

"Well, I live near Central Park."

"Oh, by golly, I live on 39th Street. You and I neighbors. Where you work in New York?"

"Oh, I worked as a butcher in a meat market over in the German section of town."

"Holy smokes, Irish! I work in slaughterhouse on 39th Street—maybe you get beef sides from slaughterhouse I work at."

Pat didn't mind being called Irish. He liked it in a way. It had a certain ring to it. But if the big Swede ended up in his outfit, he would have to insist on being called 'Sergeant'. They talked for a while, and Pat told him he'd be right at home if he was assigned to his unit. "There are plenty of Irishmen in my unit, Swede."

"I go now. My buddies back over on other side," pointing to the stern of the boat. "Good I meet you." He lumbered out of the cabin door and back to his friends.

"Hope to see you in my outfit, Swede."

Pat's thoughts reverted back to Lou Ann and the list in the back of her Bible. He had given the Bible to the guard to return to her, as he knew he was familiar with her and would probably see her again. The list of Army units he kept. He wasn't sure what he should do with it. Not knowing Lou Ann's loyalties, he kept it for evidence or proof of her activities if his worst fears about her were to materialize. He tried to put all of that behind him and focus on the future, only to experience a sinking feeling beginning in his stomach. There would be another battle—maybe many battles—ahead of him. He fumbled in his pocket for his rosary to pray that he would survive. It wasn't there. He remembered he gave it away. Have to get another, he thought, grasping the medal that hung from his neck.

The boat ride, followed by the short train ride back to camp, passed quickly. After the men were assembled and assigned to their various units, Patrick found his way back to his regiment. He was surprised to see so few men remaining in his company. His few close friends weren't there. It was bitter cold, and the other soldiers had built permanent winter quarters from logs after chopping down the surrounding trees. The small huts were only big enough to sleep four men each, and they were all fully occupied. He would have to pull rank on a few privates and corporals to build new huts. He did find a few men he vaguely knew before their regiment had been decimated. A corporal offered him a hot cup of coffee. Removing the coffee pot from the fire and pouring it into his own cup, he handed it to Patrick and jokingly said, "Hey, Sarge—you like it here so much, you shortened your vacation?"

Another soldier said, "Glad to see you're among the living."

They briefly spoke of their great defeat at Fredericksburg but not for long. Before Pat had finished his coffee, a group of new recruits came marching in. The officer in charge brought them to a halt right in front of Patrick. "This is Company B, isn't it?"

Pat saluted. "Yes, sir."

"They're all yours, Sergeant—green as grass, they are!" The officer returned Patrick's salute and quickly walked away. The small band of men stood in formation, facing Patrick, awaiting orders. As Patrick looked them over, he observed a very tall man in the back row, like a towering oak surrounded by saplings. It was the Swede. He had a broad smile on his face as he looked at Patrick.

"Attention!" Pat hollered in a loud voice. The men stood erect and listened. "I'm Sergeant O'Hanrahan, your new Squad leader." He looked at the list of names on the clipboard the officer had handed him. Murphy... O'Connor... O'Reilly—the list went on—and the very last name... Jorgenson. He took the roll call, and each man hollered "Here!" as his name was called.

"We have a lot of work to do, and it will go much easier on you if we work as a team. I have much more to tell you, but it's too damn cold to stand here and make a speech. As you may have noticed, the Army only supplies us tents; we have to make conditions more livable." He turned and motioned for the corporal standing behind him to come forward. "Corporal, take two men to supply and get some axes, matches, and any food you can hustle up."

"O.K., Sarge." He picked two men and began to leave.

"Oh, and Corporal, see if you can get some hot coffee—lots of it." Pat then ordered the rest of the men to start clearing an area of underbrush to make ready for building their winter quarters. He stomped his feet and rubbed his ears to protect himself from the biting North winds of February blowing through the encampment.

By the time the Corporal and the other two men returned, the area was cleared; and Patrick assigned the axes to the men and instructed them to begin chopping down the trees.

"Hey, Irish, they never told me I work hard like this when I join up," the Swede remarked, grinning.

Pat walked over to him. Reaching up, he placed his hand on the Swede's massive shoulder. "Call me Sarge. You have to respect these," as he pointed to the stripes on his sleeve. "When you earn three hash marks, you can call me Irish."

"Sorry, Iri… I mean, Sarge. Didn't mean no harm."

Pat started a fire and the men chopped and chopped and chopped. The big Swede was working like a machine, chopping two trees for every one chopped by the others. They took a short break to eat some hard tack, beans, and coffee; then went back to work. In three days they erected three huts, just enough to accommodate their twelve-man Squad. They had chopped the trees and trimmed them to fit together until their hands were raw and calloused. They filled the cracks between the logs with mud and twigs that they had mixed into a crude mortar. There were no windows. Just a small opening big enough to use as a doorway. They buttoned two tents together and stretched them across the top to serve as a makeshift roof. For warmth, they fashioned some empty wooden barrels into a chimney and attached it to the outside of one of the walls. A crude fireplace was then carved out at the bottom of the wall from the inside. Some men covered the dirt floor with straw or any wooden slabs they could find. These hastily built dwellings made by their own hands became their home away from home for the rest of the winter. They were proud of their handiwork.

After settling in, Pat trained the men in the use of their muskets, rifles that fired bullets called Minie' balls, named after the French inventor Claude Minie'. They drilled in maneuvers for many hours every day. The days grew into weeks and Patrick grew bored and lonely. His days were occupied with drilling, drilling, and more drilling. He taught the new recruits all that he could and only hoped that they would have courage under fire when they would first meet the enemy. He, himself, prayed every night and asked Saint Michael, his "Warrior of God", to protect him and all his men in battle. He found some relief in recreational activities. When there was snow on the ground, the regiments would face off as if in real battle, armed with snowballs, and "fight it out". Sometimes it escalated into a brawl, and many black eyes and bruises could be seen on the men afterwards. But the nights were lonely. He spent many of them reading whatever he could get his hands on, mostly newspapers from home. After dark, he would stick his bayonet in the ground and use the other end as a candleholder. He wrote home to his mother, grandparents, and Beth often. When the other men were asleep and it was quiet, he often thought of Lou Ann and was tempted to write her too. Sometimes he felt he should write her and tell her of Beth, but his love for Beth told him to just let it go.

One evening a large number of new recruits arrived in camp. The weather was cool but dry. There weren't any permanent quarters for them to sleep in, and they had just finished a long march to get there. Most of them were too tired to put up tents, so they slept on the ground with only a blanket for cover. During the night, an ice storm blew in from the North and everything froze over. In the morning, Patrick was awakened to an unusual, eerie, and unidentifiable sound surrounding his hut. He peered out to see the recruits emerging from what looked like dozens of icy cocoons splitting open, creating a crackling sound. Shortly after, this crackling was replaced by the crackling of their cooking fires as they began to prepare a meager breakfast. Now there would be more recruits to train and get into shape for the next battle with Johnny Reb.

Winter blew itself out and spring burst onto the hills and valleys of the picturesque Virginia landscape. Patrick had found a new love—nature. There wasn't much to see in New York City. Maybe a few, well-placed trees on Fifth Avenue or in Central Park, all arranged by man. But here it was in all its splendor. Vast, wild, free, and not one man's hand involved in its making. Patrick saw the hand of God in this beauty. In his free time, he would often take long walks away from camp. He marveled at the different types and array of colors of the many wildflowers. He sometimes sat down, leaning back on a tree, and observed the many varieties of birds flitting from tree to tree. He would sit very still and watch the rabbits hopping past him and darting away when he moved. On some occasions, his respite would be interrupted by a few soldiers hunting down the rabbits and small game. He didn't like that. He was well aware that they would make a succulent meal, a welcome change from the usual fare of hard tack and beans. But here he was, a soldier, a trained killer—it didn't make sense. Maybe if the rabbits could shoot at him, he could justify their being killed.

An owl he spotted one day high up in a tree fascinated him. He watched as the owl searched for prey with his keen, large, round eyes. The owl occasionally glanced at Patrick, as if to say, who-o-o-o-o are you? On a few occasions the owl swooped down on an unsuspecting rodent, snatched it from the forest floor, and returned to his perch to devour it. Patrick, who had seen many men die instantly in battle, pondered how quickly life could be snatched by the grim reaper. In that respect, he thought, mice and men were equally vulnerable. A bullet smashing into a man's body could be just as deadly as an owl's sharp talons slicing up a mouse.

Sometimes he looked in awe at the many varieties of trees. Being a city boy, he didn't know their names, but for the evergreen, which he naturally knew from Christmas. He collected leaves from other trees and pressed them in a small Bible the chaplain had given him. He hoped to take them home to show his family and Beth.

As he would return to camp, his thoughts turned to the new men in the regiment, especially in his Company. Where had all his old buddies gone? He didn't want to think of that. It was almost as if he had been plucked out of his old regiment and set down in a new one. Many new faces… but it was still the Fighting 69th! The spirit of the regiment was still very much alive. Many young boys fought and died under the Stars and Stripes and their own green Irish flag, but their spirits lived on in their replacements.

"Hey, Swede, get in step!" Patrick hollered, as his Squad was going through drill one day. The big man quickly followed orders but soon became out of step again. "Come on Swede! You're out of step," Pat hollered again.

One of the men from the Squad cried out, "Hey, big foot, don't you know your left from your right?"

Another man yelled, "Don't trip over them clodhoppers, Swede!"

"Knock it off!" Pat shouted. "Next man to speak gets an extra hour of drill—alone!"

They marched and drilled morning, noon, and night; and they came to hate it. The Swede withstood many insults and much harassment, which he accepted better than most men would have. But Pat didn't like it. He came to his defense on many occasions. His taste of battle and loss of so many comrades had had a profound effect on him. He saw himself, as he was before Fredericksburg, in the new recruits. They were all optimistic, eager, and ready to take on the Rebels. Their confidence was contagious, and he never wanted to change that. But deep down in his heart, he was a realist. He kept his thoughts and feelings about the terrible reality of war to himself. He purposely avoided making close friends and kept his comrades at arm's length—except for the Swede.

It was a clear night and a multitude of stars adorned the black Southern sky. Patrick had a large bonfire blazing in front of his hut. He leaned back on a large log to drink in the panorama of the constellations proudly displaying their diamonds in their arena of the heavens.

"Hey, Sarge, okay I sit here?" the Swede asked, his large frame casting an imposing shadow on the ground as he approached the dancing flames. He once again attempted to befriend Patrick.

"Well, maybe for a little while, Swede," Pat responded as he leaned forward to stoke the fire, causing the embers to fly into the darkness above.

"I like Army. I like this Company best, Irish," as he lowered his large frame down and sat on the other end of the log.

"How many times have I told you not to call me Irish?"

"Sorry. I forget," as he frowned and looked down, like a little boy who had just been scolded.

"All right, Private. Just don't want you getting in the habit. Next thing.... everybody will be calling me that."

"I just feel you and I neighbors in New York. Maybe I feel more like at home—sometime I miss home."

"Well, Private, we all feel that way sometimes," as he gazed up into the heavens and thought to himself that he might as well be on one of those stars, as he felt like he was a million miles from home.

"You have big family at home, Sarge?"

"Just grandparents..."

The Swede interrupted before Pat could mention his mother and brother. "I have big family. Seven brothers—three in Army like me." He went on, "We live near slaughterhouse. Smells bad. But Mama and brothers, we make good home in New York City. Papa died in accident. I make good money. I lift big beef sides and carry them to cutters. I help Mama at home, too."

Pat felt he had something in common with the big Swede... both had lost their fathers. He stood up and stared into the fire, holding his palms out to warm his hands, asking a question as he did. "Are all your brothers as big as you?"

"Oh, no, Irish—I mean, Sarge—I the biggest!" He let out a loud laugh as he added, "They call me Big, Big Brother!" By now, the Swede had gotten up and stood on the opposite side of the fire. He, too, extended his arms forward to warm his huge hands. "You good man, Sarge. You stick up for Swede."

"Just trying to keep order. You boys better learn how to get along before we meet up with the Rebs or there'll be hell to pay."

"I like others. They like pick on me. They don't hurt Swede. They good boys, by golly. All Irish... like you."

Patrick admired the patience and good nature of the big man. He was dumb and clumsy, but he had a way of accepting people for what they were and had the trust of a child. Pat believed that he would have lost his temper and taken a poke at anyone that would have taunted him as they had the Swede.

"You—how you say? See the elephant yet? I mean... you fight Rebs yet?"

Patrick's thoughts flashed back to the carnage he had been caught up in on Marye's Heights. "Oh, yeah, a few times—it's no picnic." He deliberately withheld the gory details as he looked up at the Swede's massive face reflecting the light from the flickering flames. It looked spooky—almost grotesque—a contradiction to the Swede's gentle nature.

"You kill a lot of those Rebs? I hear you Irish good fighters."

"Well, we did our best." He didn't go on any further, not wanting to relive the battle.

"I heard stupid general make big mistake in last battle here."

"You've got that right," Patrick responded without hesitation. "I'll tell you something," he said, as he stood up and stretched out his arms, yawning as he did. "You keep your head down... you're gonna stick out like a sore thumb, and we don't want those Rebs using you for target practice. Crouch down, keep low, and you'll be all right."

"We fight together, by golly. We make good team. We beat 'em good!"

"We're all a team, Swede. We'll get them on the run next time. Now go get some sleep... reveille comes early." He started walking towards his hut, then glanced back at the Swede. "Oh—and don't forget—call me Sarge."

Then the Spring rains came... and came... and came. Everything turned to mud. They drilled in mud, cooked in mud, had target practice in mud, sunk in the mud, and swore in the mud. They even changed their company street name from Maiden Lane to Mudville Mile. Some men even had their shoes sucked off their feet by the mud. They drilled by company, regiment, brigade, and division. It became monotonous and tedious, except for the division drills when they marched and drilled to the tune of a marching band. It was inspiring and it lifted their spirits. Even the Swede remained in step.

"Hey, Swede—we'll have to get you your own band for company drills," yelled one of the men.

The raw recruits hadn't met the enemy yet. But another unsuspecting silent enemy had invaded their midst: disease, diarrhea, dysentery, pneumonia, typhoid and measles. Their ranks would have to be brought back to full strength before the next battle. Patrick's job of training the new men became neverending. A stream of young boys and men flowed into camp and many became sick and had to be hospitalized. Diarrhea was the most common and sometimes fatal illness. At first the recruits would joke about it. They called it the quickstep. As time went on, it was looked upon with more respect. In fact, it became the number one killer. Men came and went and the training continued. Boredom became another big enemy. In time, the men became acclimated to the weather, many recovered from illnesses, and they began to yearn for action against Johnny Reb. Their eagerness for battle had been repressed and contained in the cold of winter. But now it was time to emerge from the deep freeze. The warmer days and soft spring rains awakened in them new life. It was time for planting and work to be done; they were eager to plow the fields—but not for planting crops. This spring the seeds of rebellion would have to be unearthed and destroyed to make way for the planting of the new seeds of freedom. It would come at a terrible cost. Rumors were spreading through the camp faster than diseases. It was late in April, and their confidence had been restored. They had prepared well for the coming battle, which they knew was imminent. "Fighting" Joe Hooker had replaced Burnside as their new general; he was confident and had developed a new plan of action that would surely "win the day" in the Army's coming battle. It was time—time for planting. But it wouldn't be rain that irrigated these new seeds of freedom. Instead, it would be blood—the blood of thousands of young men soaking the ground that would yield a great harvest that many of them would not live to see.

Patrick stepped out of his hut at Fredericksburg for the last time. He and thousands of other boys in blue broke camp. They had cleaned their rifles, received their ammunition of sixty rounds with percussion caps, and been given enough rations for three days. They filled their canteens with water; and then they prayed. This is it, Pat thought, as he stood in the drizzling morning rain looking down the long rows of huts as the men broke camp. They looked like an army of ants working feverishly.

A short while after breakfast, the drums commenced their steady beat, like rolling thunder sweeping through their ranks. By Company, Regiment, Brigade and Division, and Corps, they formed. Patrick, the Swede, and all of his squad, with names mostly beginning with "O", melded into that vast sea of blue and marched to the bands' horns blaring martial music, banners unfurled and flags flying. It wouldn't be long before they would all "see the elephant".

CHAPTER 8

▼

OPENING OF THE BALL

They marched and stopped, then marched and stopped again. The smell of battle was in the air. The duel of brothers and ideals was about to start up again. These young, ordinary men were about to find themselves doing extraordinary things. Would this conflict continue until their resources were depleted or until the last man was standing? Would their forefathers' work have been in vain? Would their experiment of a new democracy end in complete destruction? Nobody knew. All they knew was that these two great armies were on a collision course. Only brute force would determine the outcome.

Patrick's squad marched silently in step, even the big Swede, as the young drummer boy earnestly beat his drum in a syncopated cadence. The sound of many drums reverberated against the surrounding hills and engulfed the whole Army. As Patrick's regiment proceeded up the dirt road in the emerging warm, spring sunlight, a new sound intermingled with the drumbeats. It was a sound that he was very familiar with—the rattling noise of many muskets firing. The "ball had opened." The long blue line began to move faster, and then slowed down—like an inchworm spreading out and then bunching up. The noise of rifle fire was joined by the loud boom of cannons launching their projectiles into the air and screeching like a locomotive over the heads of Patrick's advancing men, only to come crashing down on the unfortunate souls in the rear. His squad moved faster now and formed into line of battle. The flag bearers were in the lead. Old Glory led the way, with the green and gold Irish banner keeping pace. When they got in range of the enemy, they opened fire. The fear that had been pent up in them on the march was suddenly released, as if it had left their long musket barrels along with their bullets. At first their lines were straight and orderly; but as the fight progressed, they began to fall apart. As some of the men dropped to their knees to reload their muskets, others advanced. In some other parts of the line, men were falling back when outnumbered by the enemy. Some fell silent as they were hit. This caused gaps in the line, so that units became intermingled and utter chaos reigned.

Patrick screamed out to his squad to straighten out, which they were able to do—for a while. But the heavy smoke and deafening din of battle permeated their senses. The lines swayed, and it soon became every man for himself. They attacked but were soon thrown back by a Rebel counterattack of great numbers of men in gray. They retreated and took cover in the woods.

"I feel good now," the Swede said as he panted and reloaded his musket. "We get 'em this time."

They reconnected with the rest of their regiment and charged once again.

"Keep down, Swede, and that goes for the rest of you men!" Pat yelled. He fired, dropped to his knees, and quickly loaded his rifle, ramming powder and bullet down into the barrel with his ramrod, then carefully replaced the percussion cap and fired again. Dropping down again to reload, he found himself kneeling on a dead Confederate who had been shot in the head. Part of his skull had been blown away, and his eyes were wide open. Patrick quickly moved away to finish reloading his musket.

"Hey, Sarge!" yelled the Swede. "You O.K?"

"Stay down!" Pat hollered back. "Keep moving!" He motioned to the rest of his squad to advance. A shell exploded just behind them, causing them to move more quickly. Pat briefly looked back and was horrified to see bodies, some without limbs, flying into the air. The terrible screams from the wounded seared his mind. Their officers in front of them on horseback were waving their swords in a forward motion to advance. Pat saw an officer and his horse fall to the ground. His horse had been shot from under him. The officer quickly got up and continued motioning the men to advance. By now, the two armies were closing on each other, and Patrick felt the excitement running through his ranks. They hollered their "hurrahs" and "huzzas" in unison, as though of one voice, as they began to run in double quick time. Patrick's fear turned to anger as he saw some of his men shot. He was loading, aiming, firing, and reloading as fast as he could. At the same time, he attempted to keep his men together.

He felt his anger turning into a wild frenzy—an urge to kill—
an overwhelming need to exact revenge—a thoughtless void of con-
science—a crazed madness that could only be satisfied with a kill!

"Hey! Wait up, Sarge!" yelled the big Swede, as he tried to catch his
breath. "Can't keep up!"

Pat didn't hear him. It was as though something had taken him over. He
had a fiendish look on his face. The sweat poured from his brow, and his face
had been covered with spatters of blood when the man next to him was shot
in the head. His uniform was covered with mud; and his face had a macabre
appearance, with black powder on his lips and mustache from breaking open
the paper cartridges with his teeth. He looked and felt like an animal! Or
worse!—a demonic savage that had lost his senses! He found his target—a
Rebel officer on horseback. He had never shot an officer before. As if in a
dream-like state, in slow motion, he deliberately loaded his rifle, took careful
aim, briefly wiped the sweat from his eyes, and squeezed the trigger. In an
instant, the officer was toppled from his mount and dropped to the ground
like a rock! The rage went out of Patrick. The kill had satisfied his thirst
for revenge—at least for the moment!

"Hey, Irish!" the Swede hollered excitedly. "You do good! You got big
cheese!"

Suddenly the Rebels retreated as quickly as they had appeared. Pat
breathed a sigh of relief. He sat down for a brief moment, still clutching his
rifle. He had a sudden twinge of fear—fear of his own emotions. What had
come over him? Urgency dispelled his thoughts. Must reload—and fast!
They may attack again any moment. My men... keep them together. He
glanced over in the enemy's direction. They were gone. He reloaded and
stood up. As the dense smoke of battle rose into the placid, blue summer
sky, his eyes beheld a panoramic view of suffering and death in the bright
sunlight, exposing all the horrors of the carnage of battle. Gazing over the
battlefield, he saw bodies strewn all over the grassy plain, some disemboweled,
some without limbs, and some writhing in pain. Deep moans were coming
from the wounded. Many boys, some who he had trained, lied motionless,
blood seeping from the many bullet holes in their young bodies. Torn flesh!
Horses with their entrails hanging out, screaming out in unearthly cries, like
nothing he had ever heard before. It was a horrible, grotesque scene. He
thought to himself, "If I never see it again—I've seen enough!" He felt like
vomiting. Fredericksburg had been bad enough, but the cold had numbed
his senses there. It was almost dark when he had passed out there, and he
hadn't been able to see much. This was different.

Patrick gathered his men together. They had become disorganized and some were missing. They regrouped with others who had straggled back from the attack. He realized they had gone too far forward. They then retreated back to the main body to form a defensive position. He wanted to move his squad forward again to attack, but he knew he would be putting his men at risk and possibly become outflanked by the enemy. As much as he wanted revenge for the slaughter at Fredericksburg, he knew an attack by so few men would be suicide. After joining the others behind the tree line, Pat, along with the rest of his regiment, sat down in the cool of the shade checking their ammunition and waiting for orders to either attack or hold their defensive position. They waited and waited. Pat wanted to attack... every minute that passed took away their momentum. He and his men became fidgety. They sat in silence, listening to the roar of battle down the line. It was only a matter of time before they, too, became part of it again.

Suddenly, a multitude of Rebs, shrieking out their Indian-like war hoops, charged from the trees on the opposite side of the clearing.

"Aim low!" Pat hollered. "Wait till they're in range!"

On they came—running—deliberately firing as they did. Each man in Pat's squad took careful aim from a crouching position or from behind a tree. "Fire!" came the order from their commanding officer. The whole regiment fired a volley, and many of the men in gray fell to the ground. They reloaded and fired again.

One of Pat's men, firing from a prone position, lay in front of Patrick. "Hey, private! Hurry up and reload!" The private didn't move. Pat bent down and saw that the boy had been shot through the head. He was eighteen years old. This was his first and last battle. The war was over for him.

The gray line advanced halfway across the clearing, and again another volley thinned their ranks. But still they came. By now, the boys in blue were firing at will— firing as fast as they could reload. It looked to Patrick like a perfect opportunity to attack, as the Confederate lines had slowed, and their reinforcements hadn't appeared. He wanted to get his men up and charging, but their officer hadn't given the order to attack. What's the matter with him, Pat thought. We can do it. He waited and fired again. Still no order. The order to attack was never given. The few Rebels whose ranks had now been decimated retreated back to the opposite woods. All was calm once again, but the battle could be heard still raging up the line.

Why can't we advance? The thought kept running through Pat's mind. He had the men count their cartridges. They still had about thirty rounds each—plenty enough for another charge. They were ready. Where was the order? After what seemed like an eternity, a messenger came running up to Patrick. He was breathing hard and seemed very excited. "What is it?" Patrick asked.

"The lieutenant!" The young man bent over, placing his hands on his knees, trying to catch his breath.

"The lieutenant what, Private? Come on man—spit it out! Take a deep breath."

The man straightened up, drawing in a deep breath. "The lieutenant's been shot! He said for you to take command of the company!" He let out a sigh of relief.

"Thanks, Private. Now return to your company." Patrick removed his hat and wiped the sweat from his brow. Why me, he thought to himself. He was trained to command a small squad of fifteen or twenty men—but a company? Two hundred men? He was forced to rethink—to think bigger. He would have to go down the line, out of his small sphere of influence, and review the whole company. He passed the word to the other squads that he was now in charge of the company and to ready themselves to make another assault. He felt a heavy weight on his shoulders. Must obey the command, he thought. Just then, a colonel rode up on horseback.

"Who's in charge here?" he bellowed out.

"I am, Sir. Our lieutenant is down. He put me in charge."

"Well, Sergeant, why are your men standing still? The enemy is over there," as he pointed with his riding stick toward the woods beyond the clearing. "Move your men out; they should be on top of the Rebels by now. There's a hole in their lines big enough to march a division through!" The colonel whipped his horse and galloped away, leaving Patrick in command. Pat had never felt so alone in his life. He positioned himself in front of the whole company, shouting orders to the squad leaders and file closers.

"Follow me!" he shouted in a deep, commanding voice. They moved out with bayonets fixed in an orderly fashion, flags fluttering in the breeze, and the little twelve-year-old drummer boy beating out the marching cadence. Patrick set the pace, avoiding haste. He wanted to charge in double-quick time but hesitated for fear of an ambush. He couldn't be sure what was waiting for them in those dark woods. Could be a trap. They marched at a steady pace; and when they reached the halfway point of the clearing, the Rebels appeared at the wood line, opened fire, and all hell broke loose! Bullets whizzed around Pat's head, and some of his comrades fell around him. He fired and urged his men forward. He ran ahead and waved his hat, motioning his men to follow. The Swede was cursing and running by his side. The men followed and charged into the woods, hollering profanities at the enemy. Their bayonets were pointed forward in defiance until there was a clash of the opposing forces. They slammed into each other with clubbed muskets and fists. It became savage and chaotic, every man attacking his nearest enemy—a struggle to the death! Pat raised his rifle, swinging the butt end of it up swiftly, striking a Rebel under the chin and knocking him off his feet. He heard a loud crack and thought he had broken the man's jaw. Pat turned to see the big Swede picking up another Rebel, lifting him over his head, and hurling him into four of the enemy soldiers. They all fell like grass under a scythe.

After a brief struggle, the outnumbered and outfought Rebels made a hasty retreat toward the back of the woods. "We whip 'em good, by golly! You do good job leading, Irish—I mean Sarge." The Swede laughed as he looked down at the Rebels he had bowled over, sitting on the ground, holding up their hands in surrender. Patrick ordered his company to pursue the fleeing Rebels. He assigned some men to take the prisoners to the rear. He and the Swede were reloading their muskets, planning to catch up with the rest of his men, when a small, beady-eyed Confederate stepped out from behind a tree. He raised his rifle and aimed at Patrick. "Watch out, Irish!" the Swede yelled, as he pulled the trigger of his rifle to shoot the Rebel. Click... click... click... The Swede's gun misfired. The Rebel shifted his sights onto the Swede, a much bigger target, and fired. Patrick, who was attempting to reload, watched as his friend fell like a large tree that had just been chopped down. The Rebel was about thirty yards away and reloading. Pat's mind raced. Should I rush him? No time. Reload and nail the bastard! He rammed a bullet down the muzzle of his musket, frantically attempting to beat his enemy. He quickly raised his gun and fired. What he saw next horrified him! In the excitement, he had forgotten to remove his ramrod from the barrel. It streaked through the air, a missile of cold steel, and impaled the Rebel on the tree behind him. Pat was struck dumb by the gruesome sight. The Rebel hung limp with his head hanging low and arms drooping to his sides. Blood poured from his abdomen and his hat had fallen to the ground. As if frozen in time, the image Pat saw in his mind's eye was of his crucified Lord hanging on a tree, blood pouring from *His* side, the same Man that dangled at the end of his rosary. He shuddered. The whole basis of his faith suddenly burned itself into his brain—the Son of God, given by the Father as an offering for man's salvation. These thoughts streaked through his mind quicker than the ramrod had sped through the air.

He noticed the big Swede move his arm. His lips were moving, as though he were trying to speak. Patrick knelt down next to him. The big man had been shot through the neck and was lying in a puddle of blood. Pat leaned closer to hear what he was trying to say. "Tell Mama... I... love..." Then he was gone. Stillness. His eyes were wide open and glassy, staring into the heavens. Patrick wanted to cry. There wasn't time—he suddenly heard the commotion of running men and muskets firing. It came from the forward position of his troops—a counterattack of the enemy! His men were being driven back in haste! He jumped up and tried to stop his retreating men. They were like a panicking mob. It was useless! The men never slowed down. A rout! Like a stampede of elephants! They had "seen the elephant" and didn't like what they saw!

Patrick didn't want to leave his big friend lying there dead, alone, without even a grave or marker. He bent down, placed his arms under the Swede's armpits and attempted to drag him back. He could hardly budge him. He pulled, using all the strength left in him, but could only make a few yards at a time. He was making no progress, and Johnny Reb was getting closer. He knew he couldn't do it, and lowered his friend's head gently to the ground. As he was getting to his feet to leave his big friend for the last time, he suddenly felt cold metal being pressed against the back of his neck.

"Say yer cotton-pickin' prayers, Yank!"

The horror of the man being impaled on the tree, his sadness at losing the Swede, and now his fear of a sudden bullet penetrating his brain were all too much. His fear quickly changed to rage. He wouldn't die like an animal without a fight. He was about to turn and attempt to overpower his captor when he heard another voice.

"Hold it, Private! Ah know the only good Yank is a dead one, but us Virginians don't have to shoot 'em in the back—we can take 'em eyeball to eyeball!" Patrick felt the barrel being removed from his neck and turned to see a Confederate officer pushing the private's gun aside. The war had almost come to a brief and inglorious end for Patrick. His time wasn't up yet!

"On yer feet, Yank." Patrick rose to his feet, and the Rebel soldier prodded him in the back with his rifle. "Git movin', Yank. Yer fightin' days are over!" Pat's Irish temper swirled around in his head. He was helpless... for now! I'll be back, he thought. I'll escape somehow—and I'll be back! That indomitable spirit he inherited from his grandfather and his faith bolstered his spirits. I'll be back—*we'll* be back, and you Rebels will have hell to pay, he thought. He remembered reading in the Bible someplace, *"For they have sown the wind, and they shall reap the whirlwind."* I'll be back!

He was led away to captivity.

Chapter 9

▼

Road to Captivity

As Patrick was being led away to prison, he didn't like the sounds of battle behind him. The Rebel yell sounded strong, as if they were driving back his comrades in blue. His concern wasn't so much for himself as it was for his men. He was marched behind Confederate lines and led to an area where other Union captives were taken. There were more there than he cared to see. No matter, he thought... escape... somehow... somewhere. He didn't see any familiar faces among his fellow captives. He guessed he must have been the only one from his company to be captured, and he knew why. Wanted to drag the Big Swede back, he thought. He sat down by himself, burying his face in his hands, and wept over his big buddy's death.

"Fall in!" shouted the Rebel lieutenant. "Line up here and empty out your haversacks." The young officer rummaged through each man's belongings as they were dumped out on the ground, confiscating all knives, weapons, money, valuables, and whatever it pleased him to keep for himself. Patrick had only a few pieces of hardtack, some dime novels, a newspaper, shaving equipment, and Lou Ann's little white flower vase. After taking the razor and newspaper, the officer held up the vase for all to see. "Well, what do we have here?" With a smirk on his face, he continued, "A pretty little vase the Yank carries around—maybe he wants to fill it with flowers to present to Bobby Lee in hopes of getting his freedom." No reaction came from Pat's fellow captives, but the Rebel guards made the most of the mockery, laughing loudly. The lieutenant's smirk, however, quickly changed to a frown as he examined the vase further. "Where did you steal this from, Yank?"

"I—I—found it."

"Yeah, sure—don't lie to me, Yank."

"What do you mean?"

"Look here!" The Rebel held the bottom of the vase up in Patrick's face. Pat, pulling his face back a little, could see a small imprint in the bottom— *CSA.*

"Either you stole it from one of our boys or confiscated it from some old lady. I don't think you Yanks are making stuff with *these* on them," as he pointed to the CSA initials on his own belt buckle. "Well, either way, you won't be needin' it where you're goin'—there ain't no flowers growin' in prison," as he threw the vase into a pile of garbage and moved to the next man.

Patrick felt humiliated and angry at first, but these emotions eventually subsided as his mind refocused on suspicion of Lou Ann's activities. Where would she get a vase made in the Confederate States of America if she hadn't been down south?

"All right, you Yanks," hollered a Confederate officer. "You'll stay here for the night."

It was getting dark, and Pat looked around at the crowd of prisoners. He estimated there were approximately two hundred enlisted men with a few officers mixed in amongst them. They were in a field, with no shelter in sight. It bordered a dirt road with a split rail fence on one side and woods on the other. It was a clear, cool night, and he could see the moonlight reflecting off the bayonets at the end of the guards' rifles. There were ten guards ringing the new band of prisoners; he had counted them. He suddenly felt hungry. The guards hadn't given them any food. Reaching into his haversack, he found a few pieces of hardtack that he had and ate them quickly. He washed them down with the lukewarm water that was still in his canteen. He was still hungry. Unrolling the blanket, carried throughout the battle on his back, he laid down on the dewy grass. Thoughts began to flow through his mind... home... Beth... Lou Ann... the Swede... the man he impaled on the tree. Too much. He fell into a deep sleep.

The next morning, he was suddenly awakened. "On your feet, you bluebellies!" hollered the Confederate lieutenant. "You've got a long march ahead of you." He waved a stick in his hand and pointed it toward a tent on the opposite side of the road. "Line up for grub over there!" The prisoners quickly lined up and followed the lieutenant. After receiving his portion,

Pat sat down on the ground and leaned back against a fence post. He looked at the cornmeal in his cup and wasn't impressed. Looks like swill that pigs eat, he thought to himself. He ate it anyway. Not much taste—something to fill me up for a little while. They were allowed to fill their canteens with water in a nearby stream; but Pat was so thirsty, he drank directly from the stream until he thought he would burst. Afterwards, he dipped his canteen into the clear, cool water and filled it to the very brim. He looked down the line at the other men on their bellies, guzzling the fresh water in the same manner. As he was getting to his feet, he noticed a young Confederate guard standing nearby. His rifle was slung over his shoulder.

"Where y'all from, Yank?"

"Who me?" Pat replied.

"Yeah—you, Yank. Where y'all from?"

"New York."

The young Rebel seemed unconcerned about anyone attempting to escape. He folded his arms and leaned back against a tree, bending his knee to prop one foot against the trunk. "Big place, huh?"

"Big enough," Pat answered.

"Had yer share a fightin'?"

"For now."

"Well, I heerd they ain't gonna exchange any more prisoners soon. Guess ya won't see any more fightin'."

"That all depends, Reb."

"Depends on what?"

"Depends on how the war goes."

"Oh, well, Yank, don't go worryin' about that. You bluebellies will be runnin' home soon, waggin' yer tails behind ya."

"That's debatable."

"What de bate bil mean?"

"I mean there's a lot more Yanks comin' your way."

"Don't mean no never mind how many come... you ain't got no general can whip Marse Robert."

"Who?"

"Bobby Lee—The Gray Fox. He can run circles around any general you got!"

"We'll see, Reb."

"Fess up, Yank. Y'all know we been whippin' ya since Bull Run."

"Don't count your chickens before they're hatched."

"Chickens? You got chickens?"

"Just a saying." Pat surmised the young guard was a raw recruit and asked him, "You seen the elephant yet?"

"What elephant?"

Pat chuckled. "You been in battle yet?"

The guard looked down at the ground and hesitantly answered with a sheepish look on his face, "Well, no, not yet." He paused. Then continued, "Just got sent up here from Richmond. Only doin' guard duty. But I'll be—how you say?—seein' elephant soon, I hope."

"Don't hope for that, Reb; you'll be better off." Pat walked back to join his comrades. He liked the young Reb—his inexperience—maybe down the road—escape. Have to get to know him better.

"All right, Yanks! Line up on the road in a column of twos! We're goin' for a stroll," hollered the lieutenant.

Pat got into line with the rest of the prisoners. He was near the front of the column and stared down the long, dusty road ahead of them. How far, he thought, will they take us? How far south, deep into the enemy's camp? No... can't... *won't* go. Escape first. Harder to escape prison.

As they were being marched away, a drizzling rain began to fall. They passed by a large tent a short distance from the road. The side walls were rolled up, and Pat noticed a high-ranking Confederate officer talking to a young lady. She wore a blue bonnet and held an open matching parasol on her shoulder. She had her back to the marching prisoners. Patrick stared and squinted his eyes as he passed by. The young lady had a striking resemblance to Lou Ann. Could it be her? He strained his neck to see her better. She never turned around. He couldn't be sure. He was marched away with the others in the rain, shocked at the thought that it *could* be her. His suspicions grew even stronger.

The guards, mostly very young or very old, walked in the front and in the back of the column. Two officers rode alongside them on horseback. As the day wore on, the road became muddy; and every time the officers galloped back and forth to check on the prisoners, more and more of the mud splattered the men.

Pat felt naked. The many long marches he had traveled on, he had had his rifle slung over his shoulder. It was his constant companion... his confidence...his equalizer. But now he was stripped of all a soldier could depend on. He felt helpless and humiliated—no longer a man—no longer a soldier—just a lowly prisoner. No different than a slave, he thought.

The men marched down the long, muddy road, sometimes slipping and falling down. At times the drizzle became a downpour, and they became drenched. The air turned cooler, and Pat began to shiver. He wrapped his blanket around his shoulders and shuffled along with the rest. As the afternoon turned into evening and darkness fell, they encamped for the night. The rain had stopped, and they were once again fed the same tasteless mush.

For two more days they marched in rain. Pat still hadn't found any chance to escape. The guards were constantly watching them. He became concerned that he would arrive at a prison and never get out.

Some time during the following night, they stopped and rested. Pat wrapped his soggy blanket around himself and lay down on the wet ground, shaking from the chill of the damp night air. An image of the Big Swede breathing his last passed before him. Those last words of his—"Tell Mama I love…"—haunted him. As he lay there, helpless and cold, he wasn't sure if he would live to tell "Mama" that the last words that came from her son's lips were of his love for her. What if the Swede hadn't hollered to warn him? It could have been he, himself, lying in a puddle of blood with a bullet through his neck. Saved my life; he trembled at the thought. Have to get control. Enough death and dying. He curled up under his blanket, trying to get warm. He would think about those happy days with Beth back home. Lou Ann was nice to think about; but when the going got tough and uncertainty of his survival occupied his thoughts, he found Beth was the one who was foremost in his mind. He had been infatuated with Lou Ann for a short while, but his feelings about her were becoming bitter. Was he a pawn in her life? Somehow he thought she had used him to carry out her espionage. But how? Getting depressed. Beth. Must think about Beth. Have to get control.

He remembered feeling "out of control" when he first saw Beth as an adult in Mr. Schuler's Meat Market. He had never met a girl who had caused his heart to flutter before. She came into his life that warm, summer evening as he was sweeping the floor and about to close the shop. He was thinking she looked familiar as he took her order.

"Do I know you?" he asked.

"I'm not sure," she replied.

"You look so familiar to me. Did you go to St. Mary's?"

"Oh, yes. Aren't you.......?"

"Patrick. Patrick's my name—Patrick O'Hanrahan."

"Oh, yes, now I remember. You sat in the desk behind me."

"Beth? Oh, my gosh! You sure look different!" He was remembering her long pigtails hanging down her back and how he was often tempted to pull one or both of them. He often wondered how she got them to hang down so evenly. He was surprised to see how she had grown up into such a beautiful young lady. The pigtails were gone now. Her brown hair was long and curly, falling gracefully from her pink bonnet over her shoulders. Her straight lines from shoulders to waist were now pleasantly adorned with soft but pronounced curves. The little girl he teased in grade school suddenly, without warning, caught his attention and would grab hold of his heart from that time forward. He filled her order and handed the wrapped package over the counter to her.

"Well, it's so nice to see you again, Patrick. Maybe we'll run into each other again."

"I'll be closing the shop in a few minutes. Would you mind if I walk you home?"

"Well, sure. That's fine with me."

He quickly finished his sweeping and locked up.

Walking her home that night, he was filled with excitement; he had never had time for girls before. This was different. Something new was happening to him. He weighed every word he spoke and discovered a slight nervousness in his voice. A warm summer breeze caressed them, as they began a journey that would test their future love and catapult them through the worst, bloody war that they and their young nation could possibly have conceived.

"Remember Miss Simon?" Beth asked.

"Oh, yeah. How could I forget her large pointy nose and that big mole on her cheek? We called her 'Simple Simon'—when she couldn't hear us, of course!"

"Oh, you boys were so mean!"

"Well, I believe I heard a few girls calling her that, too."

"Well, I don't know about that!" she said with a muffled snicker in her voice. "What ever happened to that other boy that you hung around with?"

"Oh, you mean Joshua? The kid with the red hair and freckles?"

"Yes, that's him."

"We were like brothers. His family moved to Virginia. Remember? He never came back to school after sixth grade. Yeah, I missed him when he moved away. We had a lot of fun together." He wanted to know more about her, so he changed the subject. "What are you doing now, Beth?"

"My mother and I moved back here after my parents divorced. We had moved to Georgia with my father. His business took him there. He liked the South, but Mom couldn't stand the heat. They fought all the time, so I guess it was for the best. I have a job in a small dress shop uptown. I like it a lot."

"Did *you* like it in Georgia, Beth?"

"Not really. The heat didn't bother me and it was beautiful down there, but…" She hesitated.

"But, what?" he stopped and looked at her with curiosity.

"Well, some of the people…"

"Yes? Some of the people what?"

"Oh, some of the people kind of…"

"The people kind of what?"

"Some were not very nice."

"Well, that's true all over. Every day I have a few customers who get rude with me."

"I guess it was the *reason* they didn't act nice to me."

"You mean there was a particular reason?"

"Well," she muttered in soft tones he could barely hear as she looked down at the ground, "There's a great deal of talk about war and secession and, being from the North—well, you can guess."

"Oh, that's it! I know what you mean—about the talk of war. I mean, that's all my Grandpa talks about lately. He's been talking a lot about some politician out West— Lincoln, I think his name is—and he wants to free the slaves, Grandpa says. He told me they have it worse than he did in Ireland. I don't understand all of it, do you?"

"All I know is the people in Georgia are upset. They talk about the North, States' Rights, and many talk about slavery all the time. They talk about the North as if we were the enemy. I hope we don't have a war." She stopped in front of a narrow, brick apartment building. "This is where I live, Patrick."

"Oh, I didn't realize you lived so close to my work." He was thinking he could have walked clear around the city with her and didn't want to leave her.

"Thank you for walking me home, Patrick. It was good to see you again," she remarked as she ascended the stairway to her apartment building.

"Oh, Beth," he said. "Are you going to the Fourth of July picnic next week?"

She turned back to answer him. "I hadn't heard about it."

"Oh, it's great! They have fireworks, music, games, canoe races… It's a lot of fun. Would you consider going with me?"

"Sounds exciting, but I might have to work that day."

"You mean your shop isn't closed on the Fourth of July?" he asked in a surprised tone of voice.

"I'll let you know. Goodnight, Patrick," she said with a smile as she closed the door behind her.

He didn't see her again until the third of July when she came into Mr. Schuler's market. As he was filling a customer's order and had just bent over to reach far into the front of the glass-enclosed meat counter, he peered through the glass and spotted her entering the shop. His heart pounded. Have to act casual, he thought. Hastily pulling his head from the counter, he bumped the top of it against the meat case as he did so. Pretending he hadn't noticed her coming in, he finished waiting on his customer.

"Hello, Patrick," she said as she rummaged through her purse for a grocery list her mother had given her.

"Oh, hello, Beth." He rubbed his head, glanced over at her, and smiled. She looked even prettier than the night he had walked her home. "Did you think any more about the picnic?" he blurted out.

"Mrs. Ennis at the dress shop said she wouldn't be needing me tomorrow, so I guess I can go with you," she said as she handed him her order and waited for his response.

"Oh, that's great! Can you be ready about noon?"

"One o'clock would be better. I have some chores to do for my mother."

Just then, Mr. Schuler, who had walked over and stood next to Patrick while wrapping a meat order for another customer, nudged him on the arm with his elbow. "Vas is dis girl you talk to?"

"Oh, just a friend."

"Vell, don't forget da utter customers; vork comes first, ya know." He walked back to the other end of the counter.

"Yes, sir, Mr. Schuler." Looking back at Beth, Pat smiled and raised his eyebrows, briefly glancing over at his boss, then back again. "I vill meet you at the bandstand at vun o'clock," he said in a hushed tone as he handed Beth her order, chuckling as he did.

She had heard Mr. Schuler's remark and politely nodded at Patrick. Smiling, she whispered, "One o'clock. See you then," as she departed.

Bang! Bang! Bang! Patrick woke with a start. The strong, pungent odor of exploding fireworks invaded his nostrils, as his ears began to ring. Bang! Bang! Bang! It continued and aroused Patrick to an agitated awakening. By the time he had placed his feet on the floor, he remembered his date with Beth. His agitated state quickly evolved to one of great expectation.

He shouted at the young revelers outside his window and chuckled as they dispersed in all directions. Before his youthful years would pass, he would have his fill of explosions and gun smoke, even more than he could imagine. After washing up, he dug out his only good pair of long pants and his one decent shirt. He then fumbled through his dresser for his bow tie. Standing in front of the mirror, he struggled to tie it straight. After a few attempts with no success, he finally gave up.

"Hey, Grocky! I need your help!" No answer was forthcoming, so Pat descended the stairs and found him snoozing in his favorite chair. He nudged him gently on the shoulder, awakening him. The old man let out a few grunts and groans.

"What is it, lad?"

"Need help with my tie, Grocky. Can you tie it for me?"

"Well, lad—looks like ya have an important social engagement ta be goin' to," he said with a smile as he picked up his pipe from the ashtray and clenched it between his teeth. "Turn around, lad, and let me show ya the proper way ta tie that thing." He stood behind Pat and slowly guided his hands step by step in the art of tying a perfect bow. "And what's gonna hold up yer pants?" Grocky chuckled as he lit his pipe and began to draw on it. Pat looked down and realized he had forgotten his suspenders. He bounded up the stairs, put on his red suspenders and quickly returned downstairs to the kitchen where his grandmother was cooking over the old wood-burning stove.

"Look at you, Paddy!—if ya don't look so patriotic with yer red suspenders, white shirt, and blue pants!" Teresa said with a warm smile as she continued to stir something in a large black pot.

"Smells good, Grama, but I won't be home for supper tonight." He fussed with his tie in front of the small, round mirror hanging on the wall and then meticulously combed his hair to make sure his part was perfectly straight.

"And where would ya be goin' that's so important to miss Grama's Irish stew?"

"Goin' to the carnival with a friend."

"It wouldn't be a young lady friend now, would it?"

A rosy flush came over his cheeks, as he purposely kept grooming himself in front of the mirror. "Just an old friend from school, Gram." He grabbed his cap off the tall, wooden coat rack near the back door, and walked over to give her a big kiss on her cheek, sneakily untying her apron as he did so.

"Stop that now, you fresh thing!" slapping his hands gently. "Aren't you even goin' ta have some breakfast?" She reached behind her and retied her apron strings.

"No time, Grama. Be home by eleven." He bolted out the door.

Beth stood by the gazebo where the band was playing the Star Spangled Banner. A buxom older lady was singing along with the band. His heart pounded as he admired Beth's beauty. He walked slowly toward her. She wore a long, billowy, pink dress with a matching bonnet. Her hands were folded around the handle of a small picnic basket. She smiled at him as he approached and greeted her. He would take this image of her, store it in his heart, and bring it to mind many times before a battle. It couldn't be destroyed by shot or shell and would always be there when he wanted it.

A spirit of patriotism filled the air, and the park was ringed by Old Glory fluttering in the warm, summer breeze. They walked and talked, passing by giggling children bobbing for apples and frolicking along the edge of the lake. Further down the path, the old men and veterans of the Mexican War were gathered around the beer kegs, telling war stories and talking about the current political situation. Patrick overheard Abe Lincoln's name come up as they passed by. Talk of war with the South was becoming commonplace.

"Do you really think we will go to war, Patrick?" asked Beth.

"Oh, I don't know. Mr. Schuler at the store thinks it won't happen, but my Grandpa thinks it might. I hope he's wrong. I saw my brother Mike yesterday. You know, he doesn't come home much. He's hoping for war—always itching for a fight, he is. I wish he'd stay home so we could spend more time together. I think he's traveling with bad company; he never goes to church anymore."

"He doesn't sound like you, Patrick—sounds kind of wild to me."

"Oh, he's got a good heart, but Ma said he never got over Dad's disappearance; and Grama and Grandpa couldn't handle him either."

"Did you say your father disappeared?"

"Yeah. I was very young. I don't remember him; but my older brother was about eleven, and they tell me he was very close to him."

"Oh, that's terrible. I'm so sorry. Did you ever find out what happened to him?"

"No. My mother wrote the relatives in Ireland, and she even went down to the morgue, just in case—well—you know. He never did return. We don't really know what happened to him. Where is *your* father now?"

"Well, my father's still down in Georgia. I don't know what will happen to him if there is a war with the South. He might stay and fight for their side. He always talked about the North as a dictatorship and believed the South didn't have many states' rights."

"It's very confusing to me. All I know from what I read in the newspapers and what my Grandpa tells me is that some of the people in the new territories out West want to have slaves and others say they can't. Why don't they just do away with slavery and that would solve everything."

"Well, the only thing I know is that my Pa used to say that the slaves didn't have it so bad. They always had a place to sleep and enough food to eat and didn't have to worry about starving to death."

"Funny you should say that because my Grandpa told me that people in the Old Country died by the thousands because they didn't have any food. Could you imagine watching your whole family die that way? He said that we might have starved to death if we had stayed there."

"That's horrible. But it still doesn't seem right that some people can own others— like you would own a horse or something."

"Yeah, that isn't right either, but..."

She abruptly chimed in before he finished. "Oh, all this talk of war gets me down. Let's talk about something else."

"Okay, lets go down to the lake and watch the canoe races." For the first time he took her by the hand as they strolled down to the lake. She glanced at him, smiling as she did, and gently squeezed his hand. The crowd had gathered at the edge of the water, and loud cheers were going up all around. They found a spot away from the crowd on a small, grassy knoll where they could still see well. Beth sat down, spreading her full hoop skirt demurely around her, making sure her legs were completely covered. Pat plopped down next to her and leaned on one elbow as he often did at home when Grocky was talking to him. "What's in the basket?" he inquired.

"Oh, I packed a few sandwiches for later. I didn't know if..." She stopped in the middle of her sentence.

"You didn't know if what?"

"Oh, I just wasn't sure if there were any food stands here. Never been to this celebration before."

"That was very thoughtful of you." He wondered to himself if she was being truthful or if she thought he might not have enough money with him. "When we're ready to eat, I'll get a couple lemonades for us." He didn't really have a great deal of money with him and secretly felt relieved she had brought the lunch. They sat quietly for a time, watching the canoes slipping past each other, as the crowd grew more excited with each race. Neither Pat nor Beth knew any of the racers, so they picked their favorite numbers. The canoes had a large black number painted on a white circle on the side near the front of them. Beth liked number three, and Pat always picked one with the number seven. They cheered their favorites on for a few races, and Pat found himself watching her as she sat up excitedly every time her boat surged ahead. He admired her smile and long curls hanging out from beneath her bonnet. He thought of the braids he was tempted to pull on the little skinny girl who had occupied the desk in front of him not too long ago, yet it seemed so distant now to him. They joked about their childhood antics and about some of the silly things they did at St. Mary's and recalled many of their old friends.

"What did you say happened to—Joshua, was it? You said he was your best friend."

"Yeah, we were close. We played baseball together. We sold newspapers on opposite sides of the street, and made bets on who could sell the most in one day. We went swimming in the river and did most everything together."

"Did you meet him in school?"

"Not really. I mean, I saw him in school, but I didn't really know him until…"

"Until what?"

"Well, the first time I saw him selling his newspapers right across the street from me, I wanted to go over and sock him in the nose. I remember glaring at him and trying to shout louder than him—'Get your evening newspaper right here! Read all about it!' You know, that huckster thing newsboys do."

"Oh, yes, I've heard it many times."

"Well, he shouted louder and then I shouted louder and it became a shouting match. Then just as I was really going to go and punch him in the nose, something happened that caused us to become best friends."

"How in the world did that happen? I mean—when you were so mad at him?"

"Well, this big kid comes running up to me and knocks me down, reaches into my pocket, takes all my money, and takes off running before I knew what happened." He paused a moment, picked a few blades of grass, and threw them in the air.

"And then what happened?"

"I don't know if I can tell you the rest. It's kind of embarrassing."

"Come on, Patrick. You've got my curiosity up now."

"Well, I don't know—you're a young lady and—I—well—it sounds kind of vulgar—but it's true."

"Is it *that* bad?"

"Well, I guess it's not *too* bad."

"Come on, Patrick. Tell me what happened next."

He hesitated for a moment, then briefly chuckled before he went on. "Well, I guess Josh saw what happened, and this big guy was running in his direction…" He laughed again, still not sure if he should tell her the next part. She crooked her head slightly to the side and raised her eyebrows, waiting anxiously for the conclusion of the story. He continued, looking up at the blue sky as he did. "Josh reached down into the street, picks up a horseball, and fires it smack into the guy's face! Next thing you know, Josh starts beating him with folded up newspapers. I ran over and we both jumped on him and pulled him to the ground. We beat the tar out of him. I got my money back. He got up and ran like blazes. Josh and I became good friends after that."

Beth giggled, reached into her purse, pulled out a small pink handkerchief, and held it to her mouth to conceal her laughter. "You're not spinning a tale now, are you, Patrick?"

"No, I'm not, Beth."

"Well, it sounds like blarney to me." Her giggling subsided, and she wiped a tear from her eyes.

"I swear it happened just like I said—no foolin'!"

"And that was the beginning of your friendship? Sure was a peculiar way to start a friendship." She smiled and tucked her kerchief back into her purse.

As the afternoon wore on, they enjoyed the many activities going on around them. Some men were trying to climb a greased pole, but slipped down faster than they could climb up. And the children laughed and cheered as they ran the three-legged sack races. Suddenly, the sound of exploding firecrackers going off nearby startled them, and they turned to watch the unsuspecting victims cursing and chasing the rowdy boys who had frightened them. They both were contented just being together, walking and talking and getting to know each other once again. Patrick bought two glasses of lemonade, and they sat beneath a large willow tree near the lake. Beth opened the picnic basket, laid a small linen cloth on the grass, and proceeded to place the contents on it. "Help yourself to a sandwich and some chicken, Patrick, but save room for the huckleberry pie!" His eyes lit up, as this was his favorite dessert. A warm feeling came over him as he enjoyed her home cooking, gazing into her pretty eyes, and feeling like he was sitting on top of the world.

"This is the best fried chicken I've ever had, Beth. Did you make it yourself?"

"Well, with a little help from my Mom. She's been teaching me a lot of her favorite recipes. I'm glad you like it." She picked up a sandwich and sipped the lemonade he had bought. They sat there silently for a few moments, enjoying the meal, before Pat spoke.

"Do you ever see anybody from St. Mary's?"

"No, not really. They all went their own way, I guess. I did see a few of them before we moved to Georgia, but I haven't seen any of them since I returned."

"Yeah, I know what you mean. I've only seen a couple of the boys since then, but we weren't close friends. Billy Wolf came into the market one day, and he didn't even remember me."

"Help yourself to some more chicken, Pat. Or, would you prefer a sandwich?"

He liked her calling him Pat. It made him feel like they were becoming closer friends. "Oh, I'll have one of each. Thanks. It's really good."

She watched him and admired his appetite. He finished his meal and looked questioningly over to her and then down at the basket. "Did you say you had some huckleberry pie?"

She searched in the basket for a moment; then looked apologetically at him. "Oh, no! I must have forgotten to pack it!"

"No, really? I was sure looking forward to that. It's my favorite!" He saw a smirk come over her face as she reached once again into the basket.

"Oh, wait a minute. What's this? Oh, I guess I didn't forget to pack it after all!" She pulled out a big, juicy looking piece.

"Why—you tease!!" They both chuckled as he took the pie from her hand.

The sun was going down. Patrick lay back on the soft green grass, folding his hands under his head. The mellow tones coming from a few wandering mandolin players tugged at his young, infatuated heart. He couldn't come to grips with these newfound feelings. He had only been in Beth's company a few times and already believed he wanted to spend the rest of his life with her. He had no experience in these matters, but something told him to go slow in his pursuit. He wanted to find out if she had any other beaus but didn't ask for fear of appearing too anxious.

As dusk turned to night, the lamplighter made his rounds, illuminating the park with a soft glow. In Patrick's eyes, it became like a magical fairyland; and he wanted the evening to go on forever. The band had changed from playing marching songs to softer waltzes, as young and old couples danced on the smooth, shiny gazebo floor. Patrick wanted to dance with Beth but didn't know how. His hectic young life, engulfed by survival, had no room for the niceties of life. They watched the dancing couples glide gracefully across the floor. Beth was too lady-like to ask Patrick to dance; and he was unable to do so, even though he wished he could hold her in his arms and twirl her around like the other dancers. The children's merrymaking and laughter had subsided, as they had all been taken home; and the park took on a quieter mood except for the beer tent, where a few intoxicated men were arguing politics.

War! Cries of war could be heard again and again emanating from the tent. They echoed throughout the park that night, drifting on the wind and all across the nation, as these two young lovers strolled through the park, hoping for peace for themselves and their country. It wasn't meant to be.

A loud explosion jolted them, as they suddenly saw the black night sky over the lake burst into a brilliant array of many colors streaming out in every direction. "Oh! How beautiful!" Beth exclaimed.

"Yeah, the fireworks are my favorite part of the Fourth of July." The band struck up the Star Spangled Banner again, and the park came alive with shouts of joy and patriotic slogans.

"The Union Forever!" was booming from the beer tent as if in one voice. "God Save the Union!" was heard loud and clear over and over.

Patrick escorted Beth home that evening on the horse-drawn trolley. They sat in the back, holding hands and listening to the clomp of the horses' hoofs on the hard, cobblestone street, as the music from the band faded in the distance. He walked her up the stairs to her front door and stole his first kiss. It was full on her lips, and she allowed it to last longer than she expected to. She was beginning to feel as he did. Quickly composing herself, she fumbled in her purse for her key, thanked him for a wonderful day, and said goodnight. He had the words ready to tumble from his lips, but she quietly closed the door behind her before he could ask to see her again.

The summer nights were hot and humid that year, and these two young lovers met frequently. They would often stroll around on the top of the promenade of the Distributing Reservoir on the corner of 42nd Street and 5th Avenue where the air was cooled as it passed over the water. The huge concrete structure reminded them of an Egyptian pyramid.

Summer's heat gave way to autumn's chill, and the climate between the North and South was also growing colder and more distant.

Patrick was suddenly jolted back to the reality of his captivity as a cold rain began to pelt his face. As he lay on the wet ground, he felt more distant from home and Beth than ever before. The isolation from all the goodness in his life seemed to create an emptiness that went deep into his soul and brought an exhaustion of the spirit that he had never felt before. Have to sleep. Have to sleep.

He awoke early the next morning, a ray of sunshine dancing in his eyes as the tree limb hanging above him swayed gently in the warm spring breeze. Escape. Must get free. His thoughts once again turned to the slave he had helped on the plantation—a slave who never knew freedom.

Patrick had never been incarcerated before. His grandfather had always warned him never to break the law. "Paddy, me boy," he would say, "ya wouldn't like the inside of a jail, lad. Ya'd be thrown in with some pretty bad ruffians and no tellin' if ya'd come out alive." Patrick had been a good soldier, doing what he thought was right. He hadn't minded taking orders or fighting for a good cause or any of the hardships he had to endure. It was all part of being a soldier—something done from *his* own will. But now he felt a taste of bondage, unable to move freely or speak or plan his own destiny. He had become a slave—no different than Nathan—held captive and made to go where he didn't want to go and to do what he didn't want to do. Maybe today... slip away. Today was his third day on the march—the Lord rose on the third day—have to find a way. The warm sunshine absorbed the wet and dampness from the roads and his soggy clothes and blanket. Patrick felt good as the sun's rays radiated its warmth on his face. He breathed in the fresh, clean air and sweet aroma of freshly turned earth as they passed by a farmer's field. It didn't look any different than the farms he had marched by in the North. God's earth never changes—only men change... start wars... make trouble. God's earth, he thought, never changes, just as His love for us. The sun was shining, he was still in one piece, his faith was strong... there *was* hope!

Morning turned to afternoon... and they marched. The afternoon wore on... and they marched. It was getting hot, and the sweat poured down Patrick's face. He felt exhausted, but he had to keep up with the others. He wouldn't be outdone by the Confederate guards. Sheer determination propelled him along for the rest of the afternoon. Finally, they halted. The prisoners were herded into a farmer's front yard to make camp. The house had been vacated and was in bad repair. The shutters on the broken windows were falling off, the doors were missing, and the land was overgrown with weeds. Pat removed his shoes and rubbed his sore, blistered feet. Most of the men were too tired to talk; some fell asleep. Pat dozed off briefly, his head nodding as he sat in a crouched position, resting his elbows on his propped up knees.

He awoke to the smell of food. It was getting dark. He rubbed his eyes and looked over toward the farmhouse from which the smell seemed to emanate. Standing on the ground in front of the porch stood a black man, stirring something in a large pot. He could hear the man softly humming a tune but couldn't make it out. He didn't care. All he could think of was food... smelled good. The young black man, dressed in rags, wore an old straw hat with a wide brim that looked as if it had sheltered many a head in its day. Pat watched him as he stirred the pot with a large, wooden ladle, keeping up a rhythm that seemed orchestrated to his tune. He hadn't seen many black men in his travels, but there was something familiar looking about this one. Some prisoners were milling around the yard, circled by the guards. Pat got up and stretched. He slowly moved amongst the others toward the black man. In the flickering light of the fire, he could see him wiping his brow with his sleeve while continuing to stir the pot with his other hand. Was it him? The slave from the plantation? What was his name? Nathan— yes—Nathan. No, it couldn't be. He had been freed. What was he doing here? Why was he here cooking for the Rebels? Pat moved closer to him and was about to whisper his name when a rider galloped into the yard, attracting the guards' attention. Pat quickly took advantage of this diversion.

"Nathan, is that you?"

The black man, looking startled, jerked his head around to see who had whispered his name, his hat falling to the ground. They both crouched down to pick it up. "Who yu, Massa?"

"Remember me? The plantation—got your wound fixed."

"Sa'gen—oh, yeah—Sa'gen. Whats yu doin' here?"

"Captured at Chancellorsville—I think they call it. No time to talk. Do you know your way around these parts?"

"Yassuh, ah knows these parts like the back a my hand."

"Have to escape—can you help?"

"Ah doan knows, Sa'gen." He picked up his hat and stood up, looking frightened at the prospect of trying to escape.

Pat, not wanting to look suspicious as one of the guards drew closer, whispered to Nathan, "We'll talk again. Think about it." As he moved away from the black man, he overheard some of the other prisoners talking about the rider's message.

"Did you hear that?" one of them said.

"Yeah, he said Belle Isle Prison in Richmond is all full up. Then somethin' about shippin' us further south by train."

Patrick didn't like the sound of this. Must act quickly. Now or never.

CHAPTER 10

▼

THE SLAVE

The same year that Patrick had reached the heights of the top of the Latting Tower at the World's Fair in New York City, Nathan, a young slave, struggled daily in the depths of humanity in the dirt of a Virginia plantation. He toiled in the burning sun from morning till night. This was his lot in life. Every day the overseer or driver blew his horn before daylight to summon the slaves to another day of drudgery. Every night Nathan collapsed on his makeshift bed on the dirt floor of the two-room cabin he shared with his ma and pa. He had no hope for the future. His people had been slaves for four generations. How could he ever expect things to change?

From the time he was old enough to lift a water bucket, he carried the precious liquid to the parched lips of his people in the cotton fields, in addition to feeding the animals. At the age of ten, he too, joined his family picking the cotton. He grew in size and stature in spite of the drudgery and harshness he was submerged in. By the time he was seventeen, his every thought was of escaping. He dreamt about it. But each time he did, he also thought about the terrible beatings the runaways received when caught. Besides, he feared leaving his family, for he knew reprisals would be taken out on them if he pursued his dream. He was a prisoner, chained to that existence, condemned to grovel in the dirt, to bow to his master, to wallow in the mire of slavery, and to dance to the tune of submission for the rest of his born days.

One day, as he and the other slaves stopped work for their noon meal, they sought refuge from the hot sun in the shade of the trees that lined the dirt roadway between the fields and awaited their food. An old slave named Daniel approached, leading a mule-pulled wagon containing their meager meal of peas and cornbread, along with a half-filled barrel of hot, stale water. The old man wore a smile, grinning from ear to ear. He looked around to see if the overseer was nearby. Not seeing him, he began to speak in hushed tones. "Ah heerd some white folks talkin' in town." He leaned against the wagon, still looking around, then continued. "Big white father, Abe Lincum... gonna free us." The slaves began to cheer with excitement. "Shhh—shush, you chillun. Massa cud hear!"

Nathan spoke up, "How this Abe Lincum gonna' free us?"

"Sogers—he gots lots a sogers wif guns... comin' down here."

"Glory an' 'allaluya!!" Nathan shouted.

"Shhh," the old man warned, looking around fearfully.

For the first time in his existence, Nathan had hope. Each morning as he awoke, his first thoughts were of freedom. He could only compare it with his image of heaven.

His parents and ancestors had never found any hope for freedom to pass on to him. This feeling of hope was new to him. But however it turned out to be, it would be glorious. Just the thought of not having a master greatly excited him. The hope—that's what it was—hope. He found inspiration and a new vigor in his bones.

The days passed slowly, and he waited. Days turned to weeks, and nothing happened. He began to doubt if it was true. No Lincoln's soldiers came—but *some* soldiers came... dressed in *gray*... Confederate soldiers! They came in the middle of the night. Nathan was suddenly awakened by Master Marshall, bursting through the old cabin door. "Wake up!—right away!" he said in an excited voice. "Come to the big house. You're needed there now. Hurry up!"

Nathan and his parents, Jessica and Jeremiah, scrambled to their feet. Baffled and confused, they hurriedly threw their clothes on. They ran up to the Master's big house as fast as they could. Nathan arrived in the front yard first. He stopped and waited for his parents to catch up with him. As he gazed up at the windows of the big house, he saw shadowy silhouettes flitting back and forth. Many horses were tied up at the hitching post. Standing by the front door, Marshall yelled out to them, "Hurry up!" and motioned them to go inside. Many Rebel soldiers lie on the couches and floor. Nathan saw many writhing in pain, some groaning. The housemaids and servants were scurrying around with pans of hot water and tearing up bed sheets to make bandages for the wounded. Mrs. Marshall was sitting in a chair in the corner of the room, her face chalk-white, rapidly fanning herself. Master Marshall shouted, "Jessica! Jeremiah! Get some more linen from upstairs. Nathan, go outside and take care of the horses!"

He hurried outside, took the horses to the barn, and fed and watered them. Glad I's not takin' care a dem sogers, he thought to himself. *Dey* doan wanna gives us slaves no freedom. Likes takin' care of dese horses better.

As he removed the saddles from the sweaty horses and brushed them down, he remembered back to the time when he was a small boy and how he loved feeding the mules, pigs, horses, chickens and dogs. He felt a common bond with them. They didn't holler at him or order him around—they were just there—quiet, friendly, and soothing. He would often pet them after a hard day in the fields. They provided him with a little comfort in his harsh, young life. He found other small comforts to lessen the pain of his callous existence. When he could get away from his work in the fields, he loved to steal away to his private spot—a place far back in the woods, which he had discovered earlier. It was a small clearing surrounded by pine trees, with a swift-running stream passing through it. On some occasions, after working in the hot sun all day, sometimes cutting his fingers on the cotton plants, he would come to this place and dangle his hands and   feet in the cool, clear water and dream of a better life.

He admired the large, strong steeds as he brushed them down and fed them.   The old horses and mules he was accustomed to caring for were scrawny and small in comparison. Over the next few days, some of the Rebel soldiers with minor wounds had come for their horses and ridden away. Nathan was disappointed to see them go, as he had been temporarily relieved from his work in the fields.

One evening when Nathan was feeding the black stallion, a young Rebel soldier appeared at the barn door. He stood in the dim light of the lantern hanging on the wall, leaned against the doorpost, and attempted to light his pipe. His arm was in a sling, and he was having difficulty striking the match. "Taking good care of that stallion?" asked the Rebel.

"Yassuh."

"That's good. He belongs to me." The young soldier continued to attempt to light the match without any success.

"Cud ah helps ya, Massa?" Nathan walked over to him. The soldier gave him the match, which he successfully lit and held over the pipe while the Reb drew on it until he had it going. "Dat's a fine hoss yu got dere, Massa."

"Don't call me master—I'm not your master."

"Yassuh, Mas..." Nathan caught himself. "Yassuh."

"That horse carried me through many battles. Had him for years."

"Yassuh. What yu calls him?"

"Blackjack. He's my best friend." They both stood there for a moment, silently gazing at the sleek, black steed. Looking over at Nathan, the soldier asked, "You got a name?"

"Nathan, suh."

"My name is Joshua, Nathan. Call me Joshua."

"Yassuh, Joshua, suh."

"You been on this plantation long?"

"All ma born days, Joshua, suh."

"You like it here, Nathan?"

"Yassuh."

"You ever been anyplace else?"

"Nawsuh."

Joshua told him that he, himself, had worked on a plantation for a short time as an overseer but didn't like it.

Seems too nice for an overseer, Nathan thought to himself.

Joshua bent over to lift the stallion's leg and inspect the horse's shoe. As he did so, a medal attached to a chain dangled down from his neck. Nathan had never seen such a medal. It had a star on it, overlaid with a Cross.

"Have him saddled up and ready to go at sunup, Nathan."

"Yassuh, Joshua, suh." Nathan watched as the young Rebel walked toward the big house, puffs of smoke rising from his pipe and floating upward into the dark, night sky.

The following morning, Joshua came for his horse. Nathan had him ready to go. The young soldier, his arm still in a sling, awkwardly mounted his steed. He tossed a few coins down to Nathan and thanked him for taking good care of Blackjack. Rider and horse disappeared from view. As Nathan watched them trot over the brow of the hill in the early morning haze, thoughts swam through his mind. Why dat man fights ta keep us slaves? He seem nice—show respect. Never knowed white man be so friendly. Sides, ah likes dat Cross of Jesus Lawd on dat medal!

A few days later, Nathan was sent to draw water from the well behind the big house for the rest of the slaves. He encountered a new slave walking toward the well. She was young and pretty. "Ya new here?"

"Jes' come las' night."

"Ya house servan'?"

"Yea, me an'Mama got sold to Massa."

"Ya gots a name?"

"Course ah gots a name!"

"Wha's yer name, girl?"

"Ah ain't tellin'." She pumped her pail full of water, stuck her chin in the air, and briskly walked back toward the kitchen.

"I's Nathan!" he hollered at her. She continued walking, ignoring him, as she entered the house and slammed the door.

Nathan didn't like her attitude, but then he thought... well, kinda likes it, too—needs a little tamin', dat gal.

Master Marshall was a middle aged, married man. He was a fair man, as far as slave owners could be. He didn't believe in whipping his slaves; however, a few slaves had been whipped by some of his previous overseers. When he found out about it, he dismissed them, believing that he, himself, and his slaves were better off without that cruelty. Realizing he could get more work out of them by giving them time to rest and socialize, he gave them Saturday afternoons and Sundays off. They were allowed to use the barn for dances on weekends. Nathan loved the music and dancing and looked forward to these occasions. He hadn't seen that pretty girl since their chance meeting by the well. Each Saturday night, he looked for her at the dance; but she was nowhere to be found. He couldn't help thinking that she must be "one of dem high-class, house servan's dat doan mix wid us field hands"—no matter!

He and his people, young and old, danced and sang far into the night. They had an old fiddle player and a homemade drum, fashioned from a barrel, with cowhide stretched across the end of it. Little children watched from the loft and giggled. Their little eyes, peering through the rails and glittering from the lanterns' lights, were enchanting to Nathan. Occasionally, he would stand back and enjoy watching his people whooping it up, making up songs, and creating their own dances. Sometimes, a man would get in the middle of the crowd and start dancing alone for a few minutes, afterwards picking a girl to join him. They called it "set de flo." Nathan, being young and strong, would often dance the whole night, never lacking a willing partner. When Sundays came, they would all lay around exhausted, resting up for the coming week with all its dull, hard labor in the fields.

One very warm Saturday night, Nathan came to the dance. The pretty girl from the well was standing by the barn door, fanning herself with her kerchief. There were pink bows in her hair, matching the fancy long skirt she wore; and Nathan couldn't take his eyes off her. He was wise for his young age. Knowing how uppity the young girl was, he decided to ignore her—at least for now. He walked right past her into the barn.

The fiddler cranked up the music, the drummer pounded the rawhide, and, in an instant, the barn was filled with a jovial atmosphere. The sounds reverberated to the rafters and back again; then began the hand clapping and foot stomping. Nathan was the first to "set de flo". He jumped into the middle of the crowd and danced, twirled, and stomped. A mirthful mood enveloped the slaves and seemed to fuse them into one spirit. The dance became like an oasis in the middle of the hot, dry, and unforgiving desert of bondage. Nathan saw the young girl with the pink bows standing toward the back of the crowd, clapping her hands and smiling at him. He had succeeded in getting her attention. As others joined in the dancing, he worked his way through the crowd toward the barn door to seek some fresh air, fully aware her eyes were still upon him. He decided to approach her.

"Evenin' missy," he said with a smile on his face.

"Evenin'", she responded, looking down at the ground.

"Ah's afraid ta ask yer name agin—last time ah did dat, yu run away."

"Mindy -- ma name's Mindy. Not useter talkin' ta strangers. Didn' know who ya was, standin' over by de well dat day. What yu say yer name be?"

"Nathan. Got ma name from someone in de Bible. Ma Mammy done give it ta me. Nev'r seed ya befo' dat day by de well. Where yu from, gal?"

"Massa buys us from anudder plantation near Richmon'. Ole Massa sells ev'rythin'—even sold ma Pappy..." She caught herself and held back the tears, then continued, "Massa lost his money somehow—some say gamblin' an'..." She stopped in mid-sentence.

"An' what?" Nathan asked.

"Oh, yu knows—wimmens trouble. He be mean man an' Mammy an' me be glad ta gets outa dere. How yer Massa here be? I's habn' bin here long 'nuf ta tell."

"He be purty good. Doan believe in whuppins or sellin' us off."

"Dat's good. Our ole' Massa beat de daylights outer some pore field hands fo no reason at all. Mammy an' me,—we nev'r feels dat ole cat-o-nine-tails, 'cause we's house servan's. Mammy—she do de cookin', an' ah waits on ev'rybody an' cleans de hous' fer Massa."

"Wanna dance wif me?" Nathan asked.

"Caint dance. Doan know how. Ole Massa nev'r 'llowed it."

"Ah cud shows ya." He started to take her by the hand. She quickly pulled it back and began to fuss with her hair, curling a few strands around her finger.

"Doan wanna."

"It's fun! Ya'll wud likes it."

"Gots ta git back ta Mammy over dere," as she pointed to the other side of the barn and walked away from him.

Well, leas' ah gots her name, he thought to himself. He pulled a big red handkerchief from his back pocket and wiped his brow.

The weeks dragged along for Nathan. No "Lincum's sogers" in sight. Each day was like the one before and the ones to come. Hot sun. Hot soil. Hot feet. Hot bloody fingers cut most of the time from the cotton plants. His shoes were too tight. They hurt and squeezed his feet. He discarded them. He never had much of a choice—blistered feet from small shoes or burning feet from no shoes. He preferred the latter. Each day as he baked in the sun, he hoped for those Lincum's sogers. And now... a new pleasant feeling implanted itself in him—the pretty girl standing by the well. Now she had a name—Mindy. He liked the name; it fit her petite frame and cute round face. Whenever he felt bad, he now had two pleasant thoughts to fill his days.

He saw Mindy at the secret prayer meetings in the woods, which were forbidden by the slave owners. *"Steal away, steal away, steal away to Jesus,"* they would sing in the fields on these days to spread the message that gatherings would be held those evenings. An old self-made Negro preacher would stand on a tree stump and read from the Bible. Very few slaves knew how to read or had a Bible. The one thing they did know was that Jesus was their Savior. They sang songs praising Him and believed that one day, like Moses delivering the Israelites from Egypt, He would deliver them from their bondage. Often times they had to disperse in a hurry, as the guards they posted discovered patrollers approaching.

On occasion, Nathan would get permission from the overseer in the fields to get water for the other slaves. This way, he could get closer to Mindy, working in the big house. Sometimes he would meet her at the well. Over time, he became more and more fond of her. She, however, held back her feelings for him.

After finishing his work late one evening, Nathan once again made his way to the well, bending over and pumping cool water onto his head. Mindy came from the big house, carrying out the garbage. She had something wrapped up in a napkin and handed it to him. "Ah got sump'n here fo ya, Nathan."

"Wha's ya got dere, Mindy?"

"Su'prise."

Nathan opened the napkin and found a fried chicken leg inside. "Thanks," he said with a broad smile on his face. He immediately took a large bite out of it. "Yu gits meat ta eat all de time?"

"Mos' of de time."

"*We* only gits it maybe once a week." He took another bite, then wiped his mouth with his sleeve. "Ah gots sump'n ah wanna shows ya—sump'n special."

"Wha's dat?" as she placed the garbage in the fire pit.

"Is yer work all done?"

"Jus' finish."

"Cud ya gits away fo a few minutes? I's got ta show ya sump'n."

"Well, maybe jus' a few minutes."

They walked quietly down slave row, passing the dilapidated cabins. He finished the chicken and threw the bones into the tall grass at the edge of the woods. He then led her down a dirt path into the woods.

"Where's ya takin' me, Nathan?"

"Ya'll see... not too far."

She hesitated and stopped for a moment. "Ah thinks maybe ah goes back."

"Yu be fine. Yu gonna likes it. Ah nev'r showed nobody else dis place."

She trusted him and followed him into the darkening woods. They soon came to a clearing ringed by pine trees. The rising moon cast its brilliant light upon the swift moving waters of a small stream. "Oh, Nathan, it's beaut'ful!" She walked over to the stream and sat down, dangling her feet in the cool, running water. He sat down next to her and did the same. "How yu finds dis place?"

"Ah bin comin' here fo years. Found it when ah was jus' a boy. Nev'r showed nobody but yu."

"Ah loves it!" She laid back and gazed at the twinkling stars above. "Ah nev'r did sees such a beaut'ful place."

"Ah knows yu'd loves it. Ah comes here sometimes an' dreams 'bout freedom."

"Yu a dreamer, Nathan—don' knows iffen dat dream ebber comes true."

"Oh, yea, it sho will. Lincum's sogers comin' eny day now. Dey's gonna free us." He bent over her and attempted to kiss her. She pushed him away and jumped to her feet. "Why yu allus be dat way, Mindy?"

"What yu means?" she asked.

"Ah likes yu a lot—ah thoughts yu likes me too."

She brushed off her dress and looked into his eyes. "Ah likes yu, too, Nathan—ah really does, but..."

"But what?"

"But ah don't wants no boyfrien'."

He hesitated, then holding her hand, "Ah wants ta marry yu," he stammered.

"Caint do dat, Nathan… mights git sold off to anudder Massa."

"Oh, don't yu worry 'bout dat. Massa nev'r sell us over ta nobody like some of dem udder Massas do."

"We's too young ta git married. Gotta go now—Mammy be missin'me," she said as she ran back down the dirt path.

"Wait fo me," he hollered, pulling his feet from the stream.

He arrived back on slave row just in time to see her entering the big house. Gonna marry dat gal some day, he thought. He returned to his cabin where his parents, Jessica and Jeremiah, were just sitting down to their meager meal.

The well became important to Nathan. The water not only refreshed and cooled him, but it became like a touchstone to happiness since he had met Mindy there. His universe since birth had consisted of four hundred acres of dirt, slave row, the big house, the barn and animals, and the well.

One scorching day, he was pumping water into a pail to take back to the other field hands. He knew the big house was empty, as the master was away on business and Mindy and the other house servants were in town buying supplies. He thought about something he had heard the old stump preacher reading from the Bible one night. It was about the woman at the well. Jesus had told her that he was the Living Water that lasts forever. Lawd, ah wants dat Livin' Water of yers, Nathan found himself thinking over and over again, every time he came back to the well. He wasn't sure he understood exactly what it meant—he just knew inside himself that it was something he desired. There were many things Nathan had learned from the old preacher, and he treasured them in his heart. He was quick to learn and locked on to the preacher's readings, as this was the only source of knowledge he could obtain.

As he finished filling the pail with water, he thought he heard a high-pitched noise coming from the house. It surprised him, as he thought there wasn't anyone there at the time. He dismissed it as a bird sound and began to walk away. He heard it again. It was louder and unmistakably a scream. It jolted him. He dropped the pail and ran to the back door of the house. Opening it, he listened again. A loud shriek—a woman's scream— reverberated throughout the house. Having never been allowed in the Massa's house, he hesitated for a split second. Fear overtook him. Should he or shouldn't he proceed—but he had to! A louder scream now pierced his ears. "Help me!" He threw caution to the wind; and his instincts to answer that cry for help propelled him up the stairs, as he followed the sound of the screams. He flung open a bedroom door. He couldn't believe what he saw next—Massa's wife on her back on the bed, stripped down to the waist; and a husky black man on top of her, holding her arms down as she struggled to get free.

Nathan hollered, "Git offa her!" The man turned and jumped off the bed. He had a crazed look in his eyes, as he pulled a large knife from behind him and lunged at Nathan. Quickly jumping to one side, Nathan then wheeled around and struck the intruder on the back of his head with such force that the man fell forward onto the floor. Nathan grabbed a chair to defend himself, anticipating another attack. Sweating profusely with his heart racing, he stood speechless, as his attacker lay motionless. A stream of blood seeped out from beneath the man's body on the shiny, hardwood floor. The tip of the long knife protruded from the man's back, having run completely through his chest. Nathan was frozen in his tracks, still holding the chair over his head. As he stared down at the man, he knew there would be no further attack. He slowly lowered the chair to the floor and looked toward Mrs. Marshall. She was shaking and weeping in the corner of the room, holding a bed sheet in front of her half-clad body.

"Is he—I mean—is he moving?" she asked with a quivering voice.

"No, ma'am. I think he..."

"Dead?" she interrupted in an excited and almost screeching tone.

"Ah—ah think so." He clasped his hands together in front of him to keep them from shaking.

"Turn around so I can make myself decent," she said in a forceful tone. Her instant change from fear to a take-charge attitude surprised Nathan. Still shaking, he turned around and glanced at the still figure lying on the floor at his feet. Fear and revulsion gripped him as he turned his gaze away from the dead man. "You can turn around now," she said in a calm voice, then added, "This never happened, Nathan... you understand?"

"Yassum, ah thinks so."

"This will be our little secret—not even Mr. Marshall must know of this." She sobbed briefly. "I don't know what I would have done if you hadn't come to my aid. I will never forget this, Nathan."

"Yassum. Ah didn' means ta kill him. Ah only..."

"I know. *We* know. But other people would wonder. You understand? We must never tell anyone. If people didn't believe us, they might blame you and could then hang you." That frightened him even more than he already was. "Now listen to me," she said in a commanding voice, "you take him into the cellar and cover him up. I will clean things up here. When it gets dark, I want you to slip into the cellar, take him to the woods and bury him. Don't worry about the others in the house; I'll keep them busy upstairs. And remember, don't say a word to anyone!"

"Yassum. Ah won't says nothin' ta nobody." Still shaking, he knelt down by the corpse, turned it over, and removed the knife.

"Leave the knife on the floor! I'll take care of it."

He then lifted the body, slumping it over his shoulder. Sweat streamed down his face, as he felt a warm trickle of blood on his neck. He followed Mrs. Marshall's instructions and placed the corpse in the darkest corner of the root cellar, covering it with an old quilt; and cautiously exited the back door, making sure he wasn't seen. On his way back to the fields, he saw the empty pail where he had dropped it by the well. As he picked it up, he suddenly noticed he had blood on his hands and shirt. Quickly removing the shirt, he vigorously began to pump the water to wash the blood away. He then filled the pail with water and returned to the fields.

After dark, he nervously made his way back to the cellar and quietly began performing his gruesome task. He found a spot deep in the woods, dug a shallow grave, and placed the body in it, being careful to cover it first with the old quilt. Regardless of what he thought about him, Nathan tried to show some respect for the deceased assailant. He felt some guilt for the man's death, even though he knew he hadn't intentionally killed him. He prayed for the man's soul as he knelt on the freshly turned earth beside the grave and asked God for forgiveness for killing him. "Lawd, help me. Don't lemme gits hanged. Didn' mean fo him ta die. An' Lawd, takes his soul however yu wishes ta. Mebbe he's done some good things we don't knows 'bout." After shoveling the dirt back into the shallow grave, he covered the spot with leaves and twigs and quietly walked back through the dark woods to his cabin, attempting to control his body from shaking. He had never seen a man die like that before and couldn't shake the image of the intruder lying on the blood-soaked floor from his mind.

He now had two private spots, one very pleasant and one not so pleasant. Mrs. Marshall never forgot what he had done for her and repaid him with small favors of extra food. She brought him out of the fields and assigned him new duties, taking care of the animals and the grounds around the house. Her husband never questioned her about this matter, as she always got her way when it came to the care of the grounds. Nathan was exceedingly happy to leave the fields, especially so since he was now able to see more of Mindy.

One morning, while Nathan was trimming the rose bushes in front of the big house, two riders galloped up to the front entrance and came to an abrupt halt. Mr. Marshall came out and stood on the porch. "What ya'll doin' here boys?"

"Lookin' fer a runaway, Marshall—seen anything of 'em?"

"No, haven't seen any signs of a runaway around here."

"Care if we take a look around? Yer slaves could be hidin' 'em."

"Help yourself. Better still—I'll bring 'em all in from the field and show you they all belong here. You boys can ride out and check those slave cabins awhile and make sure no one's hidin' there. But I'm tellin' you, you won't find no runaway here—I'd know about it." By the time Marshall had assembled the slaves in the front yard, the bounty hunters had returned from a fruitless search of the slave quarters. Mrs. Marshall came out of the house and stood next to her husband.

"What's all the fuss about? Who are these men?" as she pointed to the two men on horseback. She didn't wait for his response, as she grew nervous when she saw Nathan kneeling on the ground a short distance away. Pretending to check on his work, she descended the stairs and walked over to him. "Now you make sure you don't trim these bushes back too far, Nathan," as she bent over his shoulder, looking at the cuttings he had just done. "Shhh—not a word," she whispered in his ear.

"Yassum, ah be's careful with 'em."

After a feigned inspection of the roses, she returned to her husband's side on the porch. Marshall surveyed the slaves, counting and identifying them from his vantage point. Nathan focused on his work, trying to fight back images of the dead runaway on the bedroom floor with the knife protruding from his back. He began to sweat and tremble.

"They're all accounted for. All of them belong here, boys," Marshall said.

"Well, let us know if ya see him, but be careful if ya do. They say he's crazy as a loon," said the one as he spit out a plug of tobacco that landed close to Nathan's bare foot.

"Will do, boys. Hope you find him before he hurts someone," Marshall responded.

The two men rode away, satisfied that the runaway wasn't there. The slaves returned to the fields. Nathan dropped the cutting tool from his hand; and, wiping the sweat from his brow, let out a deep sigh of relief. The Marshalls went back into the house. Nothing more was ever said about the runaway slave after that. Nathan buried the incident deep in his heart—deeper than the dead man's grave! The secret was known to only three—Mrs. Marshall, himself, and God.

Life became more bearable to Nathan now. No more sweating in the hot sun, pricking his fingers on the cotton plants, and no more burning feet from hours spent in the scorching soil of Virginia.

It became obvious to everyone that Nathan and Mindy were becoming lovers. The meetings at the well became more frequent, and they were together at the Saturday night dances and whenever they had free time. Mindy felt more secure that this master would not sell her or Nathan. She, in time, had come to know most of the other slaves. Many of the older ones had been on the plantation most of their lives; and many, like Nathan, had been born there. One evening, when Mindy was sitting by the well peeling potatoes, Nathan had come over to help her with her chore. Marshall approached them, puffing on his cigar and smiling. Holding one hand on his hip, he spoke. "Nathan... Mindy... you're good workers and I guess I'll keep both of you."

"Thank ya, Massa," Nathan responded, while Mindy smiled and looked over at him.

"I think you should be married." He took a long drag on his cigar, looking out into the fields without any more emotion than if he had commented on the weather. Nathan's eyes opened wide and his mouth dropped open, as he looked over at Mindy who was becoming emotional and beginning to sob. "Don't you like Nathan, Mindy?" Marshall asked.

Wiping a tear from her eye with a corner of her apron, she responded, "Yassuh, ah does."

"Then why do you look so sad?"

"I's too..." She hesitated, looking down at the ground. "I's too young ta git married, Massa."

"How old are you?"

"Ah dunno—mebbe sixteen, Massa."

"That's old enough. Now stop sobbing. You and Nathan *will* get married next month." Marshall walked back to the house, puffing on the cigar, unconcerned, as if he had just told them to do some menial chore.

Nathan attempted to calm her down, as he put his arm around her. "Don't ya loves me?" he asked.

"Ah do loves ya—but..."

"But what, Mindy?" as he looked quizzically at her.

"But I's too..." She suddenly changed her tone. "Ah don't hafter git married!" she angrily blurted out through her tears.

"Well, ah don't wanna gits married iffen yu don't wanna, Mindy." She began sobbing more and ran back into the kitchen.

Two days passed, and Nathan hadn't seen her. She hadn't even come to the well. He finally knocked on the back door, and Mindy's mother, Hannah, answered. "What ya'll want?" she said in a stern voice.

"Is Mindy here?" he said in a low tone, looking down at the ground.

"She busy."

"Ah hav'n seed her 'round lately."

"Come in here, boy! We's hafter talk."

"Yassum."

He came in the back hall and Hannah closed the door behind him. "Yu loves ma Mindy, boy?"

"Yassum, lots an' lots."

"Well, a'right den. Ah done had a long talk wif her, an' she say she love yu, too. She say she afeared ta gits married cuz she don't wants no chillun borned as slaves—ya knows what ah means?"

"Yassum."

"But then ah talks ta Massa, and he say yu *gots* ta git married."

"But mebbe by dat time, Lincum's sogers gits us free—did ya 'splain dat ta her?" he added hopefully.

"Yea, ah did an' ah thinks she feel better. Now ya'll run along. She come out in the mo'nin' ta sees ya." As he began to leave, she touched his arm. "Oh, an' ah also 'splains ta her dat Massa cud git mad and sell us off iffen yu two don't does what he say," as she winked at him and closed the door behind him.

Mindy resigned herself to the marriage after being reassured neither she nor Nathan would be sold off, and Nathan's high hopes of being freed calmed her fears about their children becoming slaves. The coming weeks created great excitement throughout slave row. The infrequent occasions, like a marriage of two slaves, brought an atmosphere of joy to the harsh, dull lives of these poor souls. Mrs. Marshall extended her good will more than she usually did because of the debt she felt she owed to Nathan. Besides providing an abundance of food and drink for the wedding, she found a slightly used white dress in her wardrobe for Mindy to wear. Hannah fashioned a veil for her from a piece of lace given her by her mother years before. Mrs. Marshall saw to it that Nathan was given an old, three-piece suit to wear, which the master had outgrown years before.

Nathan rose early on his wedding day. It was warm and sunny, as he walked down to the end of slave row and opened the door of the last cabin. It squeaked as he pushed it open. Peering in at the litter-strewn room, he noticed the windows were covered only with old rags for curtains. The cold charcoal logs in the fireplace and the few black kettles tipped over in the corner brought back fond memories of the old couple who had lived there before. He could picture old Sarah with her gray hair tied tightly in a bun at the back of her head, making the best corn bread he had ever eaten. Her husband, Elijah, had told him and the other children many stories that delighted them. Elijah, a very thin old man who walked with a cane, never seemed to run out of tall tales. As Nathan gazed over at the blackened, well-used fireplace on the far wall, he remembered a time when he and a few other children would gather around the fireplace on cold nights. Elijah, always whittled a piece of wood, while mesmerizing them with one of his tales in a very dramatic manner, occasionally using his cane to stoke the fire. Old Sarah was constantly replenishing plates of cornbread and raising her eyebrows at Elijah's stories. The old couple had never had children of their own. Nathan and the other children had more-or-less adopted them as grandparents; and they, in turn, enjoyed the innocence of the little ones, since they had never been blessed with their own. Elijah and Sarah suffered their entire life toiling in the fields—they were born into slavery and they died as slaves. That shabby, old, drafty shanty had been their permanent home most of their adult life with never a glimpse of hope for freedom. As Nathan surveyed the humble surroundings, he thought of the past and envisioned the future. This was to be his and Mindy's home. They would clean it up and make it more livable; but only for a time, because he *knew* "Lincum's sogers" were coming. He knew in his heart his children would be born free and held on to this belief—a belief so strong that nothing could destroy it.

As he made his way past slave row and approached the big house, other slaves were beginning to gather in the front yard. To his surprise, he looked up to see Mindy coming down the front stairway, something slaves never did. She was dressed in her bridal gown; and, to Nathan, she appeared as a pure white, delicate flower. He was accustomed to seeing her in shabby clothes with an apron tied around her waist. He couldn't take his eyes off her as she smiled at him. A little girl ran up to her and placed a small wreath of wild flowers in her hands.

He momentarily chuckled to himself as he noticed Mindy's bare feet, and suddenly realized he was also shoeless. He nervously yanked at his sleeves, attempting to lengthen them, as the master's pudgy arms were much shorter than his. Nathan's husky frame could barely contain the three-piece suit, and he thought that the buttons on his vest would pop at any moment. Despite the confinement of the suit, he felt proud and better dressed than ever before.

"Gather 'round, brothers and sisters!" the preacher shouted.

Some friends who had been able to obtain passes from their masters had come from other plantations. The old preacher removed his round, black, brimmed hat, revealing a coarse crop of gray hair that matched his beard. He motioned to Mindy and Nathan to come forward. He joined their hands together and began a short ceremony, speaking so quickly that Nathan could barely understand him at times. But he did hear the words, "*What God has joined together, let no man put asunder.*" Before he knew it, the preacher pronounced them man and wife.

Following this came another ritual—an old tradition the slaves had inherited over the years when there weren't any preachers available. One of the elders stepped from the crowd and dropped a broomstick on the ground. No instruction was needed for the bride and groom, as they had seen this performed at other weddings. Nathan and Mindy stood on one side of the broomstick holding hands. The elder, a crippled old man with sunken cheeks and taut, leather-like skin, shouted out in a scratchy, high-pitched voice. "That's yo' wife!" as he pointed to Mindy. "That's yo' husbin!" He pointed to Nathan. "She yo' missus! Yu married!"

"Hold up dat sweet mouf o' yers, Missus." Nathan kissed her gently. A tear began to trickle from her eye, as he locked her arm in his to jump over the broomstick together. To some this made their marriage binding, but most believed the preacher's words had already made them man and wife, as he was "God's person." The bride and groom knew that the broomstick ritual was only that—a ritual. But they went along with it to satisfy some of the older slaves.

The celebration became more jovial as the day wore on. It was similar to their Saturday night dances except for one thing—liquor. The Marshalls had allowed them to have hard liquor for the wedding as well as providing quite a feast, which included, among other things, roasted turkeys and baked hams, quite a delicacy for slaves that got so little meat in their diet. The fiddler's music made for much dancing and singing, making such a gala event that all forgot the hardships of slavery.

Monday arrived and Nathan and Mindy's honeymoon was over. She returned to the kitchen and he, to his chores. He was still a slave, but life became more joyful now. After all, he enjoyed and cherished his new bride, as well as their new home, which he and Mindy had cleaned and made more livable—as livable as a drafty cabin with a dirt floor could be.

Early in their marriage, Mindy began to express concern about the possibility of their children being born into slavery. Lying in bed one hot summer night, unable to sleep, she was troubled. "It ain't right, Nathan. It ain't right at all."

Turning toward her and propping himself up on one elbow, he inquired, "What ain't right?"

"Yu knows. I's jus'sometimes hopin' de good Lawd gives us no chilluns. It ain't right we's have slave babies." She was about to cry.

He looked at her with a compassionate gaze, gently turning her head toward him and cradling her face in his hands. He wiped away a tear from her cheek and tried to comfort her. "Don't yu knows, honey chile, our freedoms is comin' soon—by dat time dat we gits chilluns, we be free. Don't yu worry, ah a'ready seed some 'federate sogers wif bullets in 'em from Lincum's sogers. Dey comes here one night ta gits dere wounds fixed up, befo' yu done comes here."

"Ah knows all 'bout dis here war," Mindy replied adamantly. Then, after a moment of silence, her tone softened. "But wha' iffen Lincum's sogers loses de war? Den our babies keeps on bein' slaves."

"Don't yu knows 'bout 'mancipation, gal? Big white father, Abe Lincum, done say we's be freed."

"*Ah* don't sees no freedom, does yu?"

Nathan lay back on the bed, staring at the ceiling, blackened by years of burning logs, and let out a sigh. "Ah knows Lincum's sogers comin' soon— ya knows how ya'll kin smells de fall comin' in dem late summer breezes, or ya kin smells de water when ya comes close ta de creek, even befo' ya sees it? Well, ah kin smells freedom comin' an' ah kin almos' hear thousan's of dem sogers trampin down dis way. Ev'ry night, dem footsteps gits louder— sometimes dey gits so loud, ah cain't even hears dem crickets chirpin' in de woods. Ya see, honey chile, dem babies, God willin'—deys nebber gonna calls no one Massa, 'cept mebbe de good Lawd hisself."

Mindy leaned over and kissed him, laying her head on his chest, and muttered, "Ah hopes ya'll be's right," as they both finally fell asleep in a mutual embrace with hopes and dreams of a better future.

Talk of freedom quietly spread throughout the plantation. Nathan and the other slaves were cautious and kept it among themselves. They were fearful of their owners or any white folks hearing that kind of talk. Rumors had it that some slaves on other plantations had been whipped for even mentioning freedom. Indeed, it was much closer than he could ever expect.

Nathan had just finished feeding the horses and mules in the barn. As he picked up the hoe and left the barn to work in the master's garden, he heard gunshots. He glanced in the direction of the fields and saw a line of soldiers dressed in blue uniforms emerging from the woods. Ah jus' knowed it—ah jus' knowed dey was a'comin. Glory hallelujah! Dey's finally arrived! He saw that long line of blue, bayonets glistening in the afternoon sunlight, coming fast— and so was his freedom! His heart pounded with joy and fear at the same time. Something else was pounding, too—horses' hoofbeats, and many of them. As he quickly shifted his gaze toward the long dirt road leading away from the big house, he saw a cloud of dust swirling into the air and many Confederate soldiers dressed in gray emerging from it. Once again, he had a split-second decision to make. He remembered his hesitation about entering the big house when he had heard Mrs. Marshall screaming for help. He began to run to Mindy in the house—but—no—no—she be okay inside de house. Gots ta git ta pa in de field. He bolted toward the fields, screaming his father's name, as fast as his legs would carry him. Before he could get to him, shots rang out on both sides; and the slaves scattered in all directions. He watched in horror as his father fell to the ground. Nathan disregarded the firestorm of bullets whizzing around him like a swarm of bees and continued running toward him. He bent down over him. Blood saturated his father's shirt, and Nathan ripped it open and saw the gaping wound in his chest. He frantically tried to revive him but there was no response. He was grief-stricken. He gently picked up Jeremiah's lifeless body and walked toward slave row in a zombie-like manner, seeming to be oblivious to all that was going on around him. He miraculously made it to his cabin unscathed and placed the body on the bed. Kneeling down, he laid his head on his pa's chest and wept profusely. It began to rain hard, and the sound of the gunfire outside could hardly be heard. For a time, the only sound he could hear was his own sobbing. He didn't know how long he had spent kneeling on the earthen floor, when he suddenly realized his mother, Jessica, who had recently become a house servant, and Mindy and her mother might still be in harm's way. His first impulse was to run to the big house to see if they were all safe. He opened the door to leave. It was already dark. He could hear the loud, popping sounds of musket fire. Looking toward the distant noise, the flashes from the igniting powder reminded him of fireflies. The night sky frequently lit up with great streaks of lightning that created an eerie symphonic cadence when combined with the sporadic musketry "fireflies" that provided a secondary rhythm of light to Mother Nature's grand display in the heavenly center stage. The wind-driven rain blew in his face and he quickly shut the door. He turned slowly and trembled as his gaze fell upon the still body of his Pa. He hesitated for a short time, fearing that, if he chanced running back to the big house, he would be shot. But he couldn't restrain himself. He had to see if his new bride and his mother were all right. Besides, he couldn't help his Pa anymore. His impulse drove him out the door, and he began to run with all his might. The darkness didn't hinder him, as he could find his way blindfolded—after all, he had trod that path all of his life, being confined to that tiny universe since birth. He slipped on the rain-soaked mud as he ran but never fell; that is, until a bullet struck him with such force that it felt like a sledgehammer slamming into his shoulder and spun him around before he dropped to the ground. He reached over with one hand to feel his shoulder. As he pulled it back, he could see the blood on it in the dim light coming from the big house. He crawled in the mud and finally reached the back door. Managing to get to his feet, he entered the house and stumbled up the stairway. He heard the master's voice coming from the cellar down below, "Who's that?"

"It's me, Massa—Nathan."

"Come down here, boy. Hurry up before you get shot. We're all down here."

Nathan, weakened by the loss of blood, staggered down the stairs, holding the railing to keep from falling, his left arm hanging limp at his side. Mrs. Marshall and all of the house servants were huddled in the corner. Some were crying; and Mrs. Marshall, looking very stoic, was trying to keep them quiet. Mindy ran over to Nathan, relieved that he was alive. "Nathan, ah's so glad yu's here." She hugged him, pressing her face to his chest. She hadn't noticed his bloodstained shirt in the dim candlelight. But then she felt his warm blood on her cheek and quickly pulled away from him, shocked at the sight that he was wounded. She let out a scream. "Yu shot! My Nathan bin shot! Sumbuddy help!" Mr. Marshall came over and assisted Nathan to a bench. He removed the bloodstained shirt and saw that the bullet had passed completely through the shoulder. Nathan was in great pain and winced as Marshall examined the wound.

"Hurry, Mindy. Go upstairs and get some linens and bring them down here," Marshall exclaimed. Mindy ran upstairs, forgetting all about the danger of stray bullets coming through the windows, and brought back a pile of linens. Marshall pressed the clean linens to Nathan's wounds, while instructing Mindy to wrap some bindings over them. Nathan's mother looked on and tried to console him. He leaned down, holding his head in his hand, and sobbed. He wept for his Pa. How was he going to tell his mother about his Pa's death?

"Sit here, Ma," Nathan said quietly, as he took his mother's hand in his big, calloused hand. She sat down next to him. He looked into her eyes as tears trickled down his cheeks. "Ma, I gots ta tell ya somethin'."

"Don't ya worry, boy. Yu's gonna be jus' fine."

"No, Ma—it's..." He couldn't get the words out.

"What, boy? What yu sayin'?"

He couldn't put it off any longer. "It's—Pa!" he blurted out.

She quickly stood up and looked at Nathan with fear in her eyes. "What? What, Nathan? Where's Pa?"

"He—he's in the cabin."

"Is he hurt?" Jessica asked, her voice quivering.

"Ma—he—he's..." He couldn't say it.

"He's what?" She panicked. Without thinking, she grabbed him by the shoulders to shake the words out of him.

He pulled back in pain, finally forcing the words out. "Pa's gone, Ma. He—he's dead."

Jessica let out a violent scream that pierced the ears of all present and collapsed on the dirt floor.

It was well after midnight when a young soldier named Patrick entered the house. He shouted out, "You can come out now. It's safe." Marshall ascended the stairs. "Everybody all right here?" the young sergeant inquired.

Marshall, looking unhappy that the soldier in blue was not a soldier in gray, asked where the other soldiers were.

"If you're looking for the Rebels, they skedaddled! Only ones left are the dead ones and a few wounded."

Marshall looked down at the floor as if he knew his way of life had come to an end. "Is it safe? I mean—can the slaves go back to their cabins?"

"Yes, sir, it's safe—but you'd better get used to the idea—they're not slaves anymore." Nathan and the others overheard Patrick's words and were filled with joy. They wanted to shout but could not. One of their own had been killed. Nathan knew his freedom had come, and the shackles of slavery had been undone. But his joy was tempered, for he was now shackled with grief. It wasn't supposed to be this way, he thought. He would, at that moment, have traded his freedom to have his Pa back, but now he had to take care of his mother and his new wife.

By now, Jessica had been revived and sat on the bench, sobbing and muttering Jeremiah's name over and over again. The rain had stopped, and the slaves stepped out into the darkness. The air was cool and clean, and a gentle breeze floated across the land. It was as if Almighty God had blown the hot, dry, never-ending winds of slavery back into the eternal depths of the inferno below, never to be released again.

As Nathan, Jessica, and Mindy entered their cabin, Jessica threw herself on top of Jeremiah's body, letting out an agonizing moan, and continued to sob throughout the night. It went on and on, hour after hour. Nathan and Mindy's attempts at consoling her were ineffective. Nathan, exhausted and in pain, lay down on his bed and fell asleep. When he awoke, he laid there staring at the many tiny dust particles floating in a stream of sunlight, coming through a small crack in the wall. He heard many voices outside moaning and lamenting. As he started to raise himself from the bed, a sharp pain shot through his shoulder, forcing him to lie back down. He instinctively reached over to hold it and discovered the bandages were soaked with blood. He felt sick inside as he looked over at his Pa, lying motionless and cold on the other bed. Mindy, who was standing outside with Jessica, glanced through the open door and, seeing Nathan awake, ran to his side. "Oh, Nathan! I's so sorry," she cried out. She sat down next to him, and he reached over to hold her with his good arm. He was silent; his grief made him speechless. A few moments later, a small group of mourners began to file inside to pay their last respects, embracing and trying to console the family. Many had food that they gently placed on the table before viewing the body. Mindy had placed a quilt over Jeremiah, leaving only his head exposed. The mourners' weeping and wailing continued throughout the morning and could be heard outside the dilapidated little cabin and all down slave row.

About noon, the young Union sergeant appeared at the door. Removing his hat, he walked over to Nathan. "I think you should have that looked at by our surgeon," noticing the bandages on his shoulder, wet with blood. Mindy, agreeing wholeheartedly with the sergeant, began to assist Nathan to his feet.

"Yu go wif de kind soger—yu needs new fixin's fer dat shoulder. Ah gwine stay here an' watches yo' Mammy while yu's gone." She began to nudge him toward the door.

As they walked toward the big house, Patrick spoke first. "That your kin you're mourning in there?" he asked in a quiet voice.

Looking down at the ground as they walked, Nathan responded, "It's my Pa." He tried to hold back his tears.

"I'm sorry. That shouldn't have happened. The Rebs just came out of nowhere. Well—I'm sorry. We lost a few men, too. One was a good friend of mine."

"Sorry fo yu, too, Massa."

"You can call me Patrick or Sergeant."

"Yassuh, Sa'gen'."

They walked in silence the rest of the way to the big house. The regimental surgeon had just finished attending to the wounded soldiers, lying on the expansive front porch. Nathan and Patrick climbed the stairs. "Could you look at this man's shoulder?" Pat asked.

"I guess one more won't matter… sit down here and let's have a look." Nathan winced as the surgeon removed the bandages from the wound. "Good thing you brought him here, Sarge. Have to clean this dirt and mud from the wound. Looks like the bullet went clean through. We'll fix you up, boy."

"Yassuh. Thank ya, suh."

As the surgeon finished treating Nathan, the company captain rode up to the house and called out to Patrick. "Better get a move on, Sergeant. We have to bury them dead boys and get out of here—have to join up with the rest of the Army."

"Yes, sir," Pat said, saluting as he spoke.

"You got them graves dug yet?"

"Yes, sir. I put some men on that detail earlier. It should be done soon."

"We're leaving in two hours." He galloped away.

Patrick turned to Nathan, still sitting in the chair, his shoulder all bandaged. "I didn't get your name."

"Nathan, suh."

"Well, Nathan, do you have a grave dug yet for your Pa?"

"Nossuh, Sa'gen'."

"'Course you wouldn't have. How could you dig with that shoulder? Come with me—I'll take care of it." They walked through the fields in the hot, noonday sun—that ever-glaring spotlight that burned into Nathan's skin most every day of his young life. As they walked toward the tree line at the edge of the woods, Nathan could see soldiers digging up the ground in the far corner of the field. "You know, Nathan, I lost my Pa when I was only three years old. Don't remember much about him."

"Sorry 'bout dat, Sa'gen'. Ah gonna miss my Pa bad."

As they arrived at the freshly dug graves in the shadow of the trees, three for Confederates and two for Union dead, Nathan shuddered as he looked into the deep, dark holes in the ground. Patrick called one of the soldiers over to him and ordered him and the others to dig another grave. They didn't look happy, but picked up their shovels and began to dig a grave for Nathan's father. Nathan had seen burials before, but he had never lost a close relative. This was his first encounter with real and personal grief. Patrick then turned to Nathan. "Sorry your Pa can't be buried with your people, but Marshall says that ground is full up." They stood there silently, as the soldiers labored to prepare the sixth grave.

Afterwards, the slaves carried Jeremiah's body, wrapped in the quilt, with a linen covering his face, from the cabin. There had been no time to make a coffin. The old fiddler began to play, and the mourners' song filled the air.

"Ah got shoes, you got a shoes
All a God's chillun got shoes
When ah gits to Hebben gonna put on mah shoes
Gonna walk all ober God's Hebben."

Nathan was struck by the fact that someone had placed shoes on his father's feet, which were protruding from the quilt. Tears welled up in his eyes—his father had never had shoes. At the same time the Union soldiers carried their fallen comrades and the Confederate dead to the graves and lowered them down, Jeremiah was placed in his final resting place by his own people. Nathan stood at the foot of his father's grave, his mother on his right side and Mindy on his left. He prayed for strength to overcome his grief, so he would be brave and able to comfort his mother and his new bride. He had noticed the blood stained uniforms of the dead soldiers; for a brief moment a curious thought ran through his mind. Why was the color of blood the same in all men, regardless of race, and yet their skin colors differed? As the burial teams began to shovel the freshly turned earth into the graves, Jessica quickly turned her head and buried it in Nathan's chest . Once again, she screamed and wept bitterly. Nathan thought of the many hot days that his Pa had toiled in the fields. The earth had soaked up his sweat, baked under his bare feet, embedded itself into his pores, and now he was a part of it. The old preacher read from his tattered Bible for the first time in public, having no fear of punishment for possessing it. *"I am the Way, the Truth, and the Life. He that believeth in Me shall have life everlasting."* Nathan was comforted by these words. He knew deep down in his heart that his Pa was finally free. He felt that his father had, to a degree, followed in the footsteps of Jesus, his Savior. His Pa, in his earlier days, had felt the sting of the whip, as did Jesus. The many days toiling in the master's fields had been his Way of the Cross. His humiliation for himself and his family was his Crown of Thorns. And finally, in his last hours, his body had been pierced by a soldier's weapon.

After a moment of silence, a Union private pressed a bugle to his lips and stood at attention behind the six graves. A new haunting melody called "Taps" emanated from his horn, the notes floating heavenward, as a gentle breeze rustled the leaves in the nearby woods. The Union soldiers had fashioned some crude markers in the form of crosses, each one marked with the name of their deceased, and placed them on the graves. The Confederate dead, however, could only be identified "Unknown". There was no marker for Jeremiah. Nathan vowed to his father that he would return some day to mark his grave. "Don't worry, Pa—ah's gwine come back and fix yo' up jus' like yo' deserves."

It was finished. Along with Jeremiah, slavery died and was buried that day. The cost of freedom and the opposition to it were also buried—next to Nathan's father. The Union Captain had waited respectfully until the ceremonies were completed. Mounting his horse beneath a large shade tree, he announced, "Everybody gather over here!" The slaves and soldiers turned around and walked over to him, all except Jessica, who had thrown herself on top of Jeremiah's grave, moaning and crying out his name. Nathan and Mindy hesitantly followed the crowd, while still keeping an eye on Jessica. The Captain held up a document in both hands and began to read in a clear and audible voice. Nathan stood in the back of the crowd, holding Mindy's hand, as he listened to the officer. *"Whereas, on the 22nd day of September"*— he went on with many more words that Nathan didn't understand, until he heard the words, *"All persons held as slaves shall be free."* A sudden outburst of cheers went up from the slaves. There was no mistaking these words. Nathan grabbed Mindy, wrapping his good arm tightly around her waist and raising her off the ground, taking her breath away. Nathan and many of the slaves had been confused and saddened by Jeremiah's sudden death; and, at first, somewhat fearful of the Union soldiers. They hadn't grasped the total meaning of freedom until the document had been read. Now it was official, and an unbridled surge of happiness and joy rippled through the crowd. After a few moments, the Captain shouted to the crowd for silence. When they had quieted down, he continued, *"I invoke the considerate judgment of mankind and the gracious favor of Almighty God. Signed: Abraham Lincoln."*

"Glory, glory, 'allaluya!" the slaves shouted. Once again, they laughed and cried and shouted all kinds of phrases, mostly in thanksgiving to God, to Father Abraham, and to Jesus. Nathan's strong belief that his freedom would come and that his prayers to Jesus for deliverance would be heard, had just been realized when the captain's words penetrated his ears. He knew, at that moment, that he would never forget this day for the rest of his life. He would tell of it to his grandchildren many, many times, before his final deliverance—to Heaven.

There was a flurry of activity, as Nathan and the others scurried back to their cabins and began to pack up their meager belongings. The soldiers began to march away to the beat of the drummer boy; and the first generation of a newly freed race followed, not knowing where they were going, with not much more than the clothes on their backs. But they were going—going to a place called freedom—a place that generations of their ancestors longed to go but were denied passage. They were without money; they owned nothing of material value, nor did they own any land. But they walked away with a greater treasure—one that was priceless—freedom!

The Marshalls stood pathetically on their front porch, watching their whole world turn upside down, as the slaves deliverance from bondage unfolded before their very eyes. The yolk of slavery had been broken, enslavement of body and soul castigated, and the humiliating servitude extinguished. Mrs. Marshall called out to Nathan, Jessica, Mindy, and her mother, Hannah, to come over to the porch. They left the others, some of whom began to holler insults at the Marshalls, and approached the house. Mr. Marshall stood stoic and dazed, as he watched his labor force suddenly evaporating before him. Mrs. Marshall pleaded with Nathan and the other house servants to stay. "You can't just leave this way. Can't you stay a little while longer? You have no place to go. We will pay you wages. Oh, what are we to do?" Her voice sounded as though she were going to cry. "Nathan, I helped deliver you when you were born. And, Jessica, I treated you so well. How can you leave us like this?" Mr. Marshall, who looked bewildered and embarrassed at his wife's desperation, turned around and quietly walked into the house. Hannah stuck her nose in the air and, grabbing Jessica's hand, turned to walk away. Jessica, still in shock from her husband's death, followed quietly. "Nathan, Mindy—won't you, at least, stay?" Nathan felt guilty even though he knew he shouldn't. After all, living so close to each other for years created a certain bond, even though it was distorted. Mrs. Marshall had been kind and treated him well. He had actually looked upon her as a sort-of-an-aunt. He was at a loss for words. Being a sensitive young man, he actually felt pity for her.

"I's sorry, Missus Marshall, but—we's slaves no mo'. Ya'll be a'right." Mrs. Marshall blotted the tears from her eyes, stunned at his answer and finding it hard to believe this was all happening. This sudden change in relationships was a severe shock to her. The scene was terribly awkward, and Nathan could only say, "Goodbye." He grasped Mindy's hand, turned, and joined the others, as that exodus of a freed people followed the Union Army out onto the road to freedom. Men, women, and children… young and old… healthy and sick… some still grieving… all dressed in tattered, worn clothing… mostly barefoot… walked off the plantation. The drummer boy was far down the road, at the head of the column of soldiers. His drumbeat could still be faintly heard in the rear. This armada of warriors and ex-slaves tramped down the road, kicking up a large cloud of dust; and exuberant shouts filled the air, along with songs of praise and thanksgiving to God. And into that cloud, with great expectations, walked Nathan and Mindy. Looking over at her, he smiled and squeezed her hand. "Ah done tol' ya Lincum's sogers was comin'!"

CHAPTER 11

▼

THE ESCAPE

After the guard moved away, Patrick found a spot near Nathan to sit down. He smelled the stew Nathan was cooking for the prisoners and their Rebel captors and asked him what it was.

"Chickens—ah find 'em runnin' roun' dis here yard, jus' waitin' ta jump inta dis nice warm pot!"

Pat wanted to ask him why he was not with the other freed slaves from the plantation, but couldn't take the time. Escape—his mind had focused on escaping that night. After the prisoners were fed and the fire was dying out, Patrick moved closer to Nathan. Some of the prisoners fell asleep on the ground. Two Confederate soldiers were left to guard them. Patrick spoke in hushed tones to Nathan, who had begun to clean the pots and cooking utensils. "I saw you taking food into the house. How many Rebels are in there?"

"I seed jus' two, Sa'gen'—one officer an' one young 'federate guardin' de lady."

"There's a lady in there?" Patrick asked in surprise.

"Yassuh. Ah thinkin' she be prisoner. The 'federate sogers brung her here dis mornin'. She a very pretty lady."

"Can you tell me what she looks like?"

"Well, suh, she got brown hair and she be wearin' a blue dress. An'— oh—she smell mighty sweet—like some kinda flower, ah be thinkin'."

"Like lilacs?"

"Yassuh, dat's it! Like them lilacs. How yu knows dat?"

Pat was confused. Lou Ann? Could it be? No time—get her out. Find out later. "Never mind that now... we have to get away."

"How's we gonna do dat, Sa'gen'?"

"You know what room she's in?"

"Yassuh, she be in de back room on dat side," as he pointed to the right side of the house.

Pat quickly reached over and pulled Nathan's arm down. "Don't point," he whispered.

"Sorry, suh."

"Now, tell me where the two Rebels are."

Nathan started to point toward the house but quickly caught himself. "The young 'un—he in de front room outside de lady's door, settin' in a chair."

"You said there was an officer in there, too?"

"Yassuh. He be a mean one."

"How's that?"

"Som'times he go in de lady's room an' holler at her. He holler so loud, I kin hears him, even wif de door an' window shut."

"There's a window in her room?"

"Yassuh. Ah goes by dat window when ah be gittin de wood fo' de fire, an' ah sees dat ol' 'federate officer shakin' his finger at her an' she be cryin'."

"Do you know where he is now?"

"Well, Sa'gen', ah sees his blanket roll an' bottle in de corner in de front room where de guard be."

"A bottle of what?"

"Whiskey—he drink a lot. Ah think he be mean from too much of dat whiskey in him."

"Are there guards in the back of the house?"

"Nossuh. Ah think dey's got more 'federate sogers in de barn, tho. Ah sees them som'times come out an' takes de places of de guards."

"Good. Okay, Nathan, I think I have a plan. Now listen carefully."

Just then, the young guard Patrick had met at the stream during the march South approached them. "Hey, Yank, what ya'll talkin' about? New York City?" He leaned on his rifle, slightly hunched over, and looked down at Patrick, sitting on the ground next to Nathan.

"How did you guess? I was telling this cook of yours about the fine restaurants and good food in New York."

"Well, I bet it ain't as good as my Ma's home cookin'."

"No—you're probably right. Nothing like home cookin'." Patrick could see that the young Reb wanted to hear more about New York City, but this wasn't the time for it. He opened his bedroll and laid down, yawning as he did. "Getting tired. Long march today."

"Well, don't tell nobody, but tomorrow ya'll will be ridin' in style. Ya'll gonna take a train down to a new "hotel" we're buildin' just for you boys— Andersonville. Probably won't be as nice as them fancy hotels you got in New York City, Yank!"

Pat closed his eyes and pretended to go to sleep, as Nathan finished cleaning up. Unable to engage Patrick in any more conversation, the guard walked over to the other side of the yard, hiking his rifle over his shoulder as he did. He sat down next to another guard, as though he was looking for someone else to chat with.

Patrick, still lying down, motioned to Nathan to stoop down. The embers of the fire were dying out; and in the dark shadows, Pat whispered. "Listen carefully. We can make it—we can escape tonight."

"Ah don't knows. How's we gonna do dat?" Nathan responded nervously.

"Don't worry. Trust me. Just listen. In a little while, when most of the men are asleep and the guards aren't watching closely, I'll go over to that pole over there." He pointed to a pole supporting the front porch at the corner of the house. "It's all rotted. One push and the whole thing will come down. There's always a few prisoners who can't sleep, pacing around. The guards won't suspect me. Now here's what I want you to do. When I go over and push on that pole, there's going to be a loud crash. When that happens, I want you to scream out, 'There's a man under there! There's a man under there!' The others will all wake up and gather around to see what's happening; and, when they do, you slip around behind the house. I'll meet you there. Then we'll head on out of here."

"Ah don't knows, Sa'gen'. What iffen dey catches up wif us?"

"Say a prayer. Let's ask Saint Michael to help us." Patrick's heart beat rapidly with excitement and fear, which he tried to conceal from Nathan.

"Ah 'member dat St. Michael in de preacher's Bible. He an angel. Ah be wif yu, Sa'gen'—we tries." Pat extended his hand, and Nathan hesitantly shook it.

"What's the matter? You never shook a man's hand before?"

"Nev'r done shake a *white* man's hand before."

Pat didn't know what to say. There was a moment of silence before he finally responded. "Well, that will change. Now remember... you shout, 'There's a man under there!' Then get around to the back of the house as quick as you can—but don't run—just slip through the crowd, okay?"

"Yassuh, Sa'gen'."

Pat lay down and waited. This was it! Last chance. Not gonna go on that train and rot in a Reb prison. Thoughts kept swimming through his mind. He kept looking at his watch with its cracked crystal. His captors hadn't found it hidden in his sock. Midnight—one o'clock—two o'clock. Time moved slowly. Nathan, lying on the grass behind the cooking pot, turned and whispered to Patrick, "When we goin', Sa'gen'?"

"Soon—very soon." The last hour dragged by. He looked at his watch once again. Three o'clock. Pat raised himself up on his elbows to survey the situation. Two guards were sitting together, leaning against a tree. The younger one looked like he had fallen asleep. It was just as Patrick had suspected. There were a few prisoners who couldn't sleep, milling around the yard. The few that still had tobacco lit their pipes, illuminating their faces as they drew on them. Pat got up slowly and stretched his arms. He sauntered around the yard, trying to blend in with the other sleepless prisoners, and made his way toward the rotten support pole at the corner of the porch. So far, so good—a few more yards. The guards hadn't budged. He stepped over a few snoring prisoners and prayed he wouldn't trip over one of them. Fear began to grip him, and he started to sweat profusely. Is that pole as rotted as I think? Do I have enough strength to push it over? Will the porch come crashing down?

As he approached the corner, he suddenly, for no understandable reason, thought of Abe Lincoln's words back home in New York City that wintry night so long ago. *"Faith... right makes might... dare to do our duty."* Pat dared and wrapped his strong hands around the pole. He gently tested its weakness, pushing against it slightly. It creaked. The wood was soft, and small slivers pricked his palm. He pushed then with all his might and jumped back as the entire porch roof wavered and crashed to the ground, just missing his legs as he fell down. The loud noise jolted everyone to his feet. The two Rebels inside the house ran to the front door, but the debris blocked their exit.

Nathan screamed out as loud as he could, "Dere's a man under dere! Dere's a man under dere!" He then proceeded to disappear into the crowd as planned.

Pat scrambled to his feet and quickly moved along the side of the house to the back window. It was partially open, and he quickly crawled through and began searching for the female prisoner. His eyes fell upon a figure crouched down in the corner of the bare room, but he couldn't make out her face in the dim light of the candle that was stuck on the floor. "Lou Ann, is that you?" he whispered. She was crying and didn't respond. He repeated in a little louder tone, "Lou Ann, is that you?"

Looking up at the dark figure, she responded fearfully, "Who are you?"

"It's Patrick. Shhhh." He approached her and his face became illuminated by the candlelight. She jumped up from the floor and wrapped her arms around him, still sobbing.

"Oh, Patrick! I'm so glad to see you! How did you get here? I heard the crash outside and thought we were hit by a cannonball."

"No time to talk... we're getting out of here." He grabbed her by the arm, ran to the window, and helped her climb out. Her long skirt caught on a nail and Pat pulled it free, ripping it in two. Following her out, he led her to the spot where Nathan was waiting.

"Which way do we go?" Lou Ann asked, as she held up the loose end of her dress.

"That way—north!" Nathan whispered as he pointed in a direction away from the house.

"We have to get away before they find out we're missing," Pat said. He grabbed her by the hand once again and started running into the fields behind the house. Nathan led the way, as the three fugitives ran as fast as their legs would carry them, into the black night. "Are you sure you know this country?" Pat asked, breathing hard as they ran.

"Ah knows it purty good."

"Are there any woods near here where we can hide?"

"No woods, Sa'gen', but ah knows 'bout a swamp near here."

"A swamp? Well, let's go there... maybe the Rebs won't find us there."

"Aren't there snakes in swamps?" Lou Ann panted.

"Yassum, but ah knows 'bout a man—he be called..."

Lou Ann interrupted him, as she stopped running, gasping for breath. "I can't run anymore."

Nathan and Patrick turned and stopped. "Sit down, but just for a minute," Pat said as he helped her to the ground. He and Nathan did likewise. "Stay down!" he warned.

"Now, where is this man? What's his name? Did you say he could help us?"

"He in de swamp. He be called 'One-Eye Snakeman'."

"Who *is* he?" Pat asked.

"He be escaped slave. He gots one eye burned out wif poker by his Massa. Dat Massa catches him lookin' at his wife too much. He be livin' in de swamp fo' years! Some fokes says he keep alive by eatin' them swamp snakes. Ah heerd three slave hunters look fo' him in swamp, an' only one come out alive. Dey say ole Snakeman eats the other two."

Lou Ann cried out, "Oh, that's horrible! We can't go in there! What would become of us?"

"We might not have another choice," Pat answered. "Go to prison and maybe be hanged or take our chances in the swamp."

"Ah heerd of other slaves he help escape... mebbe he help us, too."

"Is there a way around the swamp?" Pat asked, as he began to breathe easier.

"Swamp purty big. We would has ta go miles 'round—swamp be shorter way."

"How far before we get to it, Nathan?"

"Mebbe anudder mile."

"Shhhhh. Do you hear horses?"

"Sho 'nuff. Dey be comin' fo' us," Nathan answered, his voice trembling.

"Come on! We can't stay here." Pat helped Lou Ann to her feet. "Hurry!" They began once again to run with all their might. Ten minutes seemed like eternity. Lou Ann suddenly fell, tripping on her torn dress. "Lou Ann, are you all right?" As he turned to help her, he glanced up to see Rebel soldiers in the distance on horseback, holding torches and scouring the fields. "We have to keep moving."

"I can't run anymore."

"We be almos' to de swamp, Sa'gen'."

"Come on, Lou Ann. Just a little bit further." He put all good manners aside, reached over and ripped off the remaining part of her skirt.

"Patrick! How dare you?" she blurted out. "What's gotten into you?"

"I'm sorry I had to do that, but it was necessary." He bundled it up and stuffed it into his shirt, so as not to leave a trail. "Besides, you still have your petticoat to cover you."

"We better git ta dat swamp befo' them sogers catches up wif us."

They ran again; Lou Ann stumbled and fell once more. "Are you okay?" Pat asked.

"I think I hurt my ankle."

Patrick picked her up piggyback style and ran as fast as he could.

"Ah thinks we be at de swamp."

Pat set Lou Ann down and turned around to see the torches coming closer.

"I—I'm afraid to go in there, Patrick."

"We have to, Lou Ann. You don't want the Rebs to catch us, do you?"

"Well—no." She began to cry.

"Okay, we're going in."

She stopped dead in her tracks. "I can't—I'm afraid!"

He didn't reply. He simply grabbed her, lifted her up onto his back, and began to wade into the dark, foreboding swamp. She became very quiet, and he could feel her arms trembling around his neck. Nathan walked cautiously beside them. Patrick could hear the soldiers behind them coming closer. As they waded deeper into the swamp, the cold water rose above his knees and up to his chest, hiding them from view. Glancing back, he saw the Reb's torches reflecting off the edge of the water. He could hear their shouting.

"They wouldn't have gone in there, Captain. They'd be damn fools to— and if they did, the snakes'll get 'em."

"Ya'll got that right, Sergeant. Come on, boys! They must have gone in another direction."

Pat was relieved, as he heard the sound of hoofbeats trailing off into the distance. "They're gone—that was a close one! We just made it!"

Lou Ann lowered her head down and rested it on Patrick's shoulder, letting out a sigh of relief. "Thank God they didn't see us!" They continued to wade silently further into the blackness. "Are there really snakes in here?"

"Yassum, but don't ya worry." Nathan found a stick and splashed the water in front of them as they moved. "Ah scares 'em away."

After awhile, Patrick became weary. "I have to put you down for awhile, Lou Ann."

"It's okay. My ankle feels much better now." As he lowered her down, she shuddered as the cold water rose up above her knees and to her chest. She clutched his arm tightly.

"Where is this—what did you call him—Snakeman?"

"He be somewheres in de middle of dis here swamp, Sa'gen'."

Just then, the clouds began to break up, and streaks of moonlight beamed down through the canopy of trees that dangled their long, filmy vegetation from their dark tentacle-like branches. After traveling slowly and cautiously, carefully avoiding trees and pushing aside loose floating dead wood, Pat turned to Nathan. "How much further? Do you know where the swamp ends?"

"It's purty big. Mebbe..." He stopped in mid-sentence. "Did ya hear dat?"

"What? I didn't hear anything," Pat replied.

"*I* heard it—it sounded like splashing water." Lou Ann's voice trembled.

They all stood silently, listening intently for any noise, while Lou Ann clung tightly to Patrick. "There it is again—over there!" as she pointed ahead.

"Look! There's someone there," Pat whispered. " See? Over by that little shack," as he looked in the direction she was pointing.

"Hafter be dat ole Snakeman!"

They all peered over at the figure, now bending down and looking as if he was attempting to catch something in the water. Nathan cupped his hands on either side of his mouth and began to hoot like an owl. "Whoo, hoo-hoo, whoo, whoo. Ah heerd dat be's a secret call de Snakeman uses—like de owl." The old Snakeman immediately spun around and focused his one eye in their direction, the moonlight shining down, exposing his scrawny frame. He quickly climbed up into his rickety shack that set upon four stilts, which raised it above the water. Grabbing an old rifle, he fired in their direction. They ducked down further into the murky water.

"Who be comin' inta ma swamp? Git outa here befo' ah blows yer haid off."

Before they could answer, he fired another shot. Then he let out an awful, demonic-sounding laugh that echoed throughout the swamp.

"He sounds like a crazy madman," Pat whispered, as Lou Ann clutched him even tighter.

"Ah heerd he sound worse den he be," Nathan said as he attempted to control his fear.

"Try talking to him, Nathan. He might trust another black man more. Tell him you escaped Confederate soldiers and you've got a Yankee soldier and an injured girl with you."

"Yassuh, Sa'gen', ah try." He cupped his hands once again around his mouth and yelled toward the old man. "We's only tryin' ta 'scape dem 'federate sogers. Ah gots a Yankee soger an' a hurt girl wif me."

"Ask him if he can help," Pat quickly whispered at Nathan.

"Fokes says you help 'scaped slaves."

The crazed laughing had stopped and there was dead silence. They waited for a response… and kept waiting… and kept waiting. Then, suddenly, a terrible screeching yell came from behind them. The trio quickly spun around in the water to see the Snakeman jumping up and down, laughing maniacally, and splashing them with one hand while holding his rifle above the water with the other. He stopped suddenly and pointed his rifle toward them. In his high, squeaky voice, he demanded, "What you got? You got money? You got food? What you got fo' ole Snakeman?"

Lou Ann moved behind Patrick as he fumbled in his pockets for something to give the crazy old man. "I don't have any money… Rebel soldiers took the little I had."

"Who dat hidin' behin' you?"

"Oh, she's—she's my sister."

"She fine lookin' lady. Ole Snakeman—he git lonely in dis ole swamp. No one ta talk wif. I take *her*!" He grabbed for Lou Ann.

Patrick slapped his hand away, as Nathan spoke up. "You crazy ole man—you can't do dat."

Raising his gun and pointing it in Nathan's face, the Snakeman said, "Ya gonna stop me, boy?"

Reaching into his pocket again, Patrick felt for the new rosary given him by the Regimental Chaplain. "Wait a minute! I've got something!" He took the rosary from his pocket and held it in front of the old man's face. The silver Crucifix dangling at the end of it slowly twirled around, glistening in the moonlight. The Snakeman seemed hypnotized as he stared at it. He reached out to grab it with one hand, giving Patrick an opportunity to grab the barrel of the gun and pull it away from him. Nathan jumped on the old man, and they both fell beneath the surface of the water. Nathan wrapped his strong arm around the Snakeman's scrawny neck and pulled him up from the water. Patrick was surprised as the old man was spitting water from his mouth and starting that crazy laugh again.

"What's ya laughin' 'bout?" Nathan angrily demanded.

"No—ha ha ha—no bullets in gun—ha ha ha ha!"

Patrick kept the empty gun anyway. He prodded the Snakeman with it, as they all headed toward the shack. Getting closer, they saw two human skulls attached to long sticks on each side of the doorway and many snake-skins hung out on a small porch railing. Nathan held the old man tightly by the arm, while Patrick climbed up to search the shack for food.

"Let's hurry and get out of here, Patrick. I'm freezing! This is a horrible place!"

"Hold on, Lou Ann. I found some ammunition and a plate of food."

"Dat *my* snake meat!"

"Ohhhhhh. Come on Patrick. Let's just get out of here—please....."

"Yassah, Sa'gen', ah don't wants no snake food either. Hey, look Sa'gen'! Dere's a boat back dere," as he pointed to the rear of the shack.

Patrick climbed back down into the swampy water and pushed the flat-bottomed, wooden rowboat out toward them.

"Ya gotta pay me ta use dat boat!"

Patrick loaded the rifle and pointed it at the old man. "And how would you like to be paid?" The Snakeman became very silent. "You're going to take us out of here if you care about living!"

"Yassuh," he answered as he looked down the barrel of the gun and quietly got into the boat. Pat got in and helped Lou Ann, seating her next to him in the back, while keeping the gun trained on the old Snakeman. Nathan climbed up into the front. The Snakeman, standing in the middle, picked up a long pole and began to push the boat away from the shack.

"You head north, and no funny business!" Patrick commanded. The boat glided silently through the dark waters, as the Snakeman repeatedly plunged the long pole into the slimy bottom of the swamp. Lou Ann shivered in the cold, night air. Never removing his eyes from the Snakeman, Patrick pulled at his uniform jacket with his free hand to remove it, and covered her shoulders with it, wrapping his arm around her. She rested her head on his shoulder, exhausted, and fell asleep for a short time. Pat's eyes became heavy, but he forced himself to stay awake.

After many hours, the boat suddenly stopped as it came to the end of the swamp.

"We's made it, Sa'gen'!" Nathan said, as he got out and pulled the boat up onto dry land.

"Ah got ya here—now gimme ma gun back!" Patrick removed the bullets and tossed the gun to the Snakeman. After they all got out of the boat, the old man pushed it back into the swamp and quickly disappeared into the darkness, laughing his crazy laugh, which echoed throughout the misty bog.

As they walked through the fields, faint rays of daylight peeked over the horizon. "Are you sure we're heading north?" Patrick asked, as he looked toward Nathan walking by his side.

"Ah's sure, Sa'gen'. Ya knows why ah's sure?"

"No. Not really."

"Well, ya sees dat drinkin' gourd up dere?" He pointed to the sky.

"You mean the Big Dipper?"

"Yea, dat's da drinkin' gourd. Ya see dem two stars at de top of it?"

"Yeah, I see them."

"Well, all ya gots ta do is ta make a line straight out from dose two stars an' ya runs inta de No'th Star." He drew an imaginary line in the air. "We keeps headin' fo' dat No'th Star an' we's gonna git ta freedom!"

"Where did you learn all that, Nathan?"

"Ma Mammy. She learnt me lots of things. She use ta tell me dat, if'n ah eber gits free an' gits lost at night, dat ah gotta foller dat big ol' star."

"Your Mama sounds like a smart lady," Lou Ann remarked.

"She smartes' woman ah eber knowed."

"By the way, Nathan, I've been wanting to ask you… what ever happened to you?" Patrick remarked. "I mean—the last I saw you, back at the Marshall's plantation— you and your people were freed."

"Yea, dat wuz de happies' day of ma life—'cceptin fo' poor Pa, natcherly. Ah means—when we gots freed, yu Lincum's sogers wuz a sight fo' sore eyes. Well, aftah dat, poor Mama—she gots ter'ble sick on dat road ta freedom, an' Mindy an' me—we had ta take her back to de plantashun. Didn' wanna, but we's be so scared she gonna… die. Massa's wife—she be glad ta see us back, 'cause she need som'body ta chops de wood fo' de fire. Ol' Massa too old ta do dat now. She say she pay us fo' de work we does. Mindy help Missus Marshall in de house an' cook like befo'. Only till Mama gits better an' we cud find our own place."

"But how did you end up cooking for the Rebs?" Pat asked.

"Oh, aftah Mama starts gittin' better, ah gits itchy. Yu knows, ah allus wanna be one of dem Lincum's sogers an' helps ta fight fo' *all* of ma people ta gits freed. So ah says goodbye; an' befo' ah gits one day's walkin', de Rebel sogers catches me an' make me cooks fo' dem. Ah's bin cookin' dere eber since. Still wants ta be a Lincum's soger anyways."

"Well, this time you're going to make it—we'll all make it," Pat said. "Maybe we can get you in the Army when we get back to our lines. Just keep heading north. And Nathan, I know you're right about the direction we're heading 'cause the sun is coming up over there," as he pointed to the east.

Lou Ann, still holding Patrick's jacket around her shoulders, turned to look. "It's getting light out, and we're right out here in the open."

"You're right, Lou Ann. We have to get out of these fields and over to those woods."

They all began to run toward the wooded area where they sat down, feeling safe to take a few moments to rest. "Patrick, I'm so hungry. What are we going to eat?" Lou Ann asked. "We don't have any food." Pat didn't have an answer.

Nathan spoke up. "Ah heerd 'bouts some slaves 'roun' here dat helps people 'scapin'."

"We can't be sure if we're still in Reb territory or not. We'll have to be cautious."

After a brief rest, they walked for hours through the tall pines, becoming very weary. Coming upon a small stream, they dropped to their knees to drink. "I don't think I can go any further," Lou Ann said.

"Ah thinks dere mebbe is a plantashun som'wheres 'roun' here. Mebbe we cud gits somp'n ta eat."

Daylight was slowly dwindling, and the woods were growing dark. They all lay on the ground, completely exhausted, and fell asleep. In the middle of the night, Patrick was suddenly awakened by Nathan poking him on the shoulder.

"Sa'gen'—Sa'gen'—wake up! Ah foun' some slave fokes up yonder in dere cabin."

Patrick rubbed his eyes and glanced over at Lou Ann, covered with his jacket, still sound asleep. "What did you say? What about slaves?"

"Up yonder—dere's a plantashun—looks like ev'rybody done gone 'cept fo' a few ol' slaves."

Patrick shook Lou Ann gently and kissed her on the cheek. "Wake up, Lou Ann," he said softly. "Nathan says there's a plantation up ahead."

She rolled over and sat up straight, still half asleep. "Do they have any food?"

Nathan led them to the edge of the woods; faint glimmers of sunlight exposed a vast expanse of unattended tobacco fields, a large white house, and a half dozen slave cabins behind it. They all crouched down.

"What do you think, Nathan?" Pat whispered. "Did you say there were some people here who could help us?"

"Ah seed two ol' slaves—looks like dey is mebbe husbin' an' wife. Dey all bent over. Yu waits here. Ah gwine sees iffen dey gots eny food." He crawled into the tobacco fields on his hands and knees and disappeared from view.

"Are you all right, Lou Ann?" Pat asked. "Here—come over here." He sat her up against a tree with him and took her hand in his. How helpless and tired she looked, he thought to himself... so unlike the pretty, bubbly, lilac-scented girl he first met at Fredericksburg.

Again she said, "I'm hungry. I hope we can find something to eat."

"Don't worry. Maybe Nathan will find us something."

She looked at Patrick; her deep blue eyes became fixed on his momentarily, almost seeming apprehensive. She glanced down at the ground.

Before she could say anything, Patrick spoke, as he lifted her chin with his hand. "I have to talk to you about something, Lou Ann—something that's been bothering me since Washington."

"What? What is it?"

"Why were you being held prisoner by the Rebs?"

"Well, I *do* owe you an explanation, Patrick. There is something you should know about me—but—well, please, Patrick—not just now, okay? I'm just—so, so hungry—and so tired."

"Yes, *now*, Lou Ann. I need to ask you now—while Nathan's gone. Tell me—why were you being held by the Rebs?"

"Well, you see, Patrick…" She hesitated.

"Come on, Lou Ann."

"Well—I'm not sure how to tell you. You see, I'm not just a volunteer for the Sanitary Commission. I'm an… " She stopped in mid-sentence and looked over at him. He thought she looked guilty.

"What are you trying to say?" He couldn't wait any longer. He was plagued by his suspicions for a long three months. He blurted out, "Are you a spy?"

"I don't like that word!" she fired back, as she pulled her hand from his. "Agent sounds better."

"I knew it! Ever since we parted in Washington—that list of Army units in your Bible!"

"Oh, that! That was nothing… a ruse for the Confederates."

"Wait a minute! What do you mean… a ruse? What are you trying to tell me? Whose side are you on anyway?" he asked in a disquieted tone.

"Well—you *see*, I must have done my job! I mean—if you think I'm working for the Rebels…"

"Well, *are* you?" he asked in a stern voice.

"Now don't get excited, Patrick!" as she grabbed his hand. "Do you *really* think I would admit to being an agent if I was a Confederate?"

"You mean you spy for the Union?"

"*Agent*, Patrick. I gather information—mostly from Confederate officers. They trust me—or at least they *did* trust me—until they arrested me and put me under guard in that dirty old farmhouse."

"Well, how did they catch you?"

"It was the passes—they found my passes."

"What passes?"

"Oh, well, I guess I can tell you. I mean—I trust you—and it looks like my undercover work has come to an end. You see, I had forged passes to come through the Confederate lines. They had Southern Generals' signatures on them—Lee, Longstreet, Pickett, Jackson—all of them."

"How did you get them?"

"They all went to West Point before the War, and—well, there were many papers with their signatures on them still on file. We were simply able to make fake passes and duplicate their signatures."

"How did the Rebels know you had them?"

"After the Chancellorsville Battle, I was trying to get some information from a Confederate officer, when I dropped my purse on the ground and my passes spilled right out in front of him. Before I could grab them all up, he was on his knees trying to assist me and could see immediately that there was something very wrong, since I had many more than would have been expected. After looking more closely, he had me arrested on suspicion of spying and was sending me to Richmond for interrogation."

"Lou Ann, was that you talking to a Rebel officer in that tent at Chancellorsville?"

"Why, yes, how did you know?"

"I *thought* that was you—I saw you as we were being marched away by the Rebs. At least, I was almost certain that was you, but I couldn't see clearly through that pouring rain. Oh, my dear God in Heaven! You could have been hung, Lou Ann!"

"I know. You were *my* angel when you freed me from the Rebels. I was never so frightened in my whole life."

"I have so many questions—what about the vase?"

"What vase? I'm sorry, Patrick. Maybe another time… another place… I can't think. I'm so…"

Just then, Nathan emerged from the tobacco fields, still crawling on all fours. He motioned to them. "Come wif me," he said excitedly. "Dey gots food fo' us!"

"Who do you mean?" Pat asked.

"Dem ole fokes—dem slaves—dey gots food fo' us! Stay down an' follo' me. Dem fokes says dere's Rebel sogers ridin' 'roun' dese parts."

Lou Ann and Patrick followed him, as they crawled through the tobacco fields until they came to a shabby old cabin. They crawled in the open door and quickly closed it behind them, standing up as they did. Daylight began to shine through the windows, filtered by the faded, weather-beaten curtains that hung over them. Patrick looked around the small, one-room cabin, as he smelled the aroma of bacon mixed with the odor of burning pine logs in the crude fireplace. The back of an old man's head showed over the top of a rocking chair, which faced it. He continued rocking but didn't turn around. His gray hair had a yellowish tint, as it reflected the leaping flames.

Standing by the fire, the old lady turned and greeted them with a broad smile on her round face, as if they were close friends who often stopped by. "Ya'll set yo'selfs down," she said matter-of-factly, as she pointed to an old wooden table in the middle of the room. It didn't have a tablecloth; however, a tall glass vase of lilacs was in the center.

Pat leaned over them and inhaled deeply. "My favorite flower." He looked over at Lou Ann, seated across from him, and smiled. She smiled back. Nathan sat down on an old stump near the fireplace. "Come over here and sit with us."

"No, Sa'gen'. Dat's a'right."

"We want you to join us at the table," Pat repeated.

"Nossuh. Ah likes de warm fire."

Patrick wondered if Nathan was uncomfortable with the thought of sitting at a table with white people. Maybe he never had. The old lady brought a heaping plateful of hot bacon and corn muffins to the table. "Now ya'll help yo'selfs. Ah gots hot coffee fo' yu too." Pat noticed she walked with a limp as she went back to the fireplace; she seemed to be experiencing some pain.

Pat blessed himself. "Thank you, Lord, for this food."

"Yassuh, we allus thanks the good Lawd fo' our food."

"And we can't thank *you* enough," Lou Ann said, turning toward the woman, as she began to eat ravenously.

The old lady limped back to the table and poured coffee into two cracked porcelain cups. "Ah luvs de smell of dose flowers, too. Ain't dey de sweetes' yo' ever smelled? Gawd sure make dem sweet-smellin'".

"I love them, too," Lou Ann said, as she sipped the hot coffee, folding her hands around the cup to warm them.

Nathan sat quietly on the stump, eating and warming himself by the fire.

Feeling much better after eating, Patrick spoke up, as he looked over at the kind old lady. "Are you the only folks living here?"

"Yassuh. Dem Yankee sogers come and done free us slaves. Wha' a jub'lation day dat wuz! Only thing is…" She looked over at the old gent in the rocker. "Pa caint walk hisself, an' ah caint leaves him here all 'lone. Dey all done gone—Gawd bless 'em—dey all on de road ta freedom! Ah…" She started to sob, as she wiped a tear from her eye with the corner of her apron. "Ah dunno wha's gonna 'come of us. We's free—but caint go nowheres."

"*Ah* wuz on de road ta jine up wif de Yankees, Ma'am," Nathan remarked. "Den sum Rebel sogers come 'n capture me. But ah gits away—ah means, we *all* gits away," as he pointed to Lou Ann and Patrick. "But ah is *still* gonna be a Lincum's soger like de Sa'gen' here, an' ah's gonna *stay* free!"

"Ah knows *you* wuz a Lincum's soger, Sa'gen'," the old woman said to Patrick. "You gots de same uniform as dem Army boys dat freed us. Gawd bless ya. What a glory time ta be livin'! Ah only wishes ma Mammy 'n Pappy cud of seed dis day."

Pat felt helpless. The woman had been so kind to them, and he didn't have anything to repay her with. "What happened to your Mast… I mean—the owner of this place?"

"Oh, he off to de war. Only de Missus left in dat big ole house. She cry all de time. She don' knows iffen he come back. He be a big 'federate kernel or somp'n. He be gone since de war start."

"Maybe she would let you stay on if you helped take care of things around here," Pat offered.

"Missus done tol' us dat, too."

Nathan looked at the old lady compassionately. "Ah knows how yu be feelin'. Ma Mammy got sick aftah we gots freed, an' we hafta takes her back to da Massa's house. But when dis war is over, ah's goin' back an' git her an' ma wife."

The woman looked at Nathan with a surprised look on her face. "Yu is married, boy? Yu looks too young ta be's married."

"Ah jus' gots married befo' we gots free."

Pat was anxious to find out more about the whereabouts of the Rebels and to get back to friendly territory. He got up from the table and walked over to the fireplace to talk to the old man. Extending his hand, he said, "My name's Patrick. I want to thank you for all you're doing for us." The old man never took his eyes off the fire. He just kept rocking and humming a tune—or was it a moaning sound? More like a Negro spiritual, Pat thought.

"Oh, he som'times don't speaks ta no one fo' days. Don't mind him," the kind old woman said.

"I'm sorry," Pat replied. "I think we'd best be going. You've been so good to us. We don't want to cause you any trouble. I mean—if we get caught here, you…"

"Yu caint travel in de daylight."

Nathan broke in. "She right—ah heerd from some slaves we best off ta travel at night."

Lou Ann, still sitting at the table, turned to Patrick. "I don't think I could walk another mile—hardly slept—traveling in that swamp all night."

The old lady looked over at her. "Yu come thru dat swamp?"

"Yes, Ma'am."

"Yu is lucky ta be alive, girl. Ah heerd dere's ol' Snakeman in dere who eats people."

Nathan stood up. "Oh, we meets him—he jus' a crazy ol' man. We use his boat ta gits thru dat nasty ol' swamp."

The old woman looked at the three fugitives. "Now, ya'll listen here. Yu is gonna stay here taday 'n gits sum rest." She began to clean up the dishes. "Yu kin gits on de road aftah dark. Caint yu boys see dis here gal is ready ta drop over? Now ya'll gits sum sleep," as she placed three old quilts on the earthen floor and motioned to the exhausted trio to come over and lie down.

Pat was grateful for the offer, and they all lay down on the dusty old quilts that, to Patrick, looked inviting after their ordeal.

It was well after dark when the old lady woke them up. "Yu best be leavin' now."

Pat sat up and smelled the coffee that was boiling on the hearth. Lou Ann got up, tried to smooth her hair back from her face with her hands, straightened out her petticoat the best she could, and joined Patrick at the table. He was rubbing his eyes and sipping the warm brew. The old man was snoring, still in his chair by the fireplace.

Nathan sat down again on the stump and stretched his arms outward. "Dat wuz a good sleep!"

The old mammy came over to the table with some bacon and cornbread wrapped in a towel and placed it before them. "Dis here is fo' yer trip." She then handed Lou Ann an old skirt and sweater. "Here—yu needs dese ta keep warm."

"Thank you so much."

The woman continued, " Now lissen what ah has ta tell ya'll. Ah is s'posin' yu is headin' no'th."

Patrick answered, "We have to get back to our lines or find some Union soldiers."

"Ah knows de way, Sa'gen'," Nathan quipped. "We follows dat ol' No'th Star."

The mammy quickly chimed in. "Yu aint gonna see no stars *dis* night. It be all clouds—black night out dere." She opened the creaky old door of the cabin and pointed. "Now, dere's a road out pas' da Massa's big house, an' yu go follow dat road no'th," waving her finger in that direction. "Yu bes' lissen—don't make no noise. An' iffen yu hears somp'n, yu gits right off dat road an' lays down in de weeds. Dere wuz some bad, ol' bounty hunters come by de udder day. Ah heerd dem talkin' when ah wuz hidin' in de woods. Dey be ketchin' some freed slaves on de road and sellin' dem way down South."

"Do you think you're safe here?" Patrick inquired. "I mean, do you hide from them so they don't sell you, too?"

"Ah aint really skeered 'cause—ahs be'd thinkin'—ol' Pa an' me—dey caint git no money fo' us...we be too old ta work. We aint good fo' much. We done be all worked out. We got nothin' lef' but each udder."

Lou Ann went over to the corner of the room and stood behind a high-backed chair facing the wall to put on the old clothes. She returned to the table to finish her coffee, warning the couple, "Now, you be careful, too. Don't take any chances. There could still be danger if those bounty hunters are still in the area."

The old mammy replied with her *own* instructions. "Now lissen—ah gots somp'n else yu gotta know. Iffen yu comes by some ol' slave cabin where dere's blankets on de clothesline an' one of dem is hangin' half over de udder one or dere's shirts hangin' by de sleeves, yu knows dat's a signal dat dey helps runaways. Now ya'll best be gittin," as she placed the towel of food in Lou Ann's hands, threw a quilt around her shoulders, and motioned them out the door. "An' may de good Lawd protects ya'll."

They walked down the road into darkness—their ally. They walked in silence… listening…cautious… holding the quiet night dearly as a protective guard. They talked very little, and then, only in whispers, as they made their way around the curves, up and down the rises in the dirt road, and past the tall, dark trees which stood like sentinels protecting them from enemy eyes.

It seemed like many hours had passed, and they walked at a slower and slower pace. Pat suddenly stopped in his tracks. "Listen!" he said in a hushed tone. "I hear horses coming. Quick—get in the woods!"

They dashed into the woods, lying flat in the underbrush. "Who do you think they are?" Lou Ann whispered.

"Don't know if they're ours or not," Pat answered. "Sounds like about four horses. Sh-h-h! They're coming closer."

Nathan began to scratch himself and discovered in horror that he was lying on top of an anthill. He was sweating profusely but afraid to move or make a sound. As the men on horseback rode by, their voices could be heard clearly.

"Gimme my bottle back, Seth! Leave some for me!"

"Sorry, Captain, just finished the last drop." as he laughed.

They galloped away. The others followed, picking up their pace.

"Is it safe, Sa'gen'?"

"Yeah, we can get up now." Pat no sooner had the words out of his mouth, when Nathan, in a flash, jumped to his feet, frantically brushing off the hungry little pests from his body.

"Ants! Dey be all over me! Damn dose cre'tures!"

"Oh, Nathan, you scared me!" Lou Ann exclaimed. "I thought you were having a fit or something."

Nathan took off his shirt and shook it violently until he believed the ants were all gone.

"Guess we stopped in the wrong place," Pat said.

They got back on the road, and Nathan repeatedly scratched himself, constantly brushing off his clothing.

"Good thing we hid out—that was a Reb patrol!" Pat offered.

"How do you know?" Lou Ann asked.

"Didn't you hear those Dixie accents and their swords clanging as they rode off? Yep! Definitely Reb officers. Guess we've got a ways to go before we find some friendlies."

It was still dark, and they stopped to rest again. Patrick was accustomed to long marches, and Nathan had toiled in the fields from sun-up till sunset; but Lou Ann had never had the misfortune of grueling extremes and harsh conditions.

"We'll have to stop here for awhile, Nathan. Lou Ann can't keep up this pace."

"I can't go a step further," she said, as she collapsed on the road. Patrick picked her up and carried her into the woods.

"Ah don't knows how dat li'l gal done kep' up wif us *dis* long."

They found a small clearing; Patrick told Nathan to take the rolled-up quilt from his back and place it on the ground. He gently laid Lou Ann upon it, trying to cover her a little with one end. She was asleep within minutes. Patrick turned to Nathan. "We'll take turns keeping guard. Do you want to go first?"

"Ah feels okay. Ah'll take de firs' guard."

"It will be good training for you—you might be doing a lot of guard duty when you get in the Army. That's one of the first things they teach you." Pat started to hand Nathan his watch but put it back in his pocket. He didn't think Nathan could tell time; and, even if he could, he probably couldn't see it in the dark. "Just wake me in a couple of hours or when you can't stay awake any longer."

"Yassuh, Sa'gen'. Yu gits som' rest now." Nathan sat down and leaned against a tree, while Patrick lay down next to Lou Ann. He wished they could light a fire to get warm, but that would be too dangerous. He lay in the dark, his mind wandering—who was this woman lying on the quilt beside him? He had first seen her as a sweet young volunteer helping the wounded. Then as a suspected Rebel spy. And now, she was the captured Union spy he had helped to free.

Patrick was an uncomplicated young man with one goal—to survive and help bring down the rebellion. He never bargained for another love interest, let alone one involving espionage. His thoughts became like railroad tracks, running parallel. Beth... Lou Ann... Where would it all end? His head swam as he reached in his pocket for his rosary. He prayed until sleep overtook him.

Nathan awakened him sometime in the middle of the night, shaking him gently on his shoulder. "Sa'gen', wake up!" he whispered.

"What is it?" Pat asked, pulling himself up on one elbow and rubbing his eyes. "Oh... my turn to guard?"

"Nawsuh. Ah warn't gonna wakes yu yet, but ah heerd horses runnin' down de road. Dunno who dey be. Cud'n see 'em from here."

"We'll have to be quiet. Could be Rebs—or maybe even bounty hunters. You get some sleep. I'll take over the guard duty as long as I'm awake now."

"Ah's purty tired." Nathan yawned and lay down by the tree where he had been sitting.

Patrick stared into the heavy darkness. All was still except for the rustling of leaves in the high treetops and the occasional warble of a night bird. The moon seemed to blink at him as the fast moving clouds rushed by. Occasionally the "drinking gourd" came into view, and Patrick gauged that they were still heading north.

Morning dawned with gray skies and rain clouds in the distance. Patrick awakened Lou Ann and Nathan, and they ate the little food that the old mammy had given them. He had wanted to let his companions sleep longer but was anxious to get back to friendly territory. He felt that the longer they remained there, the more chance they had of getting caught. After eating, Pat rolled up the quilt, tied it with his belt, and placed it on his left shoulder. He noticed Nathan staring curiously at him. "What are you staring at, Nathan?"

"Oh, ah's jus' lookin' at dat medal yu's wearin'," he answered with a tinge of timidity in his voice.

Patrick looked down at the medal hanging from his neck on the outside of his shirt. "It's sort of a religious medal. I've worn it since I was a young boy. Is this the first you ever noticed it?"

"Yassuh, Sa'gen', but ah seed one jus' like it on a Reb soger one time."

"You saw a Reb soldier wearing a medal just like mine?" he asked in an excited voice.

"Yassuh, Sa'gen'." Nathan walked closer to Patrick to get a better look. Pat held the medal out for him to see. As Nathan observed the Cross, he asked, "Ah sees yu be a Christian, but wha' be dat star under de Cross?"

"That's the Star of David, a symbol of the Jewish faith."

"Oh, ah knows 'bout Jews from de Preacher. He done reads all kinda things from de Bible to us slaves—like 'bout Moses an' Joshua an' 'lijah......"

Before he could finish, Pat interrupted. "Did you say Joshua?"

"Yassuh, Sa'gen'. Yu knows 'bout him?"

"Wait a minute. Where did you see this Reb soldier? Was *his* name Joshua?"

"How yu knows dat, Sa'gen'? Dat *wuz* his name; cuz ah does 'member when he tol' me his name, ah thought 'bout dat Joshua dat fit de Battle of Jericho an' de walls come a'tumblin' down. De ole Preacher done tol' us 'bout dat."

Pat, very anxious to find out more, questioned Nathan further. "Where did you see him?"

"Ah takes care of his hoss—big black stallion—when de Reb sogers come inta de plantashun... all shot up an' wounded an' a sorry sight ta see."

"Oh, my gosh! It must be him."

Lou Ann walked over to see what was so special about Pat's medal. "Can I see it?"

"I can't believe it—Joshua's fighting for the Rebs! Must be in the Cavalry. It's got to be him. There can't be another Joshua wearing this medal." He looked directly at Nathan. "What did he look like?"

"Well, he was kinda short. Ah does 'member he had red hair an' a beard."

"That's him. That's Josh. We used to call him Carrot Top. Holy smokes! I can't believe it! I haven't seen him since I was a boy."

Lou Ann, still staring at the medal, asked Pat, "Where did you know him from?"

"We were best friends in grade school. His family moved to Virginia after seventh grade."

"He be nice ta me—like yu, Sa'gen'. He had same Jesus Cross on his medal."

Lou Ann looked puzzled. "Isn't that kind of strange? To have the Cross and the Star of David on the same medal? I mean—two different faiths?" she asked politely.

"Well, we were just boys back then—'blood brothers'—sworn to remain friends forever," he chuckled. "Besides, our priest told us that the Jews were our elder brothers and sisters... all sons and daughters of Abraham, he said."

"Oh, Patrick! That's beautiful!" Lou Ann remarked. "Your priest sounds like a very wise man."

"Yes, very holy and loving. Taught us about the Blessed Mother, too. He told us that Jesus performed His first miracle at Cana for His Mother when they ran out of wine. That's why I say my rosary. I figure, if Mary has that much influence over her Son, she can put in a good word for me."

Lou Ann smiled. "I believe that, too, although I have to admit I haven't said my rosary in a long time."

"Wha' dat rosary mean?"

Pat removed his rosary from his pocket and held it up for Nathan to see.

"Oh, dat's wha' yu done showed de Ol' Snakeman befo' yu grab his gun."

"Yes. Guess Jesus' Mama helped us get out of *that* fix."

Just then, it began to rain and they were reminded of their flight from the enemy. Setting out once again, they headed north, hoping to find Yankee soldiers or someone who might guide them back to friendly country. They walked in the woods close to the road. The weather grew worse, the winds picked up, and the rain blew into their faces. Lou Ann grew weaker as the day wore on. They had to stop frequently and rest. Finally, Patrick noticed that she seemed to be shivering.

"Patrick—I feel sick and feverish. I don't think I can keep going."

"Nathan, can you go on ahead? See if there is any shelter or someplace where we can get her out of the rain?"

"Yassah, Sa'gen'. Ah go sees what ah kin find." Nathan left, walking as fast as he could and disappeared in the woods.

Patrick unrolled the quilt and wrapped it around Lou Ann, holding her close to help keep her warm. She started coughing. He sat her down on a log.

"Patrick, I'm so cold."

He felt helpless. What could he do? He didn't have any matches for a fire. Besides, everything was soaking wet. He knew she couldn't go on. Nathan *had* to return.

They waited for hours. The rain had finally stopped, but Lou Ann was still cold. She was soaked through to the skin. He, too, felt the cold and wet, but it wasn't the first time. He prayed fervently, fingering his rosary beads. She was too weak and sick, so he prayed for her and for Nathan to return with good news. It wasn't long before he heard the crackling of branches. The sound grew louder—it *was* Nathan. Pat could see him approaching through the dense woods.

"Sa'gen'! Sa'gen'!" Nathan hollered. "Ah found us a place ta stay!"

"Sh-h-h-h! Not so loud," Pat cautioned. "How far is it?"

"Mebbe a hour."

"An hour? But you were gone so *long!*"

Nathan wiped his brow with the back of his hand, panting heavily. "Some ole bounty hunters—ah thinks dey wuz, ridin' up 'n ' down de road, lookin' in de woods all de time. Ah had ta lay low fo' a long time so dey caint sees me. Den ah foun' a ole preacher man, livin' in a cabin. He say he puts us up fo' de night."

"Thank God!" Patrick lifted Lou Ann onto his back once again, and they all set out for the preacher's cabin. After stopping and resting a few times, they eventually arrived at a small crossroads. Nathan pointed to the cabin on the other side, set back slightly into the trees.

"Dere it be, Sa'gen'. Ah goes fust ta make sure it still be safe."

"Just wave at us, and we'll come over. I'll be able to see you from here."

"Yassuh, Sa'gen'."

Lou Ann and Patrick crouched down and waited. She was still shivering. Patrick watched for Nathan's signal. A few minutes passed. He grew anxious. What was taking so long? Suddenly, he heard horses approaching. He grabbed Lou Ann and pulled her down with him into the thick brush.

As they grew closer, he could hear one of the riders yelling, "I saw him run into that cabin over there!"

Lifting his head slightly to peer through the weeds, he whispered to Lou Ann, "They look like bounty hunters." Fear for Nathan began to build in his heart as he watched the two men ride to the cabin and dismount. He could see them burst through the door. "Stay here, Lou Ann!"

"Be careful," she warned, while attempting to muffle her cough.

Patrick snuck over, crept up to the side of the cabin, and listened through the window.

"You comin' with me, boy!" hollered one of the men.

"Yu caint do dat—dis boy a freed man!" another answered.

"Get out of my way, old man. He's a runaway. He's comin' with us!"

Patrick picked up a small log from a pile of wood and walked over by the door, pressing himself against the walls of the cabin as he did. With his other hand, he picked up a tree branch and slapped the horses as hard as he could. They bolted and ran down the road. He raised the log over his head. Suddenly, one of the bounty hunters came bolting out the door. Patrick forcefully hit the man over the head and he dropped to the ground unconscious. Immediately, the other man rushed out and raised his rifle to shoot Patrick. In an instant, Nathan tackled the man from behind, causing his gun to drop from his hands. He began to grapple with Nathan, a violent struggle ensuing. The man withdrew a large, black-handled knife from his boot and raised it above Nathan's head. A shot rang out, and the man fell to the ground.

Patrick had picked up the gun and shot him. The preacher stepped out of the door with a look of astonishment on his face. Nathan got up and stared down at the wounded man. There was a moment of silence. Finally Patrick spoke. "Oh my gosh! Lou Ann—have to get Lou Ann! Nathan, go find the horses." Pat handed the rifle to the preacher. "Keep an eye on them."

Nathan ran down the road, while Patrick returned to the woods to find Lou Ann. She was still crouched down in the brush with his blanket wrapped around her. By the time they got back to the cabin, Nathan had retrieved the horses. Patrick quickly mounted one of them. "Nathan, lift Lou Ann up behind me!" Wasting no time, Nathan complied, then mounted the other horse. Patrick looked down at the preacher. "Aren't you coming with us?"

"Nawsuh. Ah stays right here. Dis is ma home an' ah ain't leavin'."

Patrick pointed to the bounty hunters. "What are you going to do about *them*?"

"Iffen dey tries somp'n, de good Lawd kin smote dem wif fire an' brimstone." Sitting down in the rocking chair in front of the cabin, the preacher placed the rifle across his knees and patted it like a baby. "Or de Lawd cud place dat fire an' brimstone in de hands of a li'l ole preacher man." He smirked. "Ya'll best be gittin' out of here now. Ah kin takes good care of them 'til more Yankee sogers comes."

"Well, Nathan, you've attacked your first enemy and you took 'em out good! I think you're going to make a great soldier."

"Ah hopes so, Sa'gen'. Iffen ah ebber catches up wif dem Lincum's sogers."

They turned their horses to leave. The old preacher looked up from his rocker.

"Dem Yankee sogers—dey come by here dis mornin' and done freed some slaves. Den dey all follows dem sogers down dat road. Mebbe ya cud catch up wif dem befo' de sun go down, iffen ya hurries." Patrick told Lou Ann to wrap her arms tightly around his waist and they galloped off.

They traveled all afternoon; the sun finally came out and dried their wet clothes. "I have to stop," Lou Ann said in a weak voice. They halted the horses and rested, taking advantage of the time to eat the little food the preacher man had given them. Lou Ann placed the blanket on the ground and lay down on it, exhausted, and fell asleep. Patrick had seen refuse strewn on the road for the last few miles and knew that they weren't far from the caravan of Yankee soldiers and freed slaves.

After a short while, Patrick woke Lou Ann and they continued on their journey. At about twilight, they heard singing in the distance. It was the unmistakable voice of a freed people. Shouts of jubilation! Patrick had heard this sound once before, when Nathan's people were freed. It echoed throughout the still, evening air.

As the caravan came into view, Patrick felt relieved to see friendly folk. He looked over at Nathan riding alongside him, the joy and exhilaration showing in the broad smile on his face. Lou Ann, who by now had become weaker and almost delirious from the fever, whispered, "What is it? Who are these people?"

"Friends, Lou Ann—friends." Pat could feel her losing her grip and grabbed her two hands in one of his, as he began to ride toward the columns of soldiers, hoping to find a doctor. They passed the freed slaves that numbered in the hundreds. Shouts of 'hallelujah' sang from their lips, as they waved to them. Finally arriving at the head of the column, Patrick found an officer on horseback.

"Where did *you* come from?" asked the startled lieutenant.

"Sergeant O'Hanrahan, Sir." He saluted the officer. "We've escaped from the Rebs. Got a very sick girl here. Do you have a doctor with you?"

"No, I'm afraid not, Sergeant." The officer looked over at Lou Ann. "She *looks* sick. What's wrong with her?"

"She's got a fever and chills, Sir, and she's very weak."

The officer then raised his hand and halted the wagons behind him. "Well, maybe we could at least make her more comfortable. Why don't you put her in one of the wagons where she can lie down."

"Thank you, Sir. That would help a lot." Patrick lifted Lou Ann down from the horse and laid her in one of the wagons. The lieutenant ordered a soldier to get some blankets from another wagon.

"Here you are, Sergeant."

Patrick folded one of the blankets to make a pillow for Lou Ann's head, covering her with the other.

"Where am I?" she whispered, forcing the words as though they took her last ounce of energy.

"Sh-h-h. Don't try to talk. You're safe now. We're back behind our lines now."

One of the soldiers brought a canteen full of cool water for her. Patrick held it to her lips and she sipped a small amount. "Thank God!" she whispered. "I need a doctor—Colonel Sommers—my father—a doctor in Washington..." She lapsed into unconsciousness.

Patrick was surprised that she referred to her father as "Colonel." She had told him that he was a doctor in Washington but never mentioned him being in the Army. Maybe she's confused from the fever. "Keep an eye on her," he told the private as he stepped down from the wagon.

Nathan and the lieutenant were still astride their horses. Nathan, in the process of describing their journey from captivity to the lieutenant, dismounted and stood in the road as Patrick approached. The lieutenant raised himself slightly up from the saddle, wincing as he did, and rubbed his bottom. "Too long in the saddle." Pat smiled. "Well, Sergeant, heard you had quite an ordeal. This man"—he pointed to Nathan—"was telling me all about it. Captured at Chancellorsville, were you?"

"Yes, sir."

"Yeah. That was another disaster. Guess Fighting Joe Hooker didn't have so much fight in him! When the hell are we gonna get a winning general?"

"Yeah. My company had to retreat. How them Rebs got around on our flank beats me! I thought we had 'em on the run."

"Do you think we're ever gonna win one, Sergeant? I mean—I know our boys can do it—but we need a general to outfox that old Grey Fox! That Bobby Lee beats us every time—even when we've got him outnumbered."

"I know. We lost many good men at Fredericksburg, too."

"You were in that one, too?"

"You bet—in the thick of it—Marye's Heights, they called it. A slaughterhouse it was!"

"I missed that one. Been in supply work since Antietam. Can't fight too well with *this*." He pointed down to the stump ending just below the knee of his left leg. Lost this one in that Bloody Lane along with my commanding officer and many friends, too."

"Guess I was lucky. I missed Antietam. Worked in the Quartermaster Corps then. I mean, I was there, but not in the thick of it," Pat offered.

"Yeah. They say we won that one. You couldn't prove it by me. Nope! There was just as many a good Yankee boy layin' dead as there were Rebs."

Patrick felt good talking to a fellow soldier but was very concerned about Lou Ann. "I'm not sure where we are, and that girl that we brought in—she—she needs a doctor pretty bad."

"Yeah, I've been meaning to ask you about her. Where did you find her?"

Patrick had hoped Nathan hadn't said anything to the lieutenant about her being a spy, afraid he might put her under arrest. "Didn't Nathan here," as he pointed to him, "tell you about her?"

"Just that you all escaped together, Sergeant. But I don't understand who she is."

Pat had to make up a story—and fast! "Oh, she said these Reb soldiers picked her up on the road somewhere and seems like they were planning to have some fun with her. They had her in this farmhouse where they had us prisoners camping for the night. When we overpowered the guards, she begged us to take her along. Now, a gentleman couldn't refuse a lady in distress such a request, could he?"

"No, Sergeant. I would have done the same thing if I were in your shoes. Do you know anything about her?"

"No, Sir. She got sick right after we escaped. She got *so* sick, she could hardly talk. I'm afraid she may have pneumonia. If we don't get her to a doctor soon, she may not make it. Where are we? Lost track of where we are. Been traveling through the woods the last couple of days."

"Another day's haul and we'll be over to the river. From there, we go sailing to Washington. Pick up more supplies… then back again."

"You said the river? What river?"

"Potomac—the big, wide, beautiful Potomac! Always love to get back to it. More friendly territory."

"Are we near Fredericksburg?" Pat asked.

"Just a day's ride over that way." The lieutenant pointed to the west.

"Guess we were heading more east than north. Tried to follow the North Star."

"Yeah. Can be confusing. At least you weren't heading south!"

"Yeah. Thank God for that!"

The officer handed his canteen to Patrick. "You look pretty thirsty, Sergeant."

"Thanks." Patrick took a long swallow and then handed the canteen to Nathan, who hesitated momentarily, as he looked over at the lieutenant.

"Go ahead—it's okay," he nodded to Nathan.

"Thank ya, Suh." He took a couple of long gulps and gave the canteen back to the officer.

"We'll stop up yonder for the night and get you some food. Just want to get a few more miles in. It'll be safer further on. Reb patrols thin out the further north we go." The lieutenant tied his horse to the back of the wagon and instructed Patrick and Nathan to do the same. "Come on, boys! We'll ride on the wagon for awhile. Getting' tired of straddling that animal!" They climbed up onto the driver's seat, and the lieutenant motioned to the other drivers to start the wagons moving. "Where you headin'?" the lieutenant asked as he looked over at Nathan sitting on his right.

"Ah's gonna jine up wif de Army—fight dem Rebs!"

"Yeah, I hear there's an all-colored regiment forming up north someplace. Maybe you can catch up with them."

"How does ah do dat?"

"Well, once we get to Washington, we can find out more about it. We'll get the boat up at Aquia Landing—then smooth sailing to the Capitol. What outfit are *you* with?" as he looked over at Patrick sitting on his left.

"Sixty-ninth New York."

"Not sure where they might be. Probably around Fredericksburg. Last I heard, Hooker and Lee were staring across the Rappahannock at one another. Nobody willing to make the next move."

"I'll have to see that this girl gets medical attention before I even *think* of returning to my regiment, Lieutenant."

"Yeah, Sergeant. Why don't you go to the hospital with her? You look like you could use a little medical attention yourself. You must be exhausted. A few more days before you return isn't going to matter. Besides, if you go back now, you'll probably just be sitting around the campfire twiddling your thumbs."

"I'd better check on her," Pat remarked as he crawled into the back of the wagon. He felt her forehead. She was feverish, mumbling something he was trying to make out. It sounded like, "I don't know—I don't know anything." In her delirious state, she must be dreaming she's back in that farmhouse being questioned by that Reb officer, he thought to himself. He stayed with her for a time, thinking of how their roles had been reversed. He remembered how her pretty face had been the first one he had seen after Fredericksburg—the "angel of the battlefield". There was no pretty face or sweet-smelling lilac fragrance now. Just a very gaunt, very sick girl with dark circles beginning to form under her blue eyes. He worried. Then he pulled his rosary from his pocket and began to pray. "Oh, dear Lord, be merciful. Please Lord, spare her life." He thought of that vivacious, high-spirited, bubbly, youthful presence he loved about her. He would never forget the time spent with her in the Capitol. She had pulled him out of the doldrums—that gloomy state he was in when convalescing in the hospital. Feeling that he owed her something, he would see that she received medical attention even if he were court-martialed for his absence. For now, the war would have to wait... his only concern was Lou Ann. There would be enough shooting and killing on the horizon to last him a lifetime.

And then—there was Beth...

CHAPTER 12

▼

THE COLONEL

The caravan of Yankee supply wagons slowly made its way through the rolling hills and wooded countryside. The small company of soldiers guarding the wagons had hoped not to run into any large Rebel patrol. Patrick stayed at Lou Ann's side throughout the bumpy ride, trying to comfort her as she drifted in and out of consciousness.

Nathan had joined his fellow freed slaves, who by now had dwindled in numbers. They shuffled along behind the wagons, many not able to keep up. The Yankee soldiers had given them food and water but had to continue on. By nightfall, they arrived at the boat landing and had boarded the steamer—horses, wagons, and soldiers. Nathan had re-joined Patrick and Lou Ann just before they got on the boat, the only one of the ex-slaves fortunate enough to do so. The soldiers had to form a barricade to prevent the others from boarding. There just wasn't enough room for all of them.

Patrick looked back as the steamer slowly pulled away from the shore, and he wondered what would become of the many men, women, and children left standing on the dock. Their freedom had been a long time coming. It had been a jubilant time—but what now? Where would they go? What would they do? There were some shouts of anger that quickly died out—then silence. A race of people stood there, freed by the Yankee soldiers, and now—now abandoned to fend for themselves. It seemed cruel to Patrick—not the freedom part—but that no one in the government had thought to assist them in their hour of transition. Cruel—just plain cruel. Nathan looked very sad as he leaned on the railing and watched his people, free but homeless.

Pat suddenly realized that this was the same boat landing that Danny and he and the other bloody souls from Fredericksburg had been evacuated from back on that cold, rainy day in December. He had come full-circle.

It soon came to his attention that a nurse was on the boat; Lou Ann would finally get some care. Small sips of water were given her and cold cloths applied to her forehead. The nurse feared, too, that she had pneumonia, as her cough grew worse. "She needs a doctor, Sergeant. We should be in Washington by morning, and you can get her to a hospital there. Is she your wife?"

"No, just a very good friend. Do you work in a hospital?"

"Yes. I mean I will be. I've been assigned to a hospital there in Washington, but I've been working down here since the Battle of Fredericksburg. There were so many boys wounded..."

"Yes, I know. I lost many friends. I was spared."

"You're fortunate you're still in one piece—so many lost limbs. Well, Sergeant, I have to look in on some others. Just keep applying those cold cloths and keep trying to get sips of water into her." She started to walk away.

"Oh, nurse!" She turned around. "I wanted to ask you if you knew a Colonel Sommers. He's a doctor, I believe."

"Doesn't ring a bell. Where does he work?"

"I think he must work at a hospital in Washington."

"Well, if he's a doctor, you could find him in the register at one of the military hospitals there. Do you know where Fourteenth Street is?"

"Sure do. Spent a while in a hospital there."

"Well, then, you know the general area." She stopped talking for a moment, as if she were thinking, then looked directly at him. "You know, Sergeant, I have to report for duty up at a Mount Pleasant Hospital. Why don't we take your sick friend up there? Maybe we can find that colonel for you."

"Oh, thanks. That would be great!"

Patrick watched over Lou Ann throughout the night, dozing on and off. Nathan stood all night leaning on the boat railing, looking in awe out at the broad waters of the Potomac, enraptured with the vastness and beauty of it. His plantation life had kept him in the limbo of the 400-acre plantation, far from any waterway.

The steamer chugged its way toward the dock, cut its engines, and silently glided in, grazing its side against the wood. The horses and wagons, guided by the teamsters, were carefully led down the ramp and positioned behind one another for the trip back to the supply depot. After a short exchange of words, Patrick and the nurse persuaded the officer in charge of the wagons to allow the one that Lou Ann was in to be taken directly to the hospital.

The mosquito-nettings, which covered the couches of the sick and wounded, could be seen in the darkened room, as a stout, stern looking nurse approached them. "I'm sorry, this hospital is for military personnel only." She folded her arms abruptly across her chest.

Patrick grew concerned. "Can't you at least have a doctor look at her? She's *very* sick. Says her father is a Colonel Sommers stationed in one of the hospitals here. Do you know him by any chance?"

"You mean this is Colonel Sommers' daughter?"

"That's what she said before she got so sick."

"Why didn't you say so? Everyone here knows the Colonel! About the best surgeon we have." She quickly instructed two orderlies to carry Lou Ann into a private room adjoining the ward. They laid her in a bed with clean sheets, and the head nurse began to minister to her.

The nurse from the boat turned to Patrick, waiting in the hallway. "Well, Sergeant, I guess there isn't much more I can do for her. She's in good hands now. I have to leave to report for duty. Good luck. I hope your friend will be all right."

Patrick shook her hand and thanked her. He looked over at Nathan, sitting on a bench against the wall. He seemed speechless as he gazed around, experiencing the sights and sounds of a hospital. The head nurse stepped back into the hallway. "I didn't catch your name, Sergeant."

"O'Hanrahan. Patrick O'Hanrahan, Ma'am."

"Your friend has all the signs of pneumonia. Now—you said her father is Colonel Sommers?"

"That's what she told me."

"Well, you'd better go get him... she isn't doing well at all."

"Where could I find him, Ma'am?"

She gave him directions to another hospital a few blocks away, and he and Nathan set out to find him. "I wish that teamster had stayed here with the wagon. Hurry, Nathan!"

"Ah's nebbah seed sech big buildin's likes dis befo', Sa'gen'," as he looked from one side of the street to the other.

"Yes, I guess they would look big to you, Nathan, since you've never been in a city before. Hurry!"

"Dis here where Massa Lincum lives?"

"Yes, but he lives way over on the other side of town. I'm afraid we won't see him this time. Got to find the Colonel. Then we'll see if we can find that colored regiment for you to join later."

"Yu thinks we finds dat reg'men' here?"

"No, but maybe we can get you enlisted here and find out where they are."

The pink skies in the East signaled the rapid approach of day and the streets began to come alive. They hurried along, crossing intersections and weaving through horse-drawn carriages that were beginning to fill the road. Patrick was deeply concerned about Lou Ann. He increased his pace, as Nathan kept up with him. It wasn't long before they found the hospital where the Colonel was supposed to be working. They approached a soldier sitting at a small desk in the front foyer. Engrossed in a newspaper, he didn't seem to see them enter.

"Excuse me, Private," Pat said. "Could you tell me if a Colonel Sommers works here?"

"Oh, I didn't see you come in, Sergeant. A Colonel *who* did you say?"

"Sommers—he's a doctor."

"Oh! *That* Sommers. I didn't recognize the Colonel part. We call him 'Doc' around here. He prefers it that way."

"Is he here? It's an emergency!"

"He should be here any minute. Usually comes in right on time. About another fifteen minutes maybe."

"Thanks. We'll wait."

"Make yourself comfortable." He pointed to a long bench against the opposite wall and returned to reading his newspaper.

Nathan sat down, but Patrick paced back and forth, worried about Lou Ann. He removed the watch with its broken crystal from his pocket. Only five minutes had passed. "Should be here any minute—have to get this thing fixed some time."

After a few minutes, a tall, slender officer entered the front door. He posed a striking figure in his neatly pressed uniform adorned with shiny, brass buttons. He had a thin, black mustache, trimmed to perfection and a thick crop of black hair. "Good morning, Bill," he said to the private behind the desk, smiling as he did.

"Good morning, Doc. There's someone here to see you." He pointed over to Patrick, still pacing the floor.

"Yes, can I help you?"

Patrick felt intimidated, standing there in his ragged, dirty uniform. "Colonel Sommers, Sir?" he quickly asked, saluting.

Looking at the stripes beneath the dirt on Patrick's sleeve, the Colonel responded.

"Yes, Sergeant—you look as though you just came from the battlefield. Are you hurt?"

"No, Sir—it's—it's your daughter, Sir. She's sick. I think she has..."

The Colonel quickly interrupted. "Lou Ann? What's wrong? Where is she?" he asked excitedly.

"She's in another hospital."

"Where? Show me! Do you know the name of the hospital?"

"No, Sir. It's not far from here though."

"Let's go! You can tell me what happened on the way." He turned to the private. "I have an emergency—be back as soon as I can." The Colonel headed for the front door, as he took hold of Patrick's arm. Nathan followed. "Is he a friend of yours?" He nodded to Nathan, as they climbed aboard his carriage, parked in the front of the hospital.

"Yes, Sir. He helped Lou Ann and I escape the Rebs. Nathan's his name."

"She was *captured*? How? Where?" As Patrick thought of how to explain the whole ordeal, the Colonel continued. "What's wrong with her? Has she been hurt?"

"No, Sir. The nurse said she thought it might be pneumonia."

"Oh, dear God!" He snapped the reins harder. "What did you say your name was, Sergeant?"

"Patrick O'Hanrahan, Sir."

"Oh, you must be *the* Patrick Lou Ann spoke about last winter. She visited you in the hospital, didn't she?"

"Yes, Sir. She was very kind to me."

Soon they reached the hospital. "This is it!" Pat remarked.

The Colonel jumped down from the carriage, rushed up the stairs, and flung the doors open. Before they could catch up with him, he had already found a nurse to lead him to Lou Ann's bedside. They waited outside of her room, Patrick praying that the Colonel would have something hopeful to tell him about her condition.

The weather was hot for that time of year. It was stifling in the hospital. The smells and sights brought back memories for Patrick. It had only been a few short months since he had been wounded and hospitalized.

Nathan, who had been silent most of the time since their arrival in Washington, spoke up. "Ah sho' hopes dat gal gits better. Mebbe she done gits sick from dat nasty ole swamp we wuz in."

"I hope she does, too," Patrick responded, removing his hat to wipe the sweat from his forehead with his sleeve. "Let's get some air, Nathan." They walked outside and sat on the front steps. They didn't speak for a long time.

Nathan finally broke the silence. "Yu thinks ah cud find dat reg'men' ta jine up wif, Sa'gen'?"

"Soon, Nathan. Let's wait and see how Lou Ann is doing first. Then maybe the Colonel can help you find it."

They talked about their escape from the Rebels and how lucky they were to be free.

"I was praying to God a lot, and I even asked the Blessed Mother to put in a good word for us, too."

"Ah shorely done prayed to de good Lawd, too, 'specially when dat ole porch come crashin' down. Fo' a minute, ah done think mebbe yu was under it."

People were walking in and out of the hospital doors. "We'd better move over to the side here, Nathan." It seemed like hours to Pat before the Colonel finally appeared in the doorway. Jumping to his feet, he saluted.

"Don't bother with that now, Patrick. I want to thank you both for what you've done for my daughter. It must have been a harrowing experience for all of you."

Patrick felt privileged in a way—just being an enlisted man—that the Colonel had called him by his first name.

"I'm afraid Lou Ann is very sick," the Colonel continued. "I..." He seemed to become very emotional, as though he were trying to hold back tears. Straightening up, he lifted his chin as he regained his composure. "I don't know if she will make it."

Patrick felt weak in the knees. He had experienced fear many times on the battlefield, but this was a different kind of fear—fear of losing someone he had grown very fond of. "Is there anything you can do for her?"

"We're doing everything we can. Just pray that she makes it!"

Patrick felt the rosary in his pocket and began to pray silently in his heart. The Colonel turned to go back to Lou Ann's bedside, when Patrick suddenly remembered Nathan's request. "I hate to bother you at a time like this, Sir, but Nathan here," as he gestured toward him, "wants to join the Army. We heard there's a colored regiment forming somewhere."

"Yes, I believe they're from Massachusetts. Why don't you take a walk down to the Recruiting Office and they can work out the details there. Oh, and Patrick—come back here when you're done with that."

"Yes, Sir. I sure will."

The Colonel shook Nathan's hand, wished him good luck, and thanked him again for his efforts in helping Lou Ann. As he began to walk back through the hospital doors, Patrick spoke up. "Oh, Colonel,"—the officer turned back—"where *is* the recruiting office?"

"Oh, I forgot to give you directions. Too much on my mind, I guess." He pointed to the right. "Two blocks up to Sixteenth Street. Turn left. You'll see a sign over the door. Can't miss it."

The Recruiting Office was a small storefront with a large window on each side of a center door. There were posters with patriotic slogans on the windows and a large flag hung from a pole protruding out from the building. "Can I help you?" the sergeant behind the desk asked in a loud voice. He had quickly lowered his feet, which had been propped up on the desk and tucked his shirt into his pants. There was a strong odor of liquor about him.

"This man would like to sign up for the Army, Sergeant."

The recruiting sergeant looked puzzled for a moment. "Well, I'm sure we could use him, but…"

"But what, Sergeant?" Patrick asked.

"Well, I'm sure he can shoot a gun as well as any other man, but—well—I don't know where to send him. I mean—all the others were white."

Nathan wanted to speak for himself. "Ah heerd dere's a colored reg'men' gittin' ready ta fight dem Rebs an' ah wanna jine in de fight. Dey be from Mass…Mass… Wha' de Colonel say?"

"Massachusetts, Sergeant. Colonel Sommers over at the hospital told us they're from Massachusetts," Patrick offered.

"Oh, yeah! You're right, Sergeant," the recruiter answered. "I remember now. We *did* get information about that regiment. Well, I'll take care of it." He looked at Nathan and then continued. "We'll get you in uniform. You look healthy enough to me. It might take a few days, but we'll find that regiment for you. Now, I've got some papers for you to sign. Come sit over here," as he pulled a chair over to the side of the desk.

"Well, Nathan," Pat said, as he went over to shake his hand, "you'll be a credit to the Army. I know you'll make a good soldier."

Nathan beamed at the thought, a broad smile going across his face, as he took the seat pointed out to him.

Turning to the recruiter, Pat asked, "Do you have a piece of paper I can use?"

"Sure do." He pulled a small card from the desk drawer with his name on it. "You can use the back of this."

Patrick wrote his name and home address in New York on it and handed it to Nathan. "Write me a letter when this war is over. I'd like to hear from you."

"Ah caint write, Sa'gen'."

"Well, maybe you can learn before the end of the war, or you could have someone write it for you."

The recruiter looked over at Patrick. "I guess he will have to sign the papers with an "X"."

"Whatever it takes, Sergeant. This man wants to fight!"

"We'll take good care of him. Don't you worry. Oh, by the way—what's *your* outfit?"

"Sixty-ninth New York Volunteers."

"Heard a lot about you boys. Keep up the good work!"

Patrick shook Nathan's hand once again. "Good luck, Nathan."

"May de good Lawd looks aftah yu, Sa'gen'."

"You too, Nathan," as he started for the door.

"Good luck, Sergeant," the recruiter said, as he sat down on his chair behind the desk to speak to Nathan sitting alongside. "Now, you'll start out as a private in this man's army, so get used to being called 'Private'." Nathan beamed. He was on his way to fight the good fight.

As Patrick opened the door to Lou Ann's room, he found the Colonel bending over her applying cold cloths to her forehead. Her eyes were closed, and she seemed to be asleep.

"Come in, Patrick," said the Colonel, as though speaking to an old friend.

"How is she doing, Sir?"

"About the same. Did get her fever down a bit. Still drifting in and out of consciousness, though. She really needs rest."

Pat looked at Lou Ann, her face gaunt and pale, with dark circles under her eyes. The two soldiers sat in her room, Patrick praying silently and the Colonel constantly changing the cold cloths on her forehead. The afternoon wore on, daylight became dimmer, and the room darkened. The Colonel lit a candle by the bedside, and the prospect of Lou Ann's life slipping away overwhelmed Patrick. He lowered his head into his hands and began to sob.

"That's all right, Patrick. Don't be ashamed. I know how you feel." The Colonel handed him a clean, white handkerchief. "Why don't you go and clean up? There's a washroom at the end of the hall. I'll send over to the supply room for a clean uniform for you." Patrick suddenly realized how unsightly and dirty he was. He had been so concerned about Lou Ann, he had forgotten all about himself.

Patrick returned to the room, feeling better after washing up. A while later, a private arrived with a clean uniform for him. He discarded the dirty, old, torn one that had carried him through the battle of Chancellorsville and the murky swamps of Virginia. Looking at the sleeves of the new jacket, he noticed there were no stripes.

"You can have your sergeant stripes sewn on later," the Colonel remarked. "By the way, when did you eat last?"

"Oh, I had a little something on the boat last night, just before we arrived here."

"Come on, Patrick. There isn't much more we can do here right now. We'll get something to eat. Just one minute—let me get a nurse to come in and stay with Lou Ann."

The lavish surroundings of the restaurant reminded Patrick of the Willard Hotel, where he and Lou Ann had celebrated New Year's Eve together.

"Table for two, gentlemen?" The headwaiter's bright red vest covered his white shirt, a blue bow tie matching his blue striped pants. As they followed him to their table, Patrick felt uncomfortable, even slightly inferior, as he gazed around at the plush blue carpet, gold-trimmed drapes, and finely dressed clientele.

The Colonel wanted to know all about Patrick and his involvement with Lou Ann. They talked while Patrick enjoyed the fine food and beer. After telling the Colonel all the details beginning with their first meeting at the field hospital, he ordered another beer and relaxed in his chair. He had a few questions of his own. "Lou Ann told me you were a doctor, Sir, but I didn't know you were an Army Surgeon."

"I'm surprised that she told you *that* much. I mean—you *do* know something about her activities, don't you?"

"I found out she was a spy."

"Sh-h-h! Someone might hear you."

"Sorry, Sir. Didn't realize I was so loud."

"I never wanted her in that business in the first place—not a job for a woman. It's my fault, though."

"How's that, Sir?"

Leaning across the table, the Colonel spoke very softly. "Oh, I introduced her to a friend of mine once—a Mr. Pinkerton. He does intelligence work for the Army. She thought it sounded exciting, and he thought that she would make an excellent agent, as she likes to call herself. You know, normally the enemy wouldn't expect a young woman of anything. I'm so sorry they met. She wouldn't listen to me, and now... I don't know if she'll recover." He stared blankly at the glowing candle under the frosted glass globe in the middle of the table.

"Well, Sir, I thought she was"— he lowered his voice still more—"an agent for the Rebs at first."

The Colonel chuckled. "That's a good one, Sergeant! She's a Yankee through and through! Best female patriot I've ever seen! But that's all over now. Hopefully, when she recovers, she will find a more lady-like occupation."

"Well, Sir, I guess she would have to get out of that business—I mean— the Rebs know who she is now. How did she..." He cut himself off, not wanting to ask the Colonel about details of her work.

"How did she what, Patrick?"

"Oh, it's none of my business, Sir."

"No, it's okay—go ahead."

"Well, I was just going to say—you see, this has been troubling me for some time now—how did she get that vase with the initials CSA on it?"

"Flower vase?"

"Yes, she brought me a little white vase with some lilacs in it when I was in the hospital." He looked questioningly at the Colonel.

"Patrick, you're a very observing young man. That's nothing—I brought back a few souvenirs from the Peninsular Campaign. In fact, it sounds like that same vase I gave her mother when I returned."

"Oh, what a relief!"

After a few more drinks, the Colonel set his glass down and lit up a cigar. "Lou Ann came to my wife and I when she was eight years old. Her father was a friend of mine; we fought in the Mexican War together. He was killed. Her mother died a short while later, some say of a broken heart. Lou Ann spent a few years in an orphanage. Then, shortly after the war ended, we decided to adopt her. We wanted to give her a good home. She's been a great joy in our life—we have no other children. Funny... she always had this thing for Army men. I mean, I think the uniform reminded her of her father. Would you believe she even mentioned to me once that she thought she'd like to be a soldier?"

"Well, Sir, she *has* been a soldier in a manner of speaking. I mean, she has risked her life in the duty of her country. Isn't that what all soldiers do?"

"You're a smart lad, Patrick. You're absolutely right!"

"But, Sir—you mentioned an orphanage? I—I—don't think she ever mentioned that she was an orphan!"

"Well, you know, she looks on *us* as her real parents. She was only a few years old when she went into the orphanage."

"Yes, of course. I understand."

"However, she used to speak quite often of her admiration for a Sister Agnes Mary and the other good nuns—they kind-of were her only family for a few years. And there was a time right before the war that she felt that she wanted to devote her *own* life to caring for orphans. The beauty and the gift of love the sisters had there made quite a strong impact on her. And that's why my wife and I were *so* surprised when she came home one night and announced she was going to become an actress. Then the war came along and she met Mr. Pinkerton and—well, you know the rest."

"Yes, Sir."

"I was young once, too, Patrick, and I—I realize how young people experiment until they find their way. I'm not sure if Lou Ann even realizes who she is or what she wants yet!"

Pat smiled. "Well, you know, Sir, I know she's got a big heart. I've seen her working with the wounded, myself included."

"But for now, she needs us. We'd better get back and see how she's doing." The Colonel pulled out a roll of money from his pocket and asked the waiter for the check. "This is on me, Sergeant. And—oh—by the way—not a word of this to *anyone!* If Lou Ann had such confidence in you, that's good enough for me!"

"Thank you, Sir. You have my word."

When they returned to Lou Ann's room, she was awake. The nurse was attempting to feed her without much success. Lou Ann seemed to light up for a moment as they entered the room. In a weak but audible voice, she said, "My two favorite men!", as she extended her hand out to greet them. Patrick could see that she was becoming weaker and feared she was getting worse. "I can't thank you enough for rescuing me, Patrick." She stopped to take a breath, which seemed to be becoming increasingly more difficult for her. "I think I would have been in a Rebel prison by now if it wasn't for you." She glanced around the room. "Where's Nathan? Did he make it?" she asked in a concerned voice.

"Yes, he's fine—went off to join the Army."

"Oh, I'm so glad! I know how much he wanted that."

Colonel Sommers felt her forehead and took her pulse. "You're doing fine, darling. Try a little of this," as he held a glass of water to her lips. She drank a little and lay back down. Just sitting up briefly seemed to exhaust her. The nurse left the room, and the two men sat down in chairs on the opposite sides of her bed. "Now don't try to talk, darling. Just rest." She became quiet and drifted off into a restless sleep. Occasionally, she uttered some incoherent words.

The Colonel dozed off in his chair. Patrick held Lou Ann's hand and prayed his rosary. In the late evening, the Colonel woke up and jumped to his feet. "What time is it?" He quickly pulled his watch from his pocket. "Oh, my gosh! I have to check on my patients—I can be back in a couple of hours." Heading for the door, he briefly looked back at Patrick. "Can you stay with her, Patrick?"

"Yes, Sir. I plan to stay the night."

"Thank you, lad. It means a lot to me to have someone with her." He left, quietly closing the door behind him.

Pat wondered if the Colonel had told his wife about Lou Ann. Maybe he telegraphed her. Then he remembered that Lou Ann had told him her mother lived in Gettysburg. Had she mentioned that her mother had a heart ailment? He couldn't quite remember. Too tired. Let the Colonel take care of that. He laid his head back on the chair and slept lightly, waking occasionally and checking on Lou Ann throughout the night.

During the following week, day melted into night and night into day. The Colonel and Patrick took shifts, watching over her. The fever continued to remain high. She tossed and turned, muttering meaningless phrases. Patrick struggled to understand what she was saying, but to no avail. He ate very little and prayed a lot.

On one of his brief breaks to get some fresh air, he walked around the block. There were a few poor shanties with ragged looking children playing in the yards. He saw himself in *his* poor youth. In the front yard of one of the dilapidated houses, he spotted a small lilac bush. He asked the child playing there if he could have a small branch. The little girl never spoke, but ran over and broke off a sprig. Smiling, she held it out to him. Reaching into his pocket, he handed her a nickel. She ran away, giggling and clutching her prize close to her chest, as though she had just inherited a fortune.

Patrick found a small vase and placed the lilac on Lou Ann's nightstand. Each day, he gave it fresh water, and each day he walked around the block, and each day he gave the raggedy-looking little girl a nickel for another lilac sprig until he had a full bouquet in the vase for Lou Ann.

He continued his vigil at her bedside night after night, fighting sleep and fingering his beads constantly for her recovery. The flickering candle illuminated her face, and he felt his heart drawn to her more closely than ever. "Oh, Saint Michael, help her!" His grandmother had taught him the prayer to Saint Michael following the rosary when he was a small boy, telling him of the Saint's patronage for all policemen, firemen, and soldiers. He had said it many times before battle, and now he was saying it for Lou Ann, for she, too, was a soldier. "*Saint Michael, the Archangel, defend us in battle. Be our protection against the wickedness and snares of the devil. May God rebuke him, we humbly pray; and do thou, oh Prince of the Heavenly Host, by the power of God, thrust into hell Satan and all the other evil spirits who prowl about the world seeking the ruin of souls. Amen.*"

"Is that you, Patrick?" Her voice was weak, the words slowly emanating from her dry, parched lips.

"Yes, I'm right here, Lou Ann." A faint smile from her gaunt looking face raised his hopes. He rose from his chair to kiss her on the forehead—the fever had broken. He knew she was out of danger. Tears trickled down his cheeks, as he thanked God.

"I'm thirsty."

Patrick held her head up, as he lifted a glass of water to her lips. "You're going to be fine," he said, his voice quivering slightly with emotion.

She seemed to become more aware of her surroundings as she glanced around the room. "Where's Daddy?"

"Oh, he's making his rounds. He should be back soon."

Her eyes fell upon the little lilac bouquet on the nightstand. "Oh, Patrick! They're beautiful!" She held out her arms to embrace him. He bent over and held her close.

Lou Ann made a quick recovery and was sitting up and eating within a few days. She was over the crisis, and Pat assisted her in walking each day as she gained her strength back. They talked a lot—about their escape from the Rebels, about her illness, about her father who was so important in her life. Pat was very careful not to mention her work as an "agent", not wanting to upset her.

"Hi darling. How's my girl?" the Colonel remarked, as he entered the room. He had brought Lou Ann a large bouquet of red roses and placed them on the small table next to the lilacs, dwarfing them.

"Oh, how beautiful! Thank you, Daddy." He bent over and kissed her on the cheek.

Turning to Patrick, he said, "Well, son, I guess you'll be wanting to get back with your regiment soon."

"Yes, Sir—I just wanted to stay until Lou Ann got better."

"Oh, Daddy! *Must* he go back right away?"

He didn't respond to her question. "You're a good man, Patrick. I don't know what I'd have done if you hadn't been here during this critical time."

"Well, Sir, it was the *least* I could do for her. She helped me when I was down." He looked over at Lou Ann and smiled.

"Do you *have* to leave now? Can't you stay a while longer?"

Before he had a chance to answer, the Colonel interrupted. "Patrick, would you be interested in duty right here in Washington?"

Patrick hesitated. "Well, Sir—I'm not sure what you mean."

"Well, you know, son, I *do* have some influence in these matters, and I believe I could have you assigned here permanently."

Pat looked at the Colonel, then glanced over at Lou Ann, now sitting up in bed. He didn't know what to say.

"Oh, Patrick! That would be wonderful! You'd be safer here, and we could see more of each other."

"Could I give you an answer tomorrow, Sir? I want to think a little about your generous offer."

The Colonel looked puzzled, as though he was expecting Patrick to jump at his offer. "Well, I think you're wise not to make a hasty decision. Tomorrow will be fine."

Patrick had been sleeping on a cot in the supply room for the past few nights, since Lou Ann's crisis had passed. This night, he couldn't sleep, thinking of the Colonel's offer. It was what many soldiers would dream about. Out of harm's way. Maybe he could even have Beth come and visit him—or maybe not! How did I get in this fix? The longer he had been away from Beth, the more distant she seemed. Lou Ann kept popping up in front of him. *She* was present—Beth was past. Or *was* she? He knew Beth would be worried. No communication since his capture. Must write to her and let her know I'm alive. He felt guilty. Why hadn't he written her upon his return to Washington? Too consumed with Lou Ann's sickness. His thoughts turned to Danny— lost a leg. The Big Swede—lost his life! Many others crippled or dead. But the fighting continues. Lost many battles—maybe it would be different next time. Maybe the tide would turn. He had come this far. He couldn't see himself as an errand boy in Washington while his comrades were out there doing battle. A member of the Fighting 69th!—a paper shuffler in Washington? No, sir! His spirits were up. He would fight. That's what he signed up for and he would carry it through to the end. Victory *or* defeat! He would be a part of it! At least he could say he did his part. If he took the Colonel's offer, he felt that he would be letting his fallen comrades down. He would go back, get a rifle, load it, and shoot every damn Rebel he could find until that God-forsaken contest was finished! He had decided.

He woke up early the next morning, left a note for Lou Ann next to the lilacs, expressing his joy that she was better and hoping that he would see her again. He remembered she didn't like long goodbyes. He thanked the Colonel for his offer and walked back to War.

CHAPTER 13

▼

ENEMY IN THE NORTH

Patrick didn't have to travel far to catch up with the Army. They were encamped in a little town called Fairfax Court House, not far from Washington.

"Well, Sergeant! Good to see you again. And where might you have been?" the captain said with a sarcastic tone in his voice.

"I was captured by the Rebs, Sir."

"Oh, captured by the Rebs, eh? And how did you come by that brand new uniform?"

"Well, Sir, they gave it to me in Washington."

"Washington!" the captain blurted out in a loud voice.

"Yes, Sir. I wound up there after I escaped."

"Oh! You escaped and went all the way to Washington, did ya?"

"Yes, Sir."

"And why would you be going there instead of reporting back to your outfit? You don't appear to be wounded."

"Well, Sir..." He hesitated, thinking that the captain wouldn't believe the whole truth. "You see, Sir—I was sick."

"What was wrong with you?"

"I had a high fever—almost got pneumonia. They took me to a hospital there."

"Who's *they*?"

"Oh, the supply train, Sir. They picked me up on the road."

"Now let me get this straight. First, you were captured. Then, you escaped and found a supply train that took you to Washington—is that right?"

"Yes, Sir." He remembered his promise to Colonel Sommers not to mention Lou Ann and her "activities". Besides, the captain would never believe him.

"I suppose you're going to tell me next that old Abe Lincoln took you out for a ride in his carriage down Pennsylvania Avenue while you were there."

"Not exactly, Sir." Pat knew he had said the wrong thing as soon as the words escaped his lips.

"What do you mean... not exactly?"

"I *did* see him pass by in his carriage, Sir. I mean—when I was up there in the hospital after Fredericksburg."

"Oh, yes! You were wounded then, I remember." His tone mellowed. He went on, "Well, Sergeant, if I didn't know you better, I'd be thinking you got hold of some bad liquor or you're the best damn storyteller in this man's Army!"

"Yes, Sir."

"I guess you wouldn't be back here now if you had skedaddled; and besides, I got a good report on you when you took over and led the company into battle for the wounded lieutenant at Chancellorsville."

"Yes, Sir."

"Now get out of here and back to your company. The regiment is down to one hundred and fifty men, and we need every man we can get. The old Grey Fox is moving north, and we have to catch him this time."

"Yes, Sir... this time for sure!" Patrick saluted, did an about-face, and left the captain's quarters. He thought about the captain's words. Only one hundred fifty men left—started with a thousand. Lost many at Fredericksburg—so many good men. One hundred fifty left—can't believe it!

He rejoined his company. It was June and getting hotter each day. There wasn't time to set up permanent camp. The Army was on the move. He was re-supplied with a canteen, haversack, a few days supply of hardtack, and, most importantly, rifle and ammunition. He didn't know what lie ahead, but he felt good. This was *his* place for this time. From the time he was a small boy, he took his little jobs seriously—delivering laundry for his mother, selling newspapers on the corner, and working at Mr. Schuler's Meat Market. Now his duty was to be the best soldier he could be. He got into step with his fellow Yanks and marched north to meet the enemy.

"Hey, Sarge! Looks like we're headin' toward home!" hollered one of the men, chuckling.

"Well, let's hope we don't have to chase Johnny Reb *that* far!"

"Heard the Rebs are marching all the way to Pennsylvania."

"That's fine with me. We'll give 'em a nice, warm reception!" Pat grinned.

He hadn't marched with his Regiment since he had been captured. As he glanced over the heads of the troops, he missed seeing the Big Swede's head sticking up like a sore thumb over the rest. Can't believe he's gone, Pat thought. Have to visit his Mom when I get home.

The back-and-forth remarks of the men continued for a while, as they marched in the heat along the dusty roads. They soon became quiet, and the only sounds that could be heard were the tramping of feet and the metal canteens clanging against their rifles. They drank the warm water from their canteens. On some occasions, when crossing streams, they would refill them with the cold, refreshing liquid. Some men dropped by the wayside from exhaustion, only to straggle into camp at the end of the day.

Marching north, Patrick thought. Seemed strange to him. Most of the time the Army had moved South to confront the enemy on its own soil. This time, it appeared that they would be defending their homeland. Now, he could understand, in a way, how the Rebels must feel when the Yankees occupy *their* land. Oh, well, what difference does it make? Have to fight them—North *or* South. Their Army must be defeated.

After a long march, they halted to rest and eat. Patrick's mail caught up with him—two letters from Beth and one from his grandparents. Beth had written the first one a month earlier.

My dearest Patrick,

I think of you every day. I storm Heaven with prayer for your safety every night. I just know that our merciful Lord will protect you and bring you home safely to me.

My mother is doing better now, and I am still working at the dress shop. I visited your mother and grandparents the other day, and they are doing fine.

I haven't received a letter from you recently. Please write to me when you can. I know it must be difficult for you to find the time.

I love you very much and long for the day you shall return to me.

Love always and forever,

Beth

In the second letter, Beth was very much concerned, as she still hadn't heard from him. Pat felt a tinge of guilt that he hadn't written sooner— maybe in Washington he could have taken the time. He quickly sat down in his tent and wrote a long letter back to her. He explained his capture and escape—not mentioning Lou Ann. He wondered deep down in his heart if he still wanted to marry Beth; however, her letter seemed to reawaken some of those old feelings. Could he ever end it with Lou Ann? He became more confused.

The Army was on the move once again, still heading north. The chatter between the men helped relieve the boredom of the long march, Pat thought. "Where we headin' *this* time?" one Yank hollered.

"Maybe New York City!" yelled another.

Patrick joined in. "If only we could get the Rebs into Hell's Kitchen— that would finish them off!" Laughter arose from the ranks, as they were all from New York City and knew what he meant.

As the Men in Blue marched under the scorching hot sun, dark clouds began to form in the skies ahead of them. Eventually, they were caught in a torrential downpour— a welcome relief! The fields and roads ahead of them were covered by ground fog, created by the cool rain clashing with the hot, parched soil. Silence enveloped their ranks, as they passed by the old Bull Run battlefield. The rain had washed the soil away from many graves. Pat had a feeling of revulsion as he looked at the hastily dug, shallow graves, bones and skulls protruding from them. The ground fog swirled around them, as if their spirits were crying out for justice. He felt his blood run cold.

The long blue line crawled slowly to the north, seeking the old Grey Fox and his rebellious brothers. Pat knew it was just a matter of time before the Army would once again collide with Johnny Reb. His suspicions were confirmed when they reached Taneytown, where he learned that the First and Eleventh Corps had engaged the Rebels in battle up the road in another small town called Gettysburg. Further news didn't sound good—the Yanks had been driven back through the town by the Confederates. Patrick remembered Lou Ann telling him that her folks had a home there. Hope Lou Ann isn't there now. No, she's probably still sick in the hospital in Washington. Every time he had resolved to forget her, she either came back into his life or something would remind him of her.

He sat by the fire after eating and welcomed a fresh cup of coffee that their cook had just made.

"Looks like a big battle coming up, Sergeant," one of the new recruits remarked, suddenly appearing on the opposite side of the fire.

"It's already started," Pat said, lifting the cup to his lips and letting the warm coffee slide down his dry throat. "This your first one, Private?"

"Yes, Sergeant. Hope I can stand up to it."

"Don't feel alone, lad. We all feel the same way. Some of us just keep it inside more."

"You mean, you fellas that seen the elephant before gets just as scared as us new boys?"

"Oh, yes. Well, maybe after a few battles, we just learn to control it more. But I'll tell you one thing—after you start firing that rifle, you only think about what you're doing—you know—it becomes work. You'll be fine, lad. Put your trust in God and pray. I always say the prayer to St. Michael. He's the patron saint of soldiers, you know, and he's got me *this* far!"

"Would ya—I mean—could ya teach it to me?"

"Sure lad. I'd be glad to. In fact, I'll write it down on a piece of paper so you can memorize it."

Pat picked up a partially burned paper near the fire, brushed off the singed charcoal from the edges, and wrote the prayer.

"Thanks, Sergeant," the private said, holding the prayer in front of him, as though studying it, while he walked away.

"Oh, Private, what company are you with? Never saw you before."

The private glanced back. "Company B—came in last night from Washington."

Patrick lay back on the ground, hoping to get some rest before the impending battle. He was just starting to fall asleep, when he heard someone speaking his name.

"Sergeant O'Hanrahan?"

Patrick lifted himself up on one elbow and squinted his eyes, looking up at the figure standing over him.

"Yeah, that's me."

"The captain wants to see you." Pat stood up to see the young officer, standing there with his arms folded in front of him. "Follow me." The officer walked briskly along, and Patrick followed him, while tucking in his shirt and brushing the dirt from his uniform.

What could the captain want with me? Hope it's not about my absence, he thought. A few minutes later, they arrived at the captain's tent. The young officer held the tent flap open for Patrick. "He's expecting you. Go on in."

Patrick approached the captain, sitting behind a small desk. A candle reflected bigger-than-life shadows on the tent wall. He saluted. "Sergeant O'Hanrahan, Sir."

"Can you ride a horse, Sergeant?"

"Yes, Sir, I can."

"Got an important job for you, Sergeant."

"Yes, Sir."

"One of my messengers is out of commission. I'm sending a message to Emmitsburg. Some of the high command is still there. There *is* another rider taking the same message, same destination—just in case. After you deliver the message, wait for a response and bring it back immediately. The lieutenant has a horse ready to go. Good luck, Sergeant."

"Yes, Sir." Pat stepped out of the captain's tent and saw the lieutenant holding the reins of the horse for him.

"The road to Emmitsburg is *that* way, Sergeant," as he pointed to a small, dirt road leading west of town. "You should make it there in less than an hour if you push this old nag. Did the captain tell you there's another rider taking the same message?"

"Yes, Sir, he did." Patrick mounted the horse and tucked the message securely inside of his shirt.

"Well, he left here about fifteen minutes ago. He'll probably arrive there before you, but deliver the message anyway. They will send a response back with you. The captain doesn't want to take any chances."

"Yes, Sir, the captain explained that to me."

"Good luck, Sergeant. You shouldn't have any trouble with the Rebs. We're not in Virginia now. Don't think there's any Reb patrols in the area."

"Yes, Sir. Hope you're right."

"Remember… no delays. Don't stop for anything. Now, off with you," as the lieutenant slapped the horse's rear end. Patrick kicked the horse in the ribs and galloped down the road.

The animal would often slow down, and Patrick would periodically spur him on to go faster. It was a warm, summer night. The rushing night air, streaming past his sweaty brow, was refreshing. Pat welcomed the silence enveloping him. Every place he had been, there had been noise of some kind—noise on the march, noise in the camp, noise in the hospital—and the murderous noise of battle. He thought of the silence he had enjoyed on his few treks into the woods when he was encamped at Fredericksburg. He slowed the horse to a walk on a few occasions, hoping to rejuvenate the old nag, thinking that he might not make it if he pushed too hard. For a brief time, he listened to the crickets chirping away and the night swallows singing their nocturnal refrains. How welcome these sounds were to his ears. It was such a vast difference from the screams of the dying, the burst of cannonballs, and the sharp crackle of musket fire. He drank in the peaceful sounds for the short time that he had, but the tall dark trees lining the road looked foreboding. Hope there's no Rebs in there. Wouldn't stand a chance if ambushed. Couldn't get far on this old nag. If only we hadn't lost so many horses in battle.

He eventually arrived in Emmitsburg. As he came up the road, he saw a church steeple. Upon getting closer, he noticed a few large tents pitched in the churchyard surrounded by many gravestones.

"Halt! Who goes there?" a guard hollered out.

"Sergeant O'Hanrahan. I have a message for your commanding officer from the New York 69th."

"Get down and step over here so I can see you better." He approached Patrick with a lantern in one hand and a rifle in the other. Pat dismounted and stood next to the horse. "Where's the message?" as he held the lantern up to Patrick's face.

Pat reached into his shirt and pulled out the message but didn't give it to the guard.

"Well, let's have it, Sergeant!"

"Have to give it to your commanding officer in person."

"Well, now, Sergeant, you don't be trustin' me now, do ya."

"Orders. My orders are to hand-deliver it to your commanding officer."

"Well, I guess that can be arranged." He led Patrick over to the Command Headquarters tent. There were two officers, a colonel and a captain, bent over a table, studying a map. A lantern hung from the tent pole. The colonel was clenching a small stub of a cigar in his teeth, which looked like it was no longer lit.

"Come in, son—come in," the colonel said, as he turned to greet Patrick. "What have you got for me?"

"A message from my captain, Sir. 69th New York volunteers." He handed it to the colonel, who quickly opened it and handed it to the captain.

The colonel appeared to be deep in thought, as he shifted the cold cigar from one side of his mouth to the other. "You're dismissed, Sergeant, but don't go far. We'll have a message for you to take back—maybe in an hour or so."

"Yes, Sir. Is the church open, Sir?"

"Oh, I see you're a man of the faith. That's good. Yes, Sergeant, the priest has been leaving it open all night for the troops. We'll send for you when we're ready. And—oh, Sergeant—say a prayer for our boys, if you would."

"Yes, Sir, I will. Thank you, Sir." He saluted and walked out into the warm, night air. The grounds around the church were strewn with the litter from thousands of soldiers from the 1st and 11th Corps who had camped there the previous night. Pat wondered how many had been killed in Gettysburg that day. Troops driven back through the town—doesn't sound good. He walked by the many tombstones in the front yard of the church, up the stairs, and entered through the front doors, which were wide open. He looked around and found that he was the only person there.

As he walked quietly up the middle aisle, he saw many candles on either side of the altar, lighting up the darkened church. A large Crucifix hung over the altar. To the left side, was a life-size statue of the Blessed Mother. Many flowers had been placed at her feet. To the right stood a large statue of Saint Joseph holding the Christ Child. Patrick genuflected, making the Sign of the Cross, and entered into a pew about halfway up the aisle. He knelt and gazed at the large Crucifix, pondering the Man that was nailed to it. An image of the man that he had impaled on the tree flashed before him. The guilt that he had in the beginning of the war had gradually lessened through time and battles. What did the Priest say? Self-defense. Yes—that was it. Self-defense. Again, he knew it was he or the enemy who would die. He had grown a soldier's heart.

Three little nuns moved silently up the center aisle, kneeling in the front pew before the statue of the Blessed Virgin. They took the large rosary beads that hung at their sides and began to pray in hushed tones but loud enough for Patrick to hear. He quietly removed his rosary from his pocket and began to pray along with them. As he passed the beads through his fingers, he dwelt on the Sorrowful Mysteries of Our Lord's Passion and Death. In his mind, he seemed to understand and relate Jesus' suffering to the thousands of suffering souls he had seen dying on the battlefields. He became overcome with sadness, covered his face with his hands, and wept. He knew in his heart that the suffering he had seen all around him was for the greater good of all mankind, just as the suffering of Jesus had to happen for the salvation of men's souls. The three little nuns finished praying the Sorrowful Mysteries and began to recite the Glorious Mysteries. It was a hot, muggy night, lacking even the slightest breeze. As they began to say the Our Father, a strong wind suddenly blew through the open windows. Patrick was startled for a moment. It lasted but a few seconds, passing through the windows on the other side of the church and out into the black night. When it had passed, all of the lighted candles had been extinguished except one—the one illuminating the Virgin's statue. Why would that be? Another mystery? God surely controls the winds and all of nature. He didn't believe that the wind just blew in by chance, on a windless night. He couldn't help but gaze at the only illumined object... Jesus' Mother. And *mine*, he thought—my heavenly Mother—the one I *know* loves me. He pondered this Mother standing at the foot of the Cross. The suffering in Her heart, he thought, was most certainly joined to the Heart of her Son and hammered to the tree with every blow of the executioner's mallet.

He tried to focus on the Glorious Mysteries and closed his eyes to meditate on the first of these, Jesus' Resurrection from the Dead. This seemed to provide comfort for him, as he thought of his dead comrades.

The nuns had finished praying, and the church became totally silent. Patrick meditated on his faith in the stillness of the darkened church. One of the nuns stood up and walked over to the lit candle, picked up a tapir, and proceeded to relight those which had gone out. Patrick got up, walked back down the center aisle, dipped his hand into the holy water fount, blessed himself, and quietly exited the church. He sat down on the front steps, gazing around at the tombstones surrounding the church. He could barely make out the names engraved on them. Two lanterns hung on either side of the front door, casting a dim light upon the final resting place of the many souls. What a wonderful place to be buried, he thought—on the grounds of the church. Getting up, he descended the steps to have a closer look. He could then see more clearly the first name on one of the tombstones bordering the path near the church. The neatly carved letters spelled "Joshua". The last name was concealed in the shadow from another tombstone. The marker was very old and weathered, but Patrick could still make out the dates, which were from the 1700's. Returning to the steps, he sat again. He was growing weary from the heat, and opened the buttons at the top of his uniform. Removing the canteen from his belt, he poured water over his head, hoping it would help him to stay awake. He leaned back on the steps and became drowsy, as he waited for the colonel's message. His mind began to wander, remembering his boyhood pal.

CHAPTER 14

▼

JOSHUA

It was a sad day when the young redheaded boy learned that his family was leaving New York City to move down south to Virginia. "Do they have snow down there?" he asked his father.

"No, Joshua. I'm afraid they don't get much at all."

"I don't want to leave my friends. I like it here. I won't know anyone down there."

"You'll make new friends. And, besides, you'll have longer summers where we're going.

"I don't care! I'll miss Patrick and all my friends at school—and—and—snowball wars!" He ran to his bedroom, sobbing, and slammed the door.

The first few months didn't go too well for Joshua. He was uncomfortable and felt out of place. Some of the children in his new school thought that he talked "funny" and called him "Yankee-boy". Like many young boys, he lashed back and became involved in a few fights. He did, however, take his punishment well, staying after school when disciplined by his teacher. After a short while, things did improve for him. Winning most of the fights, the name-calling stopped; and he ultimately gained respect from the other children.

The family had taken up residence in the small town of Perch, Virginia in order to be near the tobacco fields. The father, Saul, worked for a large tobacco manufacturing company and had been transferred south as a buyer for the firm. He became familiar with the farmers as he made his rounds, inspecting their crops and sometimes advising them about new techniques for growing and curing their tobacco. When Joshua turned twelve, his father began to take him along to the farms, plantations, and, at times, to the auction warehouses. At first, he didn't want to go; but after a few trips, he found himself enjoying this change in his schedule.

There hadn't been much for him to do in his new little town with his small circle of friends. The excitement and busy streets of New York City, with its crowds of people and noisy traffic, were behind him now. He soon discovered that he could make new friends wherever he'd go.

In the beginning, his father tried to teach him about tobacco. "Now, Joshua, this is what you have to look for," as he would hold a tobacco leaf in his hands, explaining all about its color and texture, prompting his son to kneel in the hot soil to study it with him. Then, on to the curing barns they would go, where the leaves were strung in bunches called "hands" and hung over five-foot poles to dry, as the sawdust fire circulated hot air throughout the barn.

Joshua's attention span wasn't too long; and when his father would become involved in conversation with an owner, he would dash out of the barn and find other children to play with. Most of the time, the farmers' children were available for games. On Sundays, the blacks were allowed to join in, their field duties being excused for the day.

On the few plantations where no children lived, Joshua found himself in the barn with the horses. Over time, he developed a great fondness for them. His trips with his father had always been in a rickety, horse-drawn wagon. Their horse, being old, was not good for riding. He envied some of the young boys who had nice riding horses of their own. His father had told him that he couldn't afford to replace Julie; besides, she was like a member of the family.

As Joshua entered his teen years, he looked for work. He had finished grade school; that was all the schooling he could get. Higher learning was only for the rich. He was determined to find any job and save his money to buy his own horse, but soon discovered that jobs were scarce. The large plantation owners had all the help they needed from their slaves. The poor farmers couldn't afford to pay hired hands. After months of searching, he gave up on looking to the farmers for work.

His parents' little two-bedroom, wood-frame house was located a mile from town. Josh often walked the dirt road to buy groceries for his mother. She suffered with arthritis and only left the house on Sundays to attend her Christian church services. Rarely, she would visit with the other ladies at the social functions, which followed the service. Joshua's father, however, being Jewish, did not accompany her on these occasions.

Joshua sat down on the wooden steps of the General Store to take advantage of the shade for a moment. His mile walk in the hot, noonday sun had made him tired and thirsty. He was attempting to work up enough nerve to talk to pretty Jenny Logan, who worked the store with her father.

In the stillness of the summer afternoon, he heard heavy footsteps approaching on the wooden sidewalk. He turned to see Old Man Sykes, the owner of the livery stable. He always wore the same, soiled, wide-brimmed hat and blue denim overalls that looked as though they hadn't been washed in years. His gray beard was long and straggly and spotted with tobacco juice, which he would let "fly" in all directions. "Whatcha all doin' there, son?" He forcefully propelled a wad of the brown liquid from the side of his mouth. It streaked by Joshua's ear, hitting the ground just in front of his feet and creating a small crater, displacing a small cloud of dust as it did. Joshua quickly moved his position a few feet to the left, hoping to get out of the "line of fire" from Sykes' future bombardments.

"Oh, hello Mr. Sykes. Just doing an errand for my mother."

"Ya wanna make twenty-five cents?"

"Yes, sir, I'd like that," Joshua said, a smile coming over his face.

"Come with me," said Sykes, as he began to walk back toward his livery stable. Joshua quickly got to his feet and followed him at a short distance, watching for any stray tobacco-plug missiles that might out-flank him. "Need someone ta keep an eye on the place fer an hour or so."

Joshua was delighted to see several horses, each in its own individual stall. Heavy-looking beams of wood held up the high roof, and a second floor covering half of the barn was piled with mounds of hay. A small room to the right of the entrance appeared to be an office.

"Now, ya don't hafta do anything," Sykes said. "Just keep an eye on things. If anybody comes lookin' fer me, just tell 'em ta come back in an hour or so."

"Yes, Sir. Can I pet the horses?"

Stopping briefly and turning back toward Joshua, Sykes said, "Yeah, but don't stand behind 'em... ya never know when they might get a hankerin ta kick ya! And—oh!—what's yer name, son?"

"Joshua, Sir."

"Well, Joshua, when I get back, if ya do a good job, I'll let ya feed 'em."

"Thank you, Mr. Sykes. I'd like that." He immediately went to inspect and pet all of the horses. He patted each one on the nose and talked to them as though they were people. He felt important, being in charge—for a short while, anyway. His brief tenure of being boss-man ended all too soon, when Sykes returned.

"That was fast, Mr. Sykes."

"Hour and a half, son."

"Gee, seemed like ten minutes to me!" Joshua was standing in one of the stalls, rubbing his hand down the horse's neck.

"You like Buttercup, son?"

"Oh, I didn't know her name. Yeah, she's a beauty!"

"Fine mare she is. Belongs ta the sheriff. Pays me good money ta take care of her."

"You mean, these horses aren't yours?"

"Only Blackjack over there," as he pointed to a stall in the corner that Joshua had somehow overlooked. "The rest are all boarded here."

"Could I see him?"

Sykes spit another plug of tobacco juice from the side of his mouth. "Sure, ya kin. In fact, ya kin feed 'em while yer at it." Taking hold of Blackjack's halter, he led the horse into the open area where the sunlight streamed through the barn doors. "Best stallion in these parts!"

Joshua gazed at Blackjack, whose sleek, black coat gleamed in the bright afternoon sun. He couldn't speak for a moment. Then he said, "He's—he's beautiful!"

"Here, son. Maybe ya'd like ta give 'em these oats." Sykes handed a bucket to Joshua.

Josh held the bucket under the horse's nose, as Blackjack pushed his mouth into it and began chomping the feed. "Have you had him long, Mr. Sykes?"

"Only a few weeks—won 'em in a card game."

"A card game?"

"You bet! That shifty old Colonel Johnson tried bluffin' me with two pair. Then *I* slaps down three Kings! Ya shoulda seen his face!"

"I've been to the Colonel's place—never saw Blackjack there."

"Oh, he came back from Richmond with 'em. He never got ta take 'em home, tho, 'cause he stopped off at that card game. Ya can't bluff old Sykes, ya know," as he flexed his suspenders with his thumbs, pulling them out from his chest and letting them snap back.

Joshua continued to hold the bucket for Blackjack, admiring the sleek, muscular contours of his strong body. He was only half-listening to Sykes.

"Ya live around here, son?"

"About a mile from here. Up on Shady Oak Lane."

"Oh! Yer Pa's that tabacca salesman, ain't he?"

"Well, not exactly. He's a tobacco buyer."

"Yeah. I know 'em. Had me shoe his horse a couple a times."

Blackjack finished eating the oats, and Joshua started to hand the bucket back to Sykes. "Ya wanna feed the others?" Sykes asked as he walked over to refill the bucket from a large barrel.

"Yes, Sir," Josh replied with a big smile on his face. Then he remembered his errand. "And then I have to get the groceries for my Ma—she'll be looking for me."

"Ya look ta me like yer right at home with these animals."

"Yes, Sir. I love horses. Hope to buy one soon as I can afford it."

"You got work, boy?"

"No, Sir. Been looking around, but nobody needs a hand."

"Well, listen—I been thinkin'—I could use a hand around here. These critters need a lot a work, ya know. Feedin', takin' 'em out fer exercise, brushin' 'em down, takin' 'em out back ta graze. I'm gittin on in years, boy, an' I been thinkin' lately—I could use a little help." He paused, then walked over to Josh who was feeding the other horses. "Ya go ta school, boy?"

"No, Sir. I'm finished with school. Don't have much to do except run errands for Ma. I could still work with my Pa, but he only makes enough to keep us. Not enough to pay me anything."

Sykes stepped back from Josh, raised his hand to his chin, and began to scratch his scraggly beard. "Tell ya what, Joshua. Why don't ya come back here in the mornin' an' maybe I kin find somethin' fer ya ta do."

"Yes, Sir, Mr. Sykes. I'd like that." Joshua finished feeding the horses, dropped the empty bucket, and started for the door.

"Wait a minute," Sykes said. "Didn't ya fergit somethin'?" He held up a quarter, then flicked it over to Josh, who stepped forward and caught it in midair.

"Thanks, Sir."

"Now don't fergit! Be here bright an' early in the mornin'. These critters like an early breakfast!"

"Yes, Sir. Bright and early." He tucked the coin into his side pocket and ran out the door.

In the excitement of his new job prospect, he passed the General Store on a run, almost forgetting the groceries. Quickly stopping, he ran back to the store, bounding up the stairs. He scurried around and grabbed up everything on the list his mother had given him, paid Mr. Logan, and streaked out the door, slinging the cloth sack of groceries over his shoulder. It wasn't until he was halfway home that he realized that Jenny wasn't at the store. No matter, he thought. Got a job. Love that Blackjack! Just maybe I could earn enough money to buy him. He couldn't wait to tell his parents about his new job.

In the following weeks, Joshua arrived at Mr. Sykes Livery Stable early every morning. He had worked into a routine, caring for the horses; and, every Friday, he received his pay from the old man and saved it. After several weeks, Sykes had delegated most of the work to Joshua. This allowed the old man more time for card games, drinking, and sleeping. After dark, Josh would lead the horses out of the barn and into a small pasture to graze. He would sometimes hop onto one of the horses and ride it bareback around the field. His four-legged friends became familiar with his voice and would respond to it when he called them by name. He also came to know their owners quite well.

As time went by, he grew to love this work of feeding the animals, brushing them, exercising them, and talking to them. But some of them were only temporarily there, as their owners would replace them from time to time. The one permanent resident was Blackjack. He had become like a black jewel in Joshua's eyes, and Sykes knew it.

One rainy day, as Josh was brushing down Blackjack, the old man burst into the barn, slamming the door behind him and shaking the rain from his old hat. "Jumpin' Jehoshaphat!" Sykes barked out. "Better start buildin' an ark—like Noah. It's rainin' cats and dogs out there!" Joshua chuckled and continued to brush down Blackjack. The old man removed his wrinkled raincoat with its large tear in the back. As he turned to hang it on a peg on the wall, Josh noticed a wet streak running down the back of his shirt and overalls. "This weather ain't fit fer man or beast!" exclaimed Sykes, running his long, bony fingers through his hair, attempting to dry it. He aimed a tobacco plug in the direction of an unsuspecting fly that had landed on a wooden post a few feet away. Splat! The drowned fly dropped motionless to the floor. "Got 'em!" exclaimed Sykes, grinning from ear to ear. He walked over and stood next to Blackjack, resting his hand on top of the horse's back. "Looks like ya found a real friend there, Josh."

"Yeah, I sure like him a lot."

"How would ya like ta own 'em?"

"I sure would, Mr. Sykes," Josh replied with excitement in his voice. "I've been saving my money, hoping maybe I could buy him from you some day."

"He's a real thoroughbred, ya know. Worth a lot! I been thinkin' 'bout sellin' 'em, ya know. He's real gentle, he is." He looked at Josh with a serious look on his face. "He needs someone who knows how ta treat 'em right."

"Oh, I'd sure treat him gentle, all right."

"Yeah, son. I noticed yer good with 'em. Well, maybe we could work somethin' out. I had a few offers, but—well—I dunno—it's jus' that some people dunno how ta treat their animals. In fact, some are downright mean. Tell ya what. I'll keep old Blackjack for a few months. Then ya let me know whatcha got saved up an' we'll see if we kin work out a deal, okay?"

Josh smiled broadly. "That's a deal!"

In the days to come, Josh would discover another benefit resulting from his new job—his proximity to the General Store… and Jenny Logan. He became a frequent visitor to the store, having conquered his initial shyness. She was the most beautiful girl he had ever seen, he thought. Her red hair, blue eyes, and delicate features were striking. Jenny was two years older than Joshua and had finished school before he arrived in Virginia. Soon he found out that she didn't have any young men pursuing her, and he thought he knew the reason. The first time that he saw her walk from behind the counter, it was quite evident she was partially crippled and walked with a limp. His initial shock stirred up feelings of pity for her, but her beauty and sweet personality eventually replaced those feelings with warm affection. It seemed that this new awakening in him was growing stronger and stronger each day.

Life was good for Josh. His interest in Jenny and his new paying job made him feel more like a man. He had also made a new friend, Caleb Snow. Caleb was a few years older than Josh and worked at his father's blacksmith shop next to the livery stable. He was part Indian, he told Josh, but the other part he didn't know. His mother had died years before, and he was raised by his father. Caleb was shorter than most boys his age but was solidly built. He had brawny, muscular arms from bending iron and lifting anvils in the forge. Joshua often needed Caleb's services to shoe the horses he cared for, bringing the two young men together on a regular basis. Caleb's father was getting older and had delegated more of the heavy work to his son, while he managed the business end of things.

Days turned into weeks and weeks into months. Joshua was determined to save as much money as he could to buy Blackjack. He had taken a second job on weekends as an overseer on Colonel Johnson's plantation. He was very young for this type of work, but the Colonel was desperate for help. His overseer had quit suddenly, so he needed immediate assistance. Joshua had no intention of leaving his work with the horses, but agreed to help out on the weekends. The Colonel had assigned one of his slaves to assist as driver during the week for the time being. He felt it was beneath him to work on his own plantation; besides, he didn't want to get his shiny boots dirty in the fields.

Joshua didn't like being overseer from the very first day. He had to be boss over the Negroes, some of whom he had played with as a child. He could feel the bitterness and resentment they had toward him. Two of them taunted Joshua and tested him to see what he would do. He asked the Colonel for advice.

"What?" shouted the Colonel. "They won't go to work, you say?"

"Well, Sir, two of them go to the fields and sit down most of the day. They won't work, but the rest of them do."

"Did you threaten them with the whip?"

Joshua wasn't prepared for this. He had heard about slaves being whipped on other plantations, but he had also heard that the Colonel never did that. "Well, no Sir. I didn't know..."

"Well, damn it! Tell 'em you'll use the whip."

"I—I can't."

"You can't what?"

"The whip—I couldn't."

"Now listen to me, boy. You can't let them slaves run *you*! You gotta run *them*! If you don't, we could have a revolution on our hands."

Joshua nodded his head, seeming to agree half-heartedly with the Colonel.

"Wait here," said the Colonel, as he stormed into the house. In a few seconds, he returned, all red-faced, crunching a cigar in his teeth and holding a whip in his hand. "This'll show 'em who's boss! Come with me, son." He walked briskly into the fields. Joshua raced along, keeping pace with him. "Which two giving you trouble, son?" As the Colonel looked over the tobacco crop, he could see the top of two of the slaves' heads barely visible but sticking up above the tobacco leaves. "Never mind—I see 'em." When the two spotted the Colonel and Joshua coming toward them, they got on their knees and pretended to be picking weeds. "Stand up, you two lazy bastards! Who do you think you're fooling?"

They jumped to their feet. "We be weedin', Massa!" one said.

"Who told you to pull weeds? Why aren't you over there with the rest of them?"

"Dunno, Massa."

The Colonel cracked the whip, snapping it just in front of their feet, as they jumped back. He cracked it again, as he bit down harder on his cigar, almost severing it in two. "Now you two get your lazy asses over with the rest of them and get pickin'! If I catch you loafing again, you'll feel the sting of this whip!"

"Yassuh, Massa," they replied simultaneously and ran swiftly to join their fellow slaves.

Looking at Joshua, the Colonel proudly displayed a confident grin, holding the whip and snapping it again. "Now, *that's* how you keep them in line, son." He spit out the stub of his cigar, which had gone out, removed a new one from his shirt pocket, tore away the wrapper, placed it in his mouth, and puffed on it until it was lit. He exhaled, watching the smoke rise slowly into the stifling, hot air. "Now, next time—if there *is* a next time—*you* bring out the whip." He continued, "Now, keep an eye on 'em!"

"Yes, Sir, I will." Joshua watched as the Colonel walked back to his house, placing one boot on the front step and brushing it off with a handkerchief he had removed from his back pocket. He then proceeded to do the same with the other boot. Josh turned and went back to the fields, bewildered and hoping that none of his childhood friends would ever feel the whip. One thing he knew for certain… *he* would never be the one holding it if they did. He had heard somewhere that one overseer on another plantation who thought as he did, had pretended to whip a slave to keep his job. He had done this by tying the slave's hands to a fence post and whipping the post instead of the slave, afterward squashing red berries on his back to make it look like it was bleeding. The owner, sitting on his porch at a distance, had been fooled by this fakery. The whole business was repulsive to Joshua. Fakery or not, he didn't want any part of it. He only lasted a few months as an overseer before he quit. The Colonel can do his own dirty work, he thought.

Now Joshua once again had more time to work at Old Man Sykes place and more time to visit with Jenny. He often dropped by the General Store to buy a drink to have with his lunch, lovingly made by his mother. One very hot afternoon, he walked into the store, removed his floppy hat from his head, and wiped the sweat from his brow. "Hi, Miss Jenny. Sure is a scorcher out there."

She was sitting on a stool behind the counter. "Hello, Joshua. You look like you could use a drink."

"Sure could, Miss Jenny," he said as he leaned his elbows on the counter top, admiring her pretty face.

She got up and limped into the back room, returning momentarily with a glass of lemonade. "Here, Joshua." She handed the glass across the counter to him. "This should help. Just made it myself." He reached into his pocket, pulled out some change, and laid it on the counter. She immediately pushed it back toward him. "That's all right—this one is free."

"Thanks, Miss Jenny. That's mighty kind of you." He picked up the glass and chugged it down in a few seconds. Placing the empty glass back down on the counter, he wiped his mouth on his sleeve. "That was great! You make the best lemonade in town."

Hearing the sound of wood being sawed in the back room, he asked, "Your Pa building something?"

"Yes. He's always sawing or hammering something. I think he's building a door for a neighbor."

"Folks say he's the best carpenter in town."

"He loves it. I mean—building things."

"Maybe he could help me build a barn for Blackjack."

"Blackjack? Who's that?"

"Oh, he's a horse I'm buying from Mr. Sykes. He's a beauty!"

"I'd like to see him."

"Well, maybe I can show him to you soon. I've been taking care of him ever since Mr. Sykes won him in a card game. Been saving up all my money to buy him."

"A card game? Oh, that's awful! That's the devil's work—I mean—gambling like that."

"Yeah, I know, but Mr. Sykes don't believe in some things—except winning at cards." Joshua picked up his coins and returned them to his pocket, as he was about to leave. "Thanks again, Miss Jenny. Have to get back to work. Mr. Sykes don't like me being away long. He's paying me by the hour."

"Oh, Joshua, don't forget—I'd like to see Blackjack some time."

"Yes, Miss Jenny. Soon, I hope. Maybe you could come down to see him some time. Mr. Sykes don't like me taking him further than the corral. Bye now." He put his hat back on and tipped it in a gentlemanly gesture with one hand, as he went out the door.

In the coming weeks, Joshua looked for Jenny to visit him, but she never showed up at the livery. Maybe she thought it unladylike… or maybe she's not interested in me. Maybe she only pretended to want to see Blackjack. Or maybe she was just being kind to me… didn't want to hurt my feelings.

When he thought he might have enough to buy the horse, Josh collected all his savings and brought them in to Sykes. He plopped down a little leather pouch full of coins on the top of an overturned barrel. Very excitedly, he said, "Mr. Sykes, here is all the money I've been saving. Will it be enough to buy Blackjack?"

The old man, who was hammering a loose horseshoe on Buttercup, turned to look at Joshua as he released the horse's front leg and set the animal's foot back down on the ground. "Well now, son," he said, dropping the hammer to the ground and removing the nails he had been holding in his mouth with one hand, while wiping his brow with a dirty handkerchief with the other. "Ya think ya got enough ta buy him? He's a fine animal, ya know." He walked over to the barrel, opened the pouch, and proceeded to dump the coins onto the top of it, catching a few that began to roll over the side. He began to count Joshua's hard-earned savings, as the boy looked on with anticipation. When he finally finished, he turned and looked at Joshua, wearing a smirk on his face. "I've got ta tell ya, son—yer doin' a good job savin' yer money. But—well, son—there's only enough here ta buy half a horse."

Joshua looked down at the ground disappointedly, as he thought he had saved enough to buy Blackjack.

"Now, don't get discouraged, son. Maybe you can save enough ta buy the rest."

Joshua replied in a weak tone of voice, "Yes, Sir," as he continued to look at the ground.

Sykes stroked his tobacco-stained beard, shot a plug of tobacco juice out of the side of his mouth, and looked as though he was deep in thought. After a few moments of silence, he looked at Joshua as he raised his eyebrows. "Got an idea, son. How's about we cut a deck of cards and see if ya git lucky?"

"I—I'm not sure what you mean," Josh replied with a puzzled look on his face.

"Ya got anything that's worth somethin'—like a ring, or jewelry, or maybe somethin' at home that's worth some money?"

Joshua thought for a moment, and then looked back at the old man. "No, Sir, I don't have nothin' worth much—nothin' that I could buy the rest of Blackjack with."

The old man looked at Joshua. "Would that be the front half or the back half now?" Sykes laughed—then laughed harder. Joshua never saw Sykes laugh so hard before. Then he began to laugh along with him. After their laughing finally subsided, Sykes stared at the medal hanging around Joshua's neck, plainly visible on the outside of his shirt. "What's that ya got around yer neck, son?"

Joshua looked down at the medal, pulling it away from his chest to get a better look at it. "Oh, I've had this for a long time. Got it up in New York City."

Sykes walked over to Joshua to get a better look. "New York City, huh? Yeah, I almost forgot—yer a Yankee, aren't ya?"

"I used to be."

"Here, let me have a look at that." He attempted to inspect the medal in Joshua's hand. "Ya know, son, this looks like it could be worth somethin'. Can ya take it off so I could git a better look?" Joshua pulled it over his head, then handed it to him. Sykes held it up. "This here chain is worth somethin'." Then taking the medal, he put it between his teeth and bit down on it. He quickly realized it had little value from the softness of the metal and immediately removed it from his mouth. "Solid as a rock! Yes, sir, this here must be pure silver. Tell ya what, son," repeating his previous offer, "What if we cut a deck of cards? If ya beat me, ya git ta take Blackjack home—paid in full! But if I beat you, I git ta keep yer medal."

The old man handed the medal back to Joshua. Gazing at it, Josh thought of his old boyhood friend, Patrick. He pondered Sykes' proposition for a moment. Knowing enough about cards to understand, at least, their face values, he figured that he would have a fifty-fifty chance of winning. He looked over at Blackjack feeding on some hay in his stall, then glanced back at his medal, still holding it in his hand. "Well—I'm not sure," he answered in a faint voice.

"Well, I won't force ya. Just thought Blackjack meant a lot ta ya."

"Oh, he *does*! He really *does*!"

"Ya know, son, that there medal won't git ya around like that fine animal will."

Joshua thought about the other boys in town who owned their own horses.

"Okay, Sir—you're right. I really want him."

"Good decision." Sykes pulled out a deck of cards that he always carried in his shirt pocket. He shuffled them and set them down on the top of a bale of hay. "Okay." He looked Joshua straight in the eye. "You first!"

Joshua nervously complied. However, his face immediately lit up as he looked at the card he had picked.

"Whatcha got?" Joshua turned the card around for Sykes to see. "King of Clubs? That's pretty hard ta beat. My turn now." The old man picked up the cards, stealthily slipping an Ace of Spades, previously palmed, in front of the selected card.

Joshua never suspected a thing. He slowly removed the medal from around his neck and handed it to Sykes.

"Sorry, son. Sometimes ya win and sometimes ya lose." He then took Joshua's medal and placed it around his *own* neck.

Joshua walked home that evening, as the sun was going down, feeling foolish and dejected. About half way home, two of the local boys, about his age, galloped by on their horses—Tom Ferris and Luke Caulfield—known troublemakers in town. "Wanna race?" one of them hollered.

"Eat my dust!" hollered the other.

They both turned in the saddle, laughing at Joshua as they passed him. It wasn't the first time they had taunted him. They had, on previous occasions, made nasty remarks, but Joshua never retaliated. This time, however, it made him more determined that, somehow, he *would* own Blackjack. He knew without a doubt that he and Blackjack could make these two ruffians "eat *his* dust"; however, it was going to take a long time for him to save enough money to buy "the other half". But he would definitely own that fine horse one day. That was for sure.

Josh went to bed that night, his thoughts bouncing back and forth, with many memories of his childhood in New York City—Patrick, their snowball wars, and the "oath of brotherhood" they had made as young boys. Amidst these thoughts, he wrestled with ways in which he could earn more money to buy Blackjack sooner.

The following morning, he had breakfast, tucked his lunch bag under his arm, slipped his hands into his pockets, and kissed his mother goodbye. He was tired and walked the mile into town slower than usual. Entering the livery stable, he went straight to Blackjack, his usual routine. To his surprise, his medal was hanging on the horse's neck. "Happy Birthday!" came a jubilant shout from behind. It was Sykes, arms folded across his chest, wearing a broad smile. He took out a new plug of tobacco, broke a piece off in his mouth, and began to chew. "Didja fergit it's yer birthday, son?" the old man asked, spitting some fresh, brown liquid of tobacco juice into a stack of hay, his one cheek puffed out with a bigger-than-usual wad.

"Yes, I guess I did," replied Joshua, "but I don't know what..."

Sykes broke in. "Well, I was thinkin' about that horse there," as he pointed to Blackjack, "and him needin' a good owner. I'm too damned old ta ride; and, if somethin' happens ta me—well—he'd probably git sold off. And no tellin' who might treat him bad. And besides, I know you'll take good care of him."

"You mean I can..."

"Yeah, Josh. He's all yours. A birthday present from me."

Joshua ran over and grabbed Sykes around the neck, hugging him. The tobacco-stained beard at that point didn't bother him a bit, as it rubbed against his face. "How did you know it was my birthday?"

"Blackjack told me!" the old man answered with a gleam in his eye.

Josh then ran back and hugged *his* horse around the neck. Looking back at Sykes, he inquired, "And the medal?"

"Oh, it's no good ta me. I'm not a religious man. I think it means more ta you— you keep it."

As Joshua stood in the stall, still holding his "prize" around the neck, Sykes walked over and gently placed his hand on Josh's shoulder. "Didja learn a lesson from this, son?"

"Yes, Sir."

"And what would that lesson be?"

"Never to gamble, Sir."

"That's right. Once ya start, ya can't stop. Look at me—ya wouldn't know it, but I was once a rich man—and now I can't stop. Nothin' much left ta lose anyway."

"Yes, Sir. Thank you, Sir. I'll always be gentle with him."

The many months that Joshua had worked in the livery stable, he had been restricted to walking the horses around the corral. He had, however, mounted Blackjack bareback at times, but only for a walk. Now, though, for the first time, he would be able to test his speed at a gallop. Old Man Sykes was so eager to see what Joshua could do with the horse, he even threw in an old saddle and bridle for the boy.

"Can I take him for a ride?" Joshua asked excitedly.

"Go ahead, son, he's all yours. See what you can make him do. And, oh—take the rest of the day off—it's your birthday."

Joshua hurriedly threw the saddle and bridle on the horse, mounted him, and rode out of the barn. He gently kicked his heels into the horse's side, let out a yelp, and bolted down the street. He galloped down to the church at the other end of town, turned, and sped back to where Sykes stood. He brought the horse to a screeching halt, covering the old man with a cloud of dust and dirt.

"Jumpin' Jehoshaphat!" Sykes removed his old, floppy hat, slapping it against his pants to remove the dust. "Gotta tell ya, boy, ya got a real winner there, son!" He spit the wad of tobacco from his mouth, wiped a few drops of the brown juice from his sleeve, then continued. "Maybe I coulda made money racin' him. Now git outta here before I change my mind."

Josh smiled. "Thanks again, Sir." He raced away, exhilarated, heading home to show his folks his prized possession.

In the coming months, Joshua worked exceptionally hard for Sykes. Some days he worked long after dark in appreciation for what the old man had done for him. Friday night card games in the hayloft had become commonplace for Sykes, Sheriff Cooper, Colonel Johnson, and Preacher John Keeper. The card game had been moved from the back of the barn since the preacher's wife had caught him "dealing with the devil", as she put it. The hayloft and its bales of hay had provided cover from the searching eyes of Mrs. Keeper, and the foursome had removed the ladder for an extra precaution. Joshua had overheard many conversations coming from that hayloft on those Friday nights, as he brushed and fed the horses, shoveled manure, and cleaned the barn. He began to hear one word spoken over and over again—WAR!

"I don't know about you fellas, but I think them damn Yankees got a lot of nerve—I mean—tellin' us how to run our country," said Sheriff Cooper.

Sykes filled the glasses with whiskey, then picked up his own glass to take a swig. "Yeah, I heard they got some rail-splitter runnin' fer president... wants ta free the slaves!"

Colonel Johnson broke in. "That's the damnedest thing I ever heard of. What's he think they're going to do for a living? Besides, he'd be taking the bread right out of my mouth. Who'd be working my fields? Just let them come down here and step one foot in this town, and I'll blow their heads off! If they know what's good for them, they won't elect that radical S.O.B. I'll go to war before I'll let them Yankees push *me* around!"

Preacher John quietly shuffled the deck and began to pass the cards around to the others, as he spoke softly. "Peace, gentlemen. We must not get angry—I'm sure, with a little negotiating, our elected politicians will work things out."

The Colonel quickly snapped back, "Well, that's easy for you to say, Preacher, but I've got everything invested in my plantation. Besides, I got it from my Daddy and he got it from *his* Daddy—been in the family for generations. I got everything to lose, but you—you lose your job, and all you have to do is tuck your Bible under your arm, find another church, and you're back in business."

"He's right, Preacher. None of us here owns blacks," the Sheriff added, "but the Colonel—he'd lose everything if them darkies become free. I got no quarrel with them Yankees; but if they think they can write something on a piece of paper and call it a law, then come down here and change everything around... I'd shoot 'em, too! No sir. The Colonel's one of us, and I'd defend his rights, just as I'd defend *yours.*"

Joshua busied himself with work, curiously listening to every word coming from the hayloft. He seldom read a newspaper; however, he had learned a great deal from that Friday night group.

That little town of Perch, Virginia, had another side to it... religion. The white, wooden-frame church with its tall steeple and large bell in the tower had become the public meeting place for its citizens. About one-third of the population attended Sunday services, even larger turnouts coming for weddings and funerals.

The first rumblings of war, oddly enough, had their beginnings in the church. At first, small groups would gather to discuss the abolition question and the growing sentiment in the North in favor of freeing the slaves. In time, their numbers grew, and eventually they filled the church to overflowing. In fact, there had been a larger attendance for the meetings than there was for Sunday services. Preacher Keeper presided over these meetings and attempted to maintain a calm atmosphere amidst the growing hostility that began to emerge amongst the townsfolk.

At first, Joshua just listened. He had seen firsthand the plight of the slaves since moving south; but he was young and impressionable, and gradually these feelings had been swallowed up in the swelling tide of rebellion. To him, it seemed it was the white folks' rights versus the black folks' rights. He knew in his heart that slavery was wrong— but then—there was the fear of invasion by the Yankees. That fear overwhelmed the town and began to overtake its otherwise law-abiding citizens. It wasn't long before that fear turned to anger, and it nourished the seeds of rebellion that permeated everything in its path, including Joshua, who was almost old enough to go to war.

Preacher Keeper would conclude all the meetings by leading his flock in a prayer for peace, but he soon became a minority. Most of the men now, upon leaving the meetings, would walk to the saloon at the opposite end of town and, after a few drinks, begin to shout slogans of war.

Joshua knew nothing of war. He only wanted to be left alone, train his horse, and pursue pretty, young Jenny Logan. He would have no peace in these endeavors, however, until he settled his score with Tom Ferris and Luke Caulfield. Their insults and taunting had increased in the past few months. One evening, Joshua had finished his chores at the livery stable early and had gone over to the General Store to see Jenny. "Hi, Miss Jenny. How are you?" He tipped his floppy hat, as was his custom.

"Hello, Joshua. I'm just fine, thanks," as she limped out from behind the counter, heading for the door. "I was just going outside to watch the sun go down. Come with me?"

"Sure, Miss Jenny. I'd like that."

Joshua held the door open for her and followed her outside. She sat down on the steps and gazed at the beauty of the pink and blue panorama before them. He sat down next to her. "Isn't it beautiful, Joshua?"

"Yes, it is."

"I come out here most every evening when there's no customers around. It's so beautiful and peaceful—it's my favorite time of day."

He looked at the sun momentarily as it slowly descended on the horizon, but his glance was drawn to Jenny. Her sky-blue eyes seemed to sparkle, and her fiery red hair shimmered in the setting sun. Holding his hat in his hands with his elbows resting on his knees, he nervously began sliding the brim through his fingers. "I've been meaning to ask you..." He hesitated.

"Ask me what, Joshua?"

"Well—I mean—are you going to the church social on Sunday?"

"Oh, yes. Ma and I baked apple pies. We go to almost every one."

"Well, maybe I could see you there and taste some of those pies you made."

"Well, you should get there early. They won't last long." She looked over at Blackjack, tied to the hitching post at the side of the building. Joshua had shown her his horse when he had first become Blackjack's proud new owner. He had offered to let her ride him then, but she had declined.

"You know, Miss Jenny, that offer to let you ride him is still open, if you ever would like to."

She quickly retorted, "No! I mean—no thanks."

Joshua looked at her, surprised at her curt response. "I didn't mean to upset you, Miss Jenny. I thought you liked Blackjack."

She softened her tone. "Oh, I think he's beautiful. In fact, I've never seen such a fine looking animal before. I just don't like riding horses."

"Well, Miss Jenny, he's about as gentle as a lamb. He wouldn't hurt a fly." Joshua got up from the stairs, walked over to Blackjack and began to stroke his neck. "I'll bet if you just sat on him, you might be tempted to ride him."

"Well—I don't know." She hesitated, as if she wanted to tell him something.

"What is it, Miss Jenny?"

"Did I tell you how I got this bad leg?"

"No, Miss Jenny." He looked at her curiously, then continued, "I didn't think it was my place to ask."

"Fell off a horse and broke my leg when I was young. It never did heal right."

"I'm sorry. I wouldn't force you. Just thought you might—well, never mind."

He no sooner had the words out of his mouth, than she quickly got up and walked over to him. "Okay. I guess one time won't hurt—I mean—just sitting on him."

Surprised at her sudden change of heart, he smiled and cupped his hands together, holding them low to provide a step for her to raise herself up onto Blackjack's back. She sat sidesaddle, straightened her dress that had slightly folded beneath her, and arched her back to sit perfectly straight, looking very proud that she had conquered a fear that she had had for a very long time.

"You okay up there?"

"I'm fine." She shifted her body in the saddle a few times until she seemed comfortable.

"Why don't you stay there a little bit? You know—maybe get the feel…"

His words were abruptly interrupted by someone yelling and shouting. Tom Ferris and Luke Caulfield galloped down the street, whooping and hollering and heading straight toward them. They came so close to Blackjack that he became spooked and reared up, causing Jenny to fall backwards into Joshua's arms. They tumbled back onto the hard, wooden sidewalk. He had broken her fall.

"Hey manure-face! That's an ugly black horse ya got there," hollered Ferris, as the two sped away.

Joshua quickly rose to his feet, angrier than he had ever felt before. He reached for Blackjack's reins to mount him, planning to give chase and punish the two ruffians. Then he realized Jenny needed his help. Bending over her, he anxiously asked, "Are you hurt?"

"I think I'm all right," she said, catching her breath.

Joshua reached down, took her by the arm, and assisted her to her feet, as she brushed off her dress.

"They'll pay for this!" he said in an angry tone.

Still sounding upset, she said, "Well, what do you expect from people like that. They tied Farmer Parsons chickens to a tree!" She began to sob and wiped a tear from her cheek. "I—I—I do appreciate what you tried to do, but I have to go back inside now." She opened the screen door, letting it slam behind her.

Joshua walked back to Blackjack and was about to mount him, swearing to get revenge on the troublemakers, when he heard someone calling his name. He turned to see a well-dressed man wearing a thin, black bow tie and a white straw hat, cocked back on his head. He carried a walking cane, and swung it back and forth as he walked toward Joshua. He looked familiar, but Josh didn't know where he had seen him before.

"Pettibone. Sam Pettibone's the name, son, but most folks call me "Slim". You don't know me. I travel the riverboats and sometimes stop by here to visit an old friend."

"Oh, yes, I think I saw you at Mr. Sykes livery stable once."

"That's right, son. Sykes and I go back a long way. In fact, he's the one that told me about you."

"He told you about me?"

"That's right, son. He told me about you and that fast horse of yours."

Joshua looked puzzled and didn't understand what he was getting at. Pettibone raised his cane, pointing it at Blackjack. "Sykes tells me that horse of yours is just about the fastest animal in these here parts, and I was wonderin' if you might consider ridin' him in one of the Saturday races."

"Well, I did hear about those races, but I don't know about racin' Blackjack. Never entered him in a race before."

"I saw what them two upstarts did to you and your lady-friend. I think they deserve to be taught a lesson, and I think you're just the fella that could do it. You know, they been winnin' those races most every month. They got fast horses, but I think you can beat 'em. Pettibone smiled and winked, adding, "And you know, son, we might make a few dollars when you do!"

"Well, I don't know. I'll think about it, Mr. Pettibone."

"Slim—call me Slim. I'll be back in town before the next race. Got to catch the boat now, before she goes upriver." He waved at Joshua with his cane and started for the boat landing, then turned and hollered, "Don't forget, son! I think that horse of yours is a winner!"

Joshua didn't have to think about Pettibone's offer for very long. He knew without a doubt that he would enter the next race and had no doubts that he would win it. The next few weeks, he took Blackjack for practice runs twice a day, morning and evening, down the dirt roads that were used for the races.

He awoke on Saturday morning, the day of the race, walked over to his bedroom window, and pulled back the curtain. Rain! Something he hadn't planned on. He suddenly felt uneasy. How would Blackjack perform on a muddy track? Maybe the race would be cancelled, he thought. He ate breakfast, went to the small barn that Jenny's father had helped him build, and walked over to his horse who was munching on a pile of hay. "Well, Jack, today you and I are going to show everybody, especially Ferris and Caulfield, what we can do." He threw the saddle over Blackjack's back, tightened it securely, and placed the bit in the horse's mouth. He hadn't told his mother about the race, because he didn't think the excitement would be good for her; and his father couldn't afford to miss a day's work.

Arriving in town, he saw a small crowd gathering in front of the blacksmith shop. Sam Pettibone, a thin, black cigar dangling from the side of his mouth, was sitting at a small table he had pulled under the shop's overhang. "Cast your bets, gentlemen! Pick a winner! Oughta be an exciting race." He noticed Joshua approaching in the drizzling rain, removed the cigar from his mouth, and announced loudly, "I do believe we have a newcomer," as he pointed his cane toward Joshua. The small crowd turned their heads to see who it was.

"Is there going to be a race today?" Joshua asked Pettibone from his saddle, looking over the heads of those gathered there.

"You bet there is, son! Rain or shine. You want to take a crack at it?"

"Yes, Sir. I'm ready."

"Well, step over here... get yourself out of the rain."

Joshua dismounted and walked Blackjack into the blacksmith shop where his friend, Caleb Snow, was hammering out a red-hot horseshoe on the top of an anvil. "You gonna race today, Josh?" He plunged the horseshoe into a large vat of cold water, which made a loud, hissing sound.

"Yeah, I planned to. Hope it stops raining, though."

Joshua took an old cloth hanging on a hook and began to wipe down his horse.

"You look like *you* need some dryin' off yourself, Josh—here!" Caleb threw a towel from his shoulders over to Joshua. "Well, you better watch out for Ferris and Caulfield—they play dirty tricks, I hear tell."

"Yeah, I know it. I'm ready for them," as he dried himself off.

Just then, Joshua heard a few cheers coming from the men gathered outside. He looked out to see his two adversaries approaching on horseback, followed by more riders. Pettibone shouted, "Fifteen more minutes to place your bets, gentlemen! I've got a list here if you want to pick a winner. And—we've got a newcomer—Joshua Halperin—riding Blackjack. Come on now! Place your bets!"

His voice suddenly lowered and Josh noticed he seemed to be whispering. Walking closer to the table, he could overhear Pettibone spreading doubts and saying that he and Blackjack were untried, never having raced before. Knowing that Pettibone had told him he was going to bet on Blackjack, believing full well that the horse was a sure thing, Josh realized that the man was attempting to make better odds for himself.

"Last chance!" hollered Pettibone. "Five minutes left to place your bets!"

Just then, Colonel Johnson approached the blacksmith shop. "Good to see you here, Joshua. I was hoping you'd race Blackjack. My money's on you." His voice dropped to a whisper. "Be careful. There are some mean riders in the race."

"Yes, Sir. I know who they are."

A shrill whistle sounded. "Race time, gentlemen! Line up on the starting line!" Pettibone hollered.

"Go get 'em!" remarked Caleb, as he walked over to shake Joshua's hand.

The rain had stopped, but the muddy "track" looked a little hazardous to Josh. After thinking about it for a moment, though, he shrugged it off. After all, he wasn't the only one racing on it. Ten horses and riders began to line up, as Joshua took his place at the end of the line. His two antagonists were three horses away from him, but he could see them whispering and pointing toward him, laughing. He ignored them and patted Blackjack on his neck, talking to him as he did. This was all new to him and his trusty steed. Excitement surrounded the scene, as the riders strained to control their uneasy horses.

"Riders—ready!" Pettibone yelled, then paused till he could see some semblance of a lineup. He then blew the whistle forcefully, while simultaneously snapping the white flag in his raised arm in a quick motion to the ground.

At first, everything was a blur to Joshua—thundering hooves, flying mud, and loud commands screamed by the riders as they bolted from the starting line. He held back slightly on Blackjack's reins, simply because he couldn't see clearly ahead of him. As the horses raced down the road, things cleared up; and Joshua could see the track and riders in front of him. He was in fourth place. He could see Ferris and Caulfield and an unknown rider running neck-and-neck a short distance in front of him. Joshua quickly wiped the mud from his face and eyes and crouched down in the saddle. "Okay, Jack, show 'em what you can do!" He gently nudged Blackjack in the ribs. The horse picked up speed and settled into a stride, as Joshua slowly let out the reins. He quickly caught up with the unknown rider, passing him with ease. He was now in third place. He glanced behind him and realized he had put a good distance between himself and the rest of the pack. Looking ahead, he saw Ferris and Caulfield rounding the turn at Miller's Crossing and heading for Conover's Creek. They looked back and waved for him to come ahead, as they laughed aloud. In quiet confidence, Joshua nudged his horse to even greater speed. Moving along more swiftly, Joshua felt as though he were just going along for the ride—almost as though Blackjack knew exactly what to do. He could feel the strong muscles of the horse fusing together into a mass of uncontrollable matter, generating unbridled speed. For a moment, it took Josh by surprise, as he hadn't known his steed's full potential until now. Before he knew it, Jack streaked over Conover's Creek and was fast approaching the two lead horses. He could see the road ahead, as it began to narrow at the crest of a hill. He quickly calculated that there was a big enough gap between Ferris and Caulfield, and he went for it. They saw him coming fast and quickly closed the gap. He was forced to drop back but tried again to pass them, this time trying to maneuver Jack to the outside of the track. Caulfield rapidly pulled his horse's reins to the right, trying to force Joshua off the road. Continuing to glance backward to prevent Joshua's passing, he failed to see the sudden descent in the road. Suddenly, Luke's horse lost its footing; he tried to pull back on the reins, but it was too late. His horse lunged head first down the hill, causing Luke to sail up and over him, tumbling forward and landing in a ditch on the part of his anatomy that had been sitting on the saddle just before. Joshua pulled hard on his reins to avoid Luke's horse and barely managed to maneuver around him. He could see that Luke's worst injury was to his pride. This time, it was Joshua who laughed—at his vanquished enemy.

In only a matter of seconds, he had Blackjack back to a smooth stride, increasing his speed as he neared the bottom of the hill.

Thatcher's Run was the last leg of the course, and he still had to catch up to Ferris, who had sped even further ahead of him by now. He was determined to catch him. He let out Blackjack's reins once again, crouched back down in the saddle, peering through the horse's ears, and spotted Ferris, profusely whipping his horse, about twenty lengths ahead of him. He "aimed" Blackjack straight toward him. He knew he could do it. The road was flat and straight all the way to the finish line. Blackjack, with his smooth, young, muscular legs pumping like pistons beneath his shiny, black coat covered with perspiration, looked like a locomotive speeding down a track at full throttle. He quickly gained on Ferris. Just as he reached the edge of town, he breezed by him like a projectile fired from a cannon. Joshua never looked back. He sped across the finish line as the crowd cheered. It took all of his strength to rein in Blackjack and bring him to a halt. He felt that his horse could go another round. He trotted him back to the finish line where Pettibone, Colonel Johnson, and Old Man Sykes, who had been awakened by the starting whistle, came over to shake his hand.

"I knew you and that horse were a great team," Sykes said, as he spit a wad of tobacco from the side of his mouth, narrowly missing Colonel Johnson's shiny, brown boots.

"You've got a winner there, Josh!" the Colonel remarked. "And to think I lost him in a card game. Never saw such a fast horse in all my born days."

"Here's your winnings," Pettibone said, as he reached up and handed Joshua a wad of bills. Josh was surprised, as he hadn't even thought of prize money; he had been so intent on beating his rivals.

As the crowd quieted down and some people began to leave, he saw Ferris sitting on the steps in front of the blacksmith shop, his head in his hands, staring at the ground. Joshua rode over to him, and, in a very matter-of-fact but soft tone, said, "Don't you think you'd better go and pull your friend out of the ditch?" Ferris was silent and never looked up.

Most of the men made their way to the saloon, as Joshua rode over to the General Store. On his way, he noticed a few children and young ladies peering out from behind some curtained windows. Josh knew that they had been restricted from watching the race, as most mothers believed gambling was a sin; but their curiosity had gotten the best of them. As he approached the store, he saw Jenny quickly withdraw from behind the window. He dismounted and walked into the store, wiping the mud from his boots on the mat just inside the door. "Hi, Miss Jenny."

"Oh, Joshua!" she exclaimed. "You look like you fell into a pigpen!"

He looked down at his clothes and hands, all covered with mud, and began to laugh. She appeared to suppress her laughter, but couldn't control it, finally bursting out and laughing with him.

Just then, the door opened and Jenny's father walked in. "What's all the laughing about?" he asked, smiling at them.

"Oh, hi, Mr. Logan," Joshua said, trying to control his laughter. "Miss Jenny thought I fell into a pigpen. I guess I do look like it," he responded, as he attempted to wipe the mud from his face and clothing.

"Well, ya looked pretty darn good comin' across that finish line ahead of the rest of the pack. Good job, son! That black horse of yours runs like the wind."

"Thanks, Mr. Logan. Once Jack got moving, he got a mind of his own. I don't think I could have stopped him if I tried." He slipped his hand into his side pocket and felt the roll of bills he had won. "Oh!" he said, looking at Jenny's father. "I want to pay you for the lumber you used for my barn." He pulled out the money, then continued. "Old Slim Pettibone gave this to me. Said I won it for coming in first place."

Logan's eyes lit up as he gazed at the money in Joshua's hand. "Ya won all that money for winnin' that horserace?"

"Yes, Sir—and I won it fair and square."

"Well, Joshua, I can't say that I wasn't pleased that ya beat out those two troublemakers and won—but—gamblin's the devil's work, ya know."

"Yes, Sir." He hesitated. "But I wasn't gambling. I mean—I didn't even know there *was* any prize money."

"I believe ya, son. Tell ya what I'd suggest to ya—give me half of what ya owe me. Then give ten percent to the church, just so's the good Lord knows your heart's in the right place."

"Well, that sounds like a real nice idea, Mr. Logan, and I'd be glad to do that, even though I don't go to that church."

"That's good of you, son. And keep the rest for a rainy day. Maybe you'll get married some day." Logan glanced over at his daughter, then back at

Joshua, smiling as he did. Jenny blushed and looked down at the floor, embarrassed that her father would say something so bold right in front of her.

Joshua got the message. It made him feel good that her father approved of him. But Jenny, herself, hadn't even shown him that she cared as much for him as he did for her. She was polite and nice, but somewhat aloof. He hoped that he could win her over one day. After settling up his finances with Mr. Logan, Joshua went home and counted out ten percent of his winnings for the church, just as he had been advised. The balance he stuffed into a sock and stashed it away in his closet.

The following evening, on his way home from work, he stopped by the church to give his donation to Preacher John. As he approached, he was surprised to see many horses tied up to the hitching post. Walking up the steps, he entered through the large, double doors and found many men talking together in small groups, as they waited for a meeting to commence. Joshua spotted the Preacher in the front of the church and gave him his donation. Preacher John seemed somewhat surprised and appeared a little bit nervous. "Thank you, son. Mighty good of you. Why don't you stop in for Sunday services? Like to see you here. Wish I had more time to talk, but I've got to get this meeting started."

As the Preacher stepped up to the pulpit and addressed the crowd, they became silent and quickly took their seats in the pews. "Gentlemen! May I have your attention, please. We shall begin our meeting by calling on our Merciful Father in Heaven to guide our hearts and minds in this hour of tribulation. I believe a reading from Psalm 120 would be appropriate." He opened his Bible and read aloud:

> *"The Enemies of Peace"*
> *When I am in trouble, I call to*
> *Yahweh, and he answers me.*
> *Yahweh, save me from these lying lips*
> *and these faithless tongues!*
>
> *How will he pay back the false oath*
> *of a faithless tongue?*
>
> *With war arrows hardened*
> *over red-hot charcoal!*
>
> *This is worse than a life in Meshech,*
> *or camping in Kedar!*

Too long have I lived
  among people who hate peace,
who, when I propose peace,
  are all for war.

Joshua looked around at the others, as he sat in the last pew of the church. For a moment, there was complete silence, then a few whispers, as some men turned to talk with one another. Sheriff Cooper, who had been sitting in the front of the church, stood up and stepped out into the middle aisle. He looked directly at Preacher John. "With all due respect, Preacher, I am the first man to strive for peace—after all, I *am* called the peacekeeper in this town." A ripple of laughter went through the church. The Sheriff continued, "I don't see a man here wantin' ta start no war, but isn't there somethin' in your Bible about people defendin' themselves? I mean—that baboon, Abe Lincoln—well—I hear he might send an Army down here ta take away the darkies and, most likely, our land, too."

Colonel Johnson suddenly stood up on the other side of the aisle, speaking loudly. "As you all know, I've seen invading Armies before. I fought in the battle of San Pasquale, you know, down in Mexico. If them Yankees send soldiers down here, no telling what will happen to our wives and daughters."

A farmer in the front row stood up, shouting. "Yeah, Preacher! What you got in that Good Book about good men protectin' their own kin and their own land?"

"Now, gentlemen," Preacher John interrupted, trying to subdue the growing, fearful rhetoric. "Gentlemen!—Gentlemen!—I think we're just borrowing trouble. No one said that soldiers were coming into our fair Southland. I think they can resolve our differences in Washington."

Then Old Man Sykes stood up. Working up a wad of tobacco in his cheek, he began to look for a place to spit but realized in a moment there would be none in the church. He "parked" it in the back of the right side of his mouth, and began to speak from the left. "I dunno 'bout the rest of ya, but I got a long musket that kin pick off a Yankee at two hundred yards; and, if one comes near my place, he's a goner!"

And so it went. Preacher John Keeper's voice and his call for cool heads had become drowned out over and over again at the weekly meetings. The men continued to visit the saloon, where secession and talk of war increased; and gradually, the God of Peace gave way to the angry gods of war. The men began to gather their firearms; and what had previously been a sleepy, peaceful little town, soon became an armed camp. The great tidal wave of war that was about to break upon the entire nation had its beginnings long back as a tiny ripple when the first slave stepped foot upon its shores.

Young Joshua had been swept up in that tidal wave. If all of his friends were joining forces to resist the coming onslaught of the enemy, he felt that his duty and loyalty was to them. He reasoned that the defense of his homeland came first. This slavery issue could be settled later.

Joshua saw Jenny again at the church social. He had his fill of pies and cakes and talked to her every chance he could get. She was busy serving food and drinks and didn't have much time for him. Most of the men folk gathered in small groups and talked for hours about secession. Joshua couldn't avoid the subject, much as he would have liked to. Colonel Johnson invited him to visit his house on the following day. He had told him that he had some business to talk about.

The burning hot sun blazed down upon Joshua, as he rode Blackjack up the dirt road toward the Colonel's plantation. As he turned off the main road onto the long road leading up to the Colonel's large white mansion, he welcomed the shade provided by the large dogwood trees that formed a canopy above him. What could the Colonel want to see me about? Could I really be going off to war? He was enjoying the quiet solitude of the cool shade, pondering all of the recent events and hoping secretly in his heart that war would not come. Just then, he heard the sound of a rapidly approaching rider coming up behind him. He turned to see Caleb Snow coming on at a gallop. "Wait up, Josh!" he hollered. Joshua halted his horse and watched Caleb barreling down on him. "WAR! We're goin' to war! It started!" His voice exploded with excitement.

"Where? Where did it start?" Josh anxiously asked.

"Fort Sumter... in South Carolina someplace. Heard we gave 'em a lickin' an' captured lots of Yankees!"

"What are you doing here?" Josh asked.

"Colonel Johnson said he wanted to see me," Caleb answered.

"Yeah, me too. Let's give him the news." They both raced toward the Colonel's house, jumped off their horses, and bolted up the stairs leading to the front door.

"What the devil's goin' on here?" hollered the Colonel who had dozed off in his rocking chair at the far end of the long, covered porch.

"Oh, Colonel!" Joshua said. "We didn't see you there. Sorry if we woke you, but..."

Caleb blurted out, "WAR! We're at war, Colonel! Didja hear?"

The Colonel jumped to his feet, wiping his sleepy eyes with his hands. "I knew it was comin' soon. There just wasn't any other way. Who fired the first shot?" he asked anxiously.

"Don't know," Caleb answered.

The Colonel looked at Joshua, raising his eyebrows as though he might know.

"No, Sir, I don't know either," Josh remarked. "Caleb just told me. Fort Sumter, South Carolina."

Caleb broke in again. "We captured a bunch of Yankees," he said with a broad grin.

The Colonel looked pleased. "Well, we'll find out all about it soon. Suppose it don't really matter now. I mean, once that first shot is fired, you can't put it back in the barrel."

At first, Joshua thought it strange, but then he realized that Colonels are made for war; and it seemed as though *this* Colonel was ready for a fight!

"My boys, you're going to make history. What happens from here on in is going to affect you and your children to come... if you ever marry." The Colonel then stepped over to the screen door and hollered, "Sarah, bring us some drinks! And don't spare the liquor!" He walked over to sit back down in his rocking chair. "Come on, boys. This calls for a drink. Have a seat," as he motioned over to two empty rocking chairs on either side of him. He continued, "It ain't every day that you enter into a civil war."

"How long before we can shoot us a Yankee, Colonel?" Caleb asked.

"Not so fast." The Colonel chuckled. "Got a lot to do first. You boys remind me of my youth. I couldn't wait to get into the thick of it. It ain't gonna be that way. We got some organizing to do. Guns—and uniforms to get. And drilling—lots of drilling."

"Do you think it will be soon, Colonel? I mean—before we get into it?" Joshua asked.

"Don't know, son. Depends on them Yankees. And our generals—they need a little time to plan strategy. Could be a matter of weeks or even months till we all get mobilized."

The screen door creaked as Sarah pushed it open with her back, a tray of drinks in her hands. She walked over to the trio, moving in quick, short steps. "Here yo' drinks, Kernel, Suh—mint ju-lips."

The Colonel hesitated. "Wait, Sarah. This won't suffice. Take these *ladies'* drinks back, and bring out my best bottle of bourbon and three more glasses."

"Yassuh, Kernel, Suh."

"This is a big day, boys. Bigger than we can imagine. This day calls for the best liquor a man can drink." They all sat silently for a moment, watching the approaching ominous dark clouds moving across the sky in their direction. Some slaves were singing a spiritual tune in the fields within plain view of the Colonel's porch. A gentle summer breeze floated across the land; its pulsating currents carried their soft, dulcet tones to the ears of the soon-to-be warriors—the ears that had become deafened to the plight of those poor souls by the war drums' loud beat.

Joshua swatted at a pesky fly that had been buzzing around his face.

"Here, Joshua. I think this occasion calls for a cigar. Besides, the smoke will drive that varmint away," the Colonel said as he handed a big cigar to Joshua, then turned and handed another to Caleb. Sarah returned with the bottle of bourbon and three more glasses, just as the Colonel had ordered. "Ah! This is more like it. Set it down here, Sarah," as the Colonel pointed to a small, round table next to him.

After doing as she was instructed, she asked, "Is dere anythin' else, Kernel, Suh?"

"No, Sarah. That will be all for now." She scurried back into the house, the screen door slamming behind her.

The Colonel proceeded to pour the bourbon into the three glasses, handing Josh and Caleb theirs. He then stood up and raised his own glass for a toast. "Here's to our beloved state of Virginia and the new Confederate States of America."

Joshua and Caleb quickly stood up and clinked their glasses to the Colonel's. "And death to them Yankees!" Caleb instantly responded.

Joshua, excited but not as angry or determined as the two others about going to war, hesitated. He glanced at the slaves in the distant field, then back at the Colonel, whose fat stomach protruded in front of him so that he could barely see his own shiny, brown boots. He felt of his medal hanging around his neck, briefly thought of his boyhood friend, Patrick, in New York City, and spoke in a soft voice. "Here's to victory and honor."

They all raised their glasses to their lips and drank to the unknown horror which was about to unfold.

After sitting back down in his large, white, wicker rocking chair and propping his feet up on the long, wooden railing in front of him, the Colonel lit up his cigar and slowly let the smoke trail into the air. He then lit Josh's and Caleb's, who followed his lead and took a seat. The small patch of blue sky had been overshadowed by the gray clouds, and a subtle mist of fine rain began to blow onto the porch and its three occupants. "I've applied to Richmond for the re-instatement of my Colonel's commission, and I'm quite sure of receiving it any day now. That's why I called for you boys to come here. I'll need some good officers, and I think you two would make fine lieutenants to fight at my side." He took another swig of bourbon. "I know you boys will need a lot of drilling and instruction in the art of warfare, but I'll see that you get it. I've been observing you both, and I believe you've got what it takes to lead. Besides, I think you'll both make good horse soldiers."

"You mean we're gonna be officers in the Army?" Caleb asked with a broad grin, as he moved his chair back from the railing and out of the rain.

"That's right, Caleb. I'll need all the good men I can get to build up our forces. I haven't been wrong in my choice of junior officers before, and I don't believe you boys will be an exception."

Joshua remained in his chair on the other side of the Colonel. He was getting wet but wasn't about to move his chair back until the Colonel did. By this time, the Colonel had finished his glass of bourbon and poured another round for the three of them. He seemed unconcerned that his highly polished boots were getting wet. "Will I be able to take Blackjack with me? I mean—to war?" Josh asked as he drank his bourbon, attempting to keep pace with the Colonel. He felt a bit woozy, as he had never drunk liquor before.

"You most certainly will," said the Colonel. "Officers ride horses, you know. You wouldn't want to be walkin' your legs off in the infantry now, would you?"

"No, Sir. I guess not."

Caleb, observing the Colonel and Joshua seemingly unaffected by the rain, moved his chair back to where it had been near the railing. The Colonel, puffing on his cigar, looked over at him. "Can't let a little rain bother you, son. We'll have our fair share of it out in the field."

The Colonel and his future lieutenants talked of war, drank their bourbon, and smoked their cigars, while the last generation of slaves labored in the fields beyond, unaware they would soon be delivered from their bondage.

The small community of Perch was joined by others; and soon regiments and brigades were formed, officers were elected to lead them, arms procured, and home-made uniforms stitched together by the town women. What they lacked in government rifles, they made up for by bringing their own personal weapons consisting of old muskets, shotguns, and pistols. Besides uniforms, the ladies made colorful flags representing the regiments and brigades for their men to carry into battle. Official meetings were conducted in the church, while unofficial meetings continued in the saloon, where the rhetoric continued to heat up against the North. The molten hot hatred and fiery anger toward the Yankees spilled over and was forged into cold steel bayonets and bullets that would kill, wound, and tear into the flesh of thousands of young men, barely old enough to shave.

Joshua began to hear more talk of prayer, mostly from the mothers and wives of men about to go to war. He believed in God but was confused as to *how* he should pray. He had attended the Christian church with his mother on occasion. And he did believe in Jesus Christ—but then there was his Jewish father. He and his father had journeyed to Richmond a few times to celebrate Yom Kippur at the temple. His father had told him that his lineage was Jewish but never objected to his going to church with his mother. Knowing he would soon venture into harm's way, Joshua did begin to pray. He found one common ground... the "Our Father". He frequently grasped his medal, holding the Star of David overlaid with the Cross, and prayed to his Heavenly Father. His earthly father, who only thought in terms of economics when it came to the war, had been concerned that the oncoming hostilities would cause him to be out of work. He sided with the South but felt he was too old to join the Army. Joshua's mother became more and more concerned about her son's plans of enlisting, but her entreaties against it were to no avail. She began to pray more earnestly that the Lord would keep him safe.

Jenny's true feelings surfaced, as she realized Joshua might indeed be leaving for war. She even offered to make his uniform, having taken measurements at the General Store a month earlier. Now the finishing touches of gold braid were about to be sewn on the sleeves, when he called upon her one last time. He entered the store where he often found Jenny sitting behind the counter. This time she wasn't there. He walked to the back of the store where her family lived in a small apartment.

"Miss Jenny, are you there?"

"Is that you, Joshua?"

"Yes, Miss Jenny. Can I see you for a minute?"

"Come in, Joshua—I'm just finishing your uniform. You can try it on and see how it fits." He pushed back the curtain hanging in the doorway and entered their small parlor where she was sitting at a table sewing. She briefly glanced up at him. "If you don't mind waiting a while, I'll be finished here; and you can try it on." She concentrated on her sewing, meticulously and deliberately inserting each stitch into the fabric, then pulling the needle out gently. As Joshua sat down on a chair at the opposite side of the table, he could tell that she enjoyed doing this for him. It gave him a warm feeling inside and hope that she was developing more affection for him. "Do you know when you'll be leaving?" she asked, looking over at him briefly, then back at her sewing.

"The Colonel says we gotta be ready by tomorrow but might not leave till the day after. Guess I'll be ready, just as soon as you finish there."

"You know, Josh, I'm..." She hesitated.

"What is it, Miss Jenny?"

"Well—I'm gonna miss you."

"I'm gonna miss you, too, Miss Jenny."

It was the first time she had called him "Josh" instead of "Joshua", and he liked that. He watched her as she continued working, neither one speaking. Gazing across the table, he thought that she looked sad. He finally broke the silence. "I don't expect to be gone too long, Miss Jenny. Most folks don't think the war will last long."

"You can call me "Jenny" if you like. I mean—I think we know each other well enough. "Miss" seems kind of formal, don't you think?"

"Sure, Miss Jenny. I mean—Jenny. I'd like that."

"Well, I hope you're right about the war not lasting long. I *do* wish that it didn't have to come at all."

"I'm with you. But I feel it's my duty. How could we just sit here and let them Yankees invade our land and do nothing about it?"

"It's a shame—a real shame that's it's come to this." She bent over the table and bit off the end of the thread with her teeth, tying a knot in the loose end of her final stitch. "Finished!" she said with a smile. "Here—you can take it in the other room and try it on."

"It looks great, Miss—I mean—Jenny."

After donning his uniform in the bedroom, he stepped proudly out before her. "How does it look?"

"Oh, Josh! It does fit you well. I'm so honored that you let me make it for you." She inspected the sleeve length, stepped back, and looked at the trousers, then stepped forward again to straighten out his jacket collar. As she placed her hands on the collar, he reached up and gently caressed them in his. He kissed her hand, then drew her closer to himself, pressing his lips against hers. They embraced and stood quietly in each other's arms, finally showing their true feelings for each other, neither one speaking for a long time. She looked into his eyes, a tear trickling down her cheek, and spoke in a soft tone. "I do love you, Josh. I think I always have. But..." She couldn't finish what she wanted to say.

"But what, Jenny? What is it?"

"It's hard for me to say."

"You can tell me, Jenny. I've loved you from the first time I saw you."

"I was afraid—I mean, I didn't know if..." She stopped again.

"Is there something wrong with me?"

"No! No—not you. It's me—my—my deformity. There—I said it!"

"Oh, Jenny—Jenny. Why didn't you tell me that before? Here all this time I thought it was something about me that you..."

She pressed her fingers to his lips, and once again they embraced. He whispered in her ear, "I'll always love you, Jenny; and, when I come back, maybe we can get..."

"I know. I know how you feel. It's too soon. I *will* wait for you, no matter how long the war lasts. I'll be here for you when you return."

"I'm so sorry. I must leave now. I could hold you in my arms forever." He stepped back a little but held her hands in his. "I have a lot to do to get ready, and Colonel Johnson says we might leave tomorrow. Maybe I can see you one more time before we go." Jenny cried as he made his way to the door.

Night had fallen when Joshua went off to war. It was a cloudless night, and the stars shone brightly in the black night sky. The cool air was charged with patriotism, shouts of victory, and cheers from the onlookers. Young ladies and old women were handing many kinds of food and drinks out to the soldiers assembling in the town square. The band played "Dixie", and white handkerchiefs were waved by the crowd as a loving farewell gesture. Black smoke, from the many torches lighting the square, drifted into the heavens. Larger-than-life shadows moved across the surrounding buildings and the ground, as the men and horses slowly moved into formation.

After a few speeches from the Mayor and Colonel Johnson, orders to prepare to march were shouted down the chain of command. The new crimson Confederate flag was unfurled, and the drums began their marching cadence. Joshua presented a striking figure, dressed in his new, butternut gray uniform, astride his strong, black steed. Jenny, always shy in a crowd, stood behind her father's storefront window, waving a small handkerchief. Joshua had been unable to have one last meeting with her. He tipped his hat and smiled at her as he rode by the window. His first kiss had been his last before leaving. It had awakened his heart to a new dimension. Why had her love for him bloomed just at that time? If only they had had more time together. These were his thoughts as he waved farewell to his pretty young Jenny.

It was as if a great tornado had touched down and swept all of the young men up into a whirlwind—a whirlwind that would bring death and destruction and leave that small town as silent as a graveyard—except for the bell high up in the church steeple. It tolled many times in the next four years, each time announcing the death of another fallen son from Perch, Virginia at the mouth of the Peddler River.

CHAPTER 15

▼

CROSSROADS OF DESTINY

All was quiet in the tiny town of Emmitsburg, Maryland, as Patrick strained to stay awake on the front steps of St. Joseph's Catholic Church while awaiting the return message from the commander. He thought it might be about troop movements, but that wasn't his concern. His job was only to deliver it and return the reply to his commanding officer. He thought he heard a voice coming from the graveyard. It sounded like someone singing in low tones. Rising to his feet, he walked down the path to investigate. Suddenly, a hand holding a whiskey bottle popped out from behind a tombstone and flopped to the ground immediately in front of him. Patrick bent over and peered around the tombstone to see a young soldier sitting on the ground, leaning against it, singing what sounded like an old Irish ballad.

"What are you doing here, Private?" Pat asked.

The young soldier looked up and raised the hand that held the bottle. "Here, Sarge! Have a swig. It's good for what ails ya."

"No, thanks. You'd better get rid of that bottle before somebody sees you."

The private raised the bottle to his mouth, cocked back his head, and took a long swallow, paying no attention to Patrick's remark.

"Are you supposed to be on guard duty?" Pat asked.

Lowering the bottle to the ground with one hand and wiping his mouth with the other, he looked up at Patrick with bloodshot eyes, reflecting the dim light from the church lanterns. "No, Sarge. I'm just a messenger boy."

Patrick suddenly realized why the captain had sent a second messenger. Just then, Pat saw a colonel approaching the church steps, as the three little nuns were descending them. One of them held a lantern by her side. "Sh-h-h! Be quiet, Private!" Patrick whispered. "It's a colonel! If he sees you, you'll be in big trouble."

Patrick stayed in the shadows, wondering what to do next. He listened as the colonel spoke to the nuns. "Good evening, Sisters." They all nodded their heads. He continued, "I guess your prayers were heard—I mean, from this morning, when we didn't know where the next battle would take place. You said that you'd be praying that it wouldn't happen here in Emmitsburg."

The older nun, looking very serious, replied, "Yes, Colonel. The Good Lord spared our little town. Now we must pray for those poor souls in Gettysburg—all the soldiers, too."

"Yes, Sister. It's already started, as you probably know from the sounds reverberating from there." As an afterthought, he added, "Would you like an escort back to your convent?"

"We'll be fine, Colonel. Thank you anyway." They all nodded once again and made their way toward the convent, their lantern light growing dimmer in the enveloping darkness as they walked.

Patrick emerged from the shadows and walked up to the colonel. "Oh, there you are, Sergeant. I didn't see you over there. Just came out to find you."

"Yes, Sir," Pat responded. "I was just looking over some of those tombstones. Some go back a hundred years or more."

Holding a piece of paper in his hand, the colonel handed it to Patrick. "Take this message back to your commanding officer. Leave right away, and don't stop for anything. It's important that you deliver it as soon as you arrive back at your outfit."

"Yes sir, Colonel." Patrick saluted and briefly glanced over at the spot where the drunken private was concealed.

"I know about the private, Sergeant. Don't concern yourself about him. He's the captain's nephew. We will deal with him. Now be on your way—make haste!"

Pat mounted his horse and sped off down the dirt road with his invaluable dispatch. He felt slightly more confident than he was on his journey *to* Emmitsburg, since he hadn't encountered any Confederates on the way there. It was after midnight; he was tired and anxious to get back to his regiment. He pushed hard all the way back to make the old nag go faster.

After arriving and handing the message to his captain, he went back to his tent and fell asleep. He had only slept a short while when he was awakened by a loud blast from the bugler's horn, announcing reveille. He opened his eyes, lit the small candle he had pulled from his haversack, and squinted at his watch with the broken crystal. Three-thirty a.m. Another march. Won't be long. Gettysburg! Just a few miles, he thought. The bonfire in front of his tent still had some glowing embers. The men quickly rekindled them enough to boil water and make coffee. Patrick slugged down a fast cup, helped the others take down their tents, and quickly got into formation. He marched along with his comrades, half awake—marching toward a little town in Pennsylvania just over the Maryland border. He had scored high in his geography tests in school and had remembered the locations of Pittsburgh and Philadelphia from his lessons and also a small town named Lawrenceville, where a cousin lived. But he had never heard of Gettysburg before Lou Ann had mentioned it. He couldn't see the thousands of men behind or in front of him, as they fast approached the little town; but he knew that he was a small part of something big—very big—something that could decide the future of his new country.

His brigade advanced up the dark, dirt road, pausing and resting briefly before arriving at dawn at a place called Cemetery Ridge. His regiment was deployed on that ridge and faced the enemy who were a mile to the west on Seminary Ridge. After positioning themselves, they rested. The sun slowly rose behind them, and they had a clear view of the enemy's position across that vast, expansive terrain. Some men played cards, wrote letters, or attempted to sleep; others prayed. Patrick lay on his back on the ground, listening to the intermittent crackle of small arms fire from their own skirmishers out in front of their lines. Not knowing when his regiment would be called into action, he fell into an uneasy sleep.

The clamor of horse drawn caissons and cannon, moving swiftly up the Taneytown Road, broke his rest. He quickly sat up to see batteries of cannon being brought into position along the ridge by their hardworking crews. He was tired but gave up on getting any sleep. Some of his men had cooked a pot of beans, which he ate along with hardtack. As he sat on the ground dunking the hard crackers into his coffee, the young private to whom he had given the Saint Michael prayer at Taneytown approached him. "Hi, Sarge. I see you're tryin' to soften up them 'teeth dullers'—almost broke my teeth first time I bit into one."

"Yeah, Private. These things are hard as bullets. Now if we could find a way to shoot them at Johnny Reb, we'd win this war in no time!"

The private laughed out loud. "That's a good one, Sergeant."

"You got a name, Private?" Pat asked, as he chewed on the hard cracker and took a sip of coffee from his metal cup.

"Michael—Michael's the name, Sergeant."

Pat looked at him, somewhat surprised. "Well, what do you know? Here I gave you the Saint Michael prayer and never even knew he was your patron saint."

"Yeah, Sarge. Guess I was named after an angel!" he remarked, chuckling as he spoke. "I didn't catch *your* name, though, Sarge."

"Patrick O'Hanrahan." He extended his hand and warmly shook Michael's. "Guess we didn't properly introduce ourselves last time."

Patrick was becoming less eager to make new friends, since the loss of the Big Swede. He tried to be sociable with his comrades, but he retained his fear of losing another close friend. He was well aware that the odds of his survival were dwindling with each battle. Only 150 men or less. Regiment getting smaller. Will any of us be left? He quickly dismissed these thoughts, as he continued eating.

"You from New York City, too, Sarge?"

"Yeah, and I can't wait for this damn war to get over so I can get back there."

"You got a girl back home?"

"Well—yes. Haven't seen her in two years, though." Pat finished his meal and got up to clean his plate, tossing out the last of his coffee and the grounds that had settled to the bottom of his cup. He felt that the conversation was getting a little too personal and purposely refrained from asking any questions about the private's life. Nor was he about to divulge any more information about his own.

Patrick slowly began to walk away from Michael, turning his face toward him as he did. "Take care now, Michael, and don't forget that prayer I gave you. I have to check out the ammunition for our squad—may be needing it soon, you know."

Many of the men had sought relief from the blazing hot sun beneath the cool shade of the maple trees. After supplying them with sufficient ammunition, Pat strolled amongst them, wiping the sweat from his brow. "Check your weapons! Be at the ready!" Standing on the ridge, gazing across the large, expansive plain between him and the enemy, he could see some cannon being placed at intervals along the opposite ridge and the glare of sunlight reflecting from a few locations. This he perceived to be spyglasses. It was only a matter of time; the waiting was the worst. The Third Corps on his left had been moving troops all morning to a spot closer to the enemy, out in front of their own established lines. By late afternoon, he heard the familiar sounds of battle coming from the forward position the corps had assumed. The "ball" had opened once again.

Patrick hoped he might get a hasty letter off to Beth, when the bugler blasted out the call to assemble. He folded up the blank piece of paper and quickly stuck it in his pocket. He assembled his men into formation and marched them a short distance with the rest of the Irish Brigade. Suddenly they halted. For a moment, he didn't know why. A small, bearded man dressed in black, stepped up on a large rock and began to speak. It was the chaplain, Father William Corby—a familiar face to Patrick. The Priest raised his right hand, and the men knelt and bowed their heads. The little chaplain called upon God to give the men courage to do their duty and gave them general absolution for their sins. Pat silently asked the Almighty for forgiveness. As Father Corby prayed, a high-ranking, distinguished looking officer, sitting erect in the saddle, slowly made his way to the outer rim of the circle of men. The rider halted, removed his hat, and bowed his head. Pat recognized him as General Winfield Scott Hancock.

As the men returned to their marching formation, Patrick could hear a loud battle in progress a short distance away. This one's gonna be a beaut, he thought. "*Saint Michael, the Archangel, be with us. Protect us in battle,*" he repeated over and over again. The intense heat of the day caused the sweat to trickle down Pat's face, irritating his eyes. He quickly wiped them with his sleeve, but the dust and dirt on it only compounded the problem.

The Brigade made its way down from the ridge, across a small stream, and through a wooded area toward a stony hill. They looked for the enemy but didn't know exactly where the Rebs were. Looking up the hill that was covered with trees and large rocks, Patrick suddenly spotted some gray uniforms about thirty yards away. "There they are!" he screamed out. A flurry of lead showered down the hill, clipping leaves and smashing against rocks. Patrick and his men returned the initial volley as they advanced up the little, stony hill. A young private, carrying Old Glory, was hit and went down. Another man picked it up and ran forward with it. Still another, pressing forward, holding the emerald green Irish banner, fell to the ground. It was immediately raised back up by another brave lad who followed behind the Stars and Stripes into the fray. The Rebels, firing downhill, were overshooting the Yanks. Charging up the hill, Patrick shot a Rebel six feet in front of him. Some close combat ensued, and a few more volleys were exchanged. The Irish drove the Rebels off the hill, taking a number of prisoners as they did. Patrick stopped and reloaded, watching the retreating Rebels running away through a large wheat field ready for harvesting. He advanced with his brigade, as they drove the Rebs back further. He could feel victory in his grasp, when, suddenly, a counterattack by the Rebs came without warning, and the Yanks were forced back to the rocks at the stony hill. Union officers urged the brigade forward, and once again they charged, driving the enemy back. Patrick tripped over a body, partially concealed in the tall wheat, and landed on his side a few inches from the dead man's face. His eyes were wide open and glaring directly at Patrick. He jumped to his feet and caught up with the rest. The flush of victory was short lived, when, in an instant, the tide turned once more when Confederate reinforcements came on, screaming their bloody Rebel yell and forcing the Yanks back to the protection of the trees and rocks again. After a few moments of reloading and catching his breath, Patrick heard the unmistakable bugler's call to charge once again. The battle seesawed two more times, and each counterattack by the enemy became more difficult to repel. The Rebels were now pressing harder and coming in on the Irish Brigade's flanks. Patrick knew there was no hope of victory now. His brief glimpse of hope in the beginning of the battle had all but vanished, as the gray uniforms increased in number and were pressing in from three sides. Some of the men on either side of him were shot dead; others ran as fast as their legs would carry them. The Rebels artillery had zeroed in on Pat's brigade, and the shells were blasting holes in their ranks. It was happening all over again. Fredericksburg—Chancellorsville—now *another* defeat. He was angry but fearful of being captured again. He was about to retreat with the others when he saw a young, Confederate officer on horseback charging down on him. One more shot. Get me an officer before I go. He knelt down, braced his elbow on his knee, took careful aim, and waited until the rider came closer. As he placed his finger on the trigger, he noticed the officer was riding a black stallion. His hat had blown off, exposing a full head of red hair. At the very moment Pat was about to pull the trigger, a shaft of sunlight reflected off an object hanging around the rider's neck, catching Patrick's eye. He remembered Nathan telling him about meeting a Confederate named Joshua who wore a medal like Pat's. For an instant, Pat lost his soldier's heart. Could that rider possibly be Joshua? The thought zipped through his mind. His human heart flashed back for a split second to two young boys whittling pieces of wood by the roadside. Can't chance it. The soldier's heart won out.

As he began to apply pressure with his trigger finger, he was suddenly blown backward by a loud explosion a short distance in front of him. A shell had almost killed him. As he lay on his back, he felt severe pain in his shoulder and neck. He felt of the wound and saw that his hand was covered with blood. Forcing himself to his feet, he saw the black stallion lying on its side, motionless. He quickly gazed around to see where the rider was. No sign of him—maybe concealed in the tall wheat. Got to get out of here. He picked up his rifle and ran to catch up with his men. Stopping once and reloading with his good arm, he fired at the oncoming Rebs, then fell back toward his own lines once again. After retreating a hundred yards or so, he stopped to reload once more but couldn't—the pain was getting worse, and the Rebels were hot on his heels. He didn't bother to shoot any more. He ran and kept running. Not gonna get captured again. He finally caught up with the rest; and they arrived back on Cemetery Ridge, which was now occupied with their reinforcements. The Rebels halted at the base of the ridge.

Darkness fell. Patrick made his way back to a hospital tent in the rear of their lines. Many wounded were carried in on stretchers; but this time, unlike Fredericksburg, he walked on his own two feet. As he entered the tent, he was immediately repulsed by the sight of a surgeon amputating a soldier's leg. The screams of agony from the victim, as the doctor performed his gruesome task, horrified him even more than the battle he had just survived. Patrick could see it would be some time before he could receive any attention for his wound. The other wounded filled the tent to capacity, many so much worse off than he, moaning and begging for water. Patrick felt so helpless. He was, however, happy to offer the small amount of water left in his canteen to one of the soldiers he thought was dying, lying on the ground.

An assistant to the doctor, wearing a blood-stained apron, finally approached. "Let's have a look at this shoulder, son." He pulled back the torn remnants of Patrick's shirt. "Looks pretty deep. You caught a shell fragment. Neck's cut in a few places, too. Here—bite down on this—it may hurt for a moment." He gave Pat a small piece of wood and picked up a large tweezer-like instrument. Pat took the wood and placed it between his teeth. The man probed into Patrick's shoulder; and, in an instant, he withdrew a large piece of metal, as Patrick bit down and broke the piece of wood in two. "Got it all in one piece, son. And you didn't let out a peep. Brave lad you are."

"Thanks, Sir," as he spit the splinters from his mouth.

The surgeon's assistant then sprinkled some powder on Pat's wounds and bandaged them up. "Lucky for you, son. No fragments in your neck. Just a few superficial cuts." He fashioned a sling and put it around Patrick's arm. "You may need this to help relieve the strain on that shoulder. You won't be doing any fighting for awhile." He scurried off to help another patient.

The smells and screams were all too familiar to Patrick. He walked out of the tent, noticing more dead bodies outside. They were lined up in rows, covered with blankets. He wanted to distance himself from all of that agony and death, as he continued walking further from the field hospital. Completely exhausted, he only wanted quiet and solitude. He didn't want to speak or listen to anyone. He found a stretch of isolated ground nearby and gingerly lay down on his good side, holding his shoulder, which was throbbing with pain. As he gazed up at the black, night sky, sprinkled with bright, little stars, visions of the battlefield unfolded in his mind. He could vividly see the whole battlefield as a huge quilt—a patchwork of blue and gray fabric—stitched together with the common thread of misery, pain, and death. It blanketed the tall wheat with bodies pressing it down. Some lay still—others writhing in pain. He imagined the unknown farmer who had planted the wheat, plowing his field in this little obscure acre on a warm, spring day, gentle breeze rustling through the trees. The farmer expected a harvest of wheat, he thought to himself. Instead, his wheat field became a harvest of death. The grim reaper had swung his giant scythe and cut down the very lifeblood of American youth—that same youth whose blood was now drowning the very wheat grown to sustain life.

The many families of these brave, slain soldiers had been robbed of their loved ones; and grief spread throughout the land, as more families, North and South, were devastated.

Patrick had heard someone in the hospital tent saying that his regiment had lost twenty-five men. Not many more than a hundred left now, he thought to himself, as he breathed in the fresh-smelling night air and finally dozed off.

A sharp pain in his shoulder woke him just before dawn. He sat up, holding his hand over the bandaged wound. The sounds of a blue jay shrieking in a nearby tree mingled with the moans emanating from the hospital tent. It seemed to him as if all of nature was crying out in agony. He got to his feet and slowly walked back toward his company. As he reached the crest of the little ridge, he could see his comrades in the gray light of dawn beginning to rekindle the glowing embers from the previous night's campfires to cook their breakfast. It was a peaceful sight. Patrick was thankful for these moments between battles, even though they were only temporary. One day, this God-forsaken war will be over—no more bullets—no more battles—no more killing—*please,* God.

A few horses were standing together under a small clump of trees, munching on bales of hay. The black horse, he thought—dead. The rider—couldn't be Joshua. *Could* it be Joshua? It seemed like a million years ago when he and Josh played and laughed together in that youthful bubble of time when summer never ended and their world was young. What happened? How will it all end? Country fractured. No victories. And now—could it be? Could it be Josh lying in that farmer's field of wheat?

"Hey, Sergeant!" He heard someone calling from behind. He turned to see his new friend, Michael, running to catch up with him. "Hey, Sarge, wait up! See you made it through that awful wheatfield."

"Well, I got out alive, but caught one in the shoulder," as he pointed to his wound.

"You caught a bullet?"

"No—shell blew up—right in front of me. Tossed me back like a feather." Pat paused for a moment. "See you came out all right."

Michael smiled. "Yep, not a scratch! Heard a few Minie' balls whizzing by me, but none of 'em hit their mark."

"Well, I guess we both got a lot to be thankful for—we're still breathing."

They walked back to their regiment in silence, as the sun rose slowly in the East, lighting up Cemetery Ridge, dotted with blue uniforms, black cannon, and white tents. So far, all was quiet. What the afternoon would bring they could never imagine. The one clear sound that drifted across the hot July wind was the pealing of a church bell in the little nearby town that Lou Ann was from.

CHAPTER 16

▼

LIGHT A CANDLE FOR ME

It was early in the morning of July 1ˢᵗ when Lou Ann awoke in her mother's home on the outskirts of the sleepy little town of Gettysburg. She was unaware that, at that time, Patrick was among the ninety thousand Union soldiers in the Army of the Potomac that were marching her way and were within a few miles. Union cavalry were even closer—and so were the Confederates!

After recovering from pneumonia in the hospital in Washington, Lou Ann was sent home to recuperate in the fresh, country air by her father, the Colonel. She was feeling somewhat better and felt a need to attend Mass in thanksgiving to the Good Lord for sparing her life. She was gradually becoming stronger after being racked by the ordeal of a deadly disease that took many lives. Her hospitalization had afforded her plenty of time to think, and she was beginning to search her heart for answers to many questions. She planned to ask God during Holy Mass for these answers. Hitching up the horse to the buggy, she rode the few miles into town to the little, red brick church named after Saint Francis Xavier. It was already warm and sunny and appeared it would get very hot that day. As the horse walked slowly along the Emmitsburg Road, the lone passenger enjoyed the beauty and serenity of the rich Pennsylvania farmland. The corn and wheat fields were ripening in the warm, morning sunlight. A farmer working in his field near the road tipped his straw hat, and she waved back at him. She began to appreciate the pleasant atmosphere she had left a few short years before. After her experiences in Washington, with its constant noisy traffic and congestion along the muddy dirt roads, she began to wonder why she had moved away from home in the first place. But something else was churning inside of her. What if I had died? Could I have done more? Can spies get into Heaven?

One night, when she had been on death's doorstep in the hospital, an older nun had come to visit her. Sister Agnes Mary had cared for her during her early childhood years in the orphanage in Philadelphia. Lou Ann seemed to remember briefly awakening at that time from her delirious, feverish state to see the nun sitting in a chair at her bedside watching her while fingering her rosary beads. The Sister had risen to her feet, placed her cool hand on Lou Ann's burning forehead, and uttered a few words. "God will heal you." After a long pause, she added, "Help the orphans." The next morning, her fever was gone—and so was Sister Agnes Mary. But the nun's few words would be buried in her heart forever. She never did find out how the little nun knew she had been sick in the hospital. Nor could she ever find out anything more about it, as no one there seemed to have seen her.

As Lou Ann's strength slowly returned, her strength of purpose also grew. There was something beyond her hopes and dreams for her own life— something that seemed much greater—something she felt that was taking on a spiritual dimension. But she wasn't sure what it was. She had turned a corner in her life—a *big* corner. God healed me—He will surely show me the way, she thought, as she continued along the old dirt road into town. She parked her buggy in back of the church, tied up the horse, and entered through the back door. She knelt down in the front pew; and after a short while, the priest appeared on the altar and began to say Mass. Father O'Brien gave a short homily about loving one another, and she then received Holy Communion. As she knelt there praying, she thanked God for her healing and asked Him for direction. "I am your willing servant, oh Lord. Show me what You want of me. And Lord, let *Your* will be done." As the priest gave the final blessing, gunshots and explosions rattled the church windows; and he quickly ended the Mass. He and the handful of parishioners scurried to the front door of the church, where they saw blue-clad Union cavalry charging down the street, heading west. They were relieved to see that these were friendly forces; however, some of the parishioners who had seen a Rebel detachment passing through town a few days prior to this, began to fear that full-blown battle would break out here. Lou Ann, however, had been staying at her mother's house on the other side of town and had not known of this Confederate presence. Some panicked and quickly ran from the church to their homes, worried for the safety of their families.

"Must get home—look after Mother," Lou Ann blurted out to the priest.

"No, my dear. It's safer here. Come inside—all of you," said Father O'Brien, as he held the door open, motioning for them to come into the church. He tried to calm them down, but more of them took off running. They tried to stay close to the buildings for fear of being trampled, as more Union cavalry raced by. A few of the ladies and older men withdrew back inside the church, but Lou Ann dashed out to get to her horse and buggy. As she rounded the corner, however, her heart sank... no horse or buggy anywhere in sight! She stopped for a moment, wondering what to do. I'll walk, she thought. Yes—I can make it. Must get to Mother.

She came back to the road and began to walk home. Just starting out, she was approached by a Union soldier. "Get off the street!" he shouted. "Go to your home!"

"My home is a few miles from here," as she continued to walk, determined to get to her mother.

"Lady, get off the street! You could get shot!" He motioned with his rifle for her to move. "Rebs comin' this way, Miss. You better listen to me and get back inside."

She wasn't about to take his advice—until a stray enemy shell sailed overhead, making a shrill sound as it passed, followed by a loud explosion when it crashed into the street a block beyond them. She turned and quickly ran back into the church. Falling to her knees in the last pew, she prayed fervently with the remaining parishioners and Father O'Brien, as the sounds of a great battle began to rage a short distance away. She prayed for her mother's safety, the soldiers, and the innocent civilians trapped within the confines of this little town.

Sometime in the late morning, a Union colonel entered the church. He walked briskly up the middle aisle to the foot of the altar where Father O'Brien was kneeling. Bending over, he whispered something to the priest, then abruptly turned and left. Father then stood up and faced the tiny band of faithful. "I've just been informed by the good colonel that our whole town is now under martial law. Our troops have everything under control and are pushing the Confederate Army back west of town. He asked me to inform all of you that all civilians must remain where they are until further notice." He went on to say, "Don't worry, you may be able to go back to your homes by nightfall. In the meantime, we do have plenty of food in the rectory."

Shortly after, the front door of the church burst open; and Union soldiers, carrying their wounded, began to file in. Father O'Brien hurried to meet the stretcher-bearers, as a captain met him halfway up the aisle. "Sorry, Father, but we're going to have to use your church for our wounded." Pausing for a moment to catch his breath, he added, "All of the other buildings are filling up fast."

"Certainly son, bring them right in. Come this way." He guided the rag-tag, bloody band of Yankee soldiers up to the front of the church. "Here now, lads. Maybe you could lay the boys in the pews—that way there will be room to walk in the aisles."

"Thank you for your cooperation, Father. It's kind of you to let us use your church."

"Well, Captain—you see, it isn't *my* church—it's *God's* church. And He opens it for everyone, especially the needy. And these poor lads are certainly needy. Are there any doctors or nurses for these poor fellas?"

"We have a surgeon coming, Father. He should be here any minute, but I have to get back to the others now. Thanks again, Father. We'll be bringin' in more pretty soon." He hurriedly left the church.

Lou Ann gazed around the church at the many wounded soldiers, some moaning in pain and some crying out for water. She couldn't remember when she had felt so helpless. In the past, when she had worked for the Sanitary Commission and visited the wounded soldiers, like Patrick, their wounds had already been attended to. Her main duties only consisted of bringing them small items, reading to them, and generally being of some comfort to them. But now, it was different—they were bleeding and dying before her very eyes.

"Miss Sommers..." She turned to see the priest motioning her to come to his side. He was bent over one of the wounded men. "Go into the sacristy, behind the altar, and get me a bowl of water and..." He stopped abruptly. "No, never mind. I can do it quicker. Here— remove this man's shirt—tear it off if you have to. I'll be right back."

She looked down at the young man whose shirt was saturated with blood. She had never pretended to be a nurse, nor had she ever dealt with raw, open wounds before. But, like it or not, the gruesome task had fallen upon her without warning. She gingerly opened the man's shirt, exposing a bullet hole in his right upper chest. The blood had oozed out and partially stuck to his shirt as it had dried. He looked up at her, the pain showing in his eyes, as she tried to separate the shirt from his body as gently as she possibly could. Without thinking, she lifted her skirt to her knees and tore off a large piece of her cotton petticoat, folding it into a thick, padded mass. She then applied it to the wound, pressing down lightly. He let out a slight moaning sound. Father O'Brien came to her side carrying a large, white, ceramic bowl containing water. Draped over his shoulder and arms, hung towels and other linens, including some of his altar cloths.

"Looks like we'll need every piece of cloth we can get our hands on." He added, "Looks like you know what you're doing, young lady."

"No, Father. I really don't. It's a little frightening to me. I never did this before."

"You're doing fine. Here—use the water." He set the bowl down in the pew next to the man's feet. "We'll have to wash around their wounds first, then apply the bandages." He soaked another towel in the water and moved to attend another soldier. She turned back to her patient. His eyes were open and staring. He had died without uttering a word. She began to cry and shake at the same time.

Just then, a small hand reached over from behind Lou Ann and shut the man's eyes. She turned to see a petite, little nun dressed in the bluish-gray garb so familiar to her from her years in the orphanage. It was the habit of the Daughters of Charity of Saint Vincent de Paul, the same order as Sister Agnes Mary, the nun who had briefly appeared at her bedside in Washington. A large rosary, secured around her waist, had a metal Crucifix attached to the end of the beads, which hung almost to her ankles. Her headdress was unmistakable—immaculately white, flaring out in two large, wing-like appendages above her shoulders.

"It's all right, my dear. He's in God's hands now." She spoke softly, an aura of quiet confidence in her slight smile. "I'm Sister Bertha. And what is your name?"

"Lou Ann, Sister," she responded in a shaky voice.

"Come with me, Lou Ann. We shall work together." She took her by the hand and moved on to another wounded soldier. The proficiency and calm assuredness in which Sister Bertha worked impressed Lou Ann. After some time of working under the little nun's guidance, she began to develop some confidence and before long was able to attend the wounded by herself, only calling upon the good Sister from time to time. In fact, she had forgotten her own weakened condition, as she had become immersed in attending the men.

As she diligently worked, washing wounds, applying dressings, and changing the bloody water in the basin, a Union officer came in carrying a small, black bag in his right hand. He approached the good priest, who was also doing what he could for the ever-increasing number of wounded being carried into the church, in addition to baptizing some of the men and administering the Last Rites to the dying. "Are you the priest in charge here?" the officer asked abruptly.

"Yes, I am," Father answered, as he finished blessing the young man he had been ministering to and closing his eyes for all eternity.

"I'm Colonel Stedem, surgeon in charge here." Wasting no time, he continued, "Where can I operate?"

The priest looked around the church; and before he could give the colonel an answer, the officer blurted out, "How about that table up there?" He pointed to the altar.

"That's not just a table, sir. That's our *Altar*."

The colonel appeared somewhat embarrassed. "I'm sorry, Priest—I didn't know."

"You can call me Father if you wish. And, about using the altar for an operating table—no—that's not possible."

"I only suggested it because it seems to be just the right size for me to do my work."

"I'm sure God wouldn't mind. In fact, I suppose, in a way, these soldiers' sacrifice and bloodletting could be joined to the ultimate sacrifice of Jesus. However, Colonel, for practical reasons, I don't think it would be good for the others. I mean, the altar is up high and in plain view of the whole church, and that wouldn't be good for all to see."

"You're absolutely right, Priest—I mean—Father. Would you have a back room, possibly out of sight?"

"Yes, the sacristy behind the altar. That would be better." Father O'Brien started up the aisle accompanied by the colonel, and they entered the sacristy through a door leading from the altar area. The room had ample space to set up an operating table, but there wasn't a table big enough to lay a body on.

"We can't delay, Father. Must find a table quickly. If we don't remove the limbs of some of these boys soon, gangrene will set in and kill them."

Father O'Brien looked around. "Nothing big enough here. How about if I bring my kitchen table over from…"

Before he could finish his sentence, the colonel had walked over to the back door and began to rip it off its hinges. He then moved two small tables, spacing them apart, and setting the door on top of them. "This will do. Sorry, Father. We'll reimburse you for your door."

Two of the colonel's assistants had entered the room, awaiting further orders. The colonel looked at them expectantly. "Well, boys, what are you waiting for? Go find the worst of the worst and let's get started. Line them up so we won't be waiting in between patients." He proceeded to set his black bag on the makeshift table, opened it and laid out a two-foot saw; two large, sharp carving knives; a small, six-inch knife; and a probe-like instrument.

Then, from the bottom of the bag, he pulled out a clean, white apron to cover his clothes from his chest down to his knees. The last items were a bottle of chloroform and two whiskey bottles. He opened one of them and took a short swig, then wiped his mouth with his sleeve. By the time he put on his apron, the first casualty had been brought in. "That's damn good liquor. Hope we have enough to go around. Now let's get at it."

A young private, loudly moaning, was laid on the table by the two assistants. He had a bullet in his knee that had shattered the bone. The assistants had torn his pant leg off, exposing the gaping wound with the broken kneecap splintered beyond repair. One assistant soaked a towel with chloroform and applied it to the boy's face. He quickly became unconscious. "This one should be easy," remarked the colonel. "It's the boys we have to work on when the chloroform and whiskey run out that get difficult. If that happens, Father, we may need your help." The priest nodded, and the surgeon picked up one of his long knives and began to cut off the boy's leg just above the knee. After hitting the thighbone, he grabbed his two-foot saw and proceeded to saw through the bone as if he were sawing a piece of wood. He then turned to the priest, his white apron spotted with blood. "We won't be needing you now, Father, but I'll call you if we do."

"I'll be out in the church, tending to the other poor lads. They'll be needin' some spiritual comfort. So many... so many..." He walked back to the growing numbers of suffering wounded.

By now, the church was half-filled with Yankee casualties. Lou Ann continued to work feverishly, doing all that she could. She was too busy to worry about her mother. Some time in the early afternoon, she heard a commotion in the streets. It grew louder by the minute. Panic filled her heart as she opened the door. Union soldiers were running in retreat through the streets, some taking time to turn and fire at the oncoming enemy, others running without stopping. A cannon had overturned in front of the church. The horse pulling it and its caisson had fallen to the ground. It was dead, and a steady stream of Yankees was jumping over it as they retreated in haste. Gunshots were heard coming from other streets, and Lou Ann could see the town was rapidly falling into Confederate hands. She quickly closed the door, only to have it flung open once again by some of the wounded inside who were still able to walk and were afraid of capture.

"Think we can make it out of here?"

"Naw—looks like the Rebs are comin' on fast—can't chance it. Lock the doors!"

They stood in silence for a moment. Trapped, Lou Ann thought. Trapped in here. Hope Mother's safe.

Sister Bertha, who had walked over to the small group, seemed unperturbed. She could see that Lou Ann was visibly shaken. "Don't worry, my dear. They don't take civilian prisoners. But these poor lads," she whispered, "I'm afraid they could wind up in a Southern prison." After a brief pause, she continued, "Now let's get back to work." She calmly walked back and continued her works of mercy, as Lou Ann followed, deep in thought. I'm not just a civilian—what if I'm recognized? I'll be taken prisoner—or worse! The Confederates might even hang me! She busied herself with her work, attempting to overcome her fear of being captured again.

As day turned to evening, the light in the church grew dimmer by the hour. Father O'Brien made his rounds, lighting candles on both sides of the church beside each window and on the main altar, reserving some to replenish those burning in the back operating room. At one point, Lou Ann went into the sacristy to get more towels. To her horror, the first thing she observed was a small pile of amputated limbs in the corner of the room. She became nauseated and began to cry. Before she could regain her composure, she was shocked to see the surgeon amputating another limb from a young private. Feeling faint, she quickly ran from the room, slamming the door shut behind her, and slumped down into a crouching position against the wall, sobbing into her open hands pressed against her face. It was becoming too much for her to handle; and now, just as she was beginning to accustom herself to the ghastly, open wounds of the men, she had been confronted with more frightful, repugnant images.

What had started out to be a peaceful morning at Mass had turned into a nightmare. Her weakened condition compounded her problems; and she prayed for strength to go on, as she gazed at the large picture of Saint Francis Xavier holding the Crucifix which hung above the altar. More casualties were brought into the church, and the moaning and cries for water increased. She continued to pray. "Lord God, help me. You who suffered so terribly for our sins, give me strength to help these poor souls." She had remembered a sermon that a priest had given at Mass once. He had called it the "Absurdity of the Cross." She had remembered that the priest had said that the world shies away from the Cross and suffering; and in so doing, it denies itself the Crucifixion Power that can only come from the Innocent Lamb of God. As she wiped away her tears, she felt a gradual renewal of strength radiate throughout her body and a more emboldened spirit settling upon her. She rose to her feet and stood for a moment, listening. Something was missing.

What was it? The clamor of battle had been raging in the streets; but now, as Lou Ann listened intently, all was quiet outside the church—all but an occasional gunshot in the distance.

She braced herself to continue her previous errand to get the badly needed linens from the sacristy, when, suddenly, the doors of the church burst open. There stood six Confederate soldiers with pointed rifles aimed toward the front of the church where Lou Ann was standing near the altar. The small band of Confederates walked up the middle aisle, searching for armed Yankees. Seeing only unarmed wounded men, the Rebel colonel and his men stopped halfway up the aisle. The officer pulled out a document from his breast pocket, and began to read aloud:

> *"By the authority vested in me by the Confederate States of America, let it be known to all citizens of this community that all of its inhabitants and property within its confines shall, from this moment forward, be subject to the authority of the Army of Northern Virginia. In addition, all Federal military personnel are now officially prisoners of war."*
>
> *Signed,*
> *Robert E. Lee, C.S.A.*
> *Commanding General*

Father O'Brien, who was praying over a dying man, got up and approached the Confederate colonel. "My God, man! What do you think you're doin' comin' into my church with loaded guns? Have ya no decency or respect for a House of God?"

The colonel, taken by surprise, didn't seem to have a quick response. After a brief moment of silence, he said, "Well, Father, I'm only following orders. Can't be sure..."

The priest interrupted. "Well, look around ya, man!" as he defiantly stared down the officer. "Ya think any of these poor devils can harm ya?"

"Can't afford to take any chances, Father."

"Well, now, I'd be thankin' ya to have your men put down their rifles. There won't be any shootin' in *this* church."

The colonel complied and ordered his men to lower their muskets. "With all due respect, Father, we'll have to bring in some of *our* wounded. We need every available space we can find."

Father O'Brien softened his tone. "We'll do what we can, Colonel. But as you can see, we don't have a great deal of space here and sorely need more medical supplies. However, we wouldn't turn anyone away, as long as the Good Lord supplies the space."

"I'll see that you get your medical supplies, and, hopefully, a surgeon, too."

"Well, Colonel, we do have a Union surgeon operating in the sacristy now, but he can use some help."

"I'll see what I can do." The officer started to walk away, then stopped and turned back to the priest. "Oh, one more thing, Father—I'll have to leave my men here. I have my orders to post guards in and around the building." Father O'Brien nodded in agreement, as the colonel left.

As the evening wore on and the steady stream of Confederate wounded were being brought in, completely filling the rest of the pews and some of the floor space, Lou Ann, Sister Bertha, Father O'Brien, and one nurse who the Confederates had supplied, worked tirelessly to care for both blue and gray alike. Father prayed and blessed the men, occasionally giving Last Rites to those whose battle had ended forever. The four Confederate guards, rifles resting at their sides, were each stationed in a corner of the church and looked on in silence.

Just finishing the care of a Union soldier, Lou Ann's attention was drawn to the back of the church by someone's anguished cries. "My babies—my babies." Walking back to the last pew, she began to attend to the distressed Confederate lying there. He had a severe wound in his side, and his shirt was saturated with blood. His eyes were covered with a bloody, makeshift bandage.

Lou Ann spoke softly to him. "It will be all right, young man. I'm here to help you." She began to wipe the blood from his side after removing his shirt.

"My babies..."

"You have children?" Lou Ann inquired.

"Yes..." He attempted to raise himself up on one elbow, but fell back, moaning. "Twin girls, Sister. My wife died when they was born. Nobody to take care of my babies," he whispered.

She was about to tell him she wasn't a nun, but stopped herself. Why? What good would it serve? Maybe he'll get some comfort thinking a Sister is here with him.

"Is it nighttime, Sister? Can't see anything."

"Yes, it is, but we have candles around the church. And many votive candles right here behind us, in the back."

"What's a votive candle?"

"Well—when we want to pray for someone, we sometimes light a candle for them, even if that person is deceased." Lou Ann remembered her years in the orphan asylum. She, too, had no parents for a time.   She began to wonder how her father was killed in the Mexican War. Did he have time before he died to think about never seeing her again? Did he die alone? Or had someone comforted him as she was attempting to do here? She finished washing and dressing the wound in his side and began to unravel the bloody bandages over his eyes, revealing a deep gash in his forehead. The boy never complained.   She washed the blood that had dried his eyelids shut, and he slowly began to blink his one eye. She cleaned around the gash and applied a fresh bandage.

"I can see!" hollered the boy. "I can see!" His other eyelid never opened. "Thank you, Sister—thank you. I thought I was blind." His sudden elation rapidly deteriorated as he grew weaker, his speech returning to a whisper.

The Confederate doctor, having arrived at the church, approached Lou Ann. "You're doing a good job, Sister."

"Thank you, but I'm not a nun," she whispered.

"Oh, I'm sorry—I thought…"

"That's all right." She got up and allowed the doctor to sit down in the pew next to the boy. "He's very weak," she whispered.

The doctor examined the young Confederate, felt his pulse, then stood up. In whispered tones, he said to her, "Make him as comfortable as possible—he doesn't have much time." He left to attend another soldier.

She found a jacket lying on the floor and propped it under the boy's head.

"Please hold my hand, Sister—I'm cold…" It was very hot inside the church. She grasped his hand in hers. "Sister—Sister…"

"Yes, I'm here."

"My babies—will you…" He coughed up some blood. "Will you—I mean—can you look after them? My name is…" He coughed up more blood.

"Yes, Private. Now try to rest."

He strained to get the words out. "My name is Clem—Haywood—Cowpasture, Virginia."

She thought of the private's request. Have I made a false promise? Oh, God, help me. How could I ever take care of his children?

The young private turned his head and gazed at a small Crucifix, about one foot in length, hanging on the back wall of the church, illuminated by many votive candles. "Is that Man hanging there Jesus?" he asked.

"Yes, it is."

"I never did see one like that—only a cross—never saw His Body like that."

"Yes, Private. He did that for love of us."

He became quiet and continued to gaze at the Crucifix. Finally he spoke. "Never did have time for religion back home." She wiped the blood trickling down his chin. "Sister, can you tell me about Him?"

"I think the priest can tell you better than I can. I'll be right back. Now you rest."

She searched the church and found the priest praying with one of the wounded. When he finished, he followed her back to the private. She was convinced that the man wouldn't live much longer and asked the priest for a paper and pencil. She had seen enough dying soldiers to know that many had been buried without identification. Her concern was also for his twin girls. Would they know where he was buried when they grew up? She wrote on the paper:

"Private Clem Haywood, Cowpasture, Virginia, C.S.A.
Whosoever lays this young soldier to rest—please mark his grave with the above information. A simple Cross will do."

Father O'Brien had a gift of joy about him. He had quietly moved from one man to another, always speaking softly and compassionately. He had a peaceful countenance and a dear smile on his face, even when things looked grim. He spent considerable time engaging the private in conversation and answering his questions. The good priest ended by baptizing him, then got up and turned to Lou Ann who was standing a few feet behind him. "He's a good boy—sincere—eager to know Jesus. I heard his confession and—well—as Scripture says, 'Only God can read the mind and probe the heart.'" Smiling confidently at Lou Ann, Father O'Brien finished by adding, "And this boy, I believe, has a good heart!"

After the priest left, Lou Ann sat down next to the private, folding the paper with his name on it and quietly slipping it into his pant pocket. He lay there with his eyes closed, a serene look of peace on his face. She was about to get up when he opened his one good eye. "Sister, please light a candle for me."

"Of course I will. Now you try to get some sleep." She stood up and looked around the church for the next person she could help. Suddenly feeling faint, she leaned against the wall for support.

Sister Bertha saw her and came to her aid. "Oh, my dear, you must get some rest. Come with me."

"I'll be all right. Just give me a minute."

"No, no. I insist you get some rest." The nun took her by the arm and led her up the stairs in the back of the church to the choir loft. Father O'Brien had carried a mattress from his house and placed it there for Lou Ann and Sister. She insisted Lou Ann lie down. "My dear, if you don't rest, you won't be able to help anyone tomorrow. I'll go and get you some soup from the priest house—you haven't eaten anything all day, have you? Now rest yourself. I'll be right back." When the nun returned with the soup, Lou Ann was already fast asleep.

Early the following morning, she awoke to the moans of many and the repugnant smells of blood and sweat permeating the stifling, hot air. She got to her feet, walked over to the railing, and looked down on, what seemed to her, a whole universe of suffering humanity. Earlier in the war, she knew that she would have run away from such misery; but something had changed in her since her own close brush with death. Many thoughts were beginning to crowd her mind and heart. It was like pieces of a puzzle falling into place. As she looked down at the many wounded and dying, she didn't see soldiers in blue and gray. Instead, she saw fathers, sons, brothers, and sweethearts. She was hungry and drank the cold bowl of soup that lay by her mattress, right where Sister Bertha had left it. Quickly washing her face and hands in a small basin of water, she readied herself for another day of caring for the wounded men. Her compassion for the soldiers seemed to increase by the hour. After only one day, she began to feel that God was calling her to a higher profession—caring for the needy was awakening something in her. She felt a spirit stirring in her soul that she couldn't explain. But there seemed to be more to it. She prayed silently for guidance for herself and for God's mercy for the poor souls she cared for. And then there was another equation entering into her "calling"... babies... orphans... I promised to look after the private's babies—must keep that promise. The promise had prompted her to check often on the private. As she approached him, still lying in the last pew, to her surprise she saw that he was embracing a Crucifix on his chest. She looked up at the wall, only to see the Crucifix was missing. Someone must have taken it down and given it to him. Probably Father O'Brien. By now, the private barely spoke. How at peace, she thought, as she washed his face and tried to give him water. He only managed a very small sip and lay his head back down. Lou Ann tried to talk with him, but his responses were unintelligible.

Father O'Brien approached. "How is he doing?"

"Well, Father, he does seem to be comfortable. I mean, it's unusual that he doesn't show any signs of pain."

"God bless him. The Lord is merciful," responded the priest.

"That was kind of you, Father—I mean—to let the private hold Jesus in his hands."

"That wasn't *me*, Miss. I thought *you* had taken the Crucifix down and given it to him."

They both knew that the private was so badly injured, it would have been impossible for him to get up and remove the Crucifix from the wall by himself. About fifteen feet away, at the corner of the church, stood one of the Confederate guards. Father O'Brien walked over to him. "How long have you been standing here, son?"

"I bin here since 'bout midnight, Father. Never left my post."

"Did you see anyone come by here? I mean, anyone attending the boy here?" as he pointed to the wounded private.

"No, sir. Nobody come by here all night. I woulda seen them, but..."

"But what, son?"

"Well—somethin' mighty scary happened 'bout three o'clock. I didn' wanna tell nobody. They'd think I was crazy. But you bein' a spiritual man, maybe..."

"What is it you're trying to say?"

"Well, Sir—I mean, Father—I was standin' right here—right where I'm standin' now. An' all of a sudden, all them candles in that rack over there started flickerin' like they was getting blowed out. But—no one was blowin' at 'em—an' there wasn't even a breeze in the church. Kinda scared me. Didn' know what was happenin'. After that, I noticed that Cross was gone."

"Did you see anyone take it off the wall?" the priest inquired further.

"No, Sir. Didn' see nobody back here all night. Only ones walkin' 'round was them other two guards and they was in the front with that nurse all night."

"Well, thanks, Private. You've been very helpful."

Lou Ann, who was listening to the conversation, looked at Father O'Brien with a look of amazement on her face. "Anything is possible with God," the priest said in a reassuring tone, raising his eyebrows. He smiled.

The second day proved to be much like the first. The only difference was that the fresh batch of wounded all wore gray uniforms. Lou Ann cared for them as tenderly as the boys in blue. She and the others did their best, moving about the men and diligently tending their wounds and comforting them with the few supplies that they had. And the grim work of the surgeon, back in the sacristy, continued throughout the day.   Occasionally screams would echo throughout the church. Lou Ann tried unsuccessfully to block them out. She labored long after midnight, until she couldn't push herself anymore, and collapsed on the lumpy, old mattress in the church choir.

On the morning of the third day, she awoke before dawn, washed her face while saying a few prayers, and hurried to her work downstairs. She still had concern and fears for her mother's safety, but a newly arrived wounded Confederate reassured her that the fighting was nowhere near the area where her mother lived, bringing her some relief.

It seemed so long ago since she had visited Patrick back in that hospital tent at Fredericksburg. So much had happened since then. For a time, she had thought that she may have been falling in love with him. She certainly enjoyed his company. But that was before—before she became deathly sick. She was developing, not just a new outlook on life, but a possible new vocation that pulled at her heart and went deep into her soul—a vocation of love and sacrifice to others. She had had feelings that she might become a Daughter of Charity, and only recently had she confronted those feelings head on. She knew there would be a great number of orphans after the war and how better, she thought, to take care of them than working as a nun in the same orphan asylum where she had been cared for. The young Confederate soldier in the last pew of the church had struck a nerve in her when he had cried out, "My babies! Who will take care of them?" The pieces of the puzzle were coming together now—but what about Patrick? She had never allowed herself to think about a long-term relationship with him because she had a secret—a secret that she had never shared with him. If they met again, she would have to tell him.

Lou Ann surveyed the carnage before her eyes. She gazed over the pitiful sight, her heart filled with sadness—not only for these men—but in a larger sense. She could see so many war orphans who would need a caring heart after the war. She immediately made a vow to God that she would become a part of that heart.

She looked over to the last pew where her young Confederate patient had been. He was gone. She ran over to see what had happened to him. A Rebel guard, seeing that she was upset, walked over to her. "Is somethin' wrong, Miss?"

"Where is the private? He was lying right here," as she pointed to the vacant pew.

"Oh, I am sorry, Miss. He passed on late last night. The Doc had him taken out along with some others."

"Thank you," she said, as the guard returned to his post. Lou Ann had known that the private was not going to live very long. She sat down in the spot where he had breathed his last and wept, burying her face in her hands to try to silence her sobs. Looking up, her gaze fell upon the spot on the wall where the Crucifix had been. Only the outline was there. The long hours of burning candles below had left their dark film of soot on the wall, but the unstained outline of the Cross was clear and defined. Jesus must have gone with the private. And now, she thought, looking at the clean spot where the Crucifix had been, he, too, has risen. I just know in my heart that Private Clem Haywood from Cowpasture, Virginia, is, this very day, in Paradise with Jesus. A feeling of joy came over her—for a short while—but then she thought of his babies. She had promised the young father—and God—that she would look after them. For a short time, she stared up at the outline on the wall, praying fervently for guidance. Tears trickled down her cheeks, as she felt overwhelmed with emotion from everything she had seen and heard in the last forty-eight hours.

Father O'Brien walked to the vestibule, grabbed hold of the end of the church bell rope and pulled down hard. As the bells chimed in the belfry above, he continued to ring them for two minutes, just as he had done every morning to notify the community that seven o'clock Mass was about to begin. He had barely completed his early morning chore, when a Confederate colonel came charging up the front steps, through the open doors, and confronted the priest. "Who gave you permission to ring those bells?" asked the officer in a very angry tone.

The priest smiled and pointed his finger toward the entrance of the church where a life-size statue of Jesus stood. "*He* did!"

The colonel turned around to see who the priest was pointing at, then turned back slowly to face him. In a sarcastic tone, the officer said, "I don't believe you will have any parishioners today. They're all hiding in their cellars." He added, "You do know you are under martial law here, don't you?"

"Yes, I am aware of that. And, do you know, sir, we are all under *God's* law—*including* Confederate colonels."

Before the colonel could answer, they heard a commotion out in the street in front of the church. An old man was arguing with a young Confederate guard, shaking his cane at him. "What is it, Private?" the colonel yelled out to the guard.

"This man was walking in the street. My orders are to keep all citizens indoors, Sir."

The old man hobbled over to the church and ascended the steps. "I am going to Mass as I do every morning; and by golly, no young whipper-snapper is going to stop me!" he said in a defiant tone.

"Well, sir," the colonel said, "we'll make an exception this time; but, when you're finished here, go back to your home. It's for your own protection."

The colonel departed, and the old man and the priest went inside to celebrate Mass. Lou Ann, Sister Bertha, and all the Catholic soldiers who could walk received Holy Communion at the Communion rail. Afterwards, Father O'Brien brought Communion to those confined to their hard, wooden pews. When Mass had ended, the priest went to the back of the church to thank his lone parishioner for attending Mass. "Good day, John. Thank you for coming—and—oh!—by the way, I admire your persistence to get yourself to Mass. But you didn't have to take such a chance."

"Well, Father, if you think *that* was dangerous, you should have been with me the other day. When them Rebs came up over that rise down by McPherson's farm, I grabbed my musket and joined our boys. That's how I got this." He pulled his pant leg up a little, revealing the bandage underneath. "Got a few of them varmints before they got me, though."

"Well, John, you're quite a courageous man, but I'd ask you to pray for peace and for those suffering boys inside."

As the old man was about to leave, Lou Ann came out to get some fresh air. "Excuse me, Father, but do you think I'd be able to get to my mother's house and see if she's all right?"

"Oh! Miss Sommers. This is Mr. John Burns. He's been a faithful parishioner here for years. Mr. Burns, this is Miss Sommers. She's been a Godsend, taking care of the wounded men."

Old John tipped his hat but skipped the niceties of a verbal greeting, quickly retorting firmly to her request, "You ain't goin' anywhere, young lady! Them Rebs all around, thick as fleas on a hound dog!"

"But I—I live just down the Emmitsburg Road, the other side of town."

"Young lady, I think you picked the worst day in all history to go down that road. Why, do you know that old Emmitsburg Road is smack-dab in the middle of thousands of Yanks and Rebs. They be fixin' for a fight an' looks like it might happen in that very spot. Yes, Ma'am, they might collide right in that very spot."

"Oh, I hope my mother's all right."

Father O'Brien took her hand in his. "Don't worry, my dear. I know your house; it's plenty far enough away from the fighting. We'll pray that God will protect her."

"Listen to the good Father, Miss. You'll be safe inside the church." He looked around to see if any Confederate guards were listening, and whispered, "Besides, our boys are gonna drive them Rebs outa here but good. You'll see. One more good battle." He smiled, tipped his hat once again, and hobbled down the church steps and out into the middle of the street. He shook his cane once again at the young Confederate guard who had tried to prevent his entering the church and began to sing the "Battle Hymn of the Republic" at the top of his voice. He defiantly stuck his chin in the air and strutted in a marching-like fashion down the center of the street in a one-man parade, impeded somewhat by his limp.

> *"Mine eyes have seen the glory of the coming of the Lord...."*

Confederate guards posted along the street seemed to admire the old man's courage, and they all tipped their hats to him as he passed them by. He turned the corner and disappeared from view, Father O'Brien and Lou Ann still smiling as they listened to his singing trailing off in the distance.

> *"Glory, glory hallelujah!*
> *Glory, glory hallelujah!*
> *Glory, glory, hallelujah!*
> *His truth is marching on!"*

The sun shone brightly, and the day was already hot and humid. Lou Ann and the priest went back into the church, and she wondered what might happen on that third day of battle and if Patrick was in that multitude of Yankee soldiers.

CHAPTER 17

▼

TIDAL WAVE OF REBELLION

Patrick found himself a shade tree in a wooded area behind his company's position, sat down, and decided to try once again to write a letter to Beth. He pulled out the small notebook pad he carried in his shirt pocket. All of his previous letters had been written on these little pieces of paper, and he would number them in proper order.

Dear Lou......

He immediately withdrew his pencil from the paper, ripped the page from the little pad, crinkled it up, and threw it away. Why did I do that? He became unsettled. Writing to *Beth*. Putting down Lou Ann's name... must be the heat! He had seldom doubted his love for Beth, but—still—why couldn't he shake loose from that pretty, lilac-scented Lou Ann? His image of Beth, standing in front of that bandstand holding the little picnic basket in her hand at that Fourth of July picnic, had never left him. But it seemed so long ago. Two years might as well be two hundred years, he thought. He suddenly realized that it was now the third of July. If I could only turn the clock back to that joy-filled time in Central Park. Two years had made a man out of him. He had been shot at and wounded, watched men be blown apart, heard death screams he never before could have imagined, even killed men. Yes, he had become a man long before his time. So far, thank God, I've survived. He took his pencil in hand once again and began to write:

Dearest Beth,

This time, he focused on Beth, expressed his love for her, told her of his experiences and the impending battle, and asked her to pray for him. He tried to be positive and to always reassure her that he would come back some day. He would convince himself that Lou Ann was just a passing fancy who sidetracked him when he was lonely. Unlikely to see her again anyway.

He finished the letter, placed the little pad back in his shirt pocket, and sprawled out beneath the shade of the little maple tree, thinking back to that Fourth of July. He could almost hear the band playing, as he thought of Beth and him holding hands for the first time and strolling around Central Park. It was high noon and the heat was becoming oppressive. He began to doze off, thinking of these pleasant thoughts of the past.

He slept for about an hour; then, suddenly, without warning, he awoke to what seemed like all the forces of the infernos of hell being unleashed. Shells screamed overhead; and loud explosions ruptured the rich, Pennsylvania countryside. Some shells had hit their targets—cannon, caissons, men, and horses were tossed high into the air.

Springing to his feet, he watched in horror as the scene before him seemed to unfold in slow motion. Rising plumes of thick, black smoke enveloped the fragments of humanity and weapons. A helpless feeling overcame Patrick as he watched the swirling objects twisting and turning in a grotesque ballet, then suddenly plummeting back to earth. In an instant, he was knocked to the ground by an exploding shell landing nearby, wincing in pain as his shoulder took the brunt of the fall. He lifted his head slightly to look for some shelter. There wasn't any. The shells were coming in a constant barrage and landing on all sides of him. The earth shook as he hugged the ground. "*St. Michael, the Archangel, defend us in battle...*" he prayed over and over again. He covered his ears and lay motionless, as though his stillness could protect him. After what seemed like hours, but in reality was only about one hour, he noticed the Rebel shells were falling further back behind the Union lines. He poked his head up once again and looked to the rear where he saw cooks' tents and supply wagons blown apart and flying in all directions. As he looked down his own lines, he watched as dozens of Union cannon fired back at the Confederates, creating a sound like rolling thunder and sending plumes of white smoke into the air, which had, by now, become thick with the acrid smell of gunpowder. He had experienced battle before but had always been moving ahead or retreating. There had been some sense of security being in motion; but this, he thought, was the worst—paralyzed—exposed—a sitting target! He could only count the minutes as he breathed in the pungent odors of battle and braced himself with every explosion that shattered against his eardrums. Then gradually he noticed that, one by one, the Union cannon ceased firing, and the enemy shells became less frequent. It was as if he had been caught in a downpour, and now the rain had become a trickle—only this rain had been filled with deadly missiles. And then... silence. An eerie quiet settled over the battlefield, and Patrick cautiously got to his feet, hoping another shell was not heading his way. He brushed the dirt from his clothes with his good arm, the other throbbing with pain from his fall.

As he walked back to his regiment, he saw Cemetery Ridge come alive once again with activity. Gun crews were bringing up new cannon to replace the ones that were destroyed by enemy shells. Other small groups of soldiers scurried to place the dead and wounded on stretchers to carry them to the rear. When he arrived back, the men who had sought cover from the bombardment were regrouping and taking up a defensive position. Patrick was just in time to hear the colonel informing them that they would be held back in reserve. He checked his ammunition and awaited further orders, as did the others. He didn't have to wait long before he heard the distant sound of drums coming across the fields from Seminary Ridge. Standing up to get a better view, he squinted in the glaring, mid-day sunlight and beheld legions of gray-clad soldiers emerging from the woods on the ridge a mile away. He watched as column after column moved into formation, unfurling their crimson flags dotted with white stars on blue bars—their Southern Cross. Stepping off smartly, still more masses of men came into view along the vast tree line beyond. Patrick remembered the big parade in New York City when he went off to war. The scene unfolding in the Rebel camp appeared no different than the many legions of blue-clad soldiers marching down Broadway two years before. He looked on in awe as his Southern brothers took up their positions for battle as calmly and deliberately as if on parade. As each regiment fell into formation, another young drummer boy set the pace as he marched alongside the men in arms. In a very short time, dozens of drums rumbled their steady beat across the open plain, like rolling thunder announcing the foreboding storm that was about to strike. The sea of gray moved together as one man. Patrick watched as they moved slowly at first, his rifle at the ready. He could still fire with his good arm. On they came—some units coming straight forward, others shifting to the left and straightening out again to merge with other regiments. It began to look as if they were planning a concentrated, massive assault on the center of the Union line, where a small group of trees were clustered together. Could they break our lines? Patrick wondered.

Just then, his colonel shouted, "Be ready for them, boys! If they break through in front, we're the last line of defense. Fix your bayonets, just in case!"

Patrick rested his rifle on his knee to fix his bayonet, wiped the sweat from his brow, and waited in silence as the enemy drew closer. They had picked up the pace and began to climb over the fences at the Emmitsburg Road. At that time, the Union cannon opened fire, blasting holes in the Rebels' ranks. Never before had Patrick witnessed such a sight. In past battles, he had only seen the immediate area around him or the enemy a few yards in front of him; but this panoramic view of the oncoming hordes of gray, with thousands of bayonets flashing in the sunlight, mesmerized him, as if in a dream. He thought that it looked like a rehearsal scene for a gigantic stage play. A moment later, he realized that the "play" was for real, when bullets began to clip the leaves from the trees located a few feet behind him.

"Keep your heads down!" yelled the colonel.

Patrick lay on the ground, pointing his rifle toward the oncoming enemy. The Rebel ranks were thinning rapidly, and Patrick wondered if any of them would reach the Union lines. As they surged forward toward the Union center, a wide gap appeared in their lines. Three Vermont regiments maneuvered into the gap and poured a devastating, flanking fire into the withering Rebel troops to the north; then turned in the opposite direction, decimating the other enemy formations. The nine-month Vermont recruits— the Green Mountain Boys—never having been under fire before—had effectively slowed the Rebels' advance. Many of them retreated, walking back to Seminary Ridge.

But the main thrust of Southern manhood was still driving toward the little clump of trees. By this time, the Union Artillery crews had switched their ammunition from shell to canister and were firing their deadly shrapnel, like giant buckshot, into the oncoming enemy at pointblank range. In his innermost thoughts, Patrick saw the Rebel onslaught as a giant wave that had been building for years, crashing down on the rocks—a wave of resentment and anger toward their Northern brothers. It was a time when Southern gentlemen would use a pistol duel to settle their differences, usually preceded by a slap on the face of the offender. The North, they felt, had slapped them in the face. That began the biggest duel the country had ever seen.

Patrick could smell victory along with the acrid smell of gunpowder— something he had hoped and prayed for in past battles. It had always been just beyond reach. The cannon spewed their fiery death, and the long blue line of Union defenders fired their muskets into the advancing Rebels who fell in droves. Many Union boys also fell, slumped over the stone wall they had crouched behind. Although Patrick's Brigade had been held in reserve, he and a few of his comrades couldn't resist stepping out and firing at the oncoming enemy, about two hundred yards to their right front. A few hundred brave, stouthearted Southern boys broke through the Union center, and hand-to-hand combat ensued. It no longer resembled two opposing armies with clearly defined lines—all order and formation in the lines had given way to utter chaos and brute force. Muskets were now used as clubs to beat their opponents into submission. When that failed, some picked up rocks to bash the closest enemy in the head. And, finally, when all forms of weapons had been exhausted, they clenched their fists and crashed the jaws of any opponent within striking range. This is what it had come to. As Patrick watched, he saw masses of men tangled together and locked in a death struggle—a struggle that would determine the destiny of a country, the slave, and possibly the whole world. From Pat's position, it looked like a huge street fight or riot. Then suddenly it ended. The biggest and strongest claimed their victory, and the vanquished slowly limped back to where they had begun their failed charge.

Patrick finally had his victory. He and thousands of blue-clad Yankees stood up and cheered, for it was the first big victory for the Union Army in two years of fighting.

They all chanted, "Fredericksburg! Fredericksburg!" Pat's nearby comrades jumped for joy. They hugged one another, and a few locked their arms together and danced an Irish jig, as their bagpipe player squeezed out a tune.

The Sixty-ninth Irish Brigade, what was left of it, rejoiced and shouted, "Long live the Union! The Union Forever!" Patrick laughed and smiled and savored the long sought-after victory. He sat down and was overjoyed to watch his comrades so full of life and happiness. Amidst the revelry, he felt a slight sadness coming over him, however. Yes, victory had come with a bittersweet taste. He remembered the many young men whom he had known for a short time who were cut down in their prime and lay in some far-off grave on a distant battlefield.

Not going to think about that. Enjoy the moment. Victory! Finally— the great Robert E. Lee had failed. What had that young Confederate guard said? "Old Mars Robert can run circles around any general you got!" Like to see that Reb guard's face now!

The rejoicing was short-lived, and the colonel soon had the men back into a defensive formation. "Be at the ready!" the colonel shouted. "We must prepare for another attack. Lee may come at us again."

Patrick lay in a prone position, holding his rifle, baking in the hot sun, secretly hoping the Rebels would try again. Maybe another charge would bring the whole war to an end.

Some Confederates were carrying their wounded. The scene had changed dramatically in a little over an hour. He couldn't believe that the strong, imposing force that had charged their lines had been so decimated and reduced to the much smaller band of bloodied, human wreckage wandering back across the open plain. Although he was elated with the victory, a feeling of pity crept into his thoughts. They *are* Americans. Used to be my countrymen. Oh, well... better them than us. Had enough defeats. Now they will have a taste of it. These mixed emotions crossed his mind as he looked over the battlefield strewn with broken men and idle weapons as far as the eye could see. His gaze swept across the farmers' fields and the gradual rise to Cemetery Ridge—there wasn't a patch of land not covered with the bodies of the dead and wounded, shattered muskets, and fallen flags. It was almost too much to comprehend. As he turned toward the little clump of trees, he saw death piled on top of itself. Some mounds of blue and gray clad bodies lie heaped together on the farmer's stone fence. Separated in life... joined in death. Strange, Pat thought. A stone fence, intended to separate the farmer's crops of wheat and corn, had become an object of unity in the long struggle. Unfortunately, it was not a union of hearts and minds, but a unity or co-mingling of blood in the gruesome contest, yet to be decided.

Patrick felt a shudder penetrate his soul. He closed his eyes and prayed. "May God have mercy." He waited in silence along with the others in the long blue line running along Cemetery Ridge. All eyes were upon Seminary Ridge, waiting for another attack. Time went by and nothing happened. By dusk, it became apparent that the Gray Fox had retired to his lair. Nightfall came and stillness settled over the battlefield. A subtle, hot breeze swept across the fields of death, as if the devil himself had breathed one last blast of treachery, inflicting pain on the dying souls to complete his malicious day's work. Campfires sprung up, and many of the Yankees began to cook their meals. Guards and pickets were sent out to observe any movement by the enemy. It had been very rare for an Army to attack after dark, so Patrick and most of his comrades stood down. Still, all were ordered to be ready at a moment's notice. To Patrick, as well as all his comrades, his rifle had become like a third arm, never leaving his side.

After another meal of white beans and hardtack, Pat sat down on the crest of Cemetery Ridge and watched as shadowy figures, holding torches, weaved in and out of the dead and wounded beyond. Some stretcher-bearers carried back the wounded; others pushed their shovels into the bloody ground, digging shallow graves for many whose battle had ended forever. After an hour or so, listening to the scraping sound of shovels and watching silent figures moving about in the eerie torchlight, Pat returned to his tent. He slept a restless sleep, unable to blot out the overwhelming images of the day.

The morning of the 4th dawned with gray skies, as Patrick stepped out of his tent. The scene hadn't changed at all. The digging and burials continued, as Father Corby worked his way from one dying soldier to another, administering the Last Rites. Thousands of Union soldiers remained behind the farmer's stone fences, still waiting for another Rebel attack. By noontime, the skies opened up and released a torrential downpour on Yankee and Rebel alike. Patrick ducked back inside his tent, listening to the heavy rain pelting the canvas and a strong wind blowing the tent flaps back and forth.

He grew bored. Funny, he thought, Army life had two extremes—battles or boredom—nothing in-between. Most of the men in his company had gathered in other tents to play cards and gamble. Patrick never gambled... it was a sin. He got up and stuck his head out into the pouring rain. It felt refreshing. The wind and rain seemed to cleanse the battlefield, blowing away the hot, stagnant smell of gunsmoke and the strong stench of death.

The day passed slowly. Patrick took his bayonet and began to whittle a stick he had found lying on the dirt floor of the tent. As he watched the wood chips fall to the floor, he thought of the time when he and Joshua sat on the roadside in New York whittling sticks and making plans to combine their medals into one. It seemed like a century ago. Could Joshua have been the Rebel charging down on him in the wheatfield? He did have red hair—and rode a black stallion, like Nathan said. And was that *the* medal hanging around his neck? Will I ever know?

He didn't have long to ponder his questions, when Michael came bursting into the tent. "Hey, Sarge! You hear? The Rebs are moving out!"

"How do you know that?" Pat asked as he looked up at the young private who was soaking wet.

"Rumors flying around camp like wildfire!"

"You mean the Rebs are actually skedaddling?"

"You bet, Sarge!"

"Well, hallelujah! Never thought I'd see the day when they would leave the field to us."

"Yeah, Sarge, some of our Cavalry spotted 'em movin' wagon trains and troops back toward the Potomac.

"Praise God!" Patrick retorted, as he threw his bayonet down, sticking it into the ground forcefully. "What a way to celebrate the Fourth of July!" Pat stood up and shook Michael's hand vigorously. "Maybe things will change now."

Pat sat down again and continued to whittle on the stick. Michael lay down on the other side of the small tent, stretching his arms behind his head, and stared up at the canvas that rippled in the wind. They were silent, as the rain came down harder, pounding against the top of the tent. Finally, Michael spoke. "You think them Rebs will be comin' back at us anytime soon, Sarge?"

"Oh, I think we did a good job on them for now. They're lickin' their wounds, but they're a tough bunch. They'll be back. Maybe not now, but we'll see them again some time." He continued, "Did you see them comin' across that field? I mean, they walked right into our guns! I tell you, Michael, I'll never forget that sight if I live to be one hundred. If we ever have a war with someone else, I hope them Rebs are on our side. Yes, sir, a braver bunch of men I never did see."

"That's for sure, Sarge. They kept comin' like we wasn't even here waitin' to blast them to kingdom come!"

The rest of the day passed uneventfully. The wind and rain continued all day and into the night.

Sunday came, and the rains still continued. Patrick hoped that he could get to Mass. It wasn't always possible when the Army was on the move, and a priest was not always available. Michael had somehow acquired eggs and bacon from a nearby farmer, and Pat had awakened to that inviting smell drifting into his tent. "Where did you get that real food from?" Pat asked, coming out of the tent, hiking up his red suspenders as he did.

"Remember that farm we passed the other day when we marched up here?" Michael asked, as he held his raincoat over the fire, attempting to keep his breakfast dry.

"I remember passing quite a few farms."

"Well, I couldn't sleep this morning, so I got up and snuck back to that farm. I offered the farmer some money, but he wouldn't take it. He seemed real happy that we drove the Rebs away and said we had earned the free food."

"You're a real resourceful lad... I take my hat off to you, Michael." Pat smiled broadly and tipped his cap.

For the first time in months, Patrick really enjoyed his breakfast, and washed it down with a hot cup of coffee. By noontime, his shoulder began to ache badly. Michael saw him wincing with pain and asked him about it. "Hey, Sarge, that shoulder botherin' you some?"

"Yeah, it don't feel so good."

"You know, it looks like it's bleedin' again." He stepped over to Patrick to get a better look and noticed the blood-soaked dressing. "I think you'd better get a doctor to look at it."

"Well, I don't like them surgeons much. They might want to take my arm off." Pat thought for a moment and finally agreed with Michael. "Well, Michael, nothin' much to do around here right now. Guess you're right." They both walked back to the field hospital and beheld many wounded men lying outside the tent in the pouring rain. "Reminds me of Fredericksburg," Pat muttered in low tones.

"What did ya say, Sarge?"

"Oh, just thinking—how come it always seems to rain after a battle?"

"Don't know, Sarge."

Patrick approached one of the surgeons in the tent. "Can you have a look at this?" as he pointed to his shoulder.

"You'll have to wait your turn, son." The surgeon pointed to the many men with more severe wounds lying on stretchers on the ground. "Have to try to save some of these boys—some won't make it."

Patrick felt guilty that he had even asked for help, as he looked at the suffering souls around him. "Come on, Michael. They've got too many serious cases here. I shouldn't even be here."

As the two Yanks started back toward their campsite, a colonel approached them from behind. "Wait up, boys." They both turned around and saluted the officer. Pat wondered what a colonel would want them for. "Come with me!" the colonel said in a commanding voice. They walked alongside the officer as he spoke. "Hope you can drive a wagon, boys. We're short of teamsters and need you to take some of the wounded into town. Have to find some shelter and get 'em out of this rain."

"Well, I've got one good arm, Sir. Guess I can manage," Pat said.

"Take the private with you, Sergeant. You'll need him."

They walked back to an area containing many empty wagons. Some soldiers were hitching up the horses. "Take your pick of wagons, boys, and get over to the hospital tent," the colonel continued. "Load up as many as you can and take them to the nearest building in town that has room." As he began to leave, he stopped momentarily and turned back toward them.

"Oh, I'll need your names to let your commanding officer know you're on this detail."

"O'Hanrahan. Patrick O'Hanrahan. And this is Private Michael Kelly, Sir. New York 69th, Sir."

"Both of you from the 69th?" the colonel asked Patrick.

"Yes, Sir—and proud of it!"

"You've got good reason to be proud of it. There isn't a better brigade in this man's army. In fact, I think your outfit has lost more men than any other that I know of."

"Yes, Sir," they both replied.

"One more thing, boys. Take your weapons with you. The Rebs cleared out of town yesterday, but you never know if they left a few sharpshooters. Now go get them boys out of the rain and find any building you can to house them."

Pat and Michael both saluted the colonel and briskly walked away.

CHAPTER 18

▼

THE REUNION

Michael took the reins, while Patrick sat alongside him, his rifle draped across his lap. After the hospital attendants loaded as many of the wounded as would fit in the wagon, they slowly drove down the Taneytown Road into town. Terrified civilians were emerging from their cellars, cautiously peering around with a look of fear in their eyes. Realizing that the Rebels were gone and blue-clad soldiers had arrived, their mood instantly changed. More and more people gathered in the streets, waving Old Glory and cheering and dancing, ignoring the steady rain. Every church bell in the little town began to ring.

"Looks like these folks had to wait a day to celebrate the Fourth of July," Pat said, turning to Michael.

"And they have a double celebration today—I mean—with the Rebels clearin' out and gittin' their town back, Sarge. Where do ya think we can find room for these poor lads?" He briefly removed his hat to shake the rain from it.

"Looks like a big building over there—maybe a library or something. Pull up over there, Michael."

Michael halted the wagon, and Patrick lowered himself to the ground, favoring his shoulder as he did. "Wait here, Michael. I'll see if there's any room in here."

A young lieutenant met Patrick as he entered the library. "Can I help you, Sergeant?"

After saluting the lieutenant, Patrick looked around at the many wounded men, lying on tables and covering the floor. Some were using books for pillows. "Don't suppose you have any room for a wagon-load of more wounded, do you, Lieutenant?"

"Sorry, Sergeant. Cramped like sardines in here. Everything's filling up. I hear the citizens' homes are even overflowing with these poor souls."

Patrick answered in a concerned tone. "Have to find *someplace*, Sir. There's many more back at the field hospital who need a dry place."

The lieutenant thought for a moment, removing his hat and scratching his head.

"You might try two blocks down and around the corner. There's a couple of churches there." He pointed down the street. "Maybe they have room in one of them."

"Thanks, Lieutenant." Patrick saluted and ran back to the wagon. "Let's go," Pat told Michael, as he gave him the directions.

"Giddyap!" Michael shouted, snapping the reins. The horses lurched forward, prompting moans from the wounded men inside the wagon. They followed the lieutenant's directions, and Michael pulled the wagon up in front of the church.

"The lieutenant was right, Michael," Pat said. "There's another church across the street. One of them must have room for these men." Pat stepped down from the wagon and entered the church. He had been exposed to repugnant smells of death and blood before; but this time, as he opened the door, the same odors assailed his senses as never before. It was a stark contrast to the rain-soaked fresh air outside. He was surprised to see Confederate wounded mixed amongst the Yankee soldiers. Guess they left in such a hurry, they didn't have time to take them all. Father O'Brien was ringing the church bells, smiling from ear to ear as Patrick approached him. "I've got a wagonload of wounded outside, Father," Pat shouted.

"What did you say?" the priest asked, continuing to pull the rope and ring the bells.

Patrick shouted louder. "I've got wounded men out there, Father," as he pointed to the street.

"Can't hear you, son. I'll be with you in a minute." He kept pulling the rope, enjoying the chimes of his own bells in harmony with the Protestant churches pealing bells across the street, all in celebration of the liberation of the town after four days of Confederate rule. Patrick watched and smiled and drank in the joy of the moment. He felt a sense of victory, and a well deserved one, after two years of defeats. It was a good feeling. Father O'Brien celebrated, the town celebrated, and Patrick could experience how the citizens felt. As the priest finished ringing the bells, he turned to Patrick and asked, "Now what were ya trying ta tell me, lad?"

Patrick shouted, "I have a..." Suddenly realizing the bells had stopped ringing, he lowered his voice. "I have a wagonload of wounded men outside. Can you take them in here, Father?"

"Well, Sergeant, we have a few spots we can squeeze them in. The Rebels took some of their own away yesterday but didn't have enough wagons for the rest." Looking at Patrick's blood-soaked bandage on his shoulder, he added, "Say, lad, ya look as if ya could use some attention yourself. That dressing needs ta be changed."

"Have to unload those men from the wagon. They need more attention than I do, Father."

"You're a good man, Sergeant—I mean—putting those men ahead of yourself. I'll get you some help to unload them, then we'll take care of that shoulder." Father O'Brien called over two guards and pressed them into service, instructing them to bring in the wounded from the wagon. Michael also helped, while Patrick knelt down in an empty pew to pray and closed his eyes. A few minutes later, he felt someone nudging him on his good shoulder. He looked up to see the priest standing by his side, accompanied by a woman. From his kneeling position, his first observation was of her bloodstained dress. As the priest stepped aside, he gestured toward the woman. "This young lady will change your dressing, Sergeant. She'll take good care of you." He walked away, and Pat slowly looked up at the woman's face.

"Lou Ann, is that *you*?" he asked in astonishment.

"Patrick! Oh, my gosh! I don't believe it's really you! I've been praying for you day and night. Are you all right? You're wounded."

Oh—my angel—my beautiful angel! His heart was speaking power-fully within him. He reached up and took her hand, gently nudging her to sit beside him in the pew. A flash of the lovely vision in blue that had lifted him from the pit of depression in the tent hospital in Fredericksburg zipped through his mind. Before he could answer her question, she lowered her head against his shoulder and began to cry. He wanted to put his arms tightly around her, as if to protect her from everything she had already suf-fered. "What—what are you doing here, Lou Ann? I thought you were still sick in the hospital."

"Oh, I'm over that now, thank God." She brushed the tears from her cheeks with the back of her hand. "Daddy thought I'd recover better here at home. I'm staying at my mother's house and..."

"And what?"

"Well, I came to Mass here a few days ago, and the Confederate soldiers took over the town. I've been here ever since."

"Oh, I'm sorry. Did they mistreat you?"

"No, but I'm sort of glad it happened."

"Glad? How could you be glad about that?"

"Well, I don't mean it the way you think. What I meant was—well—I'm glad I was here to help these poor men. There was hardly anyone here to help care for them."

As he watched her speak, he detected a change in her. It wasn't just her appearance. It wasn't the torn, dirty, bloodstained dress. It wasn't the disheveled look or the unkempt hair. There was something else—something in her face—in her eyes. He wasn't sure what it was.

She bent down to inspect his shoulder wound, and he impulsively grabbed her hand and kissed it. She smiled at him, a slight blush coming to her cheeks, but gently withdrew her hand. "Now, Patrick—we have to take care of this," as she began to peel off the bloody bandage from his shoulder. "Was it bad? I mean—was the battle bad?"

"Oh, yeah! Pretty bad! We lost quite a few good men in my outfit. I got it on the second day. In a farmer's wheatfield. A shell blew up right in front of me."

"Oh, I'm so glad you were spared!"

"I missed you, Lou Ann—thought about you a lot."

"I thought about you, too, Patrick, but... We have to talk."

Pat nodded his head in agreement, anxious to hear what she had to say.

"I did quite a bit of thinking when I was laid up at home," Lou Ann continued. "I mean—about you and me—and the future." He grimaced, as she pulled the old bandage from the wound, the dried blood on it sticking to the skin. "I'm sorry. I'll try to go easier. That's a pretty deep wound, Patrick, but it looks good and clean."

"What did you want to talk about?"

After washing his wound, she applied the new bandages, tightening them as she did. "There. I think the bleeding should stop now. You'll be okay."

He was amazed at the efficiency she exhibited in treating his wound. "Lou Ann, what did you want to talk about?"

"Well, Patrick, I know we've been through a lot together—in just a short time—and..."

"And what?"

"Well…" She hesitated for a moment. "No time to talk now. Maybe later. I have to look after those boys you brought in—some are in serious condition." She placed her open hand gently to his cheek. "I'm so glad you're all right. I'm proud of you, Patrick. You get wounded, and fight again, and keep on going from one battle to the next. You are truly brave. We'll talk later." She walked up the center aisle to attend the others.

Her small gesture to his cheek felt like a warm ray of sunshine to him in the middle of the many harsh hostilities he had undergone. This chance meeting with Lou Ann wasn't quite what he would have expected. But what would I have expected? What did she want to talk about anyway? She had said "the future". What future? He wondered if they would have *any* future together, what with the war and all. And that change he seemed to see in her—so dedicated. Yes—that's it—she's developed a dedication to help the wounded. What had happened to that fun-loving, light-hearted Lou Ann? She now appeared to be a young lady with a mission. An eagerness to do for others what they couldn't do for themselves.

He suddenly remembered Michael. He jumped to his feet and was about to go outside to the wagon when he heard his name called.

"Hey, Sergeant! Over here." Michael was standing in the back of the church leaning against the wall, his arms folded on his chest. "Didn't know you had a sweetheart down here—pretty lookin' woman, at that!" He grinned.

"Well, sort of—but not really."

Michael chuckled. "Sarge, you got a way with words—you're talkin' around me now."

"Oh, she's just a girl who helped me and was kind to me after I got wounded at Fredericksburg."

"Looks more serious than that to *me*, Sarge."

Patrick was on the verge of telling him about Lou Ann—and maybe Beth—but decided not to. He was still guarded about his personal life and really didn't want to share it with the new recruit. No—he wouldn't respond to Michael's last comment. Looking out the open church doors at the pouring rain, he breathed in the fresh air, as the wind grew stronger, blowing the rain into the church entrance.

"Listen, Sarge, you seem like you could use more time here. Why don't you stay awhile? I can take the wagon back this trip. I'll manage without you."

Patrick stared out at the rain and finally responded. "You know, Michael, you're a very decent fellow. I think you read my mind. You're right, I could use some more time here."

"Don't worry," Michael said. "If anyone asks for you, I'll tell them your wound got worse and they put you on the sick list. You should be taking better care of yourself anyway."

Patrick was glad to spend some time in the church. At least he was out of the rain. As he sat back down in the pew, he watched Lou Ann diligently attending the others. He tried to pray, but his mind kept wandering. He questioned his relationship with her. Had he been captivated by her beauty and the mystery surrounding her as a spy? Or was it his loneliness—first time away from home. Wounded. Yes—that was it. Lonely and alone. And then—there was that New Year's Eve!

Four nuns carrying baskets of food entered the church and walked up to the altar where Father O'Brien was preparing to say Mass. They were Daughters of Charity and wore the same large white headdress as Sister Bertha. They talked briefly to the priest, then knelt down in front of the altar to hear Mass, as there was no room in the pews. Father O'Brien, eliminating his homily, said a short Mass so the nuns could attend the wounded. Patrick was thankful that he was present and could receive Holy Communion. After Mass he saw Lou Ann, smiling as she approached the older nun. They embraced and spoke for a moment. The older nun then appeared to direct her companions to go into the sacristy while continuing to speak with Lou Ann. A few moments later, they returned carrying a mop and bucket, and bandages and dressings. One of them began mopping up the pools of blood on the floor, as Lou Ann and the older nun began to attend to the wounded. The other two nuns began taking the food to those who were able to eat.

Patrick was given some homemade bread with jam. He thanked the Sister, and enjoyed this delicacy, which he hadn't tasted since entering the Army. He thought about going back to his regiment, but he couldn't leave before talking to Lou Ann. It was sometime in the mid-afternoon when he felt that he couldn't pray anymore and was about to get up and go outside for some fresh air. He saw Lou Ann hastily walking down the center aisle in his direction. She approached him and motioned him to move over so she would have room to sit beside him.

"Patrick! Patrick!" she exclaimed excitedly.

"What is it, Lou Ann? You look like you've seen a ghost."

"I think there's someone you know here in the church."

"Who is it?"

"Do you remember, when we were escaping from the Confederates, and that slave, Nathan, said he met a Confederate soldier wearing a medal like yours?"

"Yes, yes. You mean Joshua? He's here?"

"I was bandaging up this Confederate..."

"Where is he?" He became as excited as she.

"Up there," as she pointed to the front of the church.

Patrick immediately got to his feet and walked up the aisle, while Lou Ann followed along. He had to step over the wounded men, as they lay sprawled on the floor. Lou Ann once again pointed to the spot where the Rebel soldier was. As Patrick approached him, he could see that his eyes were closed and he appeared to be sleeping. He was sitting in the corner, leaning his back against the wall. Pat stooped down and stared directly at him. Behind the red beard, he saw the features of his old childhood friend. "It's him! It's Joshua!" he said to Lou Ann in an excited tone. "I'd know him anywhere!"

Just then the Rebel stirred, looking dazed and not fully awake. He suddenly grabbed Patrick's medal, hanging outside his shirt, and exclaimed, "Hey! What are you doing with that? It belongs to me! Who are you?"

"Josh! It's me—Patrick. St. Mary's. Remember? New York City."

Joshua reached inside his shirt for his own medal, briefly inspecting it, then looked back at Patrick's. "O'Hanrahan! Is—is that really *you*?"

Patrick smiled. "Did you think anyone else would be wearing this kind of medal?" He reached over to shake Joshua's hand and was disturbed to see a bandaged stump. He then grabbed his other hand and shook it profusely, then embraced him with his own good arm.

Now fully awake, Joshua pulled back, and his smile turned to a frown. "You're a damned Yankee!"

Patrick quickly retorted, "And you're a damned Rebel!"

They were both at a loss for words and momentarily were silent as they stared at one another. Joshua suddenly broke into laughter, and with his good hand firmly grabbed Patrick's and shook it vigorously. Pat then began to laugh, as the two enemy soldiers were reunited and acted as if there wasn't a war going on. For a brief moment, they were just two boyhood pals whittling pieces of wood by the roadside. Lou Ann smiled and silently walked away, leaving them alone. As their laughter subsided, there followed more silence. Finally, Patrick sat down and leaned against the wall next to Josh. "I can't believe this! It's really you, Josh! You survived. I knew you were in the Reb Army and that was..."

Joshua broke in. "And how did you know that?"

"Well, I met this slave who told me he had met a Rebel soldier who had a medal like mine."

"Well, I'll be—and here we are, wearing the same medals on opposite sides of the fence. Did you say a slave?"

"Yeah. He said he took care of your horse or something."

"Oh, yeah. Now I remember. What was his name?"

"Nathan. He helped me escape after I got captured at Chancellorsville." Joshua grew very quiet and looked down at the stump where his hand used to be. Patrick looked on and tried to console him. "Sorry about that, Josh." He didn't know what to say next.

"Yeah... still got one good one left, but I feel just as bad about losing Blackjack."

"Blackjack?" Pat inquired. "Who's Blackjack?"

"Oh, you wouldn't understand. He was my best friend—my horse. He was with me from the beginning of this damned war."

"Oh, that's too bad. Speaking of best friends... remember when *we* were best friends? Seems like a century ago. What happened, Josh? I mean—this ain't right—killin' each other. You know I almost shot you?"

"Shot me? When?"

"Weren't you fightin' in that wheatfield on the second day?"

"Yeah, I was there."

"Weren't you riding that black charger, taking a bead on a Yankee when a shell exploded and blew you off your horse?"

"Yeah—how did you know about that?"

"Well, *I* was that Yankee. That shell hit me, too. That's how I got this," as he pointed to his shoulder wound. "I can't believe that happened. I mean—I came so close to shooting you."

"Well, why didn't you?"

"Normally I would have, but..."

"But what?"

"I don't know. Guess it was your red hair and that black horse you were riding that Nathan told me about."

"You're a damn fool, O'Hanrahan. I would have shot *you*."

"No—there was more than that."

"More than what?"

"At the last second, I saw something hanging around your neck that I thought..."

Josh blurted out, "The medal!"

"Yeah, that was it! Something just told me that was you."

"Well, I'll be darned! Saved by a medal! That's really something!"

"I think that it was more than just the medal."

"What's that?"

"Oh—I mean—I think God may have had a hand in that."

Josh looked over at Patrick, smiling. "You know, Pat, maybe you're right. You always were a religious lad, even when we were young boys." He hesitated for a moment, as if he were thinking. "I never went to church much. Pa took me for worship at a synagogue once or twice a year, and Ma and I went to a Christian church a few times; but I never was all that religious. Pa says we're Jews, though."

"Well, Josh, I'm not a Bible readin' man, but I know enough about my faith. I mean, when you think of it, these medals we're wearing are like a Bible."

"How do you mean?"

"Well, I don't know if I ever told you, but a priest once told me that the Jews were our elder brothers."

"Well, how does that make the medals like a Bible?"

"Well, the Star of David represents the Jews of the Old Testament and Jesus' Cross, the New Testament; and the way I figure it, our medals are like a small Bible."

"You know, Pat, you know a lot about your faith. I always liked that about you— even kinda envied it." Joshua seemed to be in pain, as he raised his arm from his side onto his lap.

Pat had laid his head back and stared at the ceiling. "Strange—very strange," he muttered in a low voice.

"Did you say something?" Josh asked.

"Oh, I was just thinking—what were the chances of both of us getting hit by the same shell? You know, we could have been killed. What if somebody found us, laying dead... both wearing the same medal, but different uniforms?" He chuckled. "That would have kept 'em guessing! I just can't believe we met this way!"

Joshua, looking down at the floor, shook his head from side to side. "I don't know—but one thing I *do* know is—I'm outta this here war. Can't ride a horse—or even shoot a gun—without *this*," as he lifted his stump slightly off his lap. "Guess your old friend, Josh, is your prisoner now."

"Prisoner? Gee, Josh, I was so excited about seeing you, I never thought of that."

"Well, I *knew* I'd come back North sometime—but not *this* way. Heard your prison camps ain't so great."

Patrick had heard stories of some Federal prison camps that were pretty bad. Some prisoners, he had heard, were half-starved to death. However, he wouldn't tell his old friend about that. As they reminisced about their childhood, Patrick couldn't help but think of Joshua rotting in a prison camp. His mind began to race, conjuring up ways to prevent this from happening. His own imprisonment was still fresh in his mind. Joshua listened as Patrick talked about various memories of the two of them back in New York City when they were young boys who had no idea about the turbulent future they had in front of them. Patrick, realizing that Joshua was becoming depressed, tried to cheer him up. Joshua listened for awhile, then suddenly blurted out, "What the hell are we doin' here? I mean—we're supposed to be enemies! Did ya ever think that, if that shell hadn't hit both of us, I could have shot you first?"

Patrick looked at him, surprised at his sudden, hostile tone. "You're right, Josh."

He remembered the incident when they had sold newspapers on opposite sides of the street back in New York. "Glad you didn't get off your shot at me first," he said with a smile. "As I recall, your aim with that horseball was perfect!"

"Horseball? What do you..." Suddenly it dawned on Josh what Pat was talking about. He began to laugh loudly.

And so the afternoon wore on as they exchanged stories about their childhood and their involvement in the war. As the church began to darken, the nuns proceeded to light candles. Lou Ann came over to Patrick, asking to talk to him in private. His arm still in a sling, he slowly got to his feet with some assistance from her. Joshua had dozed off shortly before when Patrick was in the middle of a sentence. "What is it, Lou Ann?" Pat whispered, thinking she wanted to talk about their relationship.

"Did you know they're going to remove the prisoners tomorrow?" she answered in a low tone. "I thought you would want to know, just in case you might have something else you might want to tell your friend before he's taken away."

"Who told you that?" Pat whispered.

"I overheard Father O'Brien talking to an officer who came into the back of the church a little while ago."

"Can we talk somewhere privately?" Pat asked.

"Well, there is a small room—the storage room—on the other side of the altar. What is it, Patrick?"

"It won't take long. It's—well, it's important."

"Alright, but I don't have too much time."

He closed the door behind them. She looked at him curiously and waited for him to speak. "There's so much I want to talk to you about—I mean—about you and me. But something has come up and well…" He paused for a moment.

"What is it, Patrick? What are you acting so secretive about?"

"It's about Joshua."

"You mean your old friend with the medal?"

"Yes—it's about Josh."

"Well, tell me—what about him?"

"I can't let them haul him off to a prison camp. I've heard many of them don't come back alive. Maybe we could…" He paused again, seeming hesitant to finish what he wanted to say.

"Maybe we could what?"

"Well, I was thinking that maybe we could get him out of here and over to your mother's house."

Now looking very serious, Lou Ann stared at him and asked, "Do you realize what you're saying? I mean—if you get caught—they could hang you for that—and me, too!"

"I know—but—I think we could do it without getting caught. We escaped the Rebs and didn't get caught, didn't we?"

"Well, yes, but that was different. We weren't aiding the enemy then. This is crazy, Patrick!"

"But you don't understand. We were best friends. He was even closer to me than my own brother. Come on, Lou Ann. Didn't you do things as a spy that you could have been hung for?"

"Well, yes. I have to admit to that. But that's all behind me now. I want to change my life around, but there's no time to discuss that now."

"You know, Lou Ann, I didn't want to involve you in this; but, if I can get Josh out of here, I'll need someplace to take him, and, well…" He looked at her timidly. "All I could think of was your mother's house. You did say she lived nearby, didn't you?"

"Yes, a few miles from here." She looked at him without speaking for a brief moment; then a slight smile appeared on her face. "Well, I guess I'm beholden to you, Patrick. You *did* rescue me from the Rebels."

"Then you'll help?"

"Yes, but I don't have my heart in it. Not like before."

"What do you mean?"

"Never mind now. Do you have a plan?"

"Well, haven't had much time to think about it; but, now that you're helping me, I think we can succeed. Were you planning on going back to your mother's house soon?"

"I did tell Father O'Brien and Sister Agnes Mary that, now that the good nuns were here to look after these boys, I wanted to go home. I'm worried about mother."

"Sister Agnes who?"

"Agnes Mary. She's the older nun who came in to help with the wounded. She helped care for me when I was very young."

"How do you mean?"

"Well, she runs the orphan asylum in Philadelphia where I spent some time after my parents died. She's such a wonderful person. That's the kind of work I want to devote my life to. But enough about this. We've got a dangerous task ahead of us."

For the first time, Patrick began to understand the change in her. She *was* different, he thought. She seemed to put the welfare of others ahead of herself. "We'll have to leave tonight, Lou Ann."

"How will we get past the guards?" she asked anxiously.

"Leave that to me. Do you think Father O'Brien would loan you his carriage? I mean—to go to your mother's house?"

"I can ask him."

"Good. If you can do that, I think I can take care of the rest. Meet me back here in about an hour. Let me know about the carriage." Before he left the room, he turned and looked at her. "Why is it we always seem to be escaping from someplace?"

She smiled, thought a moment, then replied, "Maybe it's a sign."

"What do you mean—a sign?"

"Oh, I was just thinking that maybe we're really trying to escape each other."

He was taken aback by her comment—but couldn't help wondering if she was right. He needed time to collect his thoughts. Could she be speaking the truth? He couldn't come to grips with an idea like *that*. He stepped over to her and grasped her hand in his. "Lou Ann, I—I have grown fond of you, but things seem to be happening so fast, I..."

"Sh-h-h," she said, as she placed her fingers on his lips. "Things will turn out fine. Don't worry." He gently removed her fingers and leaned over to kiss her on the lips when she turned her face to the side, his kiss falling upon her cheek. "We'll talk some more. Now we have to take care of your friend. I'll see you back here in an hour."

Holding the door for her, he followed her from the room, returning to his spot on the floor next to Joshua.

Pat sat down next to his old friend who was still sleeping, reached into his pocket, grasping his rosary tightly in his hand, and began to formulate his plans. He watched Sister Agnes Mary as she walked down the side aisles, opening all the windows that had been closed. The wind swept a fine mist of rain through the windows, bringing a freshness into the stale air inside and a fine shower of relief to the wounded near the side aisles. She and the other nuns had worked diligently, giving their tender care to the wounded, as well as taking care of the sanitary conditions the best they could, cleaning and mopping the floors and pews. He admired them for their tireless work, as they showed so much compassion to all of the broken and wounded men, Union and Confederate alike. And Lou Ann had worked right along with them.

It was after midnight when the nuns quietly collected their empty baskets and left the church. But before doing so, Sister Agnes Mary had told Lou Ann that she would send a few other nuns to relieve her in the morning.

A stillness enveloped the church, as Patrick glanced at his watch, the crystal still broken. Exhausted but pensive, he leaned his head back and felt the fine mist of rain from the open window above him, as it fell gently on his upturned face. Joshua awoke and looked over at him.

"I see you're awake," Pat said.

"Yeah, it felt good to get a little nap. Forgot about everything for awhile."

Patrick leaned over and whispered in his ear. "We're going to get you out of here tonight."

"What?" Joshua asked, rubbing his sleepy eyes that suddenly opened wide at hearing Pat's remark.

"Sh! We're going to help you escape."

"Who's we?"

"Oh, a friend of mine."

By now, Joshua was fully awake and was evidently excited at the prospect of escaping. "I can't believe you would take such a chance!"

"Don't worry, Josh—I owe you one anyway."

"How's that?"

"Well, if it wasn't for you, I never would have gotten my newspaper money back from that big bully!" he said with a grin.

Joshua chuckled. "How are we going to…"

"Never mind. Don't worry now. You stay right here!" He checked the time on his watch once again. "I'll be right back." He walked to the other side of the church where Lou Ann was waiting inside the little room. Patrick entered and quietly closed the door behind him.

"So far, so good, Patrick. I talked to Father O'Brien, and he gave me permission to use his carriage to go and see mother. Even said I could keep it for a few days because he's so busy around here now, he won't be using it for awhile."

"Good. Now, we're going soon; I have to get Josh out of here. I'll arrange for... Wait a minute! Is there a back door here somewhere?"

"Yes, over behind the altar."

"Can you show me?"

"Yes, follow me—it's right here, off the back hallway. It leads to the stable."

"Lou Ann, this is great! There's a carriage back here."

"Yes, that's Father's."

"Okay. So far, so good. Just give me a minute now. Let me think." Stepping back to the storage area, he gazed around the room. Boxes of votive candles, empty vases, two chalices, and altar boy vestments were stored on the shelves. A small urn labeled "Holy Water" was in the corner of the room. "What's in *here*, Lou Ann?"

"I don't know." Before she had answered, he had opened the closet door to find Father O'Brien's Mass vestments, a long black cassock among them. On a shelf above, he noticed a wide-brimmed black hat. "What are you thinking, Patrick?"

"Well, I'm wondering if we should go now or wait until morning."

She looked curiously at him for a brief moment. "Well, maybe we should wait until Father O'Brien is asleep. If he hears us, he might think it's strange for me to take his carriage in the middle of the night. I mean—he thinks I'm leaving tomorrow."

"You're right, Lou Ann." He paused. "Maybe just before sunup. That won't look so suspicious." He thought she looked worried. "What's wrong, Lou Ann? Are you afraid?"

"No," she said without hesitation. "I'm just wondering if we're doing the right thing."

"I shouldn't be involving you; but, you know, Lou Ann, if Josh died in prison, I'd never forgive myself."

She pondered his last remark. "Oh, well—I trust your judgment, Patrick. What do we..." She stopped in mid-sentence, as she watched him remove the priest's cassock from the closet and hold it up in front of himself, glancing in the mirror behind the door. "What are you doing with that?"

"Sh! Wait a minute. This is it, Lou Ann! This is how we're gonna do it!" His heart raced. He could see the way clearly now.

"Patrick! You're not going to..."

"It's the only way, Lou Ann. God forgive me, but it's for a good cause. Don't worry—I'll return it to the good Father. I figure the guards outside won't question a priest, but we've got to leave while it's still dark."

"I hope you know what you're doing."

"This will work—I *know* it will. Don't worry." He looked at his watch. Time was growing short. "I'll go and help Joshua into the room here. Can you go outside and see where the guards are posted?"

"Oh, sure. I know a few of them. They've been bringing in supplies and food for the men all day."

He returned to get Joshua, surprised that he now walked with a limp. "Did you get hit in the leg, too, Josh?"

"Yeah. The doc said a small piece of the shell was lodged in there, but he couldn't get it out. Said he was afraid of cutting a muscle or something. Pain's really bad."

"Lean on me, Josh. I want to get you in the Supply Room before the Sisters return. The guards are outside."

"What . .."

"Sh! Just hurry. I'll explain."

Lou Ann had returned to the Storage Room. Patrick pulled a chair from the corner for Josh to sit.

"Josh, this is Lou Ann. Lou Ann, meet my old friend, Josh."

"Oh, you're the kind lady who looked after me when I arrived," Josh said with a slight smile on his face. He tried unsuccessfully to get to his feet. "Darn leg—hard to stand."

"That's all right. Stay seated. I'm sorry about your wounds." Josh didn't respond—he simply nodded his head. Lou Ann quickly changed the subject. "Heard you and Patrick have known each other for a long time."

"Yes, Miss, a long time." Josh rubbed his leg.

Patrick was getting anxious to get on with his plans and nervously looked at his watch. "We can talk later. But for now, we'd better get ready to go." He saw a holy water font next to the door and dipped his fingers into it, blessing himself. Looking upward, he prayed, "Lord, help us!" Then turning to Josh, he spoke in low tones. "Now, we have Father O'Brien's carriage outside, thanks to Lou Ann here. She got permission to use it to go to see her mother." He walked over to the closet and removed the priest's long, black cassock once again. "Josh, I'm giving you my uniform to wear, and I'm going to pose as the priest. Now I know you're a good actress, Lou Ann, so you can pretend to be Joshua's sister. Just remember—you're taking your brother, who is dying, back to your mother's house."

"Sounds like a good plan, Pat," Josh said.

Lou Ann then stepped over to the holy water font, dipped *her* fingers into it and blessed herself. "Lord, forgive us for this."

Joshua looked at her curiously and asked, "Pardon me, Miss—but why do you ask the Lord for forgiveness?"

"Well, because of the priest's robe—I mean—it's deceiving to pretend to be a priest." She knew all about deception as a spy, but had reservations about using something religious, even if it was Patrick who would be wearing it.

Pat, standing with the priest's cassock and hat in his hands, smiled. "Don't worry, Lou Ann. I don't think the Good Lord will mind."

"I know, but..."

Pat interrupted. "Could you step into the hallway for a minute, Lou Ann?" he asked apologetically. "Josh and I have to change."

Raising her eyebrows and shaking her head slightly back and forth, she replied, "I hope you know what you're doing. I'll be in the church—have to get water for the men. They never seem to have enough."

Pat looked over at Joshua. "Get out of your uniform, Josh. You'll have to wear mine." He began to remove his own, tossing his sling aside. "I think I can get along without this thing." Joshua was struggling to remove his uniform with his one hand. "Here, let me help you," Pat offered. He replaced the gray with his blue. "Oh, you make a fine lookin' Yankee, Josh!"

At first, there was no response from Joshua. A few moments later, however, he remarked, "Yeah, maybe, but I feel kinda uncomfortable in this— kinda like a turncoat or something."

"Now, Josh," Pat said, as he sat down on a chair facing him, "you don't want to wind up in a prison now, do you?"

Josh shook his head and watched Patrick begin to button up the long, black cassock. "Where do you know that young lady from, Patrick?"

"Lou Ann? Oh, it's a long story. She took care of me after I was wounded at Fredericksburg."

"Fredericksburg?"

"Yeah, caught a bullet in the leg there."

"Oh, yeah? Maybe it was mine. I was there, too. We really whipped you there. I was behind that stone wall. You boys were like sittin' ducks out there." He looked down at the stump at the end of his arm. "Won't be no more fightin' for me now, though."

Pat didn't like Joshua's remarks but chose to ignore them. Finishing dressing, he placed the large-brimmed black hat far down on his brow to help conceal his identity.

"Well, Patrick, if I didn't know you, I'd think you really *were* a priest."

"That's good, Josh. Hope the guards outside think so, too."

They sat facing one another, neither one speaking. Finally, Joshua inquired, "You and that young lady—what's her name?—Lou?"

"Lou Ann."

"You and her? I mean—you seem pretty friendly with her. You sweethearts or somethin'?"

"Yeah—or somethin'."

"What does that mean?"

"Oh, we spent some time in Washington together when I was in the hospital." He decided Joshua didn't have to know the rest. No time now. "Besides, I..."

"Besides what, Pat?"

Patrick stammered for a moment. "Be—besides—I got to get through this war alive without worrying about a sweetheart." Before Joshua could ask any more questions, Pat asked, "What about you, Josh? You got a sweetheart?"

"Oh, yeah! Gonna marry her soon as I get back home."

'What's her name?"

"Jenny. She's the prettiest thing in all of Perch County."

"Perch County?"

"Yeah, Perch County, Virginia. It's at the mouth of the Peddler River."

"Well, Josh, hope you can make your way back there. Got to get you out of here first."

It was late when Lou Ann came back. Joshua had fallen asleep sitting up. Patrick, however, was anxiously pacing the floor, looking at his watch, his back to Lou Ann. "Oh, Father, I..." Pat spun around. "Pat, you frightened me. I thought for a moment you were Father O'Brien."

"Oh, that's good."

She was tired and didn't respond, as she sat down on a chair. Patrick looked at his watch. It was 3:15 a.m. "Couple more hours, Lou Ann."

Joshua, snoring loudly, never heard them talking as the early morning hours crept along. Patrick couldn't shake the feeling that he needed to clear the air with Lou Ann about Beth. But, seeing how tired she was, decided to wait until later—that is—if they were successful in their venture. She closed her eyes; Patrick wasn't sure if she was asleep. He sat down on the floor, as there were no other chairs in the room, thinking and praying about the next few hours. He also thought about the time in Washington he had spent with Lou Ann, their escape from the Rebels, and her near-death experience from pneumonia. He knew he had fallen in love with her, but he wondered if their hearts were beginning to go in opposite directions. She seemed to be having some kind of a "calling". He gazed over at her; she didn't resemble the young, vivacious girl he had dined with at the Willard Hotel. The six months that he had known her had raced by like a whirlwind. He was tired, also, and rested his head back against the wall, closing his eyes. The next thing he knew, Lou Ann was nudging him on his arm. "Patrick," she whispered. "I think we'd better leave now—it's almost dawn."

Rubbing his eyes, he glanced at his pocket watch. "Oh, my gosh! We have to get out of here right away—the sun will be up soon." He stood up and quickly walked to the back door. He stopped and turned back to Lou Ann. "Wake up Josh. I'll go and hitch up the horse."

When Pat returned, Lou Ann and Joshua were waiting by the door. Lou Ann had found a blanket in the closet and wrapped it around Josh's shoulders. "Thought this might help." They walked silently out the door, and Lou Ann and Joshua climbed into the carriage.

Patrick got into the driver's seat, turning around to speak. "Now remember—he's dying," he said to Lou Ann. "You're his sister and—well, I'll do the talking. Josh—you'd better slump down and close your eyes." Josh nodded in agreement.

Pat gently snapped the reins, and the carriage moved silently down the alleyway and into the street. Within seconds, a guard stepped out in front of them, his rifle pointing directly at them. "Halt! Where are you going?"

Patrick spoke up loud and clear. "We have a dying man here. His sister came to take him home to his mother's house. They live only a few miles from here."

"Let me see your pass."

"There wasn't enough time to get one—this poor lad doesn't have much time before he meets his Maker."

The guard removed his hat and scratched his head. "Well..." He hesitated. "I don't know. I'm not supposed to let anyone through here without a pass."

"Would you doubt a man of the cloth, lad? And—what's more—would you deny a fellow soldier from seeing his mother one last time before he dies?"

As a ray of sunlight streamed forth over the rooftops of the little town, piercing the darkness and illuminating the carriage and its occupants, the guard spoke in a different tone. "Oh, Father, I'm sorry—I couldn't tell you were a priest. I'm sure it will be all right." He lowered his rifle and waved at them to proceed. A short distance down the road, Lou Ann leaned forward and whispered, "Oh, Patrick, I think you should become an actor—you played your part so well." She smiled at him.

"Thanks. But we still have a way to go yet. Give me directions; I'm not that familiar with these streets." As they neared the edge of town, she directed him to the Emmitsburg Road. Pat turned his head toward his "passengers". "There's another guard and a log or something across the road up ahead." Joshua leaned over, resting his head on Lou Ann's shoulder, as she pulled his blanket up around his shoulders.

"Good morning, Father," the guard said cheerfully.

"Good morning, son," Patrick answered, looking out from beneath the large, wide-brimmed black hat, hoping not to be recognized.

"Where are you going, Father?"

"I have to get this boy home, Private. He's dying and wants to see his mother."

"You know what lies ahead of you, Father?"

"What's that, son?"

"Half the Rebel Army laying dead all over the road ahead. Some burial teams removing the bodies, but they haven't finished yet."

"Looks like I arrived just in time."

"Why is that, Father?"

"Well, son—I mean—I can offer up prayers for their souls and bless them and ask the Lord to be merciful as they come before Him."

"Even after they're dead?"

"Yes, my son—it's in the Good Book. You should read it some time."

"I will, Father. Be careful, though. It's a real mess—on the road, I mean." He removed the log that laid across the road; and, as their carriage passed by him, he hollered out, "Oh, Father, will you say a prayer for me?"

Pat turned his head, tipped his hat, and responded, "I've already started to, son."

"Thanks, Father."

Proceeding down the Emmitsburg Road, Lou Ann once again leaned forward. "That was a…" She suddenly stopped, then blurted out, "Oh, my God!" She quickly put her hand over her mouth. The three became horrified, as they gazed upon the mangled bodies strewn across the fields. They had to cover their noses and mouths with their hands in an effort to minimize the smell of rotting flesh. The horse, becoming spooked, recoiled and sprang from side to side, as it stepped around the dead who were lying in the road where they had fallen. As Patrick struggled to control the horse, they beheld another gruesome spectacle just a few yards off to the side of the road. A small group of Union soldiers, their noses covered with handkerchiefs, were digging a large pit for a common grave. Many corpses lined the edge of the pit, ready to be placed together in their last formation. They all wore gray uniforms. The glory and satisfaction of a Northern victory was short-lived for Patrick. He turned for a moment to look at Lou Ann and Joshua. She appeared to be stunned and shocked. Josh's eyes, filled with tears, were transfixed upon his fellow countrymen lying cold and still and laid out in orderly rows upon the rich soil of a Pennsylvania farmer's field.

Patrick tried to focus on the larger picture—a bittersweet victory, but maybe this horrendous loss of life would shorten the war. He felt pity for the dead and for his old friend, Joshua. The South, he thought, was doomed to fail. The tide had turned in those three days of killing, and the Confederacy would never quite recover. But little did he know that he would still be involved in two more brutal years of war to come. He was a soldier and Joshua was a soldier. But Joshua was an old friend, the enemy being a multitude of faceless young men dressed in gray uniforms. For now, he would take care of his friend—time enough later to confront that gray monster that roamed the countryside.

As the carriage bumped along on the narrow, dirt road, pock-marked with deep, rain-filled ruts and holes from the intense shelling of the third day, Patrick, Lou Ann, and Joshua remained speechless. The peaceful, quiet, country road that Lou Ann had traveled a few days earlier to attend Mass had become a hellish sight. In the distance, they could see the dead of both armies lying scattered across the fields, thousands of muskets, canteens, hats, and dead horses intermingled among them.

Soon they traveled through a wooded area that provided shade from the hot sun. Among the trees lay hundreds of wounded, Yankee and Rebel alike. Every clearing and space between the trees was blanketed with wounded and dead, some who had already undergone the surgeon's gruesome work of amputation. A few tents housed the lucky ones; more, however, lay in the open on blankets or straw. Ambulances were steadily bringing in more men from the killing fields.

Patrick prodded the horse along, snapping and pulling on the reins to guide the animal around the dead bodies and tree branches that had fallen to the ground from the relentless hail of bullets and shells. Some trees were completely denuded of their leaves, and many saplings were cut in two from the barrage of bullets that had sliced a path through the previously tranquil woods. Not a word was spoken by the three unlikely occupants in the carriage, as they finally rode away from the frightful spectacle of hell on Earth, with all of its repugnant sights and smells of that carnival of death. Patrick, who had wrapped a handkerchief around his mouth and nose, removed it and breathed in the fresh air that floated on a West wind coming over South Mountain.

CHAPTER 19

▼

THE SANCTUARY

After the war with Mexico, Colonel Sommers and his wife had decided that they had enough of big city life. Philadelphia was becoming congested; and, in some areas of the city, crime was on the rise. After much searching, they finally settled in a modest farmhouse halfway between Gettysburg, Pennsylvania and Emmitsburg, Maryland, very near the Mason-Dixon line. The quietude and serenity of the land, dotted with well-kept farms, was close to these quaint little towns populated with friendly folk.

Lou Ann began to cry out loud, "Oh, my good Jesus! Why? Why has it come to this? So many!"

Patrick turned and handed her his handkerchief. "I'm sorry, Lou Ann. I'm so sorry you had to see this."

Joshua, resting the bandaged stump in his lap, remarked, "That could be us, Patrick. We're lucky we made it."

Patrick snapped the reins harder, wanting to get Lou Ann away from the carnage; the horse began to trot faster.

Lou Ann, composing herself, spoke softly. "Here I thought I was learning to deal with the wounded—but—this is just too much to bear."

They continued on, as Patrick, relieved that they had passed through the horrible aftermath of the battle and successfully outwitted the guards, slumped back in the driver's seat and slowed the horse to a walk.

Joshua removed the blanket from his lap and leaned forward. "Looks like we made it, Pat. You're a great friend for doing this."

"You would have done the same thing for me, Josh—but we're not safe *yet*. How much further, Lou Ann?"

"About another mile or so. It's just off this road. I still can't believe all those poor men back there." She began to sob again.

Joshua turned to her. "Can I ask you something, Miss?"

She blotted her tears with Patrick's handkerchief. "Yes, what is it?"

"Well, why did you—well—what I wanted to ask you is—you don't even know me and yet you're risking so much to help me."

"I'm not sure—maybe it's because Patrick asked me. Besides, I know what it's like to be held prisoner."

"How do you mean, Miss?"

Suddenly realizing what she had said, she hesitated for a moment. "Oh— well..." She tried to think quickly. "I—well—I overheard some of your comrades in the church talking about being imprisoned. It wasn't pleasant." The subject quickly changed as they approached her mother's home. "Oh, Patrick, there it is!" She pointed toward a dirt road leading to a white farm- house nestled among several pines, barely visible from the road. As Patrick turned the horse onto the dirt road, Lou Ann suggested, "Oh, Patrick, I think maybe you should pull the carriage into the barn." Patrick nodded and headed for the barn, set back from the house, separated by a large vegetable garden. "Mother might have a lot of questions; maybe Joshua should stay in the barn for now. She may not understand."

They stepped down from the carriage and stood silently for a moment looking at one another. "Never thought this far ahead," Pat said. He started to unbutton the priest's cassock, reaching his hand inside and rubbing his bandaged shoulder. He was thankful that there was no new bleeding. "Guess I was so concerned about getting you out of the church, Josh. Never thought about what's next." He added, "I'll have to get out of this cassock first—don't want your mother to think I'm a priest, Lou Ann." Continuing to unbutton the robe, he realized that, since he had given Joshua his uniform, he had only his underwear beneath the priest's garb. "Lou Ann, would your father have any extra clothes in the house?"

Before she could answer, they heard horses approaching. Patrick quickly fumbled, frantically buttoning the robe back up. "Quick, Josh, hide behind those bales of hay," he said nervously, as five horsemen rode up to the barn. Patrick pretended to unhitch the horse from the carriage, as Lou Ann ner- vously walked over to greet the men, still mounted on their horses.

The officer in the middle of the group spoke up. "Good morning, Miss," he said politely, tipping his flat, wide-brimmed hat, pulled slightly down on one side.

"Good morning, Sir," she replied.

"Do you live here?" he asked.

"Yes, Sir, I live here with my mother."

Patrick, believing his avoidance of the horsemen might create suspicion, walked over and stood next to Lou Ann. "Can we help you, gentlemen?" He suppressed his fear at the sight of the stars adorning the officer's shoulder epaulet. A general! Pat swallowed hard. The general had long hair that hung down in ringlets; a silky, black, loose-fitting bowtie; and a brown mustache that drooped down on either side of his mouth. Patrick restrained himself, as he came close to saluting the officer.

"Good morning, Father," the general said cheerfully. "Are you planning to travel anywhere today?"

"Well, Sir, I've just accompanied Miss Sommers here back from town. She's done wonderful work, helping the wounded. She deserves a rest. I do plan on heading back to town soon though."

"Well, I just wanted to warn you, we've had reports of Rebel cavalry still in the area. Suggest you get back to town before nightfall."

"Yes, Sir. I'll be back long before that."

The general stared at Patrick for a moment. "You're very young looking for a priest."

Patrick was caught off guard but thought quickly. "Yes, Sir, I just graduated from the seminary; this is my first assignment." Hoping to avoid any further questions about himself, he quickly retorted, "And you, Sir, with all due respect, look mighty young for a general."

The officer beamed and seemed to appreciate Patrick's remark. "Well, Father, I'm getting old fast, though. This war takes a toll on one, you know." He then looked over at Lou Ann and asked, "Did Father here say your name was Sommers?"

"Why yes, he did, Sir."

"Would you be related to Colonel Sommers, the surgeon?"

"Why yes, General. He's my father."

"Fine man. Does wonderful work for our wounded. Met him at Bull Run. Kindly give him my best regards when you see him."

"Yes, Sir, but I didn't get your name."

"Oh, I'm terribly sorry. It's been a long night. Custer—George Custer, Miss."

He turned his horse around, glancing at Patrick. "Be careful on the road, Father." He galloped away, his entourage following closely behind him.

When Patrick was sure that the general and his men were out of sight, he removed the large priest's hat and wiped the sweat from his brow. He shook his head from side to side. "Well, what do you know? A general! First time I ever talked to a general—and Custer!—he's the big cavalry general!"

"You did fine, Patrick. You are so convincing as a priest." She laughed, breaking the tension. Pat laughed along with her.

Joshua, who had heard everything, emerged from his hiding place. "That was a close one, Patrick. First time I ever heard of a sergeant out-maneuvering a general!" he chuckled.

Pat smiled, feeling somewhat proud of himself. Turning to Lou Ann, he asked, "Would your father... Oh, never mind," as he spotted a pair of overalls hanging on a nail in the barn wall. "Can we use these, Lou Ann? I mean, can Josh wear these so I can get my uniform back? I've had enough pretending for one day."

"Yes, that would be all right, Patrick. They're Daddy's—he always wore them when he worked in the garden. I'm sure he won't be needing them for awhile—at least until the war's over."

Suddenly they heard a woman's voice shouting, "Who's out there?"

"It's my mother. I'll go to her. Patrick, you come in after you change clothes." Lou Ann ran toward the house. "Mother! Oh, Mother!"

"Lou Ann! Oh, Lou Ann, you're home! What happened to you? I've been worried sick. I thought you were dead! I've been beside myself! This horrible war came—oh, dear Lord in Heaven!" She noticed her daughter's blood stained dress as she approached the stairs of the porch. "Are you hurt? Oh, dear God! What happened to you?"

"No, Mother, I'm all right." She embraced her. "I was helping care for the wounded after the battle. Let's go inside. I'll tell you all about it." Her mother's arm was shaking as she led her into the house.

Patrick, now back in uniform, rolled up the priest's cassock and looked over at Joshua, dressed in Colonel Sommer's overalls. "Have to remember to return this to the priest, Josh," as he hid the clothing behind a bale of hay. "You hungry?"

"You bet! Haven't had a bite since yesterday."

"Yeah, me too. You stay here, out of sight. I have to go inside. Maybe Lou Ann can rustle up some food for us." As Patrick approached the house, he noticed Lou Ann standing by the door, motioning him to come inside.

They walked into the parlor where Mrs. Sommers was seated in a large, over-stuffed chair, sobbing and blotting her tears with a handkerchief, relieved to see her daughter safe.

"Mother, I'd like you to meet Patrick O'Hanrahan. Patrick, this is my mother."

"Pleased to meet you, Ma'am," as he removed his hat.

The gray-haired woman looked up at him, forcing a smile. "Come closer, son, where I can get a better look at you." She pointed to a spot on the floor in front of her chair. Blotting her tears one more time and straightening herself in the chair, she tried to compose herself. "Patrick, you're a fine looking lad. Lou Ann has told me so much about you." Suddenly noticing *his* blood-stained shirt, she exclaimed, "Oh, son, you're hurt!"

"Yes, Ma'am. Got wounded, but Lou Ann here—she took good care of me."

"I'm sorry you were hurt, son. It must have been awful. I could hear those cannon from here. Could only imagine how horrible it must have been."

"Yes, Ma'am. You're right. It *was* horrible. In fact, they're *all* horrible."

"Lou Ann tells me you two met in the hospital," Mrs. Sommers said, as she tried to change the subject to something more pleasant.

"Yes, Ma'am. After Fredericksburg. Thought I was a goner. When I woke up, it was Lou Ann's face that I saw—thought she was an angel!"

"Yes, she is a good girl. Always wanting to help people, even when she was little." She looked over at Lou Ann who glanced down at the floor, seemingly embarrassed by her mother's accolades. "And you, my boy", she continued, "my daughter said you prayed many rosaries for her when *she* was so sick in the hospital."

"Yes, Ma'am. I do believe the Good Lord heard our prayers."

Mrs. Sommers looked at Patrick curiously. "What do you mean—*our* prayers?"

He responded very matter of factly, "Oh, I meant, Jesus' Mother's and mine."

"Oh, yes, you're absolutely right. Praise God!"

"Yes, Ma'am. Praise God!"

"Oh, excuse me! With all this excitement, I haven't even offered you something to eat. You must be so hungry, both of you."

"Yes, Ma'am. Thank you, Ma'am."

"Well, you just come over here and sit right down," as she stood up and led Patrick into the dining room, motioning for him to sit at a large, round, wooden table next to a window overlooking her garden. She glanced back at Lou Ann, still standing in the parlor. "Lou Ann, you come and sit down here, too," as she pulled another chair out from the table. "You both look like you've had a terrible time of it." She hurried into the kitchen.

They ate ravenously, as the elderly woman served them an ample supply of bacon, eggs, corn muffins, and coffee, before sitting down to join them. "I have so many questions—so much to ask you both."

After a long conversation about Patrick's participation in the war and Lou Ann's harrowing experience at St. Xavier's, Mrs. Sommers wanted to know more about Patrick's background. He didn't go into detail and was becoming anxious to end the conversation, as he was concerned about getting some food to Joshua. He waited for a lull in the conversation, then spoke up. "Oh, I'm sorry, ladies, but I forgot to unharness the horse. May I be excused for a moment?" He got up from the table.

"I almost forgot about that," Lou Ann said. "We were in such a hurry, we didn't think to..."

Pat broke in. "That was delicious, Ma'am. Haven't eaten a breakfast like that since leaving home. Thank you."

"Oh, I'm glad you enjoyed it. You two certainly needed a good meal after all you've been through."

"I'll go with him and show him where the oats are, Mother—horses have to eat, too." Mrs. Sommers began to pick up some of the dirty dishes. "Leave that, Mother... I'll be right back to clean it up. Here, why don't you take your coffee and finish it in the parlor?" She led her mother to an easy chair there and returned to the dining room in time to see Patrick putting some food in a napkin for Joshua. They quietly slipped out the back door.

Joshua's eyes lit up as Lou Ann handed him the food. He didn't say anything—just sat down on a bale of hay and quickly consumed every morsel. "Thank you, Miss," he said, wiping his mouth with his sleeve. "You don't know how much I enjoyed that."

"You're welcome. My mother made it."

Patrick spoke up. "Well, now that we've all had some food, maybe we can think about what we should do next."

"Well, I can't stay here," Joshua remarked.

"I know, but it's too dangerous for you to travel yet," Pat responded. "You heard the general—both Union and Reb cavalries still patrolling the roads." They grew silent as Patrick walked over and removed the harness from the horse. Lou Ann held a bucket of oats in front of the animal who began to chomp on them.

Finally Lou Ann spoke up. "I have an idea."

"What's that?" Pat asked as he hung the harness on the wall.

"Well, it's just a thought."

"What? What are you thinking?" Patrick asked again.

She set the bucket on the floor, as the horse continued to eat, then glanced over at Patrick. "There is an old priest friend of our family at a church in Emmitsburg. He's a wonderful man. Maybe he would put Joshua up for awhile—I mean, just until the Army leaves."

"Do you really think so, Miss?" Joshua asked, looking hopeful at her suggestion.

"Well, I know he has always helped people in need."

Patrick looked at her curiously. "Would he mind that..." He hesitated. "Well, no offense, Josh, but I was going to say—do you think he would object to taking in a Confederate soldier, Lou Ann?"

Joshua's expression changed. "You *know* I ain't gonna do no more fightin', Pat," as he held up his bandaged stump. They looked over at Lou Ann, anticipating her response.

"Don't worry. I think there's a good chance he would help," Lou Ann offered.

Pat raised his eyebrows, looking over at Josh. "Well, old friend, sounds good to me! I think it's a good idea, Lou Ann. Besides, I can't think of a better one."

Joshua looked concerned. "Gee, Pat, maybe the priest would take me in even though I'm a Confederate, but..."

"But what?" Pat asked.

"Well, you know, it's not just that I'm a Confederate—but, you know—I'm Jewish, too."

"Of course I know that, Josh. Did you forget when we had these medals made?" He pulled his medal out from his shirt and looked at it. "Besides, *Jesus* was a Jew, wasn't He?"

"Yeah, you're right, I guess."

Lou Ann smiled at Joshua. "Father Pirson welcomes everyone to his church; he looks on everyone as a child of God."

"Then it's settled," Pat said. "We'll take you to the church."

Joshua got up and took a few steps, limping as he did. He stopped abruptly and braced himself against the wall. "Damn shell! Oh, sorry, Miss—didn't mean to swear. My apologies." He looked down at the floor. "Guess I couldn't even get into the infantry—even if I wanted to."

"Were you in charge of a company, Josh?" Pat asked. "I mean—you had a Captain's insignia on your uniform."

"Yeah, I started out in the cavalry, though. Liked that better. Then I got a battlefield commission, and they needed a company commander. Lost most of my men in that wheatfield—all good men! And Blackjack, too! What a hell of a war! Oh, sorry again, Miss. Didn't mean to cuss. Guess I gotta get used to bein' around ladies more."

Lou Ann nodded her head, showing acceptance of Joshua's apology. "We can't use the road. I know of a shorter way through the woods, but we'll have to walk. There's a path that only some of us locals know about."

"How far away is the church?" Pat asked.

"Oh, just a few miles."

"Well, that's not far." He suddenly realized that Joshua couldn't walk. "Do you think that you can make it that far, Josh?"

He didn't answer right away. Instead, he pushed himself away from the wall to test his legs. He fell to the floor after three steps, breaking his fall with his one good hand. Patrick and Lou Ann immediately ran over to help him. He looked up at them. "Is that a good enough answer?" he asked in a slightly bitter tone. "I'm all right," he barked at them, as he pulled himself up to his feet and sat back down on the bale of hay.

Pat, seeing Joshua so disturbed, wisely diverted his attention. "I know what we can do. You say there's a path in the woods, Lou Ann?"

"Yes."

"Is it big enough for a horse to get through?"

"I think so."

"Good—then Josh can ride."

Lou Ann thought for a moment. "I think we should leave early in the morning. I'll leave a note for mother that we went to early Mass. She likes to sleep late. I'll say I didn't want to disturb her. That way, I won't have a lot of explaining to do."

Pat looked at her with a broad smile. "You know, Lou Ann, looks like you haven't lost that "agent's" mind for planning things."

Joshua, still recovering from the fall, was staring at the ground, chewing on a piece of straw. Making sure Joshua wasn't looking in her direction, Lou Ann glanced over at Patrick, frowning and placing her index finger vertically on her lips, hoping to shush him immediately. Patrick quickly realized he had said the wrong thing in front of Joshua. Lou Ann's fears that Joshua would become suspicious at Patrick's remarks were relieved, however, as she watched Joshua staring at the ground, seemingly disinterested in their conversation.

Exhaustion began to overtake them. Joshua fell asleep in the barn, Lou Ann went to her bedroom, and Patrick dozed off on the couch in the parlor while Mrs. Sommers cooked their supper. After they had eaten, they sat in the parlor and talked. Pat felt good. He had washed up, eaten his fill once again, and enjoyed sitting on a soft chair. He felt almost human now. Occasionally they would hear horses and wagons rumbling by on the Emmitsburg Road in front of the house. Patrick observed them from the window, passing intermittently throughout the evening. They were mostly Union cavalry and batteries of cannon that he presumed were being hauled to the front. "Looks like our boys are giving chase to the Rebs! Too bad we couldn't have finished it at Gettysburg."

Mrs. Sommers, seated on a rocking chair knitting a sweater, grew more nervous each time she heard the soldiers passing by. She hastened the pace of her knitting, as she unknowingly rocked faster. "I wish the soldiers would leave here," she said. "It was so nice and peaceful before..." She stopped abruptly. "Oh, Patrick, I'm sorry. I didn't mean *you*. I mean, I'm so glad our army drove the enemy away. It's just that I guess those three horrible days of fighting... I was afraid!"

"That's all right, Ma'am. I know how you feel. I'm sorry it—I mean, that the battle had to come so close to your home. But don't worry. I know the troops will be out of here shortly. We'll probably chase the Rebs far away from here."

"Were you in the fighting very long, Patrick?"

"Well, Ma'am, a few hours, mostly in the wheatfield."

"A wheatfield?"

"Yes, Ma'am, a wheatfield—not far from a ridge, near a small hill."

"Little Round Top?"

"I don't know the name of it."

"It sounds like Farmer Rose's place. I do hope he and his family are all right."

"I don't know, Ma'am, but that's where I got hit by a shell. It blew me back, and I caught a piece of it in my shoulder. It nearly killed me and my friend,..." Almost mentioning Joshua's name, he stopped in mid-sentence.

"You were saying? A friend?"

"Oh, yes, Ma'am. A friend of mine. We were the lucky ones, though. We left many of our comrades in that wheatfield—more than I would care to count."

"Oh, that's terrible, son. How did you keep your sanity?"

"Don't know, Ma'am. Guess I pray a lot—always ask Saint Michael for his protection."

"I see you're a religious man—I like that."

"Thank you, Ma'am."

Mrs. Sommers seemed to calm down as she spoke to Patrick and listened to what he had to say. Lou Ann, who was seated on one end of the couch, spoke up. "I like that in a man, too, Mama. We never did have many church-going men here, Patrick. Mostly all women in church on Sundays."

Patrick, still standing by the front window, walked over and sat down on the couch, leaving a respectable space between himself and Lou Ann. He smiled at her.

"Speaking of church, Lou Ann, I think you did a wonderful job attending to the wounded at Gettysburg. I watched you after you took care of me."

She smiled half-heartedly, seeming disinterested and distant. Quickly changing the subject, she said, "There's something I want to tell you, Mama. Something happened to me when I was sick and almost died."

"You almost *died?*"

"Oh, Mama, Daddy didn't want to worry you with your heart condition, but I was very sick for awhile."

"Well, I knew about your pneumonia, but I didn't know that it had been *that* serious. I would have taken the first train to see you."

"That's all right, Mama. I'm fine now."

Her mother, who seemed to be having trouble concentrating on her knitting, looked over at Lou Ann. "You said something happened to you?"

"Yes, I..." She looked over at Patrick with a sympathetic look. "I'm not sure how to explain this, but I want you both to know. I guess the Good Lord allowed me   to—well—I mean, to get so sick. When I was in that delirious state of mind—from the fever, I mean—my whole life passed in front of me. I felt that—well—that I had only thought of myself and what I could do for *me*. I remembered a nun telling me something when I was an orphan. She said that, when our time comes and we go before the Lord, our hands must be full. I mean, full of good works. Then, sometime during the night, my fever broke; and I heard a soft but compassionate sounding voice say, 'Your hands are empty.'"

"Oh, my dearest Lou Ann," her Mother said, "maybe it was just a dream."

"No, Mama, it was more than just a dream—I *know* it." Patrick looked on, noticing the intensity in Lou Ann's eyes as she spoke. "You know, Mama, there's more that I have to say, and I guess this is the time to say it."

Patrick, feeling that he was intruding in family concerns, picked up his cap and stood up. "Maybe I should be leaving..."

Lou Ann quickly interrupted him. "Please sit down, Patrick," as she patted the couch cushion next to her. "I want you to hear this, too. I do owe you an explanation."

By now, Mrs. Sommers had stopped knitting and sat still in her rocking chair with her hands folded over her handiwork.

Lou Ann continued, "I had a great deal of time to think about my life while I was recuperating. When I acted in the theater, it was all pretending; and when I acted as an "agent", I was pretending to be someone else, too."

Her Mother looked at her questioningly. "What do you mean—an agent? I know about your acting in the theater, but what do you mean—an agent?"

"I wasn't going to tell you, Mama; but now that I have put all that behind me, I guess you should know."

"I don't understand, Lou Ann."

"Well, Mama..." She looked over at Patrick. "Patrick knows something about this, but—well—I did some... I hate to use this word, but—well—I did some spying for the Union Army."

"Oh, Lou Ann! You didn't!" Her mother raised her eyebrows, seemingly shocked at Lou Ann's admission.

"Yes, Mama, but it wasn't for very long. It seemed exciting at first; but when I got captured by the Rebels, it didn't seem so glamorous."

"Captured!" her mother screamed out. She slumped back in her chair and clutched her chest.

"Mama! Mama! Are you all right?"

Her mother blurted out, "Don't tell me any more. I don't think my heart could take it."

"Oh, I shouldn't have told you any of this," Lou Ann said apologetically. "Oh, I'm so sorry."

Patrick went over and stooped down next to Mrs. Sommers, speaking softly. "It's fine now, Ma'am. Lou Ann is safe at home now. This war is upsetting to all of us." The thought crossed his mind that if she ever knew a Rebel was hiding in her barn, even though it was his old friend, she would *truly* have a heart attack.

"I really didn't mean to upset you, Mother, but I just wanted you to know why I have decided to change my life around." Then she looked over at Patrick. "I wanted you to hear this, too, Patrick."

Her mother placed her hand on Patrick's, who was still stooping down next to her, his hand resting on the arm of the chair. "Oh, this war!" she said in exasperation. "Of all places, it had to arrive right on our doorstep! I wish it would end."

The elderly woman looked up at the old grandfather clock in the corner; the hour was getting late. "I don't think I can take any more excitement tonight. We can talk again tomorrow," she said, excusing herself. Proceeding to the dining room, she removed a large jug of wine from the cabinet, poured herself a glass, and tucked her Bible under her arm. Stopping halfway up the stairs, she turned back. "Oh, Patrick, you can sleep on the couch. Come along, Lou Ann."

"I'll be up in a few minutes, Mama." Pat sat back down next to Lou Ann. "I feel terrible for upsetting Mother like that. I only wanted her to know the truth."

"Oh, I'm sure she'll get over it. I guess it was just too much at one time. I mean, the war and all, coming so close. She'll probably feel better in the morning."

"I hope you're right, Patrick," she replied, as she shifted her position slightly to face him. "Do you know what I was trying to tell my mother?"

"Well, I think so. You seemed to make it clear that you want to make some changes in your life. But..."

"Yes?"

"Oh, I was just going to say—you didn't mention *how*."

She stood up and walked over to the parlor window, looking at the rising moon in the summer sky. "Orphans, Patrick. I want to devote my life to the care of orphans."

"Did you decide this after you got sick?"

"Not entirely."

Pat looked at her, as the moonlight streaming through the window cast a shimmering glow about her hair. He wanted to grab her up in his arms and kiss her and hold her forever. But gentleman didn't take such liberties. At least, he had always thought that way before the war. He had changed in some ways, though. Somehow, when he was in her presence, his resolve to be true to Beth and to tell Lou Ann about her quickly melted away. She had bathed and combed her hair but hadn't taken the time to make the curls he had been used to seeing on her. Instead, her hair hung down loosely over her shoulders, and she appeared more feminine to him that way, standing there in the moonlight. He got up and slowly walked over to her. Looking into her sparkling blue eyes, he said in a soft voice, "You're so beautiful, Lou Ann." He pulled her close to him and kissed her. At first, she didn't resist; but after a brief moment, she gently moved back and stopped his advances.

"Patrick, I know how you feel. I, too, have feelings for you, but—well— it can never be. I don't know why this happened to us." As he watched and listened to her, he knew in his heart that she was right. She continued, "I never finished telling mother about my plans, but I must tell you. Please listen to what I am trying to tell you, Patrick. First of all, I've become very fond of you, and I'm sorry if I have encouraged you in any way."

"What are you trying to say?" He anxiously waited for her to answer.

She walked over to the couch, sat down, and folded her hands in her lap. Gazing over at him, still standing by the window, she seemed hesitant to continue.

"Come on, Lou Ann—what are you trying to tell me?"

"Patrick—I have to be perfectly honest with you. You see, I really feel— well—I want to be a Daughter of Charity."

"A nun!" His mouth dropped open. "I know you mentioned that you wanted to work with orphans when we were back at the church, but you never mentioned joining a convent."

"Yes, I've decided that I want to devote my life to God and to the care of the little orphans who have no one."

Pat stood speechless as he tried to collect his thoughts. Then, after a long silence, he said, "Are you sure? I mean—have you talked to a priest or somebody about it?"

"Yes, I did speak to a priest."

"Well, what did he say?"

"He said I should pray about it and to talk with the Mother Superior in the convent at Emmitsburg. You know, Patrick, I have a confession to make to you."

"Gee, Lou Ann, I can't keep up with you. First, it's about the orphans… then you want to become a nun… what's next?"

"Well, I was hoping that you would bring it up first, but I want you to know something that I've known ever since we first met at Fredericksburg."

"And what is that?" he asked, still bewildered.

"Well, let me put it this way…" She was interrupted by a series of loud, booming noises in the distance. "What's that?" she asked, looking startled.

Patrick pulled the curtain back further, looking into the darkness. "I thought it was thunder, but there's no storm. There it is again." He listened intently. "That's cannon fire—I know that sound very well. Our boys must have caught up with the Rebs. Probably a few miles from here. Now what were you saying?" He looked back at Lou Ann.

"Patrick—I've known about Beth since we first met." The distant sound of the thundering cannon continued to resonate, as Patrick stood silent, surprised that his secret was now out in the open. Lou Ann continued, "I'm sorry, Patrick. I just couldn't bring it up before. I mean, we were both so lonely back on New Year's Eve and during your hospital stay in Washington. You see, you weren't the only lonely one. Then, when we were escaping the Rebels, there wasn't time. And, after that, well—you know—I got so sick."

Patrick looked down at the floor, feeling ashamed that she was the one to bring up Beth's name. "I'm the one who should apologize, Lou Ann. I should have been more forthright with you—but how did you know?"

"Well, I have to confess that I heard you say Beth's name over and over again before you regained consciousness in that field hospital in Fredericksburg."

"You knew about Beth all that time?"

"I'm afraid so. She *is* your sweetheart back home, isn't she?"

"Well—yes, she is—*was*—well, then *you* came along..."

"You don't have to explain. It's this terrible war. This probably never would have happened if it weren't for this war."

"I'm glad it happened. Lou Ann—I couldn't help myself. You were there for me when I was at my lowest. You were like a beautiful flower that bloomed in winter—like that sweet-smelling lilac you gave to me. You were truly my angel of the battlefield."

Lou Ann looked up at him as a tear trickled down her cheek. She dabbed at it with her pink handkerchief. "Oh, Patrick, I owe my life to you. I could have been hung as a spy or died in a Confederate prison if it wasn't for you. You were there for me when *I* was in trouble, too."

Patrick walked over and sat on the couch next to her and held her hand once again. "I wondered in my heart if it could ever be, Lou Ann. Here we are together now in the middle of this war, but my past and your future—well...

Lou Ann looked into his eyes and softly said, "It could have been different, I know, but I do believe the Good Lord has chosen separate paths for us; and in the end, we will understand His Will in a clearer light."

The distant sound of cannon had ceased, and it began to rain. They sat silently, as the wind pelted the raindrops against the windowpane.

Lou Ann broke the silence. "I'm so sorry, Patrick. I truly am."

He looked at her with a half-hearted smile. "I am, too, Lou Ann, but..." He stopped briefly.

"But what, Patrick?"

"I'll miss you, Lou Ann, but—well—maybe you're right. Maybe it's better this way."

"I'll miss you, too, Patrick, and I'll never forget you. If only..."

"Only what?" He looked at her, waiting anxiously for her next words.

"Oh—nothing. No sense looking back."

After another short pause in the conversation, Lou Ann got up from the couch, pushed her hair back over her shoulders, and stood silently for a moment, looking deeply into Patrick's eyes, as though there still was so much to say.

"Lou Ann, it's getting late!" her mother called from upstairs.

"Yes, Mama, I'm coming," she called back. "Patrick, we really should get some sleep now... we have to leave before sunup."

He jumped to his feet. "Oh my gosh, Lou Ann," he whispered. "We forgot all about Joshua—he hasn't eaten anything since this morning. I have to take something out to him."

"I'm so tired, Patrick," Lou Ann responded in a hushed tone as she walked toward the stairway. "Would you mind taking some food out to him yourself? Take what you need from the kitchen. He must be starving."

Pat rummaged through the kitchen, wrapping some food in a towel for Joshua. As he was about to leave, he noticed the jug of wine still standing on the dining room table where Mrs. Sommers had left it. He paused briefly at the door, trying to decide whether or not to take it. He remembered his grandfather taking whiskey or wine for what he referred to as his "medicinal purposes" for his aches and pains. Sure got enough aches and pains around here, he thought, rubbing his shoulder. He walked into the dining room, grabbed the jug, and proceeded out to the barn. Pushing the door open with his foot, he whispered, "Josh, are you awake?"

"Over here, Patrick."

"Can't see a thing—it's pitch black in here."

"Wait," Josh said. "I'll come over to you. My eyes are adjusted better—been sitting in the dark for some time now." He walked over and put his arm on Pat's shoulder.

"What's that you're holding, Patrick?"

"Got some food for you."

"Thanks. I could eat a whole hog—I'm so hungry!"

"I think I saw a lantern hanging on the wall before—on the back wall, Josh."

"I've got it over here, Pat, where I was sitting. Got no matches, though."

"Neither do I. I know where I can get some. Wait here. I'm going back to the house." He handed the food and wine to Joshua.

"What's in the jug?" Josh asked.

"Wine. Don't drink all of it! Save some for me!" Pat chuckled.

He quietly snuck back into the house and found the matches he had seen earlier on the stove. Returning to the barn, he lit the lantern, set it on the floor, and piled some bales of hay on top of one another, hoping to conceal the light. He seated himself, facing Josh, who was beginning to eat. Reaching over, he picked up the jug of wine, pulled out the cork with his teeth, and offered it to Joshua who immediately raised it to his lips.

"Wait!" Pat said. "Let's have a toast." Joshua lowered the jug and handed it back to Patrick, who raised it up. "Here's to us and our long-time friendship, Josh." He took a long swallow and handed it back.

"And here's to you for helping me, Patrick—and here's to better times, when this God-forsaken war will be over." He raised the jug to his lips once again with his only hand and gulped it thirstily before handing it back to Pat, who took a long swig. "Good wine."

"Mmm-hmm. Thought you'd like it, Josh." Pat smiled.

Pouring rain started up again, and they both sat quietly, listening to it beating down on the barn roof and staring at the lantern on the floor in front of them. Pat looked over at his friend, the dim light flickering on his face covered with the red beard. "Never would have recognized you, Josh—I mean, especially with the beard."

"Yeah, well you know how it is. They never give ya time to shave... always fightin' or marchin'."

"Yeah, I know what you mean. You know, if Lou Ann hadn't recognized your medal, Josh, we probably wouldn't be sitting here right now."

"Yeah, you're right. Lucky she saw it. I'd probably be headin' for a Yankee prison by now." He pulled the medal out from his shirt and looked at it.

They exchanged stories back and forth—as well as the jug. Recounting memories of their boyhood escapades seemed to lift their spirits. Pat shook his head back and forth. "I can hardly believe this, Josh. I mean, what were the chances of us meeting each other after all these years?"

"Beats me," Josh said, picking his teeth with a piece of straw.

"How did you—I mean—how was it you joined the Reb army?" Pat asked.

"I was gonna ask you the same thing—how did *you* wind up in the Yankee army?"

"Well, I guess your people fired on Fort Sumter and wanted to break up the Union. That's what I joined up for. Didn't want the States all split up."

"You mean you didn't join up to free the slaves?"

"Well, not exactly." Patrick remembered his grandfather talking in the parlor with a friend one spring evening, just after Fort Sumter had been fired on. His grandfather had been reclining on a chair near the fireplace. He could still hear his words:

"Looks like we're goin' ta war, Thomas," Grocky had said while puffing on his clay pipe.

"Yeah, Shawn. Guess we come over here at the wrong time, but what choice did we have?"

"None—woulda starved ta death in the old country."

"Yeah, guess we went from the fryin' pan inta the fire."

"Ya know, Thomas, we're too old ta fight, but I'm concerned about me grandsons, Pat and Mike. We come ta this new land with hopes an' dreams fer a better life—especially fer our young ones. Oh, I'm not sayin' that it's not a noble cause ta fight fer the black man; but, ya know, Thomas, I don't even know any black men. I kin certainly relate ta their cause, though; but, is it worth losin' a grandson an' all yer hopes fer his future? On the other hand, I wish we had someone ta fight fer us in the old country. Our lot wasn't much different than the slaves over here. Them damned landlords treated us like slaves, an' we couldn't git out from under their tyranny."

Thomas had been listening attentively to Grocky's words. He had replied, "Well, I don't have any boys that could fight, Shawn. The Good Lord, as ya know, blessed me with all girls; but I know how ya must feel. I agree with ya. And I believe that we can't have two countries here. I mean, who knows what will become of us if we crack in two."

Patrick's thoughts were interrupted by Joshua. "Patrick, did you hear me?"

"Oh, sorry, Josh. I was just thinking of something."

"You said 'not exactly'. What do you mean?"

"Well, to be honest with you, Josh, I joined up because my country called me." Pat raised the jug to his lips and swallowed once again. As he handed it back to Josh, he asked, "You never answered *my* question. Why did *you* join up with the Rebs?"

"Well, one thing for sure—I didn't join up because of the slaves. *We* never owned any. In fact, only two people in my hometown that I know owns any slaves. Only reason that I joined up was 'cause you Yankees wanted to come down here and tell us what to do."

"Do you know any blacks?" Patrick asked.

"Sure—even played with them when I was young. And once I worked as an overseer."

"What's an overseer?"

"It's like a boss-man. I had to see to it that the slaves did their jobs. Didn't like it, though. The Colonel wanted me to be too hard on 'em. Didn't like it at all. Only lasted a short time; then I quit."

Patrick detected some sympathy for the slaves in Joshua's words. However, Josh seemed resigned to the fact that the institution of slavery was acceptable. Pat looked over the lantern illuminating Josh's face and asked, "Do you *believe* in slavery, Josh?"

"Well now—never did give it much thought."

"Well, you said you played with them when you were younger and worked as an overseer. Didn't you ever stop and think how bad it was for them? I mean—being owned by others—like animals or something."

Joshua looked back at Patrick as if he didn't have an answer. Then, after a long silence, he explained, "Well, Patrick, when we first moved down here, it did seem strange. But then, after awhile, it was just a way of life. Nobody ever said it was wrong, but I'm sure about one thing."

"What's that?"

"I never woulda picked up a gun and went to war if I thought it was just about someone keeping their slaves. The way I heerd it was that you Yankees was comin' down here and takin' all our rights away—some even said you'd be takin' our land away and molestin' our women folks."

Pat looked surprised. "Gee, Josh, I guess you folks heard a lot of nonsense about us Northerners. After listening to you, it's no wonder the South went to war. Well, isn't it strange—here *I* didn't go to war to *free* the slaves and *you* didn't go to war to *keep* the slaves. And yet... that's what it's come down to."

"Seems so."

"But you know, Josh, don't mind tellin' you—after seeing some slaves a while back living like animals, afraid to speak, fearful of their masters—I *know* we have to win this war."

"Only thing *I* know is that it ain't *my* war no more. All I care about is goin' home and seein' my Jenny."

"Jenny?"

"Yep. Gonna marry that gal—no matter *how* this war comes out!"

"Well, I hope you get home safe, Josh, but I'm gonna see this thing through to the end, God willing."

Josh handed the jug back to Patrick who drank some more. By this time, they weren't feeling any pain. Pat suddenly broke into laughter.

"What's so funny?" Josh asked.

"Oh, I was just thinking how we first met when we were youngsters. There I was, laying on the ground after that bully mugged and robbed me, just thinkin' about the money he stole; and when I looked up, I see him runnin' away toward you and you winding up with something in your hand. Next thing I know..." Patrick started laughing again—so hard he couldn't speak.

Then Joshua began to laugh with him, blurting out, "You should have seen that scoundrel's face... all covered with horseshit!"

Patrick, who by now was standing, was bent over at the waist, holding his stomach and laughing uncontrollably. Attempting to sit down on a bale of hay, he lost his balance and slipped onto the floor, looking stunned for a moment. Josh laughed harder; Patrick joined him. After a few minutes, he suddenly realized that they might wake up Lou Ann's mother. "Josh," he said, "we have to quiet down. We might wake up the mother." They both attempted to control their laughter with little success. Patrick wiped the tears of laughter from his eyes, as they continued passing the jug back and forth. As the hour grew late, they emptied the jug; and finally they both sprawled out on the barn floor and Josh fell asleep. Pat's thoughts, watching Joshua in deep slumber, now turned from childhood antics to the stark reality of the many souls, both Northern and Southern, who slept the Eternal Sleep in the nearby fields of Gettysburg.

The next morning, Patrick was awakened with a gentle nudge on his arm. Lou Ann's pretty face was the first thing he saw. He remembered when he gazed upon her image at Fredericksburg and thought she was an angel. After collecting his thoughts, he believed that this could possibly be the last time that he would awaken to her pleasant countenance.

"Patrick, wake up! We'd better get started." He sat up, held his head in his hands for a minute, then rose to his feet, brushing the hay from his hair and clothing. "You look like you had a hard night, Patrick," Lou Ann quipped as she smiled and picked up the empty jug from the floor. She walked over and woke up Joshua, immediately noticing the bandage on his stump was soaked with fresh blood. "We'd better change that dressing—I'll be right back." When she returned, she had two fresh, hot cups of coffee, some muffins, and clean bandages. She also gave Joshua a shirt that she had taken from her father's closet. "Here, Joshua, you can put this on."

Josh began to put on the shirt, which was too big for him. "Your father must be a big man, Lou Ann," he remarked, as he rolled up the one sleeve with his good hand. It suddenly dawned on him that he couldn't roll up the other sleeve. He lowered his head and shook it back and forth, looking dejected. Lou Ann did it for him and proceeded to change his dressing.

Pat sat down next to him, as they sipped the hot brew. After a few minutes, he said, "We'd better saddle up the horse for Joshua before your mother wakes up, Lou Ann." He gulped down his coffee, grabbed a muffin, and stuck it in his mouth. With some help from Patrick, Joshua mounted the horse. Lou Ann led them to a narrow path behind the barn, Patrick following her on foot, leading the horse. They journeyed for a short time, pushing back overhanging branches and plodding through the muddy path, as the horse's hoofs created a rhythmic, sucking sound in the saturated earth. Before long, they emerged from the woods and entered a vast open area. A short distance away, they could see a little white church on top of a small hill. "That's the church I was in before the battle," Pat offered. "I recognize it with all those gravestones around it."

"Saint Joseph's—that's where we're going," Lou Ann remarked.

"Can I help you?" the housekeeper asked, as she opened the rectory door, drying her hands on her apron, seemingly disturbed at being interrupted from her chores. Her brown hair, mixed with strands of gray, was tied neatly in a bun at the back of her head.

"Is Father Pirson here?" Lou Ann inquired.

"I believe he's in the study," the housekeeper answered abruptly. "Who shall I say is calling?"

"Miss Sommers."

"I'll tell him you're here." The screen door slammed behind her.

The front entrance to the priest's home, located across the road from the church, had a large front porch with a few rocking chairs on it. Patrick assisted Joshua down from the horse and helped him over to one of the chairs, then sat down himself and began to rock. "Nice place," Pat said, as he looked over to Lou Ann, waiting at the front door, seeming to be deep in thought. "Something wrong?" Pat asked.

"No. I was just thinking that housekeeper must be new here... I don't recognize her."

Just then, the priest appeared at the door. He wore a long, black cassock, and was opening the top button, wiping the sweat from his neck and forehead with a white handkerchief. "It's a hot one!" he said, smiling at Lou Ann. "Good to see you, Miss Sommers."

"Good morning, Father," she said. "May I speak with you for a moment? Oh, excuse me—this is my friend, Patrick, and his friend, Joshua. This is Father Pirson."

"How do you do, gentlemen?" He held open the screen door. "Won't you come in?" Patrick assisted Joshua who was leaning on him, hobbling into the study. "Oh, you're hurt!" the priest remarked, pulling over a chair for Josh to sit down.

"Yes, Sir," Joshua answered, as he slowly sat down, wincing in pain.

"Can I get some cold drinks for you? You all look so hot from your travels."

"Thank you, Father. We would really appreciate that," Lou Ann responded.

Father Pirson went into the kitchen and returned shortly with three glasses of lemonade. After handing them the drinks, he sat down behind his desk. His broad smile showed two rows of perfectly aligned, very white teeth. "Now then, how may I help you?"

Lou Ann sat up straight in her chair, trying to steady the glass in her hand, anxious about the huge request she was about to make to the priest. "Father—I..." She didn't know what to say next.

"What is it, my dear?" the priest asked in a kindly tone, attempting to put her at ease.

Just then, Patrick spoke up. "Father, if I may..."

"Please do."

"Well, Father, it's a long story; but I'll be as brief as I can. You see, Joshua here is an old friend of mine. We grew up together in New York City." Patrick went on to explain how they lost contact when Joshua's family moved south, and how they met once again on the battlefield at Gettysburg. "Lou Ann thought you might be able to help. Do you think it's possible, Father, that you could put Joshua up for a short time, just until his wounds heal? I know it's asking a lot, but I just can't let my friend be taken to a prison camp."

The priest leaned back in his chair, raising his eyebrows, attempting to digest it all. "That's some story! Sounds like the Good Lord was watching over the two of you. Amazing—just amazing!" He looked over at Joshua. "Well, son, I'm sorry about your injury; I guess you won't be doing any more fighting now, will you?"

"No, Sir," Josh replied.

Turning to Lou Ann and Patrick, the priest offered, "I admire you both for helping your friend—you've put his welfare ahead of your own. You took quite a chance, you know." He got up from his chair, walked around to the front of his desk, and leaned back against it, folding his arms in front of his chest. "Patrick, I don't know that you and Joshua were ever really enemies; but you know, the Good Lord taught us to love our enemies, and I believe you are doing just that—now how could *I* do any less?"

Patrick stood up and shook Father Pirson's hand, thanking him in earnest. Lou Ann's face lit up with joy, as she, too, offered her thanks. Joshua began to reach out his hand to the priest, suddenly realizing once again there was only a stump. He quickly retracted it and extended his other hand. "Thank you, Sir," he said.

"You can call me Father Al," the priest said in a gentle tone. "I could use some help around here anyway. I mean—after your injuries heal, you may be able to help me with some odd jobs. We have plenty of room in the church cellar. I'll set up a cot for you—it's nice and cool down there."

"I'll do what I can, Father—but my leg—well, I can't walk on it yet."

"Don't worry, son, we'll have a doctor look at it in the morning. I have to say Mass now." Looking over at Pat and Lou Ann, he added, "I'll take good care of Joshua. Now you'll have to excuse me."

Joshua indicated that he wanted to sit on the front porch and await Father Al's return. Patrick helped him into the rocker. "Goodbye, old friend," Pat said, as he put his arm around Joshua's shoulder. "I know you'll be in good hands here."

"Thanks, Patrick. I'll never be able to thank you enough—and you, too, Lou Ann—for everything you've done for me."

"If I can be of any help, Joshua, I'll be just down the road at Mother's house."

"Good luck, Josh," Pat said. "I hope you make it home alright—I mean, when you're well enough to travel."

Lou Ann and Patrick went into the church where Father Al was beginning to celebrate Mass. Patrick prayed the Good Lord would keep them all safe and for a speedy end to the war. After Mass, he and Lou Ann returned to her mother's house by the same route.

Pat was becoming concerned about getting back to his outfit and knew that there wasn't much more to discuss with Lou Ann. It had all been said. They stood in the shade of a large oak tree outside the barn, as a gentle warm breeze played with a few strands of Lou Ann's hair. Pat reached over and gently pushed them away from her cheek. "Well, Lou Ann, I guess this is it. I mean, we probably won't see each other again."

"Patrick, I want you to know that—well—you will always be in my prayers and I will never forget you."

"Goodbye, Lou Ann."

"May God go with you, Patrick."

He walked down the road and out of her life, never turning back to see the tears trickling down her cheeks. Two young souls drawn into the Great Conflict, whose hearts had collided like ships in the fog of war, were now to part and drift to unknown shores.

CHAPTER 20

▼

THE REBEL AND THE PRIEST

And so, Patrick, Lou Ann, and Joshua went their separate ways. Pat caught up with the Army of the Potomac, now pursuing Robert E. Lee and the Confederate Army around Williamsport, Maryland. Lou Ann petitioned the Daughters of Charity in hopes to be accepted in that Order, while still attending the wounded in and around Gettysburg. And Joshua remained at Saint Joseph's Church in Emmitsburg, Maryland, helping Father Al as much as he could while his wounds healed.

Joshua had a great deal of time to think. At first, he was discouraged, having difficulty understanding how he had gone from a brave, courageous cavalry officer leading his men into battle to a lowly, crippled custodian living in a church cellar. But as time went by, he slowly healed from his wounds and depressed state. Father Al encouraged him whenever he could, trying to keep him busy with chores around the church and grounds. The good priest also had the local blacksmith fashion a metal hook and attach it to Joshua's arm, enabling him to better perform basic functions. The doctor had determined that a muscle had been torn in his leg and that it had not healed properly. He was, however, able to walk with a limp. After witnessing many boys losing their legs in the war, he was grateful that he still had both of his, even if one was defective. He painstakingly forced himself to learn to write with his left hand. When he became fairly proficient at it, he wrote to Jenny and waited for her reply. He hadn't mentioned anything about his injuries; he wanted to wait until he returned home.

Many weeks passed when, one cool morning as he was cutting the grass around the tombstones which surrounded the church, Father Al called out to him from the front porch of the rectory. "Joshua, there's a letter here for you." Josh quickly limped over to the porch. "Hope it's good news, Son."

"Thanks, Father." Joshua sat down on the front steps and immediately ripped it open with his hook. As he began to read, he felt the warmth of Jenny's love enveloping his heart. He had forgotten that feeling that was so contrary to the cold calculations of killing and death, which he had faced on a daily basis. He hadn't heard from her in a very long time, as it was common for mail to take months to arrive due to the rapid movement of the armies. For all he knew, her past letters could be in the hands of the Yankees. He read her letter over a few times, as if each reading would somehow bring her closer to him. As he pondered the words she had written—how much she loved and missed him and prayed for his safe return—he wondered how he would support her if she accepted his hand in marriage. A strange thought occurred to him as he envisioned their wedding day—it troubled him somewhat. They would both be limping down the aisle. This certainly was not the way he ever would have pictured it to be. But he *was* in love—and that was enough to overcome *anything.*

As the weeks passed, he tried to keep a low profile. Neither he nor Father Al had divulged his secret to anyone. On a few occasions, when curious parishioners would ask where he was from, he would simply say, being careful not to lie, "I'm from New York City... got injured at Gettysburg... going back home as soon as I can travel." If asked about his accent, he would say, "Lived in Virginia a few years—guess I picked it up there."

Things returned to normal in the little town of Emmitsburg, as the Union and Confederate armies moved south, skirmishing with each other. The wounded in and around Gettysburg were gradually shipped to hospitals in Washington, and the many dead were disinterred to a new national cemetery located on Cemetery Ridge, where much of the fighting had taken place.

Joshua tried to avoid conversations about politics and the war, as he still had sympathies for the South. His home, his family, his friends—*were* the South. He guarded his feelings well and secretly held out hope for the cause. After all, many of his friends had paid the ultimate price—like Caleb Snow—killed at Bull Run. Yet, deep in his heart, he knew what the outcome would be.

By summer's end, he had come to feel at home in his small corner of the church cellar. After traveling and fighting in the Virginia countryside for two years, it was peaceful and calm. Some days, after working in the hot sun, it

was a welcome relief to go down into his cool corner, recline on his cot, and dream about Jenny and home.

Before long, the cool days of autumn brought a new chore to his work. Two large stoves in the cellar had to be fired up every morning before Mass. He would stoke the fires and feed them with wood provided by a nearby farmer. There was a vent near his cot on one of the pipes which led up into the church near the altar. When he would open the vent, he could hear the priest's voice clearly resonating from upstairs. He never paid much attention to Father Al's words until one morning, lying down on his cot to rest after his chores, he heard the priest giving a reading from the Old Testament. *"The Lord replied to Joshua: 'Stand up. Why are you lying prostrate?'"* It startled him. He had only heard the last part and thought he was being summoned by the priest. He stood up and walked over to the vent pipe, listening attentively to every word. From that day forward, he listened to the good priest's readings and sermons. He even learned the words to many songs and would sing along from his little corner of the cellar.

It took a little time before he learned to cope with his hook, but did well in his work at the parish, cleaning and maintaining the church and the grounds. The priest was pleased with his work and found him to be a real asset.

"Joshua," Father Al said as he handed him an envelope, "you've been doing a fine job here—please accept this. I want to pay you for your labor."

"Oh, Father, I couldn't take anything. You've done enough just putting me up here."

"No—I insist. You've been a great help to me. Besides, you should have a little spending money."

"Well, if you insist, Father, but you've provided me with all I really need."

By November, Father Al was wearing a black sweater daily. Joshua had noticed a hole in the right elbow the size of a quarter. He had learned from the housekeeper that Vincentian priests took a vow of poverty. He felt uncomfortable with the fact that Father didn't have a better sweater to keep him warm, and decided to save some of his earnings for the priest to get a new one. By the middle of the month, he approached him with an envelope in *his* hand. "Please accept this, Father. I would like you to use it for a new sweater." The priest was gracious in his acceptance of Joshua's gift.

As Joshua was replacing some of the burned out candles on the altar one morning after Mass, Father Al returned from the sanctuary. "Good morning, Joshua."

"Good morning, Father. I enjoyed your sermon last Sunday." He placed two new candles on either side of the altar.

"Thank you, but I didn't realize you had attended Mass."

"Well, Father," Josh replied, looking down at the floor, "I didn't."

"Then how did you hear my sermon?" asked the priest.

"I have a confession to make, Father. You see, I can hear your voice down in the cellar during Mass."

"Oh, I see," said the priest with a look of surprise on his face.

Over the past few months, Joshua had learned a great deal about the Catholic faith, just from conversations with the good priest and listening to his sermons from his quarters.

Father Al looked directly at Joshua who was beginning to step down from the altar with his box now containing the used candles. "Would you be interested in joining our church, Joshua?"

Joshua hesitated. "Well, Father, I'm—I'm not sure. To tell you the truth, I've been thinking about it, but I don't think I'm ready just yet."

"Well, Son, if you have any questions about the faith, I'm here for you."

"Thank you, Father. I'm grateful for your concern."

As he began to leave, Father Al remarked, "Oh, by the way, Joshua, did you know that the President is coming to Gettysburg next week?"

"You mean—Lincoln?"

"Yes, President Lincoln. He's coming to give a speech at the battlefield. Would you be interested in accompanying me there?"

Joshua had mixed feelings. He hadn't revisited that field of death since the battle. "I'm not sure, Father—I've got too many bad memories of that place."

"Well, let me know if you decide to come. It should be a momentous occasion."

The days had grown colder; Josh could be seen working in and around the church in a blue winter overcoat, left behind by a Union soldier that hot day in July just before the great battle. One evening, while tending to the fire, he opened the furnace door and peered inside at the glowing embers. Suddenly, a spark blew out and burned him on the side of his neck. He quickly brushed it off, letting out a few profanities. It was a small burn but gave him some pain, nevertheless. It was miniscule compared to the pain he had already endured from his wounds. As he stepped back, still looking at the hot coals, his thoughts turned back to the heat of battle. The shrieks and cries of wounded men falling and dying all around him revisited his senses. In the few short months since the battle, he had not only begun to heal from his wounds but, slowly, he was putting the war behind him. Now, in an instant, it all became real again. It was like opening a raw wound. He didn't like it, and he began to deal with feelings he thought he had overcome. The peace he had been experiencing became replaced by bitterness once again—bitterness he had kept buried deep within him, never revealing it even to his good priest friend.

The night before Abraham Lincoln was due to speak at Gettysburg, Father Al once again invited Joshua to go with him to hear the President. This time, Joshua agreed to go.

He awoke early and tended to his first chore, maintaining the furnace fire for the small group of parishioners attending morning Mass. After the service, he donned the long blue overcoat, hesitating momentarily before leaving the cellar. He stood for a few moments, as if he were unsure of something. Finally, he walked over to the back wall of the cellar, reached up on top of one of the stovepipes, and grasped a revolver that he had hidden there. He had successfully concealed it in his boot when captured and had intended to keep it for self-defense or hunting. He carefully placed it in the deep side pocket of his overcoat and walked over to the priest house where Father Al had prepared a light breakfast of coffee and cornbread.

"Come in, Joshua. Looks like you could use a hot drink on such a cold morning."

"The coffee smells good, Father."

"Come in and sit down." The priest gestured him to sit at the large, rectangular dining room table. "Help yourself," he said, as he placed the plate full of cornbread in front of Joshua.

"Thank you, Father," Josh replied as he removed his overcoat and hung it over the back of another chair. He helped himself to the food and coffee, as the two of them enjoyed the breakfast, neither one speaking for a short time.

Finally, Father Al inquired, "Are you feeling all right, Joshua?" as he looked across the highly polished table at his guest.

"Oh, yes, Father. Why do you ask?"

"You look deep in thought—is something bothering you?"

"No—guess I'm not fully awake yet."

"Well, Son, guess we better get going. Maybe we can get a good spot to hear the President."

"Excuse me, Father... I have to use the backhouse before we go. I'll only be a minute."

"Take your time, Son."

When Josh returned, he put his coat back on and climbed into the buggy, as Father Al took the reins and started up the dirt road to Gettysburg. Josh pulled up his collar, shielding himself from the cold November wind, and placed his one hand in his coat pocket. The cold, metal hook on his other arm didn't need warming. He leaned back in the buggy, as they made their way toward the battlefield and the President. Father Al seemed excited and did most of the talking. Joshua, however, remained silent for the short journey. As they came into view of the battlefield, they could see a large crowd gathering on Cemetery Ridge. The priest drove the buggy off the road and halted beneath a large shady tree. As they climbed down from their seat, they were jolted by thunderous cannon a short distance away, fired to salute the arrival of the President. The horse, startled, reared up, but Father Al soon had him under control. Joshua froze in his tracks for a brief moment, as though he were going to live the battle over again. The Marine Band blared out Marshall music; and in the midst of mounted cavalry and marching infantry with glittering bayonets, rode Abraham Lincoln, his head bent forward as if in deep concentration. They stopped at a platform draped with red, white, and blue. The President was assisted down from his horse and directed by soldiers to a rocking chair that had been placed in the center of the platform. After walking across the rough fields and around open graves, Father Al and Joshua moved through the crowds toward the speaker's platform. With the priest leading the way, they were able to find a spot about twenty feet from the front.

Joshua became fidgety as he stood in the crowd, trying to stay warm and shifting from one foot to the other. He listened to the noted orator, Edward Everett, speak for what seemed to be a very long time to him, his own thoughts blotting out much of the speech. Where's the tribute to *my* fallen comrades. They fell here, too—where's *their* tribute? Was it all for nothing? No matter... for me it's over—or *is* it?

In his one pocket was his cold, metal hook attached to his flesh and blood arm. In the other pocket, his good, unscathed arm still had a strong hand attached to it—and *that* strong hand clutched a cold, steel revolver that could possibly change the outcome of the war dramatically—and he was very aware of it. His mind raced. He knew what the outcome would be for him, but was it worth the sacrifice? Could he save many lives? And what about Jenny? And his parents?

The loud applause for the great orator jerked him back to a sober state. He had felt like a drunken man whose thoughts had overpowered and confused him, leaving him shaking more than any battle he had ever experienced.

The Marine Band once again began to play. Then the President, holding some papers in his hand, slowly rose to his feet. He spoke in a high, clear voice: *"Four score and seven years ago..."*

Joshua began to sweat—a cold sweat in the brisk autumn air. The pressure mounted as he stood alone, surrounded by Yankees. He grasped the revolver tightly and placed his finger on the trigger. He felt caught up in a vortex, as though he were in the eye of a hurricane. An uncontrollable force seemed to be moving the revolver from his deep pocket. Lincoln's speech seemed distant and garbled at first; and then he clearly heard the words uttered by the bearded President—*"that this nation, under God, shall have a new birth of freedom."*

Like a sudden burst of sunlight breaking through the clouds of a stormy day, Joshua felt a warm presence enveloping him and remembered Father Al's words: "The good Lord taught us to love our enemies."

Josh released his tight grip from the revolver and let it sink back into the bottom of his pocket. What did I...? I'm not an assassin—a soldier, yes—but not an assassin. A great weight had been lifted from him. He felt as if he had just awakened from a horrible nightmare.

The President had finished his speech and stood there for a moment overlooking the wounded soldiers, the freshly dug nearby graves, and the vast battlefield, as an immense swell of applause arose from the crowd. The President took his seat once again, as the Gettysburg Ladies' Chorus began its much practiced memorial dirge followed by prayers and benediction.

"Good speech and to the point, wouldn't you say?" remarked Father Al.

"Oh—oh yes, Father," Josh answered.

"Well, Joshua—it's hard to believe that so many died here. When will we ever learn? And what a terrible cost!"

The crowd began to disperse as the ceremonies ended. Riding back to Emmitsburg, the air grew colder as the horse trotted south, away from the killing fields. Father Al turned toward Joshua and asked, "And what did you think of Mr. Lincoln's speech?"

"Well, Father, to tell you the truth, I—I'm a little bitter. I mean—all I could think of was waste—a terrible waste of lives."

"It does seem that way, doesn't it?" As an afterthought, the priest added, "And they were so young—most of them—like yourself."

"Father," said Joshua, "I have to confess something to you."

"Well, Joshua, you know that the sacrament of Confession can only be received after Baptism, and you're not baptized."

"I know that, Father, but..."

"But what, Son?"

"Well, Father, I feel that I *have* to tell *someone*..." He stammered. "Father—I—I almost..." He searched for the right words. "You see—I have a gun—and..."

Before he could finish his sentence, the priest interrupted, reaching into his own pocket, then opening his hand to reveal six bullets. "I know what you want to say, Joshua, but it's all right—I know." He smiled at him, then added, "I saved these for you. Thought you might need them for smaller game on your journey back home."

Joshua was dumbfounded. He didn't know what to say. Finally, after recovering from the priest's revelation, he spoke. "How did you know?" He looked at Father Al curiously, as he removed the gun from his pocket and examined the empty cylinder.

"Well, Joshua, I have a confession to make, too. You see, I discovered the gun when I moved your coat to another chair while you were in the backhouse. Didn't want to spill anything on it." Joshua looked down, feeling ashamed. The priest handed the bullets back to him. "You did the right thing, Son. I hoped you would—I just couldn't chance it though."

"I would have done the same thing in your position, Father."

They continued their ride back to Emmitsburg in complete silence. The subject was never mentioned again.

That pivotal year of the Civil War, 1863, President Lincoln proclaimed the last Thursday in November as *"A Day of Thanksgiving and Praise to Our Beneficent Father."*

Joshua had stayed in Emmitsburg longer than he had planned; he would leave right after this new official holiday. Although he wanted to go home much earlier, he prolonged his departure because of his injuries. He finally realized that he had healed as much as possible and had learned to use his hook to a high degree of proficiency. He knew, however, that he would have to live with his game leg for the rest of his days. It was time. Jenny would have to accept him as he was. He developed enough courage to go home, crippled and defeated as he was; but he was leaving with new hope for the future—for now there was something wonderful in his life—his newfound faith. Father Al had baptized him into the Catholic faith a few days after their trip to Gettysburg. He wanted to get home for Christmas, as it now had new meaning for him. After all, it *was* Jesus Christ's birthday, and he wanted to celebrate it with his loved ones.

Thanksgiving had mixed blessings for the farmers and occupants of the little burgs called Emmits and Gettys. They were very grateful that the horrendous battle had not obliterated their towns; however, their crops had been decimated. What the troops hadn't eaten, the hordes had trampled underfoot. The harvest had been very meager.

Many fields, normally producing an abundance of food, had become the final resting place of young Americans from both North and South. For the fallen brave, there would be no future. But Joshua *would* have a future. He began to pack his few belongings and prepared to leave. He took the holiday afternoon to walk through the town that had harbored him for four months. He passed by the Motherhouse of the good Daughters of Charity who had a school there for young women, some of whom were boarded by wealthy Southern families and gave the poor Sisters much difficulty when the Union forces occupied the town, shouting unpleasant remarks from their windows and yelling for the Southern cause. He had grown to love the little town, noted for Mother Seton's first parochial school in the United States. He visited her grave, and later spent time at the Grotto of Our Lady of Lourdes way up on the hillside, where he sat by the spring of fresh water contemplating all that had happened to him. He had always found great peace there, and he prayed his own prayer of thanksgiving to God for his life.

The leaves were falling and the North wind blew them around his feet as he approached the rectory early in the evening. Father Al ushered him into the rectory that General George Meade had temporarily used for his headquarters before the great battle. "Happy Thanksgiving," said the priest with a smile.

"And the same to you, Father."

"Come in, my boy. We have a fine dinner prepared."

After they were seated, Joshua looked across the table at his priest friend, a solemn countenance on his face. "I've decided to leave for home tomorrow, Father."

Father Al didn't seem very surprised, as Joshua had hinted to him recently that he wouldn't be staying much longer. "Well, Joshua, I'll be sorry to see you go. You've been a great help to me and you'll be sorely missed." Blessing himself, he prayed, "Now let us give thanks to God for the food we eat and the blessings He has bestowed on us and ask Him to continue to bless us and all our loved ones. And for peace to come to our beleaguered land. In Jesus' name, we ask. Amen."

Joshua prayed along silently, head bowed and hands folded in prayer. After the priest finished his blessing, Josh spoke up. "And, Father, thank you for everything you have done for me."

"You have repaid me more than you know, Joshua. Your Baptism into God's holy Church brings me great joy. Now, let's eat."

They ate the feast that Father Al's cook had prepared—turkey, dressing, and all the trimmings one could ask for. Joshua hadn't had a meal like that since prior to the war. He didn't talk—just savored every bite until he couldn't eat anymore.

"Care for some pumpkin pie?" asked Father Al, not waiting for his reply before sliding a generous piece over to him.

"Oh, Father, I don't know if I could..."

"I'm sure you can find room. I never pass up a piece of fresh baked pumpkin pie— you know, my cook only makes it once a year."

"Well, it sure looks good," as he picked up his fork and began to eat. "Guess I can manage it."

Their relationship had been a friendly one, but Joshua had never really discussed his personal life with Father Al. Now that he was leaving, almost without thinking, he opened up and told the priest about everything—his home and childhood, his work—and Jenny. They finished their meal with hot coffee and retired to the parlor where they sat in soft chairs and had a glass of wine. Father proposed a toast to Joshua's safe journey home. They talked very little about the war, as Father knew it was still a sore subject to him and wanted his last night there to be a pleasant experience.

The hour grew late. Joshua got up from his chair, stretched his arms, and glanced out the window. "It's dark out already. Where did the time go? Well, Father, I'd best be getting to bed now; I'll be traveling all day tomorrow."

"Oh, Joshua, I have something I would like you to have. Come with me to the barn."

As they entered the barn, the priest lit the lantern and walked over to a stall that housed his one and only horse. He held up the lantern so Josh could see better. "Now, Son, I would like you to have old Shamrock here—let's say, as a token of my appreciation for all the work you've done around here."

"Oh, Father, I couldn't. I mean—that's your only..."

"Now, Joshua, I insist. Don't you worry about it. I have some generous parishioners who I'm sure will donate other transportation for me. Besides, you can't *walk* all the way home."

"I can't thank you enough, Father. I'll be leaving at sunup, so I guess I won't see you in the morning."

The priest gave him a firm handshake and blessed him. "Oh, by the way, Joshua, I just wanted to let you know that the money you gave me a short time ago has been put to good use. You see, I was able to buy enough food to provide two poor families with Thanksgiving meals."

Josh had noticed during dinner that Father was still wearing his old sweater; now he knew why. The priest and the Rebel walked out of the barn. The full moon illuminated the church and all of the surrounding gravestones, and Joshua inhaled the crisp autumn air, as he shook hands with Father one final time and retired to his "home" in the cellar.

He was up early the following morning, picked up his worn haversack, put on his blue overcoat, mounted Shamrock, and headed for home. He was grateful for Shamrock, but was still saddened by the loss of his trusty steed, Blackjack, who had carried him through many battles. The wreckage of war was behind him. Many of his comrades would not be returning home, he thought. His future was uncertain; the South, as he knew it, would never be the same again. After Gettysburg, he felt that their cause was doomed. But there was one thing that he was certain of that had not changed—Jenny's love. And that love was like a magnet drawing him back to Perch, Virginia, at the mouth of the Peddler River.

Christmas—must get home for Christmas.

CHAPTER 21

▼

FIRE AND RAIN

By November, Patrick had become fully entrenched in soldiering once again. His involvement with Lou Ann and his old friend, Joshua, had ended. About the same time Lincoln was making his address at Gettysburg, General Meade and the Army of the Potomac were skirmishing with General Lee and his Army of Northern Virginia near Germanna Ford. Since returning to his unit in July, Patrick hadn't seen much action. Guard duty, drilling, and boredom were taking its toll on him; he was anxious to get that long war over and done with. The "cat and mouse" game between the armies continued, accomplishing nothing for either side.

The winter blew its cold winds over the encamped armies, with the temperature dropping below zero that January. Patrick, like all of his comrades, would have to wait until spring before seeing any action. Time moved slowly, and he would just have to wait it out. The armies were like two gigantic, killer beehives lying dormant until the spring thaw, when each would release its swarm and attack the other with thousands of stingers to annihilate the enemy.

Each day, Patrick sloshed through the mud, drilling in formation with his regiment. He ate, slept, and whenever possible, attempted to keep warm by the fire pit in front of his tent. On some days, when enough snow had covered the ground, some of the men occupied themselves with snowball wars, as in past winters. Patrick, by this time, had lost interest in these mock wars, finding no recreational value in them. About the same time, however, a new sport came on the scene—at least, it was new for Patrick— baseball.

It was reported to have been invented by Abner Doubleday, a Union general; and Patrick loved it. To him it was a competition where one team could win the day without killing its opponent. On warmer days, after drilling and marching, Pat would often organize a team from his own company and play against a team from another company. Regardless of his exhaustion from drilling, he became rejuvenated on the baseball field. He was very good at batting, even though his old shoulder wound sometimes gave him pain, and eventually earned the nickname "Slugger". The new sport helped him through the long, dreary winter.

As the months went by, his thoughts of Lou Ann grew less and less— or was he purposely trying to keep her out of his mind? He found himself beginning to look for letters from Beth and news from home. It had to be several months since he had heard anything. Had *she* found another? But then, of course, he hadn't written her either. He thought maybe he should write more to her—maybe make up for what he considered to be lost time during his preoccupation with Lou Ann. Generally, he slept well at night, but the thought of future battles sometimes kept him awake and wondering if he would survive the war. There was little danger from the Rebel army at this time; however, the old enemy within—disease—took its toll once again and many young boys would succumb before ever firing a shot. His thoughts often turned to home during cold, winter nights, when sometimes it seemed like his small, half-cabin half-tent would be blown away by the strong, northerly winds. On occasion, the winds would blow through the cracks of the small structure and extinguish his candle, which was mounted on the rifle end of his bayonet, implanted firmly into the frozen earthen floor. He would relight it and continue writing letters home—including to Beth. It had been two years since he had left for war. At times, she and home had seemed like a dream that he saw through a misty fog that had grown more hazy during the time since he left. He became discouraged at times but concealed his feelings when writing to them. "Oh God!" he would pray, "take this terrible loneliness from me. Help me to face whatever comes and give me the strength to do my duty."

The bleak winter was drawing to a close, and the camp became alive with rumors of the next offensive. The biggest news buzzing among the men was about a new commander named Ulysses S. Grant. Word had it that he had won many battles in the West along the Mississippi River. The Army of the Potomac, however, had lost many battles to the Confederates due to the poor leadership of its generals. Hope grew amongst the men that maybe they would finally have a leader who could bring them more victories.

The sun shone brightly when the army broke camp that spring day. The line of supply wagons covered with white canvas stretched for miles and the columns of blue-clad Union soldiers seemed endless. And somewhere in that great sea of blue marched the 69th New York and Patrick O'Hanrahan, now a seasoned veteran at the ripe old age of twenty. They were moving south with many new replacements to fill the ranks, and one of the new soldiers in the Army of the Potomac *was* the recently appointed Lieutenant General U.S. Grant. As they moved in formation and crossed the Rapidan River, hopes were high throughout their ranks. The snake-like column moved down the road that led through the woods. Suddenly, the sun seemed to be swallowed up as they entered the dark, forested area. At first, the shade was welcomed by Patrick, as the sun had become blistering hot. And then, as they marched deeper into the Wilderness, an uneasy quiet pervaded the ranks, as all eyes began to search the woods surrounding them. All that could be heard was the tramping of thousands of feet and the ever-present clanging of canteens banging against shouldered rifles. Patrick felt jittery; he wasn't accustomed to the confinement of thick woods on either side of him. Most of the previous battles had been out in the open where he could see the enemy. Pat was no general, but he didn't think that this was a good spot to engage the enemy in battle. Could we be walking into an ambush? Oh, well, the generals must know what they're doing. Besides, the Rebs are probably miles away.

On his return to his regiment after his two stays in Washington, he had found the ranks depleted. He had felt as though he was in a new army and considered himself lucky to find a few familiar faces still present for duty. It wasn't the same army he had started with in '61. Most of his old buddies were either dead or injured or had long-since gone home after finishing their three-year enlistments. Patrick, however, had reenlisted, unlike some who felt they had done enough. Some of the new men were substitutes—mercenaries who went to war in place of others who had paid them three hundred dollars or more. Many, however, deserted when the going got rough. But the cause hadn't changed, and Patrick was determined to see this war through to its conclusion.

At the head of his column, the color bearers proudly carried Old Glory and the new regimental, emerald green flag, boasting its golden harp. The old one was so tattered and full of bullet holes, it had to be replaced after the horrendous defeat at Fredericksburg. And behind these flags marched O'Reilly, O'Connor, Murphy and O'Grady, O'Flaherty and Finnegan, O'Shaunessey and Rafferty—and Patrick O'Hanrahan.

By this time, the third year of warfare, Pat had begun to withdraw from close friendships. Although he lived in the close quarters and marched and fought beside the others, he had a fear that he couldn't overcome. Ever since losing his friend, the Big Swede, he continued to fear the loss of others with whom he might develop a close friendship.

Through the shady stillness of the surrounding woods marched this Grand Army of the Republic. When a lone voice, an Irish tenor, barely audible, sang out, *"Mine eyes have seen the glory of the coming of the Lord,"* a rippled effect occurred throughout the ranks when, from this one small voice, arose a hundred more, singing the next line strongly. And in a matter of seconds, Regiment, Division, Brigade, Corps, and the host of the entire Army of the Potomac was singing the "Battle Hymn of the Republic". And they marched deeper into enemy territory with lifted spirits.

The singing was short-lived and suddenly replaced by the shrill bugle calls to march at double-quick resounding down the line. The "ball" was opening once again.

Patrick's pulse began to race, and he quickened his step along with the others. Soon the sounds of battle could be heard up ahead. The unmistakable crackling sounds of muskets and smell of war were upon him once again. Before long, he could see the officers on horseback racing down the line, swinging their swords as pointers, directing regiment upon regiment into the woods on the right. Orders were being shouted to company commanders whose troops were quickly swallowed up into the dense forested area. "Follow me!" Pat heard his captain shouting; and into the woods he ran, echoing the same command to *his* squad.

"Stay close! Keep the men on both sides of you in view! Keep it tight—together!" It became evident to Pat before long that the color-bearers were unable to carry their flags through the low-lying branches, which hindered their progress. They were furled and passed to the rear, the bearers taking up muskets in their place. Patrick could hear the battle coming closer, as thousands of rifles angrily barked out up ahead; but he couldn't see more than twenty feet in front of him. He felt like a blind man trying to feel his way forward. This was all new to him. He became fearful of shooting his own men but had no time to dwell on these fears, as bullets began to whistle overhead, clipping the leafy tree limbs and smacking into nearby trunks. Then, suddenly, the trees ahead were interspersed with gray uniforms, and he could finally see the muzzle flashes and accompanying white smoke spewing from their hot barrels.

"Fire at will!" he heard his captain shouting. And all up and down the line, a crescendo of musketry fire was returned. The gruesome task was once again in progress. For awhile, neither Reb nor Yank gave up any ground. The opposing lines just picked their targets and banged away at each other. Then the bugler blasted out the call to attack. Patrick and his men moved out along with the rest of the regiment, and the Rebels turned and ran. He had experienced this exhilarating feeling before. It was a good feeling—firing and getting the enemy on the run. But he became cautious; his own ranks were becoming disorganized. Some men had advanced too far ahead and were out of sight. All cohesion seemed to be dissipating. Must bring these men together. He began to depend more on his hearing than on his sight. He followed the sounds of battle. A few Rebel prisoners were being taken to the rear, as Patrick's squad caught up with the others at the edge of a small clearing. He was grateful that they stopped where they did, so that he could regroup the men. He wasn't too happy, though, on learning that the enemy had taken up a position on the other side of the clearing.

"Hey, Sarge!" hollered Private O'Malley. "Didja get lost?"

Pat's earlier fears now turned to anger. He walked over to the private, ignoring some incoming fire, and stared down at the young soldier, who was in a crouched position. He then placed his foot on the man's shoulder and forcefully pushed him to the ground. The young private sat dumbfounded; he had never seen that side of his sergeant before. A bullet suddenly grazed Patrick's arm, tearing his sleeve; and he, too, took up a crouching position. Looking around, he counted his squad members. "Looks like we didn't lose anybody yet." Then he shouted, "Damn it all! You men stay together in formation—you got too far out in front…" His words were cut off as a hail of bullets flew in from the Rebs across the clearing. Two of his squad members went down with mortal wounds. The others fired back. The enemy must have been reinforced with more men, he thought, as their firepower seemed greatly increased to him. He knew it was a prelude to a counterattack. It wasn't long before the gray masses came charging across the clearing, yelling their war whoops like Indians on the warpath. This wasn't the first time Patrick had heard this ungodly sound, and he knew that the shrill screeching of these thousands of Rebels could instill great fear in the hearts of many of his men. The Yanks fired one volley and took down a few Rebels; but the enemy's force was overwhelming, and the blue line broke and ran for their lives. Pat tried to control his squad in an orderly retreat, but it was too late. The woods became filled with individual Yankees scrambling through the trees and underbrush, hoping they were retreating back to their own lines.

The woods were so thick that some lost their direction and fell into enemy hands; however, most of them made it back to safety, where some officers had set up a reinforced, defensive position, ordering their men to begin putting up breastworks. As others arrived, they, too, joined in that work, Patrick and his squad included. Order was restored, and the soldiers lined up by regiments behind the newly formed barricade, rifles loaded and ready for the Rebs. A few came into view there and were quickly cut down. Their ranks had also become fragmented, men becoming disoriented and going in different directions.

Private O'Malley came over to Patrick and apologized for making the wise remark earlier. "Sorry, Sarge... didn't mean nothin' by it."

"Forget it," Pat said. "Not used to my men getting out of my sight. Can't see a damn thing in these woods."

Time moved slowly, as Patrick lay in a prone position, his rifle pointed outward over the top of the hastily built breastworks, waiting for another Rebel attack. He was hot and periodically removed his hat to wipe the sweat from his brow. There wasn't a breeze, and the air hung heavy with acrid gunsmoke. The men had refilled their canteens from a nearby stream, and Patrick obtained more ammunition for them. All they could do was wait. They were mostly silent, except for a few soldiers up and down the line making small talk to ease their anxieties. There wouldn't be much time to pick a target when the Rebs would come into view, as their field of vision was much smaller than on the open plains. But they were ready. A few Yankees who had had difficulty finding their way back came running to the lines; some limping from leg wounds hobbled up to the breastworks and tumbled over them to safety. And right behind them came the enemy. The colonel shouted, "Let 'em have it boys!" The long line of Yanks opened up with a thunderous volley of lead spewing out of a thousand musket barrels. Not a man was left standing, and the ground was covered with gray-clad bodies. What had been the predator a short while before had now become the prey. Soon more gray uniforms came charging, and again they fell like autumn leaves. A few retreated, but soon there came more charging Rebels. And again, not one made it to the breastworks. Patrick was firing and reloading as fast as he could, frantically attempting to be ready for the next charge. And then, things were quiet. Ten, fifteen, thirty minutes went by—no more attacks. What are they up to, Patrick wondered. And as he lay there sweating, mouth all blackened from biting open the paper powder cartridges with his teeth, and viewing the ground in front of him strewn with dead Rebels, he felt good at first that the enemy had been repulsed. Once again his thoughts went back to Fredericksburg, where he had lost so many friends and thousands of Yankees had been annihilated on that plain in front of Marye's Heights. But then, despite having developed a soldier's heart, his Christian heart became saddened as he viewed the still bodies in front of him and, worst of all, those barely clinging to life writhing in pain. Cries were heard for water and some of them were calling out for their loved ones.

Orders filtered down from Command Headquarters to hold their position, while another regiment of Union soldiers on their left was ordered to advance. The 69th reinforced their breastworks and waited. Pat watched as the other regiment moved out toward the enemy's position and disappeared into the woods. Before long, he could hear his comrades engaging the enemy up ahead. He sniffed the air and smelled something new. It wasn't the familiar smell of gunsmoke. At first, he thought someone had started a fire for cooking. Impossible! Who would be cooking? It was definitely wood burning. After all the campfires he had been around, he couldn't mistake *that* smell. The wind soon picked up, blowing in his direction and carrying smoke through the trees, over the breastworks, and into his position. The sounds of battle grew louder. Patrick knew it didn't sound good; he believed his comrades were being driven back once again. It wasn't long before a few Union soldiers came running back to the safety of the breastworks. What happened next horrified him. It was Gettysburg all over again—at least, the climax of the third day's battle there. Maybe not on such a grand scale—but just as fierce! Hand-to-hand combat. Blue and gray soldiers emerged from the woods locked in mortal combat. Some Rebels were shot on the run, and others grappled with the men in blue. Screams were heard, as cold, steel bayonets slid through the soft flesh of both armies. The 69th opened fire and killed many Rebs, but more came rushing from the woods along with still heavier clouds of black smoke. It was becoming so thick, it was difficult to distinguish friend from foe. The wind fanned small fires that had begun to break out. Soon large flames licked the tall, dry, pine trees and swept to the top in seconds. Some men were overcome by smoke and fell in their tracks. Others continued their death struggle with bayonets, clubbed muskets, and fists, paying no attention to the oncoming flames. Suddenly, the breastworks were ignited, and a wall of fire began to consume the dry logs. Pat and the others pulled back and fired through the flames at any distinguishable enemy. Patrick shuddered. Two Rebels leaped over the burning barricade, their clothes catching fire, yelling their eerie war cry—like demons emerging from the fires of hell. Pat steeled himself, took careful aim, and shot one of them. The other came at him; and he prepared to use his bayonet, when the man fell at his feet consumed in flames screaming in agony, then suddenly became silent. Pat was repulsed by the smell of burning flesh, as this was a smell he had never experienced before. Suddenly, the gunfire ceased. Some Rebels scattered in different directions, some were captured, and some, along with the Union dead, lie on the scorched earth in front of the breastworks.

The wind began to blow in a different direction and took the fire along with it. There was a flurry of activity amongst the Union soldiers, who immediately began to put out the fires on the breastworks and surrounding underbrush. They dug up dirt with their bayonets and threw it on the fires, and used whatever pots and pans they had carried in their haversacks to carry water from a nearby stream.

When they finally succeeded in extinguishing the fires, they responded to screams coming from the woods in front of them. Several badly burned men, both Reb and Yank, had somehow survived the inferno. Some wished they hadn't. The few that Patrick helped carry back to his lines died before arriving there. The screams diminished as the sun began to set, and finally the woods became silent. Pat walked back to a spot that the fire hadn't reached behind the breastworks, found a patch of tall green grass, and sprawled down into it—hot, dry, and exhausted. Many of the men did the same. Most plunged into the stream and refilled their canteens. "You boys get back on that line," the captain shouted. "Johnny Reb may come at us again."

Returning to the smoldering breastworks, Patrick looked at the burned bodies of both armies. Some had their rifles still clutched in their hands, permanently melding flesh and weapon into one for all eternity. He leaned up against a nearby tree and vomited. The men buried the dead in hastily dug graves, gave water from their canteens to the survivors, rebuilt their breastworks, and waited. Coughing was heard all up and down the line, as some smoke lingered in that forest of death. Exhausted and choking, Pat laid down looking into the darkening woods toward the enemy's position, rifle propped up in front of him, and soon fell asleep. Skirmishers had been sent out into the woods; and Patrick knew that if the enemy came near, ensuing gunfire would awaken him. Many others also dozed off from sheer exhaustion.

Daylight grew dim, and the remaining remnants of tall, blackened trees created weird, finger-like images against the darkening sky, as if they were desperately reaching toward Heaven, pleading to the Almighty for mercy. Patrick awoke in the dead of night to the sound of distant sporadic gunfire. He rubbed his eyes and went back to sleep—the sleep of a sentinel—with one eye open. The black night air was heavy with foul odors of everything repulsive to the human senses. He thought back to Fredericksburg once again,

292   *ONE NATION UNDER GOD*

where he had almost frozen to death. And again to Gettysburg, where a soft, summer breeze blew the stench of battle away. But here—here in this hellish ash pit of death—Mother Nature would not give up the slightest breeze. Will we have to fight our way out of here? Will we be driven out? Retreat? Or will we even get out of here at all? He prayed his daily prayer again—"*Saint Michael, the Archangel, defend us in battle . . .*"

The next morning, Patrick awoke with a feeling that something was crawling on his hand. He was still holding onto his rifle that lay on top of the breastworks. As he opened his eyes, he saw that it was a beautiful butterfly adorned with brilliant yellow and subdued brown wings. Pat lay very still. The creature slowly fanned its wings, but didn't fly away. It was a welcome sign of life and color against the harsh backdrop of the blackened, burned out woods and the charred remains of many young Americans. It gave him hope. There *was* another world out there—a world of peace, of love, of serenity— a world of skating in Central Park and summer picnics—a world of young ladies and gentlemen walking hand in hand down Broadway—and so much more. Patrick wasn't a great believer in signs or omens. But this time, he did suspect that this beautiful butterfly might be a harbinger of good things to come. He considered this small incident to be a subtle sign from God that he would be spared and return home one day. He attempted to preserve the moment, lying as still as possible so that he could view this little, colorful creature longer, when a tiny drop of sweat fell from his forehead and landed on his hand right next to it. In a heartbeat, the creature flew away.

Pat looked down the line at his squad. Some of the men were just awakening and others were stretching, as they began walking around behind their breastworks. No fires for cooking—that's for sure, he thought to himself. He removed his haversack from his back and pulled out some hardtack. He was hungry and thirsty and wished he had a cup of coffee to soften up the almost impenetrable thick cracker.

About mid-morning, orders arrived to advance toward the enemy. Patrick filled his canteen, re-supplied himself and his squad with ammunition, and once again prepared for an attack on the Rebels. The long line of blue spread out, the 69th Irish Brigade taking its place amongst the great assembly of soldiers; and the command was given to move out. Uncertain where the enemy was, they began to move cautiously over the blackened, burnt forest floor. Patrick surveyed the terrain ahead of him, looking for the enemy and, at the same time, being careful not to step on the burnt bodies that never made it out of the inferno. He turned to the man on his right and suddenly noticed it was Michael, the soldier he had given the Saint Michael prayer to. "Michael! What are you doing here?"

"Hi, Sarge. Oh, I was sent over here to help fill your ranks. They said you lost a few men."

"Yes, we did. We need every man we can get."

Pat felt better about the terrain, as he could see further in all directions, the fire having consumed the underbrush and many trees. Suddenly, musket fire crackled a short distance ahead and, within seconds, the 69th was engaged with the enemy about one hundred yards directly in front of them. It wasn't long before the battle heated up, and some of Pat's men fell, mortally wounded—no foliage for cover.

There was a spontaneous new development beginning to take place—something that hadn't been present in earlier battles. The men all up and down the line of battle began to drop to their knees and dig out the dirt with their bayonets. Some young glory-seeking officers shouted, "Stand up and fight!" The men kept digging. Pat, himself, began to dig. Now this makes more sense, he thought to himself. They hollowed out small trenches and fought from a prone position. The days of glory with massive frontal assaults would be gone forever. Pat fired and reloaded along with the rest. As he lay on the charcoal-black ground, his uniform became covered with black soot. Sweat poured from his brow; he wiped his forehead with the back of his hand which, by now, was also covered with soot. Along with his blackened mouth from the cartridges, he took on a macabre appearance. Both sides laid down an unrelenting fire upon each other for the remainder of the afternoon.

By early evening, the colonel rode up behind the men shouting, "Fix bayonets!" Patrick had no sooner attached his own bayonet to his musket than the colonel was shouting his next command. "Charge!"

"Now, steady boys! Remember, stay together!" hollered Patrick to his squad.

As if one voice, thousands of Yankees, having the same grotesque appearance as Patrick, rose up shouting their huzzas and hurrahs and charged the enemy lines. They resembled the burnt bodies and appeared like an army of dead soldiers with wide-open white eyes running toward the frightened enemy, who retreated in haste. A few Confederates stood their ground and were summarily shot or bayoneted.

Patrick shot a Rebel in the arm who, although wounded, came at him with his own bayonet, lunging at Patrick who deflected the man's weapon and clubbed him under the chin with his rifle butt. The big man, now unarmed, got up, seemingly unshaken, and stared defiantly at Patrick. Pat couldn't shoot him, as he hadn't had time to reload. He could only run him through with his bayonet—but he couldn't do it. For a brief second, the Yank and the Reb, standing only a few feet apart, glared at each other. The big Rebel, with lightning speed, thrust his hands around Patrick's neck. They both fell to the ground. Before Pat realized what was happening, the big man was kneeling over him. He drew a long knife from his boot and raised his arm to plunge it into Patrick's body, shouting, "Death to all Yankees!" Then a shot rang out, and Pat heard a cracking sound. A bullet smashed through the Rebel's skull and blood spurted into Pat's face, as the man fell in a heap on top of him. Pat rolled the Reb's body aside and looked up to see Michael, smoke drifting from his rifle barrel.

"You all right?" asked Michael in a soft voice.

"Yeah—yeah, I'm all right. I owe you my life, Michael," Pat replied in a shaky voice.

Michael extended his hand and pulled Patrick up, handing him his rifle. "You had that Reb dead to rights, Patrick—can't give them no leeway!"

"Yeah, you're right. That won't happen again," Pat replied as he pulled his cap from beneath the dead Rebel, brushed it off, and placed it back on his head. "Better catch up with the rest of the men."

They ran ahead to join their regiment, who had run the enemy off. Proceeding through the woods, they entered into the thick underbrush area that had escaped the fire. The officers halted the men, as they were once again becoming disorganized. They were losing daylight and feared an ambush in the darkening woods. Once again, they began digging shallow trenches. Nightfall came and Pat could hear the far-off fighting diminishing until it finally ceased. All was quiet on both sides.

After another long restless night, Patrick awoke to the inviting aroma of coffee. Private O'Malley had started a small cooking fire and brought a cup of the very welcomed beverage to Pat. "Morning, Sarge. Thought you might like some coffee."

Patrick sat up in the shallow trench and slowly began to sip the brew. "Thanks, Private. Tastes good." He hesitated for a moment, scratched his head, and yawned, then continued, "You know, Private..." He wanted to apologize for pushing the young private to the ground but thought it would compromise his authority. Don't want to get soft, he thought to himself.

"What was that?" asked O'Malley.

"Oh, nothing. You make a mean cup of coffee." He took another sip.

"Thanks, Sarge." He looked apprehensive, as though he had something on his mind.

Patrick looked up, squinting from a bright ray of sun that had broken through the canopy of trees above. "Something bothering you, Private?"

"Well, Sarge, as a matter of fact, I did want to ask you something."

"Fire away."

"Well..." He stammered for a moment, then blurted out, "Do you think I could carry the colors next time?"

Pat hesitated. Then he stood up, took another sip of his coffee, and looked directly into the private's eyes. "You know that job has a high rate of casualties. Do you know how many good men went down carrying the colors?" Then he added with a smile, "Besides, who would make that good coffee for us if you got hit?"

The private looked somewhat downcast and mumbled something inaudible.

"You know, Private, I'll put in a good word for you with the colonel."

O'Malley looked up with a broad smile. "Gee, thanks, Sarge," as he scurried back to his cooking fire.

As the day wore on, the men ate whatever scraps of food remained in their haversacks. By late afternoon, Patrick grew restless. *Don't like this waiting—let's get on with it.* He paced back and forth behind the lines, then returned to his position and once again readied himself for an attack from the Rebels. It never came. *What are they up to?*

Shortly after dark, the order to withdraw came down from Command Headquarters. Pat assembled his men, and the entire brigade shuffled back through the black forest. The general mood amongst the men was as black as the dark night sky. As they slowly made their way through the thick underbrush, low-hanging branches scraped their faces. "Retreating again," mumbled some of the men. After marching back over the hard-won ground where so many of their comrades had perished, Pat couldn't help wondering what had been accomplished. Finally they reached the narrow road and assembled with their entire division. "Right back where we started from!" somebody yelled, causing a low murmur of grumbling to ripple through the ranks.

Just then a lone rider galloped down the road, heading south. He was somewhat slouched down in the saddle, his uniform and boots splattered with mud and the front brim of his soiled hat hanging low over his brow. "That's General Grant!" someone shouted excitedly.

"That's a general? He looks like one of us," another shouted.

And yet another voice could be heard, "He's going the wrong way. He's moving toward the enemy!"

A colonel rode up, hearing the last remark from the ranks, and shouted out, "No soldier, he's going the *right* way—we've got ourselves a mover and a shaker this time!"

Their mood changed instantly, and a thunderous cheer arose from the ranks, as the men believed that they had finally acquired a *fighting* general. The command was given, "Forward march!" and Patrick, along with the multitude of Yanks, smiled, as hearts were lifted and confidence restored. Now—maybe now, he thought—we can drive old Robert E. Lee from the field once and for all. South—they were moving south. They didn't realize it yet, but this lone rider with the floppy hat, at this juncture of time, didn't recognize any other direction.

They marched through the night, and in the morning found the enemy waiting for them in a strong, defensive position. This time, Private O'Malley got his chance to carry the colors; Patrick made sure of that. When the young soldier was handed the flag, he grasped the wooden pole tightly with one hand, then the other, as he smiled and proudly looked up at the golden harp upon its emerald green background. He took his place next to O'Shaunessey who stood holding the Stars and Stripes, the warm spring breeze catching both flags and unfurling them into the wind. Pat felt a surge of pride and honor as he gazed upon the colors and his fellow soldiers, some of whom would be making the ultimate sacrifice for God and country. And then it began.

Through the fields they charged, colors flying, muskets firing, men dropping, shot and shell exploding—and on they raced! As they neared the Rebels' line, bullets pierced both flags with increased rapidity. Patrick, running alongside the colors, could hear the quick thrusts of flying lead tearing the fragile fabric that they held so dear. The Rebels broke and ran. O'Malley jumped over their breastworks; and he, along with O'Shaunessey, made it into the enemy's position. They were followed by those of their regiment who had survived the charge. Pursuing the Rebels far behind their works, it began to look like a rout. Before long, however, the enemy reinforced its second line of defense, and soon the Yanks advance ground to a halt. As it did, Patrick heard a loud crack just off to his right. Turning, he saw, as if in slow motion, Private O'Malley going down, his flag falling on top of this brave color-bearer. A bullet had cut the flagpole in two and struck O'Malley in the head. The young private had fallen, still grasping the flagless half of the pole in his hand. Patrick picked up the flag and continued the charge. He had only gone a short distance when the colonel ordered them to halt. The Rebels secondary fortifications were too strong, and the charge quickly ended. The remaining Yanks retreated with no time to pick up their dead and wounded, as the hail of bullets was still coming in from the men in gray.

And so it went—charge after bloody charge—attack by the Yanks and counterattack by the Rebels. Day after day, the carnage continued, as more men breathed their last. And then the rains came, and the fighting grew even more deadly. The 69th became entangled with the Rebels in close combat at a salient in the enemy's lines. Patrick found himself only a few feet from their entrenchments, firing point blank into a mass of gray-clad soldiers who were separated from the Union troops by a wall of logs they had hastily built. Men from both sides thrust their steel bayonets through separations in the logs, spearing each other and withdrawing their blood-soaked weapons, only to try again to kill one another. As the day wore on, the torrential rains drenched both blue and gray alike. Men fell in droves into the muddy quagmire, mortally wounded, only to be trampled down by more soldiers replacing them. The ghastly screams and moans of the wounded were drowned out by the din of battle, as they began to sink deeper into the sludge until they became like human mortar piled on top of each other, laying the foundation of freedom for generations to come. Small rivulets of blood began to course their way through the soggy mud, and soon the crimson liquid flowing from Yank and Reb alike co-mingled into channels of the lifeblood of American youth.

Darkness fell and still they fought with ferocity, until well past midnight. As the deadly flashes of fire from a thousand muskets lit up the dark battlefield, the pungent odor of gunsmoke invaded Patrick's nostrils and burned his eyes. Finally, some time during the night, both sides, exhausted and drained of their last bit of energy, ceased the struggle. Except for a few shots ringing out, the battle, for now, had run its course. Patrick collapsed where he stood. His whole body ached. His arms were weakened by the loading and firing all day long of his single-shot muzzle loader and the many thrusts of his bayonet into the enemy's breastworks. He never really knew how many of the enemy he had killed. He lay on the bloodstained earth and closed his eyes. The ugly scenes of the battle raced through his mind. He tried to dismiss them but to no avail. He opened his eyes, hoping they would go away. The rain had tapered off to a mere drizzle; he turned his face upward, washing away the splattered blood, black soot, and sweat. It felt refreshing, as though the Good Lord was cleansing him from the stench and filth that always accompanied men who do battle. Then suddenly, he was startled by someone gripping his ankle. He quickly sat up, and through the darkness could barely see a hand protruding from the mud beneath. Jumping to his feet, he grasped the man's hand in his own and pulled the half-dead soldier from his muddy grave. Just then, orders came down the line for the whole brigade to pull back and reorganize their ranks. Patrick somehow mustered up enough strength to lift the man over his shoulder, attempting to carry him back to the new position a few hundred yards to the rear. He had difficulty holding on to him, as the man's body was covered with slimy mud. He gripped the soldier's belt and held on to it tightly as he sloshed through the muck. The man moaned with each step that Patrick took. What seemed like forever to Pat actually took only about fifteen minutes, and finally he reached the rest of his brigade gathered in a clump of trees. He gently laid the soldier down in a tiny clearing in the center and, bending over to assist him, wiped the mud from his face. He looked familiar, and Pat tried to recall the face as he began to wipe the worst mud from the man's clothing. Gray. It was gray. A Reb. Then he realized it was the young Rebel soldier who had guarded him back at the farmhouse where he had been held captive. The young boy in gray opened his eyes and muttered the word "mother" as he began to fade away. At the last second, he seemed to recognize Patrick and words whispered from his lips in his last exhaled breath: "Newww... Yorrrk..." Patrick wept. He had liked the young lad who had seemed so naïve. He remembered the boy recruit who was so anxious to "see the elephant" and who had bragged about his mother's home cooking. Well, Patrick thought, he got to "see the elephant" but would never taste his mother's home cooking again. This crazy war— maybe *I* killed him... Don't understand. As Patrick's mind and body were totally beyond the point of exhaustion, he collapsed and fell into a deep sleep.

The next few weeks were like a blur to Pat. He didn't know the names of some of the battles he had participated in, although someone had mentioned the last one being called Spotsylvania. Someone else had called it The Mule's Shoe. More battles followed, some bigger than others. There were skirmishes, attacks, more counterattacks, and short marches from one fight to another—until they came to a place called Cold Harbor. It wasn't cold—and it wasn't a harbor. All Pat could see was a country crossroads. More rain, mud, fighting and death. They were still moving south, but at a terrible cost. Early one morning, Pat fell into line with his brigade, preparing, along with the other divisions, to charge the enemy, not knowing their line was almost impenetrable because of heavy reinforcements. The Yankees were decimated and thrown back in only half an hour, seven thousand of his comrades lying dead or wounded on the field. He, however, was lucky. He came out of it with only two small flesh wounds to his arm. More attacks followed but were also unsuccessful.

Once again, the men in blue marched away from the battlefield, avoiding Lee's Confederates; and slipped around his flank in the middle of the night, heading south.   Knocking on the door of the city of Petersburg, although surprising the Rebels, they hesitated. Patrick found out later that the Union officers had overestimated enemy strength there, and wrongly decided against a full-fledged attack.

It was the beginning of a long, hot summer followed by a very cold winter. The siege had begun. Rebel and Yank began to dig large trenches and throw shot and shell each other from these well-fortified positions. It appeared that the days of glory, flag waving, and massive frontal assaults had *truly* come to an end. Both armies were reluctant to attack each other, since formidable works of long wooden poles had been secured in the ground in front of the trenches, sharpened to points.

The long marches on the hot, dusty roads seemed to be behind them. At first, Patrick was thankful for that. His feet, blistered from the countless miles he had tramped, had had time to heal. The insane frontal assaults had ceased, and the Stars and Stripes were firmly planted in the Union ramparts a few short miles from Richmond. But now, calloused hands were replacing his blisters. Patrick's musket had become a part of him—for three long years, he had shouldered it, marched with it, ate with it, and slept with it. But now, it was replaced with a shovel. Day after day, week after week, he dug trenches. He still carried his musket wherever he would go, but his primary tool was now the shovel. He almost preferred the blistered feet and long marches to the drudgery of digging, especially when it rained and the ditches became a quagmire, making it an almost impossible task.

On one occasion, when he shoved his spade into the hard Virginia clay, he thought of his grandfather who had dug ditches back in New York City just to put food on the table. He wondered how his Grocky had been able to do it at his age. He soon discovered one good thing—he had more free time for letter writing and reading. Since he wasn't constantly on the move anymore, letters would come more quickly. Sometimes he received two letters a month from Beth; and he, in turn, promptly responded, beginning to shower her with affection once again. His whirlwind romance with Lou Ann had ended; however, the memories *still* lingered. She had been a blessing to him at a time when he needed someone. How could he forget that lilac-scented, pretty girl that he first gazed upon after being dragged from the battlefield at Fredericksburg? When he pondered his relationship with her and all that they had been through together, he would eventually, though quite unwillingly, sober up to the reality that she *was* planning to become a nun. Still, things that happen to a lonely soldier far from home are never *completely* forgotten.

Feelings for Beth had never really ceased but did lie dormant and unattended for a time. He felt guilty, for his heart *had* strayed away from Beth. He remembered their promises to one another on that steamer that had slowly cruised up the Hudson River before the war—how she had agreed to marry him after the war was over, and how she said she would accept his medal as a token of his love on their wedding day.

Summer turned to fall, and fall into winter. Christmas came and Patrick attended Mass for the first time in many months in a small, wooden chapel erected behind their lines. He thanked God for many things as he knelt in silence after receiving Holy Communion. An inner peace came over him as he prayed. He began to believe that the division in the country would soon come to a close, as the Confederate Army was desperate and seemed close to defeat. The simple, small chapel was plain and crudely constructed; however, the chaplain had placed an evergreen tree decorated with a few ornaments next to the left side of the altar. And beneath it were small statues of the Baby Jesus, Mary and Joseph. A sheep and a camel completed the scene. After Mass had ended, Patrick knelt down at the altar railing and gazed upon the little figures. Looking upon the Holy Family, he longed for home and hearth and his own family. He hadn't celebrated Christmas at home for four long years, and he prayed that he would be home for the next one.

1865 came, and the men made their own New Year's celebration. A few Irishmen were able to obtain some whiskey and ended up dancing the Irish jig and falling all over themselves until dawn. Only one fight broke out, and both pugilists missed more punches than they had thrown. Patrick had a good laugh and enjoyed every minute of the festivities. There was an abundance of food; and music was provided by O'Connor's fiddle, Finnegan's harmonica, and a few Irish tenors thrown in.

The following morning, it was back to the muddy trenches. Pat learned to hate trench warfare. Besides the dirt and mud to contend with, there was the constant sniper fire that occasionally killed soldiers who had forgotten to keep their heads down. This, along with the enemy shells that would come in at any time during the day and night, made it miserable for him. Sometimes, when he was on guard duty alone in the dark of night, his only company was the few, large, black rats that scurried through the trenches across his feet. But he didn't complain, for he had heard that the Rebels, half-starved to death, were reduced to eating the creatures. In fact, he had also heard from some Rebel prisoners that butcher shops in Richmond had rats for sale hanging in their windows.

The siege continued through the long, cold winter; and Patrick resigned himself to the harsh conditions and the boredom. He began to feel more confident that he would survive the war. In the past, when he had laid his head down at night, he was never entirely sure. A certain amount of fear had always been his constant companion. But now, his thoughts were taken up with plans for his homecoming—long overdue plans that had begun four years ago on a boat sailing down the Hudson River on that beautiful starlit night. His letters from Beth had given him hope for a new life and a new world. Besides avoiding the sniper fire and shells that dropped behind their lines, Patrick had been involved in only two attacks against the Rebels since the beginning of the siege, neither being successful in penetrating their strong fortifications. The Union forces had taken only light casualties and the siege continued.

Finally, the warm, spring sunshine fell upon the trenches; and the two opposing armies stirred. April came, and Patrick found himself on the march once again. General Lee and his army broke out to the west, and U.S. Grant was hot on his heels. Patrick felt good about leaving the filthy trenches behind and being on the open road once again. The fighting was much different now. Instead of the enemy attacking, they were retreating. A few times, they had put up a stiff resistance; and more blue and gray fell mortally wounded. Day after day, there continued skirmishes and firefights, but they were short lived. Each time the fighting ceased, a forced march began. Mile after mile, along the dusty roads, Patrick observed hundreds of abandoned Rebel muskets discarded by the roadside along with something else he had never seen before—vanquished sons of Dixie, half-starved, thin and gaunt, sitting by the roadside with their heads in their hands. The end was near. Old Virginia, the Mother of Presidents, had been named after a virgin queen of England. Many battles had raged upon her fertile soil that ran red with blood. Now, however, it was slowing to a trickle. She had no more to give. She was being beaten into submission and was in her final death throes, along with her rebellious sister states. The Old South was about to collapse, never to rise again.

CHAPTER 22

▼

GRIEF AND GLORY

The Yankee hordes were driving their Southern American brothers back through the fields and streams of the beautiful Virginia countryside. There was no more time to write letters, to cook, or even to boil a cup of coffee. Patrick had thrown down his shovel and picked up his musket once again. It had only been one week since the Union Army had evacuated the trenches around Petersburg and Richmond to pursue Lee's army, which was moving west. Suddenly they halted near a large, red brick house with stairs leading up to a front porch. Patrick believed it was in preparation for an attack on the flank of Johnny Reb. As he loaded his musket to make ready for another fight, a rumor shot through the ranks that General Lee and General Grant were talking terms of surrender. Pat was stunned! He couldn't believe his ears. An explosive cheer went up from the ranks and reverberated across the fields, being returned in echo by the surrounding hills. Patrick had thought the end was near but had never believed it would come so quickly. Is it true? Could it really be finished?

The men were told to be at ease; however, they were to be ready to move on a moment's notice. They sprawled out beneath some shade trees, and Pat drank the warm water from his canteen, placing his musket on the ground near his side. He listened to his comrades who were all smiling and chattering amongst themselves. They reminded him of a group of schoolboys who were about to begin summer recess. The cheerfulness was so prevalent, unlike the solemn silence that usually preceded a battle. A quiet surge of joy and relief overwhelmed Patrick, and he finally knew with certainty that he would be going home. He silently prayed to the Almighty in thanksgiving for sparing his life.

"Hey, Sarge!" one of the men called.

Pat looked over to see a private lying in the grass, looking up at the blue sky and chewing on a long piece of grass. "What is it, Rafferty?"

"I called ya twice—ya look like yer dreamin'. Thinkin' about yer girl and home, are ya?"

"Yeah," Pat answered.

"Yeah, me, too. Can't wait ta get back ta New York City an' civilization again."

Patrick listened as Rafferty rambled on, talking about his home and family. He was only half-listening, however, thinking about his own future and becoming a civilian once again. He took another sip of water from his canteen, then spit it out. It was late morning; and the water, by this time, had become hot. He, like the others, was waiting for orders, hoping that the rumors of the surrender were true.

Early in the afternoon, Pat, along with many of the men, although extremely excited over the possible surrender, began to doze off on the outer edge of the well-manicured lawn from the sheer exhaustion of the forced marches and fighting.

He was abruptly awakened by the sound of galloping horses. Looking up, he saw three Confederate officers approaching the house. One officer dismounted from his gray horse. He was impeccably dressed in a clean, butternut gray uniform, a sword hanging from his side, shined black boots, and a wide-brimmed, gray felt hat. Patrick was impressed with this striking figure who rode in so gallantly and erect in the saddle. "Look! Look!" Rafferty shouted. "It's the old man himself—Lee!"

General Lee handed Traveler's reins to one of the other officers and, without fanfare, ascended the stairs where he was ushered into the house by a Union officer. Patrick and his comrades looked on silently, waiting for the other player of this gigantic chess game to arrive and checkmate his opponent. Soon, a Union officer, followed by a dozen others, came galloping up the same road. The high-ranking officer at the head of the group wore a floppy black hat and carried no sword. His uniform was splattered with mud and his boots were dirty. It was General U.S. Grant. Strange, Patrick thought, Lee looks like the victor and Grant like the vanquished. He was awestruck by this momentous event unfolding before his very eyes. He knew it was of great historical importance and, even though the war had dragged on for four long years, everything now seemed to be happening so quickly. He had never imagined it happening this way—he was overwhelmed that he would be present right here at the exact moment that this horrible conflict would come to an end. Grant slowly and deliberately ascended the stairs and entered the house. Patrick thought he looked like a man returning home from a hard day's work.

About four o'clock in the afternoon, General Robert E. Lee emerged from the house, mounted Traveler, and began a slow ride to his camp, head bowed though seated erect in his saddle. His loyal soldiers, tears in many eyes, lined up on either side of the road, touched his horse, and waved their farewells to their beloved leader. Union artillery fire began a victory salute; and the men in blue cheered, jumped up and down, hugged one another, and threw their hats in the air. The grand emotion electrified the Union ranks. General George Meade was seen racing down the road on his battle-hardened horse waving his hat and shouting, "It's all over, boys! Lee surrendered! It's all over!"

The excitement was short-lived, however, as an order soon came from General Grant, read by Patrick's colonel:

> *"The Confederates are now our prisoners, and we do not want to exult over their downfall. The war is over. The Rebels are our countrymen again."*

It was finished. Patrick was filled with emotion. On the one hand, he felt a great sigh of relief and joy; but a sadness befell him as he watched some of his brave adversaries weep and fall to the ground, covering their faces and crying profusely.

That night, campfires sprung up all over the quiet little community of Appomattox Court House, extending far out into the countryside. The men were supplied with food; and after the many days of forced marches and battles, they ate ravenously. Whiskey bottles had made their way into camp, and the Union troops celebrated all night long. Patrick hadn't had a drink of hard liquor since that New Year's Eve he spent with Lou Ann back in Washington. When a bottle was passed to him, he took a few swigs; it burned as it slid down his throat but felt good inside. He slept like a baby that night.

Next morning, Father Corby held Mass for the Irish Brigade in a field not far from the surrender site of the heavily bearded Mr. McLean's house. When it came time for the homily, the priest began to speak in a solemn but joyful tone. "Gentlemen—God is good. Our Almighty God has brought our righteous cause to victory. Now all men shall be free, and your sacrifices and hardships have been the instrument of that freedom. And what a terrible price we have paid. We shall offer up our Mass for our fallen comrades and those of our Southern brothers, for they, too, are God's children. The time has come for healing and to bring them back into the fold. Yesterday, the day the hostilities ceased, was Palm Sunday. Did you know that palms are a sign of victory and triumph? For, according to John 12, Chapters 12-15, '*The crowds, seeing Jesus mounted on the colt of a donkey entering Jerusalem, spread out palm branches before him.*' We have won a great victory and I see a significant parallel to the ultimate victory of our Lord and Savior Jesus Christ over sin and death. Let us rejoice and be glad. Return to your homes and continue to pray for our nation, that we may one day be in wholeness and love before the Lord and our children will be raised in goodness and holiness. Bless us now, dear God, as we place these intentions in your Sacred Heart through the intercession of the Blessed Virgin Mary, Your Mother and ours. Amen."

Patrick had heard homilies about Palm Sunday many times before; but this time, the words of the priest had profound meaning. He never realized that palms had been a sign of victory. For the next few days, he pondered the priest's words and prayed in thanksgiving to his God that the killing was no more. He used his time in writing letters to Beth and his family.

Three days after Robert E. Lee capitulated to U.S. Grant, the formal surrender of the Confederate troops took place. The long gray line marched proudly up the road with their crimson "Stars and Bars" and other battle flags flying in the warm, spring breeze. Patrick thought that they looked as though they were about to embark on another battle. But this final battle would produce falling tears instead of flying bullets. He could see in the eyes of the vanquished that fighting back the tears was possibly their greatest battle of all. They stacked their arms and furled their flags for the last time as delicately and reverently as if they were cradling a newborn babe. Pat stood in formation with his blue-clad comrades, and every man stared into the eyes of the gray-clad men facing them from across the road. Not a whisper was heard. Joshua Chamberlain, now a Major General, did the honors of accepting the surrendered arms and flags. Patrick looked at him with admiration. He had learned that the then-Colonel Chamberlain and his 20th Maine had held off the Rebels in that pivotal battle on Little Round Top at the same time his 69th had fought its bloody struggle in the wheatfield below.

Chamberlain shouted a command, and the Yankees snapped their first and last salute to their conquered foe. And in a brief moment of time, it was over. Patrick looked on as the proud Rebel soldiers, who just moments before had marched up the road looking as such a formidable force, had dissolved and began to wander off into the fields, hills, and roads of the Virginia countryside as aimless, homeless, and scattered vagabonds drifting off into oblivion. The once strong, proud Army of Northern Virginia had ceased to exist. He wept for his adversaries, no longer there and gone forever. He couldn't explain it, but he nevertheless wept. And, as he looked around, he saw that he was not the only one weeping—many men in blue did the same.

That night, Pat didn't take time to pitch his tent. He lay on his back and surveyed the night sky. He marveled at the constellations of stars. Their patterns never changed—unlike the stars that had fallen from Old Glory. But now they would be returning to their rightful place. His imagination wandered. Men change, governments change, ideas change; but the everlasting stars stand fast in the universe—like bright, peering eyes watching the folly of mankind.

The last march began on Good Friday. The Union Army was proceeding back to City Point on the James River for their final journey by boat back to Washington. Spirits were high. The rigid formation of men in war on the march to battle had changed to a relaxed gait, and they were filled with merriment. Thousands of boots tramped out of step, each man marching to his own drumbeat and soon to be dissolved into civilian life. The few who had consumed too much liquor passed out by the roadside, but most of them joked and talked and discussed their plans for the future. Patrick, however, talked very little. He was daydreaming about Beth and seeing his family once again. First thing I'm going to do, he mused, is take a nice, warm bath; sleep for two days; then put on some clean clothes and go see Beth.

The Army of the Potomac stopped at sundown and made camp one last time before arriving at their destination. Patrick ate the white beans and hardtack, a fare he soon would certainly not miss. He thought about sitting at a table once again and enjoying a good home-cooked meal. He could hear the regimental band off in the distance playing "Tenting Tonight", "The Star Spangled Banner", "Yankee Doodle", and "The Girl I Left Behind Me." A favorite amongst the men, "The Battle Hymn of the Republic", wasn't played. There would be no more battle cries for these men. Patrick felt better than he had in four long years. He became melancholy and sat by the fireside, having no apprehension for the 'morrow. The music floated through the camp on a subtle breeze—and all was right—but not for long. Suddenly it ceased, and an eerie silence followed for a moment. Then an officer rode frantically through the ranks shouting, "Lincoln's been shot! Lincoln's been shot!"

Pat quickly rose to his feet. His heart sunk. "No—no—it can't be!" he hollered.

He and many of his men gathered together, all asking the vital question, "Is he—is he—dead?" No one knew.

"This *can't* be—the war is over!" Patrick exclaimed to the others.

One angry private yelled, "We shoulda killed all of them bastards!"

The camp became so infuriated that they were ready to shoot any stray Rebel soldier on sight. After awhile, they began to settle down into a somber mood and all returned to their campfires, waiting to find out if their President was alive or dead. The joy of victory had changed to one of gloom by one small bullet from an assassin's gun. The following morning, when they were breaking camp, they received the final blow. There wasn't a rider shouting or even a formal announcement made. Like the creepy fog of death that killed the first-born of Egyptians in Moses' time, the news spread throughout the camp. "He's dead! Honest Abe is dead!" At first, Patrick thought he was having a nightmare; but, as he jumped to his feet, he saw some soldiers standing around weeping and lamenting over their Commander-in-Chief's death. The nightmare was real. He was overwhelmed with grief. The tall, bearded man in his stovepipe hat, whom he had first seen in New York City, was gone. He had remembered his sad-looking eyes and the friendly smile the President had given him when he and Lou Ann had briefly passed him in his carriage in Washington. Before long, a few men who had been drinking began to shout. "Let's finish them off!" The inebriated men sparked anger and violence in the others; and before long, a crowd of soldiers had picked up their muskets, ready to do battle once again. Pat didn't join them. He suddenly realized that a catastrophe would have occurred if the assassin's bullet had found its mark during the surrender, when both armies stood only feet apart at Appomattox. The unruly crowd of incited soldiers wanted revenge for Lincoln's death. But, after swearing and voicing their anger, it soon became apparent that there wasn't anyone around to fight.

A colonel arrived on horseback and shouted loudly, waving his sword in the air. "Put your guns down! The war is over—there is no more Rebel Army. Any man who fires his weapon will be court-martialed. Haven't you seen enough killing?"

Some men grumbled as they slowly moved back to their campsites. A few vowed to kill the assassin if they could ever get their hands on him.

Patrick couldn't get the image of Abe Lincoln out of his mind—that noble, distinguished, yet pleasant air he had about him. This great man who seemed to be sacrificed for freeing the slaves reminded Pat of another man who had willingly sacrificed Himself for all men to be freed from the slavery of sin. Both slain on Good Friday, he thought.

Easter Sunday came and went without any fanfare or even a Mass for the men. They marched all day toward Washington, one step closer to home.

Pat prayed silently as he marched and gave glory to God on this holy day of Jesus' Resurrection.

The following night Patrick shuffled up the ramp of the steamboat, exhausted from the march. He wondered how many miles he had trodden in the last four years over the embattled Virginia turf. The soldiers found themselves a spot to lie down on the over-crowded decks and fell asleep. As Pat tossed and turned, he felt a hard object beneath him. Realizing it was his ammunition pouch, he pulled out his last remaining bullet. Getting up, he gingerly stepped over the others and moved to the railing where he held the bullet up to his eyes for a moment before forcefully throwing it over the side with all his might. He watched as it tumbled end over end in the bright moonlight until it finally plunged into the dark, cold waters. A few ripples spread out from the splash; and then, in an instant, they were gone and the waters once again became placid. He squeezed into a spot on the deck once more and fell back asleep.

The following morning the soldiers disembarked the steamboat and set up camp in a large, open field within sight of the Capitol Building in Washington. Thousands of small, white tents sprang up all around the government buildings, and the "invasion" of Washington began. The discipline that had kept the Grand Army of the Republic going for four years was quickly evaporating. Patrick was relieved that the many long drills and marches had ceased, but there was something new developing—idle hands. Each regiment still held morning roll calls; but for much of the day, the men were left to their own devices. Pat played baseball, caught up with his letter writing, and was becoming very excited about going home. Others played cards and gambled, hoping to accumulate a "nest egg" to take home with them. And some got drunk. The taverns were full every night. Some bartenders even offered free drinks for the victorious Yankee soldiers. And so, the men indulged themselves night after night. The "ladies of the night" also prospered.

Patrick visited the taverns on a few occasions and celebrated with the rest, but he knew his limitations. He always made sure he could walk back to camp unassisted. The 69th Irish Brigade surely knew how to celebrate—and brawl! It was commonplace to walk down the streets of Washington and see some drunken men being tossed out of a saloon after a barroom fight and landing on their posteriors in the middle of the street. The very next night, these same men would be drinking and singing together with arms resting on each other's shoulders. And so it went—night after night. But they had earned it. In a few short days, the men would be released from duty and go home. But first, they would march in the victory parade down Pennsylvania Avenue as the final climax to the four grueling years of killing that left the nation in mourning. It had begun with a shot fired in anger at Fort Sumter, South Carolina and ended with another shot also fired in anger at the sad-eyed man in the stovepipe hat. Some men just went home before being released from duty. The officers and guards looked the other way.

One morning, Patrick sat on a log outside his tent sewing a few tears in his uniform with his "housewife," a small kit of needles and thread, which had been issued to each soldier upon entering the army. The men were told to repair and spruce up their uniforms the best they could, so as to look good for the fast approaching parade. He became frustrated, as he was having difficulty threading the small needle. When he held it up to the bright morning sky attempting to insert the thread into the tiny hole, he could see the Capitol Building in the distance. After many unsuccessful attempts, he finally succeeded in slipping the thread through the eye and gently pulled it through. Looking back once again at the Capitol, brilliantly shining in the bright sunlight, he remembered that day when he and Lou Ann had toured the city just at the time the dome was being completed. While admiring his neat sewing job, he noticed a private emerge from his tent a few yards across from him. Pat couldn't remember his name, as the man had recently been assigned to the regiment. He only knew that he was from upstate New York. The private fixed his bayonet to the end of his musket, then forcefully plunged it into the ground.

"Hey, Private! What are you doing?" Pat shouted.

"Goin' home, Sarge," he responded with a grin on his face.

"What do you mean? We have to stay for the parade."

"Not me, Sarge. Got planting ta do. Can't wait. My wife needs me. She wrote me and said there's not enough food for her and the children." Pat was at a loss for words. "Parade or no parade, my family has ta eat," the private went on to say as he briskly walked away.

I can't argue with that, Pat thought to himself. Something in the Bible—what was it? Something about soldiers turning their swords into plowshares?

The big day of the victory parade finally arrived late in May, and Patrick awoke to the irritating sounds of the regimental band tuning up. Great excitement filled the air, for this parade would be the final act to a long sought-after victory for the North. Pat was ready. He had washed his clothes, mended the tears, and would march in a tattered but clean uniform. They formed their ranks in expansive, open fields near the Capitol—division by division, brigade by brigade, and corps by corps, they maneuvered into position.

Thousands of men, horses, cannon, and caisson came together for their last march. The trumpets blared, the drums thundered, the flags unfurled—and down Pennsylvania Avenue they marched. And in that azure sea, came the 69th Irish Brigade, each man wearing a green sprig of boxwood in his cap, led by its officers on horseback, with Sergeant Patrick O'Hanrahan proudly carrying the Stars and Stripes. Dancing in the wind beside it, the green banner with the golden harp was upheld by O'Shaunessey, smiling from ear to ear. The bands played the "Star Spangled Banner", the throngs jammed the sidewalks, and onlookers lined the rooftops. Along the parade route, some schoolchildren cast rose petals at the feet of the marching soldiers, and cheers swelled up from every throat, rising to the heavens. What a glorious day, Patrick thought, as his brigade passed by the reviewing stand. He looked up at the dignitaries, among them U.S. Grant and President Johnson. Immediately, he felt a sense of loss. It wasn't supposed to be that way—the Tall Man in the Stovepipe Hat should be sitting there. One hundred and fifty thousand men of the Grand Army of the Republic marched for two days down Pennsylvania Avenue; and instead of marching into battle, they marched into history. The mightiest army in the history of the world would dissolve and evaporate into thin air, and the country would breathe a sigh of relief. It was finished.

The men returned to their campsites and waited for their release papers. After dark, they began to stick candles in the end of their musket barrels, lighting them, pointing them heavenward, and parading around the grounds. Patrick joined them and thought of them as thousands of votive candles lit in thanksgiving to God that the war was over and that the North had been victorious. They marched in precision formations, executing the drills that had become as commonplace as eating and breathing. They marched forward, and to the right flank, then to the left flank, then reversed their direction to the rear. And so it continued far into the night. Patrick thought of the many drills and marches on the dusty roads he had tramped for the last four years. Strange, he thought—the very same men who had always complained about drills had taken it on themselves to voluntarily march there in the open fields with flickering candles instead of bullets in their guns.

Although they were all anxious to get home, there seemed to be a gnawing sadness in parting. Beyond the horrors of war, the deprivations and pain, there was something else—comradery? Had the Army become like a family to them? Pat couldn't explain it, but he felt it deep down in his soul. Had living on the edge, not knowing who would be left standing after a battle, been a cohesive bind? Or was it the close proximity to others that had its effects? No one understood it, nor could they explain it. After many hours of this "march", it *would* be finished. The Grand Army of the Republic would go out of existence. Patrick thought of it like a death—it had been more than just an army. It had taken on a life of its own; and no matter how many of its members had been killed or wounded, it continued to evolve and move and have its being—and completed the work it had set out to do. Little by little, the candles were extinguished, as the soldiers retired to their tents one last time.

Next day, Pat watched as tents were folded, and the ranks began to thin out. As more men received their release papers, the landscape became checkered with open spaces. Some men in his regiment stopped and shook hands with him as they parted. They wished each other good luck and then they were gone—and Pat waited. Another day passed and more men departed. And the field grew more barren of tents and men. Patrick began to grow concerned that his papers might be lost. On the night of the third day, he looked around and observed only a few tents remaining with isolated campfires burning. All of the men in his outfit had already gone. As he sat in front of his campfire all alone, boiling coffee, he decided to search for an officer, if any were still there, and inquire about his papers. If not, he was going to leave—papers or no papers. As he was about to remove his coffeepot from the campfire, he was startled to see a figure standing by the fire. "Oh, Michael! Where did you come from? Haven't seen you in quite a while."

Michael stood on the other side of the fire, smiling, his face illuminated by the flames. He held out a piece of paper in his right hand. "Thought you might be looking for these, Sarge," he said in a calm voice.

Patrick took the papers and quickly read them. "Oh! I've been waiting for these—where did you get them?"

"Guess they were mis-sent to another regiment, along with some others. The colonel asked me to find you and give them to you."

"Thanks so much, Michael. I see you made it through in one piece."

"Yeah, through the grace of God."

Patrick was about to offer him a cup of coffee, when a strong gust of wind came out of nowhere and swept across the fields. His tent was partially knocked down, and he turned to see the canvas whipping in the wind and beating against the ground. He was about to secure the tent from blowing away, when he distinctly heard Michael's loud, clear voice—"May God go with you." Patrick turned back—Michael was gone. The coffeepot flipped over onto the ground, and the hot embers flew across the open field, growing cold, just as the hot winds of war had blown away and become cold—as cold as the six hundred thousand young Americans who lay beneath God's green fields stained with their blood, purifying the nation. And just as quickly as the wind had kicked up, it stopped. Dead calm followed, and the flapping sound of the tent had ceased—and yet—Patrick heard a softer flapping— more like the wings of a bird ascending into the dark, night sky. Where had Michael gone? Why did he leave so quickly? Didn't see him go. He realized he was still holding his release papers tightly in his hand. Then an astonishing thought zipped through his mind. Saint Michael, the Archangel? Could it be? At first he became afraid. Things like this never happen to *me*. Then, in an instant, he felt a warm glow envelop him. He quickly gathered his belongings, folded his tent, and picked up his rifle. As he walked toward the train station, he wondered. Where did Michael come from? Said he came from another company. Only appeared before or after some battle. He *had* saved my life. Would anybody ever believe me? He walked in a daze, struggling with his heavy load and finally reached the train station where the supply wagons were lined up in a row.

"Over here, Sarge!" hollered a supply sergeant standing beside one of the wagons.

Pat walked over and dropped his folded tent at the feet of the soldier. "I'll take that, too," said the sergeant, as he pointed to Pat's musket. "You won't be needing that any more."

Patrick handed over his weapon as though he were parting with an old friend. After all, it had been his only protection for those four long years. Then, when he wondered how many of his fellow Americans in the South had been killed with it, he wanted no part of it.

Most of the men had already departed for home. The trains had been jammed with the constant throng of soldiers for three days. But now, the trickle of the remaining few was minimal. He sat on the platform waiting for the next train, his haversack still on his back. He reached into it, only to find a few crumbs, and then threw it away along with his canteen and ammunition pouch. He looked at his release papers, carefully folded them, and tucked them into his jacket. As he gazed around the train station, he saw a few soldiers sleeping on benches. Looking down the long platform, he spotted a little sign at the end that read "To Gettysburg." It had never crossed his mind to go anyplace but home to New York City and Beth. She had been his first and only love—until Lou Ann came along. But Lou Ann was becoming a nun. And why would he want to go back to those killing fields near her home anyway? He got to his feet and slowly walked down to the little sign, sat down beneath it, leaning back against a pole, and fell asleep.

CHAPTER 23

▼

THE LILAC THAT NEVER BLOOMED

Patrick was suddenly awakened by the loud hissing sound of the train's engines as it pulled in and stopped by the platform in front of him. He watched as a few men boarded the train. He didn't move. Should I or shouldn't I? Before long, the conductor hopped up onto the steps of the train and hollered, "All aboard! Last train to Gettysburg!" He watched as it started to move, engines laboring to gain momentum; and he sat still as the cars slowly began to pass him by. Finally, the caboose, trailing along, rolled out beyond the platform. The great spurts of steam spit out by the engine began to cloud his view. Then, without another thought, he sprang to his feet, jumped off the platform, and ran like blazes after it. It was beginning to move faster—but so was he. As he ran faster and faster, he began to gain on it. He sprinted through the steam into the dark night, keeping his eye on the red lantern swinging back and forth on the back of the caboose. He felt exhilarated—free—unencumbered. No rifle, haversack, ammo, canteen, or all of the accouterments that he had dragged around with him those four long years. Wherever he wound up, he would feel free to live once again. He was happy that the slaves had been freed—and now he felt liberated also. He was free from killing; free from the fear of dying; free from long, exhausting marches; and, most of all, free from his own constant fear of turning his back to the enemy.

When he finally caught up with the train, he grabbed the iron railing and pulled himself up onto the back of the caboose and sat down to catch his breath as he watched the station behind him slip from view. He hoped never to return to the South again and wished that the horrible memories of the war would some day fade from his mind. He remained sitting there on the platform as the train made its way out of the busy railroad yards of Washington and into the quiet Maryland countryside. The cool night air felt good at first—but then, as the train got up a good head of steam, it billowed out more smoke, bringing tiny cinders trailing off to the rear, which irritated his eyes. He got up and moved inside the caboose but couldn't get through the locked door to the passenger cars ahead. A conductor was sleeping on a small cot in the corner. Patrick sat down on a well-worn bale of cotton in the other corner, which looked like previous occupants had used it as a chair. As he gazed around the inside of the caboose, he noticed a newspaper lying on the floor next to the conductor. Pat picked it up, unconcerned about disturbing the loudly snoring trainman, settled back down on the cotton bale, and pored over the front page. He had just begun to relax when he suddenly jumped to his feet, still holding the newspaper in his hands, his eyes glued to the front page. "Oh, my gosh! The assassin—Booth. It's him—the actor! Oh, my gosh!" He mumbled the shocked words, continuing to stare at the picture of the little man with the mustache and goatee, remembering his meeting with him that night at the Willard Hotel when Lou Ann introduced them. He looked at the snoring conductor and could hardly contain himself. He wanted to tell someone, but he had no one to share it with—for now anyway. Never before had he taken much interest in newspapers. This time, however, he read every article about Lincoln's assassination; the subject filled most all of the paper.

As the night wore on, his eyes grew weary; and he finally rested the newspaper on his lap and laid his head back against the wall. The only sounds he heard were the conductor's snoring and the constant clackity-clack sound of the heavy metal train wheels rolling over the steel tracks as it chugged its way North. As he began to fall into a light slumber, his mind became flooded with past battles. The train wheels seemed to be saying:

FRED--RICKS--BURG, CHANCE--LERS--VILLE, GET--TEYS--BURG, PETE--ERS-BURG over and over again.

It seemed like only moments had passed when the train jerked to a stop. "Gettysburg!" And again a loud shout—"Gettysburg!" Patrick got to his feet, exited the back door of the caboose and stepped down onto the platform. It was still dark, but he could see a glimmer of daylight on the horizon. He glanced up at the sign hanging from the roof of the station illuminated by a small lantern next to it—GETTYSBURG. After a brief time, the train pulled away and disappeared once more into the night. He was the only one to disembark, and he stood there for a moment listening to the crickets chirping in the fields. He thought about the tens of thousands of soldiers that had descended upon that little town on the fateful day in July two years earlier; and now—now he stood here alone. A survivor—alone with his memories.

The sleepy little town was quiet and peaceful—a stark contrast, he thought, to the pitched battle that had swept through it and severely frightened its inhabitants. As he walked through the dark streets guided by an occasional lantern hanging next to someone's doorway, he saw an elderly gentleman wearing a wide-brimmed, straw hat, approaching in a wagon. The man reined in his horse and stopped next to Patrick. "Whatcha doin' out here at this hour of the mornin', son?"

"Going to Emmitsburg," Patrick answered.

"Ya got quite a hike, son. Emmitsburg's nine miles south." He took a closer look at Patrick's uniform. "Oh, I see yer a soldier."

"Yes, sir."

"Ya from Emmitsburg, son?"

"No, sir, just going to visit someone."

"Didn't figure ya was from these parts—sounds like yer from up North."

"New York. I'm from New York."

"Well, son, I can't tell ya how grateful I am that you boys saved us from them damned Rebels. I mean—ya did fight in that battle, didn't ya?"

"Yes, sir. Sure did."

"Well, hop in, son. Least I kin do is give ya a ride. Just havta stop an' git some seed fer plantin' down at the granary." Patrick hopped up and sat next to the farmer, watching as the old man lit his corncob pipe and snapped the reins of his horse.

Pat helped load up the wagon with a dozen bags of seed and they were soon on the road to Emmitsburg. They had only traveled a mile or two when the farmer turned to Patrick. "Didja eat anything yet, son?"

"No, sir. Not since yesterday."

"How would ya like a good, hearty breakfast?" He drew on his pipe, slowly letting the smoke escape from his mouth.

"Well, I don't want to impose on you. I mean, you're good enough to..."

"Don't say another word, son. My place is just up the road and the wife's makin' a big breakfast anyway. One more won't make no nevermind."

The sun began to rise over the neatly checkered fields separated by the stone fence boundaries dividing the crops. They entered the farmhouse, where Patrick was introduced to the man's wife, busily setting the food on the table. "Dig in," said the farmer.

"Aren't you forgetting something?" the wife inquired.

"Oh, yes." The farmer bowed his head and clasped his hands in prayer. "Thank ya, God, for this food; and we pray for a good harvest this year—and, oh, Lord, we thank ya for that terrible war being over and bless this young lad fer his part in it. Amen."

Patrick blessed himself and answered, "Amen." The farmer's wife joined them at the table, and they all sat quietly, enjoying their breakfast. Pat was having his fill and didn't refuse a second helping when the lady of the house offered it to him. He enjoyed the peaceful view of the farmer's fields from his seat opposite the window.

The old man pushed himself away from the table and lit up his pipe once again as his wife served them coffee. "I didn't catch yer name, son."

"Patrick—Patrick O'Hanrahan, Sir."

"Oh, don't call me sir—the name's Rose—most people call me Farmer Rose."

Rose? Pat wondered where he had heard that name before. He sipped the hot brew and was thinking about getting to Emmitsburg but didn't want to sound anxious. He gazed out the window at the expansive farmlands. "You have a beautiful place here, Mr. Rose."

"Thanks, son. It wasn't so beautiful two summers ago—fiercest damn battle ya ever saw. My wheatfield was covered with dead bodies—both Yanks and Rebs!"

"Wheatfield?" Pat asked, surprised. "Did you say wheatfield?"

"Why—yeah. Why?"

"Excuse me," Pat said excitedly, as he quickly got up from the table, went to the front door, and stepped outside. What he couldn't see in the dim light earlier, became very visible to him now. Then it dawned on him. Rose—Lou Ann's mother had mentioned that name.

The old man had followed him outside. "What is it, son? Ya look like ya seen a ghost!"

As Pat surveyed the landscape, he saw the large boulders and the little hill just beyond—Little Round Top! "Oh, my gosh! It's where..." He realized this was the exact field on which he had fought. "I—I'm sorry, Sir, if I seemed rude, but I had to see for myself. I fought here—I mean—my brigade fought here. I didn't realize that this was where it happened."

"Yer lucky, son. We buried many of yer boys. It musta been terrible—bein' in the thick of it."

Patrick remembered many of his friends who fought and died there; and the vision of Joshua riding that black stallion charging down on him seemed like a dream that was unreal. "I can't believe it! I mean—it looks so peaceful now."

"Yeah, son. I'm not complainin', but we had no harvest back in '63. Them poor boys was scattered all the way up ta my peach orchard. Took weeks fer the Negroes ta bury all them bodies—had one grave that they put fifty of 'em in. No identification on many of them poor souls."

Patrick looked over the "killing fields" and became silent. The old man went inside and left him to his memories. After a short while, he stepped back outside. "Ya ready ta go ta Emmitsburg now, son? Got a lotta plantin' ta do today." Farmer Rose's voice suddenly yanked Pat from his thoughts.

"Oh! Oh, yes—I'm ready. Thanks."

They both got back into the wagon and started out, heading up the Emmitsburg Road. After going a short distance, the farmer stopped next to a split-rail fence. There was a large mound of dirt, which was raised up higher than the rest of the surrounding turf. Pat remembered a similar scene of a mass grave of Confederates being dug on his last ride down this road with Joshua and Lou Ann. "Here they are, son—the men I told you about."

Patrick looked on and saw a weathered, wooden cross at the head of the grave, painted with some lettering which read:

"50 Union Dead"
G.
A.
R.

He shuddered and said a silent prayer. He didn't just see a meaningless number, but the faces of those with whom he had eaten, marched, and fought.

"Sorry, son. It must be hard for ya."

"I'm all right." He wiped some tears from his eyes. Then, with a half-smile, he looked over at Farmer Rose and added, "Don't want to hold you up. Can we go now?"

As they rode along, the old man talked of the battle in great detail, sounding as if he, himself, had fought it. He talked about the horrible wounds and dismemberment of bodies and about the many dead horses—and worse—the half-dead horses that had to be shot and put out of their misery. Pat had heard enough, but couldn't think of a kind way to shut the old man up. If

Farmer Rose had seen the many mangled bodies that *he* had seen from Fredericksburg to Petersburg—well—Patrick didn't want to hear any more. He tried to concentrate on seeing Lou Ann one more time. Why? He really didn't know. He was half-listening to the farmer rambling on.

Farmer Rose regularly snapped the horse's reins, keeping the brown mare trotting all the way, so as to waste no time getting Patrick to his destination. Where will I find her? Pat inquired in his own thoughts. Two years had passed since he had seen or heard from her. The last thing she had mentioned was about entering a convent—but where was it? Someplace in Emmitsburg—the priest would know.

Pat asked Farmer Rose to drop him off at Saint Joseph's Church, thanking him for everything. The old man wished him good luck and rode away back to his farm to plant another crop of wheat.

Patrick knocked on the rectory door, but there was no answer. He sat down on one of the three wicker rocking chairs on the long front porch and gazed at the many gravestones surrounding the church across the road. He recalled that night, before the great battle, when he had prayed silently in that church, along with the three little nuns who had quietly shuffled in and knelt in the front pew.

As the midday sun rose above the high steeple of the white stucco church, he recognized Father Al coming across the road, dressed in his long, black cassock and black hat. Pat rose from his chair as the priest ascended the steps to the porch.

"Good morning, son, and what can I do for you?" asked Father Al.

"Hello, Father. Do you remember me?"

The priest looked curiously at Patrick for a moment, then exclaimed, "Oh! Oh, yes—now I remember. Miss Sommers' friend. Patrick, isn't it?"

"Yes, Father."

"Well, I'm so glad to see you made it through the war all right." He smiled. "You know, I prayed for you. And Miss Sommers—I mean, Sister Mary Michael—requested I say a Mass for your safe return."

"Sister who?" Patrick asked anxiously.

"Oh—Sister Mary Michael. That's her religious name—Miss Sommers, I mean."

"You mean she's become a nun—already?"

"Well, not exactly. She's a novice now, studying to become a Daughter of Charity."

"So she really did pursue it," Patrick said under his breath.

"What was that?" asked the priest.

"Oh, nothing, Father. I was just thinking—umm—Lou Ann said she wanted to join the order—but..."

"But what, Patrick?"

"Well—I didn't know if she went through with it or not." Pat thought about the name she had taken for the order—Michael—Sister Mary Michael. Strange. Another Michael in my life. Too many to be coincidence.

"Oh, yes, Patrick. She's very dedicated and truly has a calling. I've seen her caring for others—especially the orphans. I think she'll make a fine Daughter of Charity." He looked directly at Pat, then added, "You're a long way from New York, Patrick. I presume you're on your way home now."

Pat was surprised that the priest remembered where he was from. "Yes, Father. Just wanted to see how Miss Somm..." He caught himself. "I mean, Sister Mary Michael—was doing. She helped me through some tough times, you know."

"Yes, I know, Patrick. She told me all about you."

"She did?"

"Yes, and it was all good."

Patrick was always shy about receiving compliments. He looked down, as he rubbed his fingers across the brim of his hat, which he was holding in his hands. "I thought I might see her once more before I head for home."

"I understand," said Father Al with a smile. "You can find her over at the convent. It's only about a ten minute walk down the road," as the priest pointed in a southerly direction.

Pat put his cap back on and prepared to leave. "Well, Father, I can't thank you enough for your prayers and—oh! Father, I almost forgot to ask you about Joshua. Did his wounds heal? Did he stay with you very long?"

"I'm glad you mentioned that. I almost forgot something, also. Wait here a minute." Father Al went inside the rectory and returned momentarily, holding a letter in his hand. "I'm glad you mentioned Joshua. Here's a letter that he sent for you. I've been holding it for some time now, hoping that you'd return here. He wasn't sure of your address, so he sent it to me, expecting you might pass through on your way back home to New York.

"I'm glad he thought to send it here." Patrick quickly opened it and began to read.

"Why don't you sit down here, son? Looks like a lengthy letter. You look thirsty—I'll get you a drink."

"Oh, thank you, Father." Pat sat down in the rocking chair with his mail, as the priest went back into the rectory.

Dear Patrick,

I hope this letter finds you in good health and unharmed by this God-awful war. I have sent it to the good priest, Father Al, who gave me refuge in his church. You most likely will not receive this until some future date, possibly when the war is over. As I write this, the fighting is going on around Petersburg and Richmond. You may be in the trenches there right now. I fear that the end is near for my people, but I will be glad when the killing stops.

I want to tell you that I am very thankful for what you and Miss Sommers did for me. It was a great risk for both of you. Please extend my thanks to her and to Father Al for helping me when I was wounded and about to be shipped off to prison.

Speaking of prison, after leaving Emmitsburg and heading for home, would you believe I was captured by my own people? You see, I was wearing a blue overcoat and they mistook me for a Yankee. I was sent to Andersonville Prison in Georgia. I shall not attempt to describe the filth and degenerate conditions of that prison, for it is sufficient to call it a cesspool. Fortunately for me, the authorities discovered their mistake and released me after four weeks.

I married my Jenny and work for her father in the General Store here. I am perfectly contented but am trying day by day to put the horror of the war behind me. This town is small but the war casualties are big. Each day we hear about another boy who won't be coming home. I don't imagine your losses would be felt as much in a big city like New York.

Some good news: I am so happy to tell you I am a baptized Catholic now, and I thank God for my new faith. You see, I often think of that fateful day when we met so tragically in that wheatfield in Gettysburg. I really believe those medals we wore saved us both. We shall never know if one of us would have been killed—or maybe both of us—if that shell hadn't exploded between us. I truly believe it was Divine Providence that spared us both. I don't think we really knew the significance of the medals when we were young boys; but now, when I look at it, I understand so much more what you were trying to explain to me in that church in Gettysburg—I mean, about the Star of David representing the Old Testament, and the Cross, signifying Jesus as our Savior in the New Testament—well, like you said—it kind of represents our entire Bible.

Well, old friend, from one soldier to another, I wish you all the
best and hope you return safely to your home in New York City. Please
write to me and let me know how you are doing. My address is:
    Joshua Halperin
    C/O Postmaster
    Perch, Virginia

        Warmest regards,
        Josh

Father Al returned with a glass of lemonade, and Patrick drank it as he rocked in the big wicker chair. They talked briefly of the war and Pat shared Joshua's letter with him. After a short while, the priest excused himself to get back to his duties. Pat thanked him again for all he had done for Joshua, then began walking to the convent to find Lou Ann. He was impressed with the neatly manicured grounds around the church, remembering how littered with debris it had been two years before from the thousands of Yankee troops that had been encamped there.

As he approached the convent, he was surprised to see a large, brick building looming in front of him. It occupied a sizeable plot of land in the middle of beautiful cultivated farmlands. How peaceful, he thought to himself. The cannon and muskets and death and dying had been swept away, leaving a paradise that had escaped him on his march to battle. He ascended the convent steps and knocked on the front door. As he waited, he noticed a life-size statue of Our Lady on the front lawn near the doorway, appearing to be made of marble. She was clothed in a long, white robe that partially covered her feet. A blue sash hung over her right shoulder and swung down, crossing over her lower body, becoming fuller as it did. She wore a golden crown upon her head and held the Christ Child, also crowned, in her arms, his feet standing on a globe.

"Can I help you, sir?" came a timid voice from the opened door.

Patrick turned to see a petite little nun wearing the large, white headdress of the Daughters of Charity. He remembered the good nuns' habit, for they had worked diligently caring for the wounded at Gettysburg. "Oh, Sister! I didn't hear you open the door. I was just admiring your statue on the lawn."

"Oh, thank you, sir. That's Our Lady of Victory. We recently dedicated it in honor of the Mother of God. You see, we prayed for her intercession to her Son to spare us and bring victory to our righteous cause."

"Well, Sister, I see your prayers were answered. Thank God!"

"Yes, we pray in thanksgiving every day to our Merciful Father in Heaven." The little nun smiled and looked at Patrick, inquiring, "And how may I help you, sir?"

"I'm looking for Lou Ann—I mean—Sister Mary Michael. Is she here?"

"No, I'm afraid she isn't here today."

"Do you know where I might find her?"

"Are you a friend of hers?"

"Well, yes I am."

"Well, I guess she wouldn't mind if I told you she was visiting with her mother today."

"Oh, yes, I know her mother's house. Thank you." He tipped his hat. "Good day, Sister."

"Good day, sir." She quietly closed the door.

Before long, he found himself standing in front of Lou Ann's mother's house. Said goodbye before. What draws me? This is crazy. He turned and began to walk away, when he heard a young lady's voice cry out, "Is there something I can help you with, sir?"

He swung around to see a nun standing on the front porch. She wore a habit that looked similar to the Daughters of Charity, but there was something different about it. Instead of the flaring white, firmly starched headdress that the professed sisters wore, her head was covered with a dark bluish-gray hood bordered by a narrow band of white cloth, which hung down a few inches in the front of her shoulders. "Is that *you*, Patrick?"

"Yes—yes, it is. Lou Ann?"

She descended the steps and quickly made her way to the road where Pat stood. He was cautious, as he *still* couldn't believe it was actually Lou Ann. He hadn't been prepared for such a drastic change in her appearance. "Oh, Patrick! I'm so glad to see you! Thank you, Lord, for bringing him back safely," as she folded her hands in prayer and looked up at the gray skies forming overhead. She leaned over to him and gently kissed him on the cheek. "Let me look at you," she said with a light-hearted lilt in her voice, stepping back and extending her arms to grasp his hands in hers. There was no mistaking her sparkling blue eyes and pretty face, but Patrick saw a new radiance about her—a peace in those eyes and a joy that had touched him before she had spoken a word.

For a moment, he was speechless. He didn't exactly know how to relate to her. The only nuns he had ever known were his teachers at St. Mary's Grade

School. He felt awkward and not sure how to act or what to call her. He finally blurted out, "Lou Ann— it's so good to see you again! Oh! Should I call you Sister now?"

"Well, actually, my new name is Sister Mary Michael—or at least it will be when I take my final vows. But my family still calls me Lou Ann. They probably always will. But—well, never mind my name—it seems so trivial right now. Oh, Patrick! I mean, I'm just so thankful to see you're back unharmed."

"Well, there were a few times that I didn't think I'd make it—but the good Lord spared me."

"Yes, Patrick, God is good."

He fumbled for words but couldn't express himself. She slowly released her hands from his and seemed to compose herself from the exuberant emotion that had overtaken her on seeing him once again.

"I am *so* pleased to see you, Patrick. I thought you would have gone directly home—well—you haven't seen your family or..." She stopped in mid-sentence.

"You were going to say—Beth? Yes, I am anxious to go home—but..."

"But what, Patrick?"

"I don't know. I feel something—I mean—I just had to see you one more time." After a slight pause, he mustered up the courage to say what he really felt. "You see, Lou Ann, I think I really... Well, I mean, I still care..."

She put her fingers over his lips before he could say any more. "I know. I know, my dear Patrick. I had hoped that we could have gotten on with our lives in the last two years—but some things take more time."

After the words had tumbled from his lips, he felt embarrassed. Why had he stopped to see her? Didn't he want to marry Beth? But she had been so distant—he hadn't seen her in four long years. His young heart had been so turned and twisted and confused within the confines of that gigantic, bloody war, with all of its horrors, mutilations, death, and depravation, that he was fortunate to still have his sanity.

"You have gone through so much, Patrick. I understand how you feel. I mean, being away from home for so long." Lou Ann seemed to sense the emotion in him and quickly changed the subject. "Could you help me hitch up the horse and carriage? Maybe you would like to ride into town with me; I have to get some supplies for Mother."

He nodded his head to comply with her wishes. She ran into the house and returned with a small shoebox in her hands. As they traveled along the road to Gettysburg, Lou Ann talked about her two years at the convent and her plans to work with orphans. It was clear to Pat that she was very excited about her new life. She did most of the talking as they began to pass through the battlefield. His attention was riveted on the peaceful farmland that, two years earlier, had been the site of the bloodiest battle of the war. His mind swirled with images of men falling down, bodies flying through the air, and shells exploding, decimating dozens at a time. As he listened to Lou Ann, he gradually began to realize that his place was back home in New York City. What am I doing? Living in the past. Everything around *here* is dead— including plans with Lou Ann. She no longer exists. Now I'm sitting next to Sister Mary Michael. He realized that he had been looking back instead of forward and that he had been living with a fragile memory for two years.

"Would you mind turning down this road for a minute, Patrick? I want to show you something."

"No, I don't mind."

After a short ride down the quiet country lane, they came to a large oak tree.

"Stop here, please," she said.

Pat brought the horse to a stop and wondered why she had brought him to this out-of-the-way place. He remained seated and watched as she walked over to a small mound of earth beneath the large oak. Just then, the skies opened up and a heavy downpour ensued. Lou Ann quickly hopped back into the carriage and wiped her face dry with a handkerchief she pulled from her sleeve. The flimsy cover over the carriage protected them from most of the rain, but a fine mist blew in from the side. He watched the horse bending down, chewing on the grass, totally unfazed by the rain rolling off his back. Neither one spoke for a few minutes, as Patrick waited for an explanation from Lou Ann. Finally she spoke. "You must be wondering why I brought you here."

"Well, I can see that it must be someone you know who's buried here." He attempted to read the writing painted on a small wooden cross, but couldn't make it out in the driving rain.

Lou Ann read it for him. "It says, 'Pvt. Clem Haywood, C.S.A.'"

"Did you say C.S.A? You mean, he was a Rebel?"

"Yes, Patrick—but he was just a young man who left two little orphan girls behind."

"Well, how did you come to know him?"

"From the church."

"What church?"

"You remember Saint Francis Xavier Church in Gettysburg?"

"Oh, yes, of course. How could I forget?"

"Well, I tended his wounds there, and I promised him I'd look after his little girls. He knew he would never see them again—he was dying, and there wasn't much I could do for him."

"That was very kind of you, Lou Ann—I mean—Sister," as he attempted to show respect for her new title. "But how do you expect to take care of them? I mean—well— you live in the convent, don't you?"

"Well, yes, I do. But you see, Patrick, that's only where we *live*. The other sisters and I—we do our works of charity outside the convent and we have a large orphanage in Philadelphia where this man's girls will have a good home. And, what's more, I can visit them often."

"That's wonderful. Those little girls are lucky to have you."

"I give thanks to God for the opportunity to make a difference for those less fortunate." The rain continued to pour down on the thin canvas top of the carriage, and Sister Mary Michael continued, "You see, Patrick, I thought you might understand what I'm about now and how I want so desperately to help others. That's why I brought you here."

Pat glanced over at the little mound of earth and the crude wooden cross. He began to get the sense of a holy woman who had a burning desire to help others. She seemed to be completely transformed from the young, worldly girl he had met three years earlier. "Well, Lou—I mean, Sister..."

"Oh, never mind the Sister title for now. We've been through a lot together. I'm sorry, Patrick—you were about to say?"

"I think I *do* understand you more now. I can see that you really do have a calling, and I know that you will touch many lives in this work you're doing. You know, Lou Ann, I guess I somehow always knew—I mean, deep down somewhere—that you had so much to give." He turned and looked at her, staring into those beautiful blue eyes, and saw a love, not just for himself, but a love that was bigger and more encompassing than he could have imagined—a self-less love—a love for mankind that could not be captured, contained, or shared with only one—but with all.

"I'm so glad you understand, Patrick," as she turned her gaze to Private Haywood's grave and then stared out through the rain that fell onto the Battlefield of '63, as though she were praying silently for the thousands of others who took their last breath on the hills and fields surrounding that little town. The rain slowed to a drizzle, and a few, bright rays of sun peeked out through the gray clouds. "Oh, look, Patrick! A rainbow!" as she pointed Heavenward. He looked up and saw the most beautiful double rainbow that he had ever seen. It stretched from Cemetery Ridge to Seminary Ridge and beyond. She continued, "A priest told me one time that whenever we visit a shrine, we will see a rainbow—and I truly believe this place is a shrine."

Pat looked at her curiously for a moment and wondered how she could see these killing fields as a shrine. After pondering her words, he finally said, "Well, I guess Abe Lincoln did say something about this being hallowed ground when he spoke here."

"Yes, Patrick, and not only that, but consider the cause. Could men have fought and died for a greater cause than to set a whole race free from bondage?"

"You're right, Lou Ann. There is no greater cause than freedom. Many of my friends died for that cause, and I will never forget them."

The rain had completely stopped, and the sun shone brightly on the peaceful, Pennsylvania landscape. Pat pulled his watch with the cracked crystal from his pocket, asking, "Do you know what time the trains arrive here? I mean, is there one heading north that comes today?"

"I see you *still* have that broken crystal in your watch. I remember it from that New Year's Eve we spent together in Washington."

"Yes. Never had a chance to get it fixed, but I will when I get home."

"I believe there is a train that stops about three o'clock; we can find out for sure in town."

"I would like to be on it. Can't imagine going home—feels like a million years since I left. You know, Lou Ann, speaking of that night in Washington, I couldn't believe my eyes when I saw Lincoln's assassin's picture in the newspaper."

"Oh, wasn't that horrible? And to think, *I* introduced him to you. Remember? At the Willard?"

"Yes. Remember I told you at the time that he seemed to me like a sinister character? Booth—I remembered that name."

"Yes, I do. You have a good perception of people. And to think I worked with him on the stage—but we must pray for him."

"Well, he got what was coming to him. What a cowardly act—sneaking up on Mr. Lincoln and shooting him from behind."

"I know." She hesitated for a moment, then spoke in very soft tones. "But we must forgive him. Didn't Our Lord forgive *His* killers?"

"Yes, He did, but—I'm sorry, Lou Ann, I have a tough time with this one—Booth, I mean."

"Then you must pray for that. I will pray for you to receive that grace of forgiveness."

Patrick looked at his watch once again. Two o'clock. "Well, Lou Ann, I think we should be leaving. Don't want to miss the train." She nodded in agreement. Pat snapped the reins and headed for town. When they got near Cemetery Hill, he slowed the horse to a walk, as he noticed a few gravediggers working there.

"It's so sad," Lou Ann said. "I mean, they're still finding some poor souls scattered about."

"You mean they're moving them to that hill?"

"Oh, yes, they're making a new military cemetery here. I believe I heard that they are burying the soldiers in plots that are designated by states. You know, they were taken from all areas of the battlefield to be buried together in one large resting place." Patrick watched as the gravediggers dug into the rain-soaked earth and noticed many wooden crosses lined up in rows. Some had names. Many were marked "unknown". He thought for a moment, deciding whether he should go and search for men that he knew from his brigade who had fallen here. It didn't take him long to make up his mind. Too many lost—seen enough. Besides, there's no time. I might miss my train. He quickly snapped the reins once again and, in an instant, had the horse moving at a trot. As the soon-to-be Sister and the veteran soldier proceeded to the little town of Gettysburg, Patrick knew for sure that this *would* be the last time that he would see Lou Ann or that place. He began to put it all behind him and tried to concentrate on the future, bringing his heart back to New York City where he had left it four long years before.

Lou Ann picked up the supplies for her mother in the shops, while Patrick sat in the carriage, looking down the quaint, little street, once filled with sharpshooters, infantry, and death at every intersection. It seemed to him that it had never happened. The calm and peacefulness of the place concealed the terror that had struck the hearts of the residents on those three fateful days under that hot, July sun two years earlier. Completing her shopping, Lou Ann returned to the carriage, and they rode the few, short blocks to the train station.

"That's right, son—three o'clock every day, rain or shine," said the stationmaster standing on the platform looking at his watch, then down the tracks. "'Bout fifteen minutes before she rolls in, give or take a few minutes. We're still trying to get things back to normal—I mean, since the war and all."

Another fifteen minutes before the final farewell, Patrick thought. He would say goodbye to everything, including a lost love, battles won and battles lost, death as a daily companion, and all manner of hardships he would never have thought possible to endure. As the train pulled up to the platform, Pat stepped down from the carriage. He had no luggage. His only possession was the soiled, blue uniform on his back and a pocket watch with a cracked crystal. The sadness he had felt when he said goodbye to Lou Ann two years earlier at her mother's house wasn't quite the same. Without realizing it, he had matured. He began to understand reality and became more in tune with the world around him.

"I wish you all the best, Patrick, and I would ask you to pray for me."

"Yes, Lou Ann, I will. And I would ask you to do the same for me." He caught himself, as his mind began to drift back to all that they had been through together. Must look ahead. He handed her the reins and kissed her hand as he did so.

"Oh, Patrick, I almost forgot." She reached down to the floor and pulled up the little shoebox that she had brought along. "Here's a little something for you. Thought you might enjoy it on your journey back home."

"Thank you, Lou—I mean, Sister Mary Michael. I guess you'll have to get used to that name." He smiled, turned, and began to board the train. Before he reached the top step, he heard the carriage moving. He looked back to see a cloud of dust as she rode away in haste. He smiled as he remembered back to that day when she had hastened her goodbye to him in Washington, forgetting her Bible. She never did like long goodbyes, he thought, his eyes tearing slightly.

He boarded the sparsely occupied train, seating himself next to a window in the front of the car. He guessed that by this time most all of the soldiers had gone north and returned to their homes. A few civilians reading newspapers and two sleeping soldiers were seated toward the rear. He liked it that way… he wanted to be alone to think about his future. As the train chugged along, he looked at the small shoebox on his lap and decided to open it. Inside, he found a rosary. She remembered I was always losing mine, he thought. Next to it was a small jewelry box. He opened it to find a shiny, new, gold pocket watch. How easy it was to see the numbers on the face. The last item that he removed was a small Bible. As he picked it up, he noticed something was between the pages—it was a fresh sprig of lilac. As he sniffed the sweet fragrance, he read softly from that page—"Apocalypse, Chapter 12, Verse 7-9."

> *And there was a battle in Heaven; Michael and his angels battled with the dragon, and the dragon fought and his angels. And they did not prevail, neither was their place found any more in Heaven. And*

*that great dragon was cast down, the ancient serpent, he who is called
the devil and Satan, who leads astray the whole world; and he was cast
down to the earth and with him his angels were cast down.*

At this point, Patrick knew without a doubt that his daily prayer to Saint
Michael had been heard. After all, he *was* returning home in one piece, when
six hundred thousand others wouldn't be returning home at all. Besides, he
pondered, too many Michaels cropping up—too many to be coincidence.

His mind raced back to the first time he had met Lou Ann in that cold
field hospital tent near the battlefield of Fredericksburg in December and to
every meeting he had with her right up to the present. He couldn't remember if he had ever shared his devotion to Saint Michael with her. She knew
very well of his devotion to the Blessed Mother, as he always tried to pray his
rosary daily. But he thought hard and long and couldn't remember speaking to her about Saint Michael. And yet, she had taken Michael for her new
religious name. And now, this Bible chapter and verse... His imagination
began to soar as he stared out the window watching the small farms passing
by. He thought about his friend, Michael, who seemed to evaporate into thin
air back at his camp in Washington. Now he began to wonder about Lou
Ann—his "angel of the battlefield." No—it couldn't be.

He suddenly felt hungry. But he could wait. He had gone without food
many times when the Army had made long marches and gone directly into
battle. His excitement grew as he concentrated on returning home. How
will I act? Will Beth look the same? Have I really been unfaithful? Only
kissed Lou Ann a few times. Did I kiss an angel?

The train wheels clicked over the tracks as the sun went down, and his
eyes closed to a chapter in his life that would remain emblazoned in his heart
and mind forever.

CHAPTER 24

▼

THE SILENT SENTINEL

The hard, stiff seats and the creaking sounds of the railroad cars as they bent their way around the huge mountains of Pennsylvania did not deter Patrick from a sound sleep. He did, however, awaken to the blaring sunlight that poured into the window and onto his face. He squinted and gazed down at the river running alongside the tracks, watching as it cascaded over rocks and glistened in the early morning sunlight. He felt groggy and opened the window. The cool morning breeze flowed in, and he took a deep breath of the fresh, spring air. But that didn't last very long. He knew that he was almost home when the foul odor of the stockyards and slaughterhouse floated on the wind through the open window. But it was a welcome smell that told him he was fast approaching his home in New York City.

The train rolled to a stop, and the conductor shouted, "New York City!" Pat stepped down from the train and onto the long platform. He gazed around at the many buildings and cobblestone streets radiating out in every direction. It felt strange and confining to him; and for a brief moment, he longed for the open roads and expansive outdoors that he had traveled for the past four years. He had no desire, however, to follow them any more, as they had all led to violent battlefields. Walking past the shanty homes near the slaughterhouse, his thoughts turned to the Big Swede. Sure he said he lived around here somewhere. But for him, I'd be dead now. Have to visit his mother soon... promised him. Better get settled first.

The city was awakening and the shop owners were setting up their goods outside. Trolley cars, omnibuses, and horse drawn carriages emerged onto the streets; and the clatter of hooves and shouts from the hucksters grew louder as he advanced into the heart of the city. An army of pedestrians invaded the sidewalks and scurried in many directions. He found himself dodging the hordes of civilians that brushed by him as he made his way toward home. At first he felt threatened. It had been a long time since he had walked the streets of New York. He had grown accustomed to orderly marches in formation with thousands of men down long, dusty roads. They had all moved together in the same direction. Now he was alone—an army of one—a solitary member of society guiding his own feet and marching to his own drumbeat.

After the initial shock of the city, Patrick began to enjoy his newfound freedom. Instead of chasing the enemy, he would chase his dream—the dream that he had always harbored deep in his soul to settle down and raise a family—providing that he would survive. And he had! *Where should I go? Home? Or maybe see Beth? Too scraggly to see her. Maybe go home first—get cleaned up. Should probably see Beth, though.* He stopped at a fruit stand and gazed at the many fruits displayed in large, wooden bushel baskets. He couldn't remember when he had last eaten any fresh fruit. He still had money in his pocket, as the Army paymaster had caught up with the soldiers in Washington, D.C. He picked up an orange and an apple and reached into his pocket to pay the short, fat, balding man with the stained apron and the long, black mustache hanging down on either side of his mouth.

"You a soldier?" asked the little man as he looked at Patrick's worn uniform.

"Well, yes. I mean, I was."

"You no havta pay me—you do plenty for our country. You take and eat in good health."

"Thank you, sir. Thank you."

The fruit peddler turned and went to attend to another customer. Patrick noticed his own image in the storefront window. He hadn't seen himself in a mirror in many months. He was surprised at the man he saw—scruffy beard, hair hanging down over his ears, and leathery-looking countenance. He struggled with himself as he bit into the apple, savoring the juicy fruit, while making his way through the teeming masses. He would be passing right by the dress shop where Beth worked. *How can I* not *stop? But I look so awful!* He felt his heart begin to pound as he turned down Amsterdam Avenue. *She doesn't even know I'm back.*

The moment had arrived—the long, sought-after moment—that moment in time that he had thought and prayed about since the war began. He stood outside Mrs. Ennis' Dress Shop and peered through the window, cupping his hands on either side of his face to block out the glare and stared between two manikins dressed in ankle length dresses and wide-brimmed hats. But he didn't see Beth. As he walked over to the door and pushed it open, a tiny bell rang overhead. A tall, thin, elderly, well-dressed woman with metal-framed spectacles perched low on her nose, a cloth measuring tape hanging down from her shoulders, and a few straight pins protruding from her mouth, turned to see who had entered. Removing the pins, she smiled and greeted him. "May I help you, sir?"

Patrick quickly removed his cap and attempted to smooth his hair over with the palm of his hand. "I was looking for Miss Wheeler. Is she working today?"

"Yes, sir. She's in the back room. I'll get her for you." She turned and took a few steps toward the back, then inquired, "Oh, who shall I say is calling?"

"Patrick's the name, Ma'am." He watched as she headed for the back room, her full skirts rustling as she walked. As he looked around the shop at the many dresses and hats, he could hear the muffled voices coming from the rear.

Suddenly, he heard his name shouted. "Patrick! Is it really *you*?" Beth came bursting through the curtained doorway, stopping abruptly a few feet from him. For a brief moment, she seemed unsure that it was he, as she stared at his face, then spontaneously threw her arms around his neck. He found himself hugging her back and kissing her and wouldn't release her until she pulled herself away. The old feelings resurfaced anew, his heart swelling with the warmth of her love. "Let me catch my breath! Oh, my dearest Patrick—I—I—just thank God you're back!" She laid her head on his shoulder and sobbed.

Mrs. Ennis pretended to busy herself, arranging dresses on a rack.

"Oh, Beth," Pat said, "I'm so happy to see you!"

"Oh, Patrick—I—I can't believe it's really you! My prayers have been answered. Oh, thank God you're back unharmed." She wiped her tears away and turned to Mrs. Ennis. "Oh, I'm so sorry, Mrs. Ennis. This is Patrick. Patrick... Mrs. Ennis."

"A pleasure to meet you, Patrick. Beth has told me much about you." The elderly woman pushed her glasses up on her nose as though to get a better look at him. "You're every bit as handsome as she said you were."

"Thank you, Ma'am. She has spoken highly of you, also. I mean—in her letters."

"Why don't you take the rest of the day off, Beth—you two must have so much to catch up on."

"Oh, thank you, Mrs. Ennis," replied Beth as she quickly went over to the coat rack, grabbed her purse and flopped her bonnet on top of her head. "Thank you again," as she grabbed Patrick's hand and whisked him out the door.

Beth clutched his arm as they strolled down the street, stopping at brief intervals to hug one another. Some onlookers occasionally exhibited disapproval. Patrick didn't care. He had earned the right to show his affection, even if it was in public. The young couple walked many blocks until they found themselves in Central Park. They sat down on a bench, holding hands and gazing into each other's eyes. "This is where it all started, Beth. Remember that Fourth of July?"

"Oh, Patrick, I can't recall the number of times I've thought about that day. I only had those few memories of you. I think they gave me hope."

"Oh, that reminds me..." He removed the medal from his neck and held it up in front of her. "Will you accept this now and..."

Before he could finish, she said, "Oh, yes. Oh, yes, my love. I promised I would."

He gently placed the medal around her neck and proudly proclaimed, "Then it's official. We are now engaged."

He kissed her and held her close, not wanting to release her from his embrace. And the world seemed to stand still. All was well. The war was over and now, finally, they could plan their future together. They strolled by the lake and reminisced about the happy times before the war when they had skated hand in hand in that winter wonderland.

Shadows formed across the open grassy areas of the park; and before they realized that daylight was fading, the little lamplighter began to make his rounds. "Oh, Patrick, it's getting late. Mother will be looking for me," Beth said.

"Yes, I know, and I should be getting along myself... haven't seen my family yet." He walked her home and they stood on her doorstep talking for another hour. "I don't want to leave you, Beth. It's been so long."

"I feel the same way, my dear Patrick; but we can spend the rest of our lives together." They embraced again, neither one wanting to let go. They kissed and finally parted. But this time, it would only be for hours, not for years.

Patrick walked the many blocks to his home, taking in the sights and sounds of the big city. Might take some time getting used to, he thought to himself. When he finally arrived back home, he wasn't quite sure if he should knock on the door or just walk in. After being away for so long, he felt peculiar inside, as if his absence had somehow estranged him from the household. He decided to knock on the door. At first there was no answer. He knocked again. After a few minutes, the door slowly opened; and a young bearded man with a peg leg leaned against the doorframe. He stared at Patrick for a brief moment. "What can I do for...? Patrick! Is that you?"

"Michael!" Pat exclaimed. "You made it back, too!" Pat wrapped his arms around his brother, hugging him so hard that Michael almost toppled over, but for Pat steadying him.

"Who's there?" came his grandmother's voice from the kitchen.

"Oh, just a beggar, Gram!" Michael replied.

"Well, don't let him go away hungry, Michael. I've got some food here that he can have." She poked her head around the kitchen door and recognized the "beggar" immediately. "Patrick!" she shouted. "Praise be! You're back!" She wiped her hands on her apron and ran toward him. Michael stepped out of her way as she flung her arms around Patrick and began kissing him about his face. He hugged her and picked her up off the floor, her feet dangling in midair. "Praise be ta Jesus—the Lord is good! He returned my two grandsons home safely." She cried and smiled simultaneously as she grabbed them both by their hands. "Come and sit down." She led them over to the couch. "We're going ta have a celebration."

"What's all the fuss about, Mother? A man can't even git a decent nap around here," Grocky complained as he emerged from the back bedroom, hiking up his suspenders over his shoulders and rubbing his eyes. As his gaze fell upon Patrick, he looked astonished. "Paddy, me boy, is that *you*? I can't believe me eyes!"

"Yes, Grocky, it's me."

The old man walked over to Pat, who stood up and grabbed his hand firmly in his own. "Let me look at ya, son," as he took a step back. "Yer lucky yer still in one piece! I mean, ya still got all yer movin' parts. Yer brother here wasn't so lucky," as he looked over at Michael sitting on the couch, his peg leg extended outward. "Come sit down, me boy; we have a lot ta talk about. Mother, bring us some drinks—this is a special occasion!"

"An' how should ya be askin' now?"

"Would ya *please* bring us some drinks, Mother dear?"

"That's better," she said, smiling as she went into the kitchen.

Pat and Mike smiled at each other, as Grocky shook his head from side to side. After looking back to see if she was out of hearing range, he looked at his two grandsons and whispered, "I think she believes she's been liberated, along with the slaves!" They all chuckled.

Grocky had many questions for Patrick. He wanted to hear about every battle. Pat obliged but left out many details that he wanted to forget. After a few beers, their mood became more relaxed. Before long, Pat switched the conversation over to Michael. "Enough about me," he said. "I haven't heard much about you and your travels, Michael."

Michael placed his hand on his peg leg and spoke softly. "Lost it in the battle of Atlanta." Patrick noticed that his demeanor seemed to have changed dramatically from the feisty brother he had left four years earlier.

"I've been meaning to ask you, Michael—how did you wind up in Sherman's army?"

"Well, you know, Pat, after my enlistment was up, I heard about the substitute thing. A fella paid me three hundred dollars to go in his place. Never shoulda taken it. Three hundred dollars for a leg!" He shook his head in disgust.

Grocky set his pipe down in the ashtray and sniffed the inviting aroma of roast beef coming from the kitchen. "Well, Paddy, looks like ya got here just in time fer Grama's roast beef dinner."

"Who's settin' the table?" Grama called out from the kitchen.

"I'll do it, Grama." Pat set the plates around the large, rectangular, oak table.

"Yer one short, Patrick," his grandmother said when she returned from the kitchen.

"How's that, Gram?"

"Well, yer mother will be comin' home from work soon."

"Mama? Working?"

"Yer mother's doin' good, Paddy. She recently got a steady job cleanin' the church and school."

"Did she—I mean..."

"Yes, Patrick, she stopped drinkin'. Grocky and I figured that she got so afraid that you and Michael would—well—you know. She started goin' ta church and prayin'. She's a changed woman, she is. Praise be! Ya see, Paddy, some good things come outta a bad situation.."

"I'm so glad to hear that, Grama. And I know your prayers had something to do with that."

She didn't answer but smiled at him as she set another plate on the table and returned to the kitchen. Grocky took his place at the head of the table, and Grama brought out a roast beef on a large platter, setting it down on the middle of the table and seating herself next to her husband. "Come and git it, boys!" shouted Grocky in a joyful tone.

Patrick offered to help Michael up from the couch, as he stood over him with his hand extended. "I can do it myself," Michael said as he motioned Pat away and pushed himself up with great ease. Pat walked to the dinner table, while Michael hobbled over on his peg leg as if determined to show him that he was not, in the least, handicapped.

"Well, now, lads," Grocky exclaimed, as the boys took their place at the table, "we got a lot ta be thankful fer, and..."

Just then, the front door opened and Patrick's mother, Bridget, came into the living room. As she removed her faded pink scarf from her head, she began to speak before looking around the room. "Smells good, Grama. I'm really hungry. I could eat a horse." Suddenly, her eyes fell upon Patrick. "Oh! Patrick—you're home! You're really here—I can't believe it!" She ran across the room. Pat quickly got to his feet and embraced her, as she kept repeating his name. "Patrick! Patrick! Thank God! Oh, Patrick!" She began to cry.

"Yes, Mom, I'm here to stay." After their long embrace, they looked at each other. He saw a tired lady—her clothes were dirty and her hair straggly. She was much thinner than he remembered, but there was a rosy glow about her face; and he noticed her tear-filled eyes to be clear and sharp. She had lost that "alcoholic look" that drains the soul, he thought. After another long embrace, Pat pulled a chair out from the table for her. "Here, Mom, have a seat." Bridget sat down and began wiping away her tears with a napkin.

"Well, now," Grocky said, "praise be! We're a family once again. Now let's say grace," as he began to make the Sign of the Cross. "Oh, Lord," he began, bowing his head and folding his hands, "we thank ya fer this food and fer sendin' our boys home to us safe and sound and fer endin' this terrible war and we pray fer all the brave lads that won't be comin' home and fer their loved ones—in Jesus' name."

They all responded, "Amen!"

Patrick feasted on the roast beef and mashed potatoes with gravy and all the rest of the trimmings until he couldn't eat another bite. In fact, he was so engrossed in the meal after the many years of army food that he became oblivious to the conversation going on around him. When he finally finished and sat back in his chair, setting his napkin back on the table, he looked up to see the whole family staring at him. They had all finished ahead of him. A spontaneous laughter broke out, and Patrick became slightly embarrassed at first. Then he began to laugh along with the rest.

A warm glow seemed to radiate throughout that humble home in that spring of 1865. The family had been reunited after four long years of fear and uncertainty. It was a microcosm of the whole country with one exception. Many less fortunate families had an empty chair at their dinner table—some even had more than one. The blood had been let— families had grieved— the arms laid down—and the slaves freed. And now, it was time to pick up the pieces and test the nation's resolve to reunite and heal the deep wounds.

Realizing that they had run out of beer, Grocky motioned to Patrick. "Here's a quarter, Paddy," as he dropped it into a gallon-size tin bucket and handed it to him. "Go down ta McGinty's and have Old Tom fill 'er up with beer. What kinda celebration would it be without a little suds?" As Pat made his way to the door, the old man hollered, "And don't fergit ta take the quarter out before he fills 'er up! Last time, he filled 'er up, not knowin' the quarter was in the bottom." Pat chuckled and went on his mission.

After he returned, hours of exchanging stories were shared amongst the family.

Grocky talked of his promotion to captain on the police force. Bridget was anxious to share about her church and the many nice friends she had made there. Michael was less talkative. In fact, Patrick had to ask him questions in order to bring him into the conversation. Pat saw a striking change in his brother. He had become so quiet and sullen—so unlike the belligerent, rowdy brawler he had remembered. Pat was surprised, however, to learn that he was holding a job as a ticket clerk at the railroad station—a job well suited for a one-legged man, he thought. Patrick himself talked about seeing Lincoln in Washington and about the friends he had lost in battle. He had no intention of reliving the battles or mentioning Lou Ann, though. And Grama—well, Grama just sat quietly, her hands folded on her lap, smiling from ear to ear, contented to sit in silent prayer, thanking the Almighty that all of her "chicks" were home in the nest.

Patrick hadn't courted Beth for very long before the war started, and he had never brought her home to meet his family; however, they had become good friends while he was away. Beth had visited them regularly, sharing some of his letters with them; and they had become quite fond of her.

The ladies retired early; and Pat, Mike and Grocky stayed up late, all sharing the "suds" from McGinty's. Michael finally fell asleep in the chair, and Patrick began to doze off shortly after. But, before doing so, he was elated to hear his grandfather telling him that he would get him a job on the New York City Police Force. Sometime during the night, he awoke and shuffled, half-asleep, to his bed and literally flopped down in his uniform. The last thought he had before falling into a deep sleep was how wonderful and soft the mattress felt. For hundreds of nights, he had had only a blanket—sometimes wet from rain—between his body and the hard earth.

He arose early the next morning to the sounds of the city outside his window. During the time he had been gone, the growing metropolis had spread its business tentacles outward, and commerce had encroached on this otherwise quiet street. After removing his uniform and hanging it up, he sat down on his bed and gazed into the small closet, viewing his few civilian clothes that hung there. He looked at his mended and faded blue uniform and felt like he had shed his skin—like a snake, he thought. He had more meaningful memories to carry with him for the rest of his life than most men experience in a lifetime—and he was just twenty-one years of age! He decided to save the uniform, if for no other reason than the fact that it was the only tangible thing he had to show for his service to his country. He hadn't won any medals or awards. The only mementoes he had were his scars left from the bullet wounds. He sat there in his underwear and rubbed his hand over the scar tissue on his leg and shoulder. He never looked for any honors or rewards, but thought of his many fallen comrades—and considered himself fortunate. He also thought of those who would have to limp around on one leg, like his brother—or worse, be confined to a wheelchair for the rest of their lives. He, himself, had been shot, blown up, marched in all kinds of weather until he thought he'd collapse, eaten food containing bugs, watched friends die in agony—and lived to tell about it. He was only a single soldier, one of thousands of young men who did his duty, stayed the course, and saw it through to the bitter end. His great reward, as he saw it, was his life—a life spared to be lived, to marry and raise a family, to love and be loved, and to proclaim to the next generation that freedom for all men had come at a terrible cost—a cost so great, it couldn't be measured.

Peace had come, killing had ceased, and Patrick, for the first time in his adult life, began to experience peace in his own soul. He had great hope for the future, now knowing full well in his heart that this future *was* with Beth. Since returning home, he had come to realize more than ever just how much he loved her. He had felt love for Lou Ann, but it had seemed like an unreachable love—like a firefly that briefly lights up the dark night, then vanishes. But he was young and so was she, and the war had spun around their fragile relationship, as if they had been in the eye of a storm. Now the storm was over, and Patrick and Beth began to make plans for their future together.

The warm breezes of summer swept across the shanties, mansions, and rapidly rising commerce buildings of New York City in that year of 1865;

and plans for a wedding were in the air. No longer did Patrick have to live on memories of home and Beth—memories that he knew very well could have been the last images he would have had of them had he met the same fate as his fallen comrades in arms. Now he could make plans with a real-live sweetheart who would become his wife, raise his children, and provide a happy home for a family that, until now, had been a distant dream.

In the first few months after coming home, he and Beth visited their memories at Central Park, the Distributing Reservoir at 42nd Street and 5th Avenue, and also rode the steamboat up the Hudson River where he had first proposed marriage to her. They had arranged with Father Flaherty at St. Mary's Church for a December wedding. Patrick had saved enough money from his Army salary to rent a small, one bedroom apartment a few blocks from his mother and grandparents' apartment. He was also looking forward to becoming a member of the New York City Police Department, thanks to his grandfather. It was a glorious summer for the soon-to-be newlyweds. All the horrors of war were behind them, along with the fears and anxieties that latch on to the human soul like a blood-sucking parasite during wartime.

Fall arrived and Patrick donned another blue uniform—this time, it was the uniform of the New York City Police. He had fought for years to *make* the peace—now his duty was to *keep* the peace. His family and Beth were happily impressed to see him in his new garb. They fussed over him and showered him with compliments.

"Oh, Patrick! How handsome you look!" Beth offered.

"Faith and begorrah, Paddy me boy! Ya look almost as good as me in that uniform! Proud ta have ya as a member of New York's finest!" Grocky remarked, a hint of glee in his eye.

And Grama—she just stood there proud as a peacock, grinning from ear to ear.

As for Patrick, it was just another uniform. The fact that he had a steady job was the most important thing to him. This time, he would carry only a nightstick with him— the nine-pound rifle was history. Instead of facing hordes of gray-clad soldiers firing at him, he would confront thieves, thugs, burglars, and murderers. Not on hillsides or valleys of Virginia, but on city streets and alleyways in New York City. It didn't take him long to learn the basics of the job... he had a good instructor—Grocky!

"Now, ya can't be too easy with these hoodlums. They're a wily bunch, ya know," Grocky would say.

One of Pat's first assignments, however, was in Germantown, a low-crime area where Grocky had walked the beat when he was a rookie. As Pat familiarized himself with the territory, he saw that Mr. Schuler still had his meat market there. The first day he made acquaintances with all of the storeowners, before walking into his old employer's market.

"Yes, Officer? Can I help you?" the old German said.

"Don't you remember me?" Pat asked, as he pushed the peak of his hat back a little with his nightstick.

"Vhy..." The old man hesitated for a moment, then suddenly blurted out, "Vhy—you're Patrick! My helper boy—from before da var! I didn't know dat ya vas a policeman now! Ya vent to var. I remembered."

"Yes, Mr. Schuler. I've been assigned to this beat, and I thought I'd let you know I'll be checking in here from time to time."

"Jus' like yer grampa used ta! Vell, I'm so glad to see ya. Ya growed up so much and ya got through da var so goot, I see!"

"Yes, sir, I was one of the lucky ones."

"Can I get ya some sausage—or maybe some livervurst? I remember ya like dat livervurst a lot."

"No, thanks, but I guess we'll be seeing a lot of each other in the future."

"My, my! I can't believe yer a policeman now."

Just then, a customer entered the store, and Mr. Schuler began walking over to wait on her. "It's goot to see ya again, Patrick."

"Good seeing you again, sir." As Pat walked toward the door, he overheard the old man speaking to the customer.

"Dat boy used to vork for me, and now, he's a policeman! Can ya believe dat?"

As time went on, Patrick became more comfortable with his new job. He met many nice people on his beat and encountered mostly petty thieves who he arrested and escorted to the police station. He tried to uphold the letter of the law and wanted to make Grocky proud of his work there. In time, he became known to those in his precinct as "Officer Pat". The children, especially those he called his little street vagabonds—the homeless and the orphaned—became very fond of him, as he always looked out for their welfare and often passed out fruit to them that the merchants of the area had given him. Those little ones looked up to him, and he wanted always to set a good example for them. In a few short months, he found himself beginning to understand Lou Ann's deep desire to care for orphans.

His return to civilian life had been an easy and joyful adjustment for him, as his wedding day grew closer. But there was one loose end he had put off until now. He had made a promise to his friend, the Big Swede. He had wanted to forget the horrors of war and all the sadness that comes with it; however, he knew that he couldn't rest until he had fulfilled his promise. He would go to visit the Swede's mother that evening after supper. Beth wanted to spend the evening with her mother anyway, trying to finalize some of the wedding plans; so he was free to do something on his own. It was a long walk to the Swede's neighborhood. He could have taken the trolley car, but he wanted to take the time to think about what he would say. He was apprehensive. *Haven't felt this uneasy since going into battle. Have to muster up a little courage.* He had passed by a few saloons and decided to stop in the next one he came to. *One beer won't hurt,* he mused, stepping up to the long, mahogany bar. The tall, thin bartender with the long, black handlebar mustache wiped his hands across his long, white apron. "What'll it be?"

"Glass of beer."

"Comin' right up!"

A moment later, the bartender returned and placed the glass down on the bar in front of him. Patrick laid his money down next to it, and lifted the glass to his lips.

"Ya from around here, son?" the barkeep asked.

"Yes, sir, not far from here."

"Haven't seen ya in here before."

"I've been away—fightin' a war, you know."

"Oh, another veteran, huh?"

"Yes, sir."

"Call me Slade." Patrick nodded and took a long swig of the cold brew. "We get a lot of boys back from the war in here—I see you're one of the lucky ones."

"How's that?"

"Well, ya got all yer limbs—many of the boys come in here missing arms and legs.

"Yeah, I guess I am lucky all right."

"If ya don't mind me askin'—did ya see much action?"

"Yes, sir—I mean Slade—from Fredericksburg to Petersburg."

"You were at Fredericksburg?"

"Yeah—it wasn't pretty."

"Ya know, there was a boy who used ta come in here after Fredericksburg—lost a leg there. Nice lad, he was. Came through all that fightin' and wound up gittin' run down by a trolley car."

"That's a shame."

"It was a sad case, it was. They said his crutch got caught in the rails an' he couldn't get out of the way fast enough."

"Terrible."

"Yeah, son, he came in here a lot, hobblin' on those crutches. Poor lad came home ta find out his mother had died an' his sweetheart took up with another man —almost drank hisself ta death. I used ta say ta him, 'Danny— now ya better slow down.' He just couldn't get over his sweetheart goin' off like that."

Patrick quickly set his glass down on the bar and stared at Slade. "Did you say his name was Danny?"

"Yeah. Short fella. Dark hair. Think he said he was with the 69th."

"Oh, my gosh! I knew him! We were in the hospital together. I can't believe he's dead!"

Slade looked down for a moment. "Sorry, lad. Didn't mean ta be the bearer of bad news." He filled up Patrick's glass again. "Here, lad, this one's on me." He went to the end of the bar to wait on another customer. Pat sipped the cold brew, saddened by the bad news. He remembered Danny on that rain-soaked train and how excited he had been about seeing his girl again. He had almost forgotten about going to see the Big Swede's mother. When he had entered the saloon, he was wishing that he had some memento of the Swede's to give to her—a letter or anything that she could keep as something belonging to him. But all he had to give her were the last words of her big soldier son— "Tell Mama I love her."

Soon the bartender returned. "I'm sorry about yer friend—didn't know ya knew him."

"Well, we met in the Army. Never knew him from the neighborhood." Patrick removed his handkerchief from his pocket to blow his nose and to catch a tear that had escaped his eye. "You say his sweetheart ditched him?" Pat asked, slipping the hanky back into his pocket.

"Yeah. Felt sorry fer him. He drank away the little money he had. He couldn't find work—ya know—having only one leg. He ran up a bar bill that he couldn't pay. Then one night he reached in his pocket and handed me a medal—ya know—a medal he received fer bravery. I told 'im I couldn't take it, but he insisted—it was the only thing of value he had ta pay me with. So I finally took it ta satisfy 'im—never meanin' ta keep it, ya understand. But he never came back fer it. I found out a few days later 'bout the accident. Guess his troubles are over now." Slade reached over to the back bar and picked something up, placing it in front of Patrick. "Here, ya see? I still have it." Pat looked down and picked up the medal, inspected it, then placed it back on the bar. Slade continued, "An' that's all that's left of the man—can ya believe it? He escaped that terrible battle only ta get run over by a trolley car!" He pushed the medal over toward Patrick. "Here, lad. Why don't you take it? I mean—he had no family an' I think if anybody should have it, you should."

"No, I couldn't take it. I wouldn't feel right." Pat finished his drink and asked for another. As Slade went to refill his glass, Pat stared at Danny's medal. What would *I* do with it? Then it suddenly dawned on him that this could be something he could give Swede's mother. Oh—but—that would be a lie!

After the third drink, Pat found himself loosening up somewhat and sharing his whole story about the Swede with the bartender.

"Ya say the big fella saved yer life?" Slade asked.

"Well, yeah. If he hadn't hollered to warn me, that Rebel would have shot *me*!"

"Well, then—I don't know how much you know about the Bible, but there's somethin' in there that says that the greatest thing a man can do is lay down his life fer another. Wouldn't ya say that *he* deserved a medal?"

That was all Patrick needed to hear. After all, he thought, who would it hurt? What good would that medal be collecting dust on the back bar of a saloon, when it could bring a little joy to a grieving mother? "Thanks, Slade. You're a good man. Better be on my way." He picked up Danny's medal and put it in his pocket.

"Come again, son. Oh, I didn't catch your name."

"Patrick—Patrick O'Hanrahan." He turned and smiled. "Thanks again, Slade. You've been a great help." He exited through the swinging doors.

Walking through the city, the sounds of traffic in the streets seemed distant, as he concentrated on his meeting with Mrs. Jorgenson. A cold autumn wind began to blow, and he felt a chill as he stuck his hands in his pockets, clutching the medal that seemed, for a brief moment, to be his. Eventually he arrived in the shabby section of town where the Swede's mother lived. He removed a piece of paper from his pocket and checked the address, found through a contact at police headquarters. After knocking on the door, he waited. The unpleasant smell of the stockyards and slaughterhouse permeated the air. He jumped back, as a large black rat scampered past his feet, then knocked once again.

The rickety old door creaked open, and a short, stocky woman with gray hair peered out. "Who is it?" she asked in a guarded tone.

"My name is Patrick O'Hanrahan."

"What is it you want?" she asked curtly.

"I was a friend of Sven's. We were in the war together, Mrs. Jorgenson."

"Sven? You knew my Sven?"

"Yes, Ma'am. He was in my company."

The old woman opened the door wide and grabbed his hand. "Come in. Come in. My Sven—he was such a good boy. Tell me... No—we talk inside. Come. Come, I get you a drink." She led him up a flight of stairs and into the parlor. He gazed around the room at the dilapidated furniture and realized that his own home wasn't that bad. "Sit down. I get you some tea."

"Oh, thank you, Ma'am."

As she walked over to the stove, situated at the other end of the parlor, he felt at a loss for words. He remained standing, feeling uneasy. It wasn't long before she had returned, carrying a tray containing a pot of tea and two cups. "Sit... sit," as she placed the tray on a table and motioned him to a large overstuffed chair—the stuffing protruding from one of the arms. He cautiously sat down on the edge of the chair, taking care not to disturb the loose stuffing with his hand. She sat down opposite him, looking pensive.

Pat hesitated, then said, "I'm so sorry..."

"Drink—drink the hot tea."

He complied and began to sip the hot brew. "I'm so sorry about your son, Mrs. Jorgenson. He was a brave fellow."

"How you know him?"

"I met him on the boat in Washington—I mean, when he first came into my Brigade. I—I..." Pat wondered how to tell her how her son died—or, even if he should.

She looked at him, trying to hold back the tears that were already welling up in her eyes. "Did he—well—were you with him when he..." She burst out crying.

"Yes, I was with him when he died."

"Did he suffer?" She wiped the tears from her cheeks with her calloused hands.

"No, Ma'am, he didn't." He got up and walked over to her, placing his hand on her shoulder. "I want you to know how brave your son was. He—he saved my life!" She looked up at him and placed her hand over his, waiting to hear more. "Well, he was shot trying to warn me before he..." He took her hand and held it tightly between his own, as he crouched down in front of her. He couldn't bring himself to explain any more detail to her, but he did add, "Well, Ma'am, he wanted me to tell you—I mean, his last words were—

'Tell Mama I love her.'" She began to sob uncontrollably. Pat felt helpless. He reached into his pocket and brought out Danny's medal. He didn't say anything at first. He just remained there, allowing her to grieve. After a few minutes, she apologized for her outburst and grew silent. He turned her hand upward and placed the medal in it. "Here's something Sven would want you to have. It's a medal he won for bravery and courage in the face of the enemy. Few men receive such a medal—it's a great honor."

She looked at it for a brief moment, then clutched it to her breast. The agony that filled her heart was intoned in her words—"Sven! My boy! This is all I have left of him!" Patrick couldn't find any more words of consolation. He held back his own tears. "I'm sorry, son. I—I know you did your best," she said as she looked down again at the medal in her hand, wiping away her tears with the other.

Patrick slowly rose to his feet. "If there is ever anything I can do for you, Ma'am, please contact me. I'll give you my address if you like. I don't live far from here."

"Thank you. Thank you. You are a good boy—to take time to come see me—but I be okay. I got other big sons who take care of their Mama. I be okay."

"Well, I'd better be going now. I'll come and visit you again."

"I like that," she said, forcing a smile.

Patrick descended the rickety stairs and exited through the old, creaky door. The smell of the crisp, cool fall air began to improve as he distanced himself from the Swede's home and the stockyards. At first he felt guilty about leaving Mrs. Jorgenson so quickly. Maybe I should have stayed with her longer. Oh, well, did my duty anyway—kept my promise to the Big Swede. As he walked through the dimly lit streets toward home, his thoughts turned to the future.

Wedding arrangements were finalized and December came quickly. A light snowfall dusted the ground with a pure-white beauty, as the church bells resounded their harmonizing blend—and Patrick's heart pounded as he watched his bride-to-be walk slowly down the middle aisle of Saint Mary's. A small group of family and friends were gathered in the little white church for the ceremony. He and Beth made their vows of marriage during Holy Mass, tears of joy and love filling her eyes as she spoke the words of Holy Matrimony to her beloved. The pride Pat felt in his heart as he beheld her was overcome only by the sanctity and depth of the commitment they were making to one another. Life, he thought—we belong to each other for life. Mr. and Mrs. Patrick O'Hanrahan. The Consecration during the Mass seemed to draw a parallel in his heart of the consecration they were making to one another. He giving his life to her... and she giving her life to him—as God gave His life for all. How beautiful, Pat thought. Afterwards, they honored the Blessed Mother by placing a white rose at the foot of her statue on the side altar, where they brought this consecration of their marriage to her.

As the bride and groom walked back down the aisle and out the rear door, they were showered with handfuls of rice by the well-wishers present at their happy occasion. The priest had recruited a few boys from the parish to sweep a path through the light fallen snow from the church to the school hall where a reception was to be held. It began as a small, quiet celebration. An odd mix of musicians consisting of two fiddlers, a banjo player, and a drummer, somehow blended together to fill the hall with merriment. Patrick took his new bride by the hand, stepped onto the dance floor, and, for the first time in his life, danced with her. He remembered his first date with her in the park on that Fourth of July before the war. He had wanted to dance with her then, but didn't know how. He *still* didn't know how, but he did his best. After a few glasses of wine, however, it seemed to come more natural to him. In fact, he began to wear out his new bride, but he wanted to keep on dancing. He grabbed his mother and danced her around the floor next, and even got his Grama to dance one time. In between the dancing, he joined Grocky and the men at the bar, set up at the side of the hall, for a "wee nip", as Grocky called it.

The war and all of its horrors were beginning to fade, and Patrick felt new life invigorating his soul. The future looked bright. About half-way into the celebration, the doors of the hall burst open and in came a tall, husky, red-faced man wearing kilts and playing an Irish tune on a bagpipe. He was followed by a dozen policemen in uniform marching behind him; and behind that column, two more of New York's Finest rolled in a large keg of beer. Patrick knew immediately that this was Grocky's doing. The noise grew louder, the beer flowed like water, and it was a fine celebration. At one point, when Pat had been talking to his grandfather at the bar, Grocky reached into his coat pocket and pulled out a letter, handing it to him. "Paddy, me boy, almost fergot ta give ya this. It came in the mail this morning. Didn't want ta bother ya on yer wedding day, but could be important, so I thought I'd best give it ta ya."

Pat took the letter and began to open it, as he took his seat next to Beth at the head table. "What's that you have there?" she inquired.

"I don't know yet." As he removed the letter from the envelope, he glanced first at the signature on the bottom—it was written in a very primitive way. Nathan. He turned to Beth. "Oh, it's from Nathan!"

"Who?"

"Nathan. Someone I met when I was in the war. Oh, how great! I'm so glad to hear from him!"

"Can you read it to me?"

"Why, sure, I guess so." He held the letter in both hands and began to read out loud, competing with the noise surrounding them. "Oh, it says here that, because Nathan doesn't know how to write, the letter is being written *for* him by his pastor, Rev. John Jefferson."

Dear Sargean'

Ah hopes y'all be home safe from de war. Ah wants ta thank y'all fer helpin' gits me inta Lincum's army. Ah gots wounded an' receives a medal fer brav'ry at battle of Fort Wagner. Lost half are men an' are kernel. It was mitey bad. But now dis ole war be's over an' ahs home wif my Mindy. She done give birf ta a baby boy. Da fust born inta freedom—prase da Lawd! Ah's so happy. We done got areselfs forty acres an' a mule. Da dirt be's rich in dis here bott'm land. Good fer growin' crops. Ah saves yo address eber since ya'll rote it down fer me in Washin'ton. Ah wud like fo' ya ta writes me a letr an' tell me ya'll be's al rite. Ah nebber fergits yer kind ways wif us wen we meets ya'll at da Massa Marshall plantashun._

Pat didn't read the rest of the letter out loud. He would have had a lot of explaining to do, and this was his wedding night. He ended it quickly by reiterating to Beth it was from "Your friend, Nathan" before glancing once more at the last line.

An' how be dat sick gal we 'scaped from da Rebel sogers wif? Miss Lu Ann.

He folded the letter and placed it in his pocket.

"Who was he?" Beth asked with a puzzled look.

"Oh, he was a slave. His father was killed and he was wounded in a battle on their plantation. I helped him get bandaged up."

"And you got to know him?"

"Oh, he traveled with many of the slaves. They followed the Army and—well, I helped him join up."

"Sounds like he really liked you. I mean—appreciated what you did for him."

"Yeah. He was a good man."

"You haven't told me much about what happened to you all that time, Patrick."

"Later. Plenty of time for that later. Come on—let's dance." He grabbed her once again and whirled her around the dance floor. Images of the slaves and the war flashed through his mind. He looked at his bride and into her eyes and saw only love. It was strong enough to blot out the past. He felt "born again"—into a world of hope and promise, as they embraced and danced the night away.

They left the reception early, slipping out the side door to the waiting carriage which Michael had arranged to drive his brother and his new bride to their small, humble, second-floor, rented apartment. They couldn't afford a honeymoon, but they didn't care. They had each other. The snow was getting deeper and the carriage wheels made ruts in it, as the horse's hot breath spurt out small clouds of wispy vapor in the cold, December air. Patrick thought how much he had always loved winter. He hadn't seen a heavy snowfall since joining the Army in '61.

Upon entering their apartment, they removed their coats. "It's freezing in here!" Beth said.

"I'll put some more wood on the fire." Pat opened the door of the small, black, potbelly stove in the middle of the room. "Guess Michael didn't make a good fire this afternoon—it's down to embers. He should have put an extra log on it." He placed more wood over the embers, stoking them with a poker as he did. Rubbing his hands together, he blew on them to get them warm and waited for the fire to take hold.

Beth had gone over to a small, round table at the foot of their bed and picked up a Bible. "Is this your Bible, Patrick?"

"Yes, Beth."

"Oh. I never saw it before," as she began to leaf through it.

"Well, I brought a few of my things over last night. You know—last minute stuff."

She stopped at a page containing a dry sprig of lilac and held it up. "Where did you get this old flower? Looks like a lilac."

"Oh, I got that from…"

"From where?"

"A nun gave it to me. She cared for me and treated my wounds after Gettysburg."

"Were there nuns tending the wounded? I thought nurses did that."

"Oh, no. The Daughters of Charity were the ones there—at Saint Francis Xavier. They used the church for a hospital. All the buildings in town were filled with the wounded."

She placed the dried lilac back in the Bible and came over to him, wrapping her arms around him from behind and hugging him. "I love you so much, Patrick." He turned around and embraced her, holding her tightly. After a moment, she looked into his eyes, squeezed his hand, and said almost apologetically, "I'll be right back. I have to change," as she walked into a small dressing room.

The night had become illuminated by the gaslights on the street, as he glanced out the front window in time to see two young lads having a snowball war below. He thought of Joshua and himself when they were youngsters—before the war—before they lost their innocence. He undressed and got into bed, nervously awaiting his new bride.

Beth returned and lay down next to her husband, and they consummated their marriage. Afterwards, she rested her head on his chest as he propped his head up on his folded arm beneath it, stroked her hair, and kissed her forehead. Reaching her hand up, she caressed the side of his cheek. They were lost momentarily in their little world of happiness, their hearts filled with the beautiful joy of love.

"Was she pretty?" Beth asked.

"Who?"

"The nun—you *did* say she was a nun, didn't you?"

"Yes, I did—and yes, she *was* pretty. In fact, she looked a little like you."

"Well, I'm glad she helped you so you could come back to me. I thank God for that."

Beth's eyes closed and she began to fall asleep. Pat looked out the window at the large, wet, glistening snowflakes floating down, when he heard the melodious voices of Christmas carolers beneath his window. With all of the excitement of the wedding, he had almost forgotten about Christmas—and here it was, only two days away. He closed his eyes and listened as the sweet refrains of "Silent Night" drifted up into the cold, night sky. *Sleep in Heavenly Peace—Sleep in Heavenly Peace.* For the first time in four years, he felt true peace. He remembered reading somewhere that, when a soldier retires and melds into civilian life, he becomes a "Silent Sentinel", guarding his memories for the rest of his days.

He prayed that his seed would grow into new life, that his offspring would flourish and prosper in that wounded nation; and that that nation would heal and once again become one nation under God.

"If we ever forget that we are One Nation Under God, then we will be a nation gone under."

-President Ronald Reagan
August 23, 1984

. . . AND THERE WAS A BATTLE IN HEAVEN;
MICHAEL AND HIS ANGELS. . .

LaVergne, TN USA
23 February 2010
174009LV00009BA/44/P